# THE ABSTINENCE TEACHER

Also by Tom Perrotta

*Little Children*
*Joe College*
*Election*
*The Wishbones*
*Bad Haircut: Stories of the Seventies*

# TOM PERROTTA

## The Abstinence Teacher

FOURTH ESTATE · London

This edition first published in Australia in 2008
First published in Great Britain in 2008 by
Fourth Estate
An imprint of HarperCollins*Publishers*
77–85 Fulham Palace Road
London W6 8JB
www.harpercollins.co.uk

First published in USA in 2007 by St. Martin's Press

Visit our authors' blog: www.fifthestate.co.uk

1

A catalogue record for this book is
available from the British Library

ISBN  978-0-00-726100-0

Printed in Great Britain by Clays Ltd, St Ives plc

All Fourth Estate books are printed on 100% recycled paper
with Blue Angel environmental accreditation.

Blue Angel is one of the world's first and most respected
environmental accreditation programmes. This high-quality
recycled paper, made from 100% post-consumer waste, has
been manufactured according to stringent controls.
For more information visit www.blauer-engel.de

Find out more about HarperCollins and the environment at
**www.harpercollins.co.uk/green**

*For Joe Gordon*

# Acknowledgments

*Listen to advice and accept instruction, and in the end you will be wise.*

—PROVERBS, 19:20

In the course of writing this book, I've been lucky to receive invaluable advice and instruction and assistance from Maria Massie, Elizabeth Beier, Dori Weintraub, and Sylvie Rabineau—my gratitude to them all. Carol Luddecke of the Lentegra Mortgage Group provided me with an insider's perspective on the mortgage business. My friends Mark Dow and Kevin Pask were intrepid companions at a Promise Keepers' weekend in Baltimore. As always, though, my biggest debt is to my wife, Mary Granfield, and to our kids, Nina and Luke, who give me lots of good reasons every day to abstain from work and have a little fun.

*And if anyone causes one of these little ones who believe in me to sin, it would be better for him to be thrown into the sea with a large millstone tied around his neck.*

—THE GOSPEL OF MARK

# PART ONE

# Some People Enjoy It

# Miss Morality

ON THE FIRST DAY OF HUMAN SEXUALITY, RUTH RAMSEY WORE A short lime green skirt, a clingy black top, and strappy high-heeled sandals, the kind of attention-getting outfit she normally wouldn't have worn on a date—not that she was going on a lot of dates these days—let alone to work. It was a small act of rebellion on her part, a note to self—and anyone else who cared—that she was not a willing participant in the farce that would unfold later that morning in second-period Health & Family Life.

On the way to homeroom, Ruth stopped by the library to deliver the grande nonfat latte she regularly picked up for Randall, the Reference Librarian, a fellow caffeine junkie who returned the favor by making the midday Starbucks run. The two of them had bonded several years earlier over their shared revulsion for what Randall charmingly called the "warmed-over Maxwell Piss" in the Teacher's Lounge, and their willingness to spend outlandish sums of money to avoid it.

Randall kept his eyes glued to the computer screen as she approached. A stranger might have mistaken him for a dedicated Information Sciences professional getting an early start on some important research, but Ruth knew that he was actually scouring eBay for vintage Hasbro action figures, a task he performed several times a day. Randall's partner, Gregory, was a successful real-estate broker and part-time artist who built elaborate dioramas featuring the French Resistance Fighter GI Joe, an increasingly hard-to-find doll whose moody Gallic good looks were dashingly accentuated by a black turtleneck sweater and beret. In his most recent work, Gregory had painstakingly re-created a Parisian café circa 1946, with a dozen identical GI Jeans staring soulfully at each other across red-checkered tablecloths, tiny handmade Gauloises glued to their plastic fingers.

"Thank God," he muttered, as Ruth placed the paper cup on his desk. "I was lapsing into a coma."

"Any luck?"

"Just a few Russian infantrymen. Mint condition, my ass." Randall turned away from the screen and did a bug-eyed double take at the sight of Ruth's outfit. "I'm surprised your mother let you out of the house like that."

"My new image." Ruth struck a pose, jutting out one hip and sucking in her cheeks like a model. "Like it?"

He gave her a thorough top-to-bottom appraisal, taking full advantage of the gay man's license to stare.

"I do. Very Mary Kay Letourneau, if you don't mind my saying so."

"My daughters said the same thing. Only they didn't mean it as a compliment."

Randall reached for his coffee cup, raising it to his lips and blowing three times into the aperture on the plastic lid, as though it were some sort of wind instrument.

"They should be proud to have a mom who can carry off a skirt like that at . . ." Randall's voice trailed off diplomatically.

". . . *at my age*?" Ruth inquired.

"You're not that old," Randall assured her. "And you look great."

"Lotta good it does me."

Randall sipped his latte and gave a philosophical shrug. He was a little older than Ruth, but you wouldn't have known it from his dark curly hair and eternally boyish face. Sometimes she felt sorry for him—he was a cultured gay man, an opera-loving dandy with a fetish for Italian designer eyewear, trapped all day in a suburban high school—but Randall rarely complained about the life he'd made for himself in Stonewood Heights, even when he had good reason to.

"You never know when opportunity will knock," he reminded her. "And when it does, you don't want to answer the door in a ratty old bathrobe."

"It better knock soon," Ruth said, "or it won't matter *what* I'm wearing."

Randall set his cup down on the Wonder Woman coaster he kept on his desk, next to an autographed picture of Maria Callas. The serious expression on his face was only slightly compromised by his milk-foam mustache.

"So how are you feeling?" he asked. "You okay about all this?"

Ruth shifted her gaze to the window behind the circulation desk, taking a moment to admire the autumnal image contained within its frame: a school bus parked beneath a blazing orange maple, a bright blue sky crowning the world. She felt a sudden urge to be far away, tramping through the woods or wandering around a strange city without a map.

"I just work here," she said. "I don't make the rules."

RUTH SPENT most of first period in the lounge, chatting with Donna DiNardo, a Biology teacher and field hockey coach in her late thirties. Over the summer, after years of being miserably single, Donna had met her soulmate—an overbearing optometrist named Bruce DeMastro—through an internet matchmaking service, and they'd gotten engaged after two magical dates.

Ruth had been thrilled when she heard the news, partly because of the fairy-tale aspect of the story, and partly because she'd gotten tired of Donna's endless whining about how hard it was to meet a man once you'd reached a certain age, which had only served to make Ruth that much more pessimistic about her own prospects. Oddly, though, finding love hadn't done much to improve Donna's mood; she was a worrier by nature, and the prospect of sharing her life with another person provided a mother lode of thorny new issues to fret about. Today, for example, she was wondering whether it would be a hardship for her students if, after the big day, she asked them to address her as Ms. DiNardo-DeMastro.

Although Ruth felt strongly that women should keep their names when they married—she hadn't done so, and now she was stuck with her ex-husband's last name—she kept this opinion to herself, having learned the hard way that you could only lose by taking sides in matters as basic as this. She had once offended a pregnant friend by admitting—after persistent demands for her *honest opinion*—to disliking the name "Claudia," which, unbeknownst to her, the friend had already decided to bestow upon her firstborn child. Little Claudia was eight now, and Ruth still hadn't been completely forgiven.

"Do whatever you want," Ruth said. "The students won't care."

"But DiNardo-DeMastro?" Donna was standing by the snack table, peering into a box of Dunkin' Munchkins with an expression of naked longing. She was a heavyset woman whose body image anxieties had reached a new level of obsession now that she'd been fitted for a wedding gown. "It's kind of a mouthful, isn't it?"

"You're fine either way," Ruth assured her.

"It's driving me crazy." Donna lifted a chocolate Munchkin from the box, pondered it for a moment, then put it back. "I really don't know what to do."

With an air of melancholy determination, Donna backed away from the donut holes and helped herself to a styrofoam cup of vile coffee, into which she dumped two heaping spoonfuls of nondairy creamer and three packets of carcinogenic sweetener.

"Bruce hates hyphenated names," she continued. "He just wants me to be Donna DeMastro."

Ruth glanced plaintively around the room, hoping for a little backup from her colleagues, but the two other teachers present—Pete Fontana (Industrial Arts) and Sylvia DeLacruz (Spanish)—were ostentatiously immersed in their reading, none too eager to embroil themselves in the newest installment of Donna's prenuptial tribulations. Ruth didn't blame them; she would've done the same if not for her guilty conscience. Donna had been a kind and supportive friend last spring, when Ruth was the one with the problem, and Ruth still felt like she owed her.

"I'm sure you'll work something out," she said.

"If my name was Susan it wouldn't be such a big deal," Donna pointed out, drifting back toward the Munchkins as if drawn by an invisible force. "But Donna DiNardo-DeMastro? That's too many D's."

"Alliteration," agreed Ruth. "I'm a fellow sufferer."

"I don't want to turn into a joke," Donna said, with surprising vehemence. "It's hard enough to be a woman teaching science."

Ruth sympathized with her on this particular point. Jim Wallenski, the man Donna had replaced, had been known as "Mr. Wizard" to three decades' worth of Stonewood Heights students. He was a gray-haired, elfin man who wandered the halls in a lab coat and bow tie, smiling enigmatically as he tugged on his right earlobe, the Science Geek from central casting. Despite her master's degree in Molecular Biology, Donna just didn't look the part in her tailored bell-bottom pantsuits and tasteful gold jewelry. She was too earthbound, too well organized, too attentive to other people, more credible as a highly efficient office manager than as Ms. Wizard.

"I don't know, Ruth." Donna peered into the Munchkins box. "I'm just feeling overwhelmed by all these decisions."

"Eat it," said Ruth.

"What?" Donna seemed startled. "What did you say?"

"Go ahead. One Munchkin's not gonna kill you."

Donna looked scandalized. "You know I'm trying to be good."

"Treat yourself." Ruth stood up from the couch. "I gotta look over some notes. I'll catch up with you later, okay?"

After a very brief hesitation, Donna plucked a powdered Munchkin out of the box and popped it into her mouth, smiling at Ruth as she did so, as if the two of them were partners in crime. Ruth gave a little wave as she slipped out the door. Donna waved back, chewing slowly, her fingertips and lips dusted with sugar.

THE SUPERINTENDENT and the Virginity Consultant were waiting outside Room 23, both of them smiling as if they were happy to see Ruth come clackety-clacking down the long brown corridor, as if the three of them were old friends who made it a point to get together whenever possible.

"Well, well," said Dr. Farmer, in the jaunty tone he only trotted out for awkward situations. "If it isn't the estimable Ms. Ramsey. Right on time."

Glancing at Ruth's outfit with badly concealed disapproval, he thrust out his damp, meaty paw. She shook it, disconcerted as always by the change that came over the Superintendent when she found herself face-to-face with him. From a distance he looked like himself—the handsome, vigorous, middle-aged man Ruth had met fifteen years earlier—but up close he morphed into a bewildered senior citizen with rheumy eyes, liver spots, and unruly tufts of salt-and-pepper ear hair.

"Punctuality is one of my many virtues," Ruth said. "Even my ex-husband would agree."

Ruth's former husband—the father of her two children—had taught for a few years in Stonewood Heights before taking a job in nearby Gifford Township. He'd recently been promoted to Curriculum Supervisor for seventh- and eighth-grade Social Studies, and was rumored to be next in line for an Assistant Principalship at the middle school.

"Frank's a good man." The Superintendent spoke gravely, as if defending Frank's honor. "Very dependable."

"Unless you're married to him," Ruth said, doing her best to make this sound like a lighthearted quip.

"How long were you together?" asked the consultant, JoAnn Marlow, addressing Ruth in that disarmingly cordial way she had, as if the two of them were colleagues and not each other's worst nightmare.

"Eleven years." Ruth shook her head, the way she always did when contemplating the folly of her marriage. "I don't know *what* I was thinking."

JoAnn laid a cool, consoling hand on Ruth's arm. As usual, she was done up like a contestant in a beauty pageant—elaborate hairdo, gobs of makeup, everything but the one-piece swimsuit and the sash that said "Miss Morality"—though Ruth didn't understand why she bothered. If you were determined to live like a nun—and determined to broadcast this fact to the world—why waste all that time making yourself pretty?

"Must be so awful," JoAnn whispered, as if Ruth had just lost a close relative under tragic circumstances.

"Felt like a ton of bricks off my chest, if you want the truth. And Frank and I actually get along much better now that we don't have to see each other every day."

"I meant for the children," JoAnn explained. "It's always so hard on the children."

"The girls are fine," Ruth told her, resisting the urge to add, *not that it's any of* your *business.*

"Cute kids," said Dr. Farmer. "I remember when the oldest was just a baby."

"She's fourteen now," said Ruth. "Just as tall as I am."

"This is where the fun starts." He shook his head, speaking from experience. His middle child, Andrea, had been wild, a teenage runaway and drug addict who'd been in and out of rehab numerous times before finally straightening out. "The boys start calling, you have to worry about where they are, who they're with, what time they're coming home—"

The bell rang, signaling the end of first period. Within seconds, the hallways were filled with platoons of sleepy-looking teenagers, nodding and muttering to one another as they passed. Some of them looked like little kids, Ruth thought, others like grown-ups, sixteen- and seventeen-year-old adults. According to surveys, at least a third of them were having sex, though Ruth knew all too well that you couldn't always guess which ones just from looking at them.

"Girls have to protect themselves," JoAnn said. "They're living in a dangerous world."

"Eliza took two years of karate," Ruth reported. "She made it up to her green belt. Or maybe orange, I can't remember. But Maggie, my younger one, she's the jock. She's going to test for her blue belt next month. She does soccer and swimming, too."

"Impressive," noted Dr. Farmer. "My wife just started taking Tai Chi. She does it with some Chinese ladies in the park, first thing in the morning. But that's not really a martial art. It's more of a movement thing."

The adults vacated the doorway, making way for the students who began drifting into the classroom. Several of them smiled at Ruth, and a few said hello. She'd felt okay right up to that point, more or less at peace with the decision she'd made. But now, quite suddenly, she became aware of the cold sweat pooling in her armpits, the queasy feeling spreading out from her belly.

"I was talking about spiritual self-defense," said JoAnn. "We're living in a toxic culture. The messages these girls get from the media are just so relentlessly degrading. No wonder they hate themselves."

Dr. Farmer nodded distractedly as he scanned the nearly empty hallway. His face relaxed as Principal Venuti rounded the corner by the gym and began moving toward them at high speed, hunched in his usual bowlegged wrestler's crouch, as if he were looking for someone to take down.

"Here's our fourth," said Dr. Farmer. "So we're good to go."

"Looks like it," agreed Ruth. "Be a relief just to get it over with."

"Oh, come *on*," JoAnn said, smiling at Ruth to conceal her annoyance. "It's not gonna be *that* bad."

"Not for you," Ruth said, smiling right back at her. "It's gonna be just great for you."

SOME PEOPLE *enjoy it.*

That was all Ruth had said. Even now, when she'd had months to come to terms with the fallout from this remark, she still marveled at the power of those four words, which she'd uttered without premeditation and without any sense of treading on forbidden ground.

The incident had occurred the previous spring, during a contraception lecture Ruth delivered to a class of ninth graders. She had just completed a fairly detailed explanation of how an IUD works when she paused and asked if anyone had any questions. After a moment, a pale, normally quiet girl named Theresa McBride raised her hand.

"Oral sex is disgusting," Theresa declared, apropos of nothing. "You might as well French-kiss a toilet seat. You can get all sorts of nasty diseases, right?"

Theresa stared straight at Ruth, as if daring her to challenge this incontrovertible fact. In retrospect, Ruth thought she should have been able to discern the hostile intent in the girl's unwavering gaze—most of the ninth graders kept their eyes trained firmly on their desks during the more substantive parts of Sex Ed—but Ruth wasn't in the habit of thinking of her students as potential adversaries. If anything, she was grateful to the girl for creating what her grad school professors used to call "a teachable moment."

"Well," Ruth began, "from what I hear about oral sex, some people enjoy it."

The boys in the back of the room laughed knowingly, an attitude Ruth chalked up more to bravado than experience, despite all the rumors about blowjobs being as common as hand-holding in the middle school. Theresa reddened slightly, but she didn't avert her eyes as Ruth continued with the more serious part of her answer, in which she discussed a few basic points of sexual hygiene, and described the body's ingenious strategies for separating the urinary and reproductive systems, even though they shared a lot of the same real estate. She finished by enumerating the various STD's that could and could not be transmitted through oral-to-genital contact, and recommending the use of condoms and dental dams to make oral sex safer for both partners.

"Done properly," she said, "cunnilingus and fellatio should be a lot more pleasant, and a lot cleaner, than kissing a toilet seat. I hope that answers your question."

Theresa nodded without enthusiasm. Ruth returned to her lecture, removing a diaphragm from its plastic case and whizzing it like a miniature Frisbee at Mark Royalton, the alpha male in the back row. Acting on reflex, Mark snatched the device from the air, and then let out a melodramatic groan of disgust when he realized what he was holding.

"Don't be scared," Ruth told him. "It's brand-new. For display purposes only."

IT WAS her own fault, she thought, for not having seen the trouble brewing. The atmosphere in the school, and around town, had changed a lot in the past couple of years. A small evangelical church—The Tabernacle of the Gospel Truth—led by a fiery young preacher known as Pastor Dennis, had begun a crusade to cleanse Stonewood Heights of all manner of godlessness and moral decay, as if this sleepy bedroom community was an abomination unto the Lord, Sodom with good schools and a twenty-four-hour supermarket.

Pastor Dennis and a small band of the faithful had held a successful series of demonstrations outside of Mike's World of Video, convincing the owner—Mike's son, Jerry—to close down a small "Adults Only" section in the back of the store; the church had also protested the town's use of banners that said "Happy Holidays" instead of "Merry Christmas." Tabernacle members had spoken out against the teaching of evolution at school board meetings, and initiated a drive to ban several Judy Blume novels from the middle-school library, including *Are You There, God? It's Me, Margaret,* one of Ruth's all-time favorites. Randall had spoken out against censorship at the meeting, and had been personally attacked in the *Stonewood Bulletin-Chronicle* by Pastor Dennis, who said that it should come as no surprise to find immoral books in the school library when the school system placed "immoral people" in positions of authority.

"They've given the inmates control of the asylum," Pastor Dennis observed. "Is it any wonder they're making insane decisions?"

But the good guys had won that battle; the school board had voted five to four to keep Judy Blume on the shelves (unfortunately, the books themselves had been repeatedly vandalized in the wake of this decision, forcing the librarians to remove them to a safe area behind the circulation desk). In any event, Ruth had foolishly chosen to view these skirmishes as a series of isolated incidents, storms that flared up and blew over, rather than seeing them for what they were—the climate in which she now lived.

Her second mistake was thinking of herself as invulnerable, somehow beyond attack. She'd been teaching high school Sex Ed for more than a decade and had become a beloved figure—or so she liked to think—for the unflappable, matter-of-fact candor with which she discussed the most sensitive of subjects. She believed—it was her personal credo—that Pleasure is Good, Shame is Bad, and Knowledge is Power;

she saw it as her mission to demystify sex for the teenagers of Stonewood Heights, so they didn't go through their lives believing that masturbation was a crime against nature, or that oral sex was the functional equivalent of kissing a toilet seat, or worse, perpetuating the time-honored American Tradition of not even knowing there *was* such a thing as the clitoris, let alone where it was located. She was doing what any good teacher did—leading her students into the light, opening them up to new ways of thinking, giving them the vital information they needed to live their lives in the most rewarding way possible—and in doing so, she had earned more than her fair share of respect and affection from the kids who passed through her classroom, and some measure of gratitude from the community as a whole.

So when Principal Venuti told her that he needed to talk to her about an "important matter," she showed up at his office without the slightest sense of misgiving. Even when she saw the Superintendent there, as well as a man who introduced himself as a lawyer for the school district, she felt more puzzled than alarmed.

"This isn't a formal interview," the Superintendent told her. "We're just trying to get the facts straight."

"What facts?" said Ruth.

The Principal and the Superintendent turned to the lawyer, who didn't look too happy.

"Ms. Ramsey, did you . . . umm . . . well, did you *advocate* the practice of fellatio to your students?"

"Did I what?"

The lawyer glanced at his yellow pad. "Last Thursday, in sixth-period Health? In response to a question by a Theresa McBride?"

When Ruth realized what he was talking about, she laughed with relief.

"Not just fellatio," she explained. "Cunnilingus, too. I would never single out just the one."

The lawyer frowned. He was a slovenly guy in a cheap suit, the kind

of attorney you sometimes saw on TV, blinking frantically, trying
to explain why he'd fallen asleep during his client's murder trial.
Stonewood Heights was a relatively prosperous town, but Ruth sometimes got the feeling that the people in charge didn't mind cutting a
few corners.

"And you're telling us that you advocated these practices?"

"I didn't *advocate* them," Ruth said. "If I remember correctly, I
think what I said is that some people like oral sex."

Joe Venuti let out a soft groan of dismay. Dr. Farmer looked like
he'd been jabbed with a pin.

"Are you absolutely certain?" the lawyer asked in an insinuating
tone. "Why don't you take a moment and think about it. Because if
you're being misquoted, it would make everything a lot easier."

By now it had finally dawned on Ruth that she might be in some
kind of trouble.

"You want me to say I didn't say it?"

"It would be a relief," admitted Dr. Farmer. "Save us all a big
headache."

"There were a lot of witnesses," she reminded them.

"Nobody had a tape recorder, right?" The lawyer grinned when he
said this, but Ruth didn't think he was joking.

"I can't believe this," she said. "Are people not allowed to like oral
sex anymore?"

"People can like whatever they want on their own time." Joe Venuti
stared at Ruth in a distinctly unfriendly manner. Before being named
Principal, he'd been a legendary wrestling coach, famous for verbally
abusing several generations of student-athletes. "But we can't be advo-
cating premarital sex to teenagers."

"Why do you guys keep saying that?" Ruth asked. "I wasn't advo-
cating anything. I was just stating a fact. It's no different than saying
that some people like to eat chicken."

"If you said that some people like to eat chicken," the lawyer told her, "I don't think Mr. and Mrs. McBride would be threatening a law-suit."

Ruth was momentarily speechless.

"Th—they're what?" she spluttered. "They're suing me?"

"Not just you," the lawyer said. "The whole school district."

"But for what?"

"We don't know yet," said the lawyer.

"They'll think of something," said Venuti. "They're part of that church. Tabernacle, whatever."

"They got some Christian lawyers working pro bono," Dr. Farmer explained. "These guys'll sue you for wearing the wrong color socks."

AFTER LIVING the first forty-one years of her life in near-total obscu-rity, Ruth had been shocked to find herself transformed into a public figure—the Oral Sex Lady—a person she barely recognized. The story was first reported in the *Bulletin-Chronicle* ("Sex Ed Crosses Line, Family Says"), and then picked up by some larger regional papers be-fore getting an unwelcome moment in the sun of a big-city tabloid ("Oral Sex A-OK, Teacher Tells Kids"). Ruth was contacted by nu-merous journalists eager to get her side of the so-called scandal, and although she was itching to defend herself—to rebut the malicious and ill-informed Letters to the Editor, to put her "controversial remarks" in some sort of real-life context, to speak out about what she saw as the proper role of Sexuality Education in the high-school curriculum—she had received strict instructions not to comment from the school dis-trict's lawyer, who didn't want her to jeopardize the "sensitive negotia-tions" he was conducting with the McBrides' legal team.

The gag order remained in effect during the emergency school board meeting called to address the crisis, which meant that, after issuing a terse, abject apology to "anyone who might have been offended" by anything she'd said "that might have been inappropriate," Ruth had to sit down and shut up while speaker after speaker rose to accuse her of recklessness and irresponsibility and even, in the case of one very angry old man, to suggest that she had more than a thing or two in common with "a certain lady from Babylon." A handful of parents spoke up on Ruth's behalf, but their support felt tepid at best—people were understandably reluctant to rally around the banner of oral sex at a school board meeting—and their statements were regularly interrupted by a chorus of boos from the Tabernacle contingent.

The bad taste from this experience was still strong in Ruth's mouth when she got to work the next morning and found a notice in her mailbox announcing a special schoolwide assembly on the subject of "Sexual Abstinence: Saying Yes to Saying No," presented by an organization called Wise Choices for Teens. At any other point in her career, Ruth would have barged into the Principal's office and told Joe Venuti exactly what she thought about Abstinence Education—that it was a farce, an attack on sexuality itself, nothing more than officially sanctioned ignorance—but she was well aware of the fact that her opinion was no longer of the slightest interest to the school administration. This lecture was damage control, pure and simple, a transparent attempt to placate the Tabernacle people and their supporters, to let them know that their complaints had been heard.

So Ruth buttoned her lip—it had become second nature—and went to the assembly, curious to see what the students would make of it. After all, Stonewood Heights wasn't the Bible Belt; it was a well-to-do Northeastern suburb, not liberal by any means, but not especially conservative, either. On the whole, the kids who grew up here believed in money, status, and fun; most of them would readily admit that they were a lot more focused on getting into a good college than the Kingdom of Heaven. They traveled, drove nice cars, wore cool clothes, and surfed the web on their camera phones. It was hard to imagine them being particularly receptive to the idea that an earthly pleasure existed that they weren't entitled to enjoy whenever and however they felt like it.

Ruth wasn't sure what kind of spokesperson she'd been expecting, but it certainly wasn't the young woman who took the stage after a warm welcome from Principal Venuti. The guest speaker wasn't just blond and pretty; she was *hot*, and she knew it. You could see it in the way she moved toward the podium—like a movie star accepting an award—that consciousness she had of being watched, the pleasure she took in the attention. She wore a tailored navy blue suit with a knee-length skirt, an outfit whose modesty somehow provoked curiosity rather than stifling it. Ruth, for example, found herself squinting at the stage, trying to decide if the unusually proud breasts straining against the speaker's silk blouse had been surgically enhanced.

"Good afternoon," she said. "My name is JoAnn Marlow, and I'd like to tell you a few things about myself. I'm twenty-eight years old, I'm a Leo, I'm a competitive ballroom dancer, and my favorite band is Coldplay. I like racquet sports, camping and hiking, and going for long rides on my boyfriend's Harley. Oh, yeah, and one more thing: I'm a virgin."

She paused, waiting for the audience to recover from a sudden epidemic of groans and snickers, punctuated by shouts of "What a waste!" and "Not for long!" and "I'll be gentle!" issuing from unruly packs of boys scattered throughout the auditorium. JoAnn didn't seem troubled by the hecklers; it was all part of the show.

"I guess you feel sorry for me, huh? But you know what? I don't care. I'm happy I'm a virgin. And my boyfriend's happy about it, too."

Somebody coughed the word "Bullshit," and pretty soon half the crowd was barking into their clenched fists. It got so bad that Principal Venuti had to stand up and give everyone the evil eye until they stopped.

"You probably want to know why I'm so happy about something that seems so uncool, don't you? Well, let me tell you a story."

The story was about a carefree girl named Melissa whom JoAnn had known in college. Melissa slept around, but figured it was okay, because the guys always used condoms. One night, though, when she was having "safe sex" with this handsome stud she'd met at a bar—*a guy she didn't know from Adam*—the condom just happened to break, as condoms will.

"The guy looked healthy," JoAnn explained. "But he had AIDS. Melissa's dead now. And I'm alive. That's reason number one why I'm glad to be a virgin."

It turned out JoAnn had a lot of reasons. She was happy because she'd never had gonorrhea, like her friend, Lori, a straight A student who didn't realize she was sick until prom night, when she discovered a foul puslike discharge on her underwear; or the excruciatingly painful Pelvic Inflammatory Disease suffered by her ex-roommate, Angela, who'd let her chlamydia go untreated, and was now infertile; or herpes, like her old rock-climbing buddy, Mitch, who couldn't walk some days because of the agony caused by the festering sores on his penis; or hideous incurable genital warts like her otherwise-cute-as-a-button neighbor, Misty; or crabs, which were not actually crabs but lice—real live bugs!—having a party in your pubic hair, like they'd done to her ex–dancing partner, Jason.

"Oh, my friends used to tease me a lot," JoAnn said. "They called me a prude and a Goody Two-Shoes. Well, you can bet they're not teasing me now."

And there was one more thing. JoAnn was glad she'd never gone through what her friend Janice had, never had to pee on a stick to discover she was pregnant by some jerk she'd met at a frat party and would never have even spoken to if she hadn't been so drunk she could barely walk; never had to drive to an abortion clinic with this same jerk, who despised her as badly as she despised him; never had to lie there in a hospital gown while some creepy doctor did his business with a vacuum hose; never had to live with the responsibility of making a baby and then not allowing it to be born.

"I can sleep at night," JoAnn declared, "and that's more than I can

say for a lot of people I know. I can sleep because I don't have any regrets. I'm a strong, self-sufficient individual, and I can look myself in
the mirror and honestly say that my mind and my body are one hundred percent intact. They're mine and mine alone, and I'm proud of
that."

It was standard-issue Abstinence Ed, in other words—shameless
fear-mongering, backed up by half-truths and bogus examples and inflammatory rhetoric—nothing Ruth hadn't been exposed to before,
but this time, for some reason, it felt different. The way JoAnn presented this stuff, it came across as lived experience, and for a little while
there—until she snapped out of her trance and saw with dismay how
easily she'd been manipulated—even Ruth had fallen under her spell,
wondering how she'd ever been so weak as to let herself be duped into
thinking it might be pleasant or even necessary to allow herself to be
touched or loved by another human being. Why would you, if all it
was going to do was make you vulnerable to all those afflictions, all that
regret?

After a short Q&A, JoAnn concluded her talk with a slide show. Instead of the gallery of diseased genitalia that Ruth had expected,
though, Stonewood Heights High School was treated to a series of
photographs of JoAnn and her boyfriend vacationing on a Caribbean
island. If you didn't know better, you might have thought they were
on their honeymoon—two happy, attractive young people frolicking
in the ocean, drinking out of coconut shells by the pool, kissing beneath a palm tree, clearly reveling in each other's company (now that
she'd gotten a glimpse of JoAnn's fearsome bikini cleavage, Ruth was
convinced that her breasts had indeed benefited from cosmetic surgery). The final image showed the boyfriend alone—a buff, shirtless,
all-American guy—standing by the water's edge in his swimming
trunks, a surfboard tucked under his arm.

"As you might imagine," JoAnn said, "it's not easy saying no to a
superhot guy like Ed. But when it gets hard, I just remind myself of

my wedding night, and how amazing it's going to be when I give my-self to my husband with a pure heart, a clean conscience, and a per-fectly intact body. Because that's going to be my reward, and mark my words, people—it is going to be soooo good, oh my God, better than you can even imagine."

The lights came on, and the students applauded enthusiastically, though Ruth wasn't quite sure if they were applauding for the hot sex JoAnn would have in the future or her commitment to avoiding it in the here and now. Either way, Ruth had to grudgingly admit to herself that she was impressed. JoAnn Marlow had somehow pulled off the neat feat of seeming sexy and puritanical at the same time, of imper-sonating a feminist while articulating a set of ideas that would have seemed retro in 1954, of making abstinence seem steamy and adven-turous, a right-wing American variation on Tantric sex. It was a little scary.

But it was over. Or at least Ruth thought it was, until she walked out of the auditorium and saw Dr. Farmer and Principal Venuti and several members of the school board standing in the hallway, looking pleased and excited.

"Wasn't that extraordinary?" Dr. Farmer asked her. "What a great role model for the kids."

"Informative, too," said Venuti. "Lots of medical facts and whatnot."

The board members—there were five of them, enough for a vot-ing majority—nodded in enthusiastic agreement, and Ruth saw that it would be useless to quibble with JoAnn's facts or find fault with the way she'd presented them. The situation had clearly progressed beyond the point where facts were of any use to anyone, so she just nodded po-litely and went on her way.

At least this way she had a heads-up, and didn't feel ambushed a month later when the school board announced that the high school would be revamping its Sex Education curriculum over the summer, with the help of a dynamic nonprofit organization called Wise Choices

for Teens. Later that same meeting, it was also announced that the McBride family had decided not to file a lawsuit against the Stonewood Heights School District after all.

A PALPABLE current of electricity moved through the classroom as Ruth perched herself on the edge of the metal desk, primly crossing her legs at the ankles. Tugging at the hem of her skirt, she found herself momentarily startled—it was something that happened a lot these days—by the sight of her calves, which had been transformed by all the running she'd done over the summer. They looked lovely and unfamiliar, almost as if she'd borrowed them from a woman half her age.

She'd started exercising in late spring, at the height of the scandal, on the suggestion of her ex-husband, who thought that a vigorous aerobic workout might alleviate the tension headaches and insomnia that had left her groggy and short-tempered, in no condition to function as a teacher or a parent. He reminded her of how riding a bicycle had gotten him through the darkest days of their divorce, when he missed their daughters so much he regularly cried himself to sleep at night.

"You can't brood," he told her. "You gotta go out and do something positive."

It was the best advice he ever gave her. She started small, half-walking, half-jogging a few laps around the middle-school track, but her body responded right away. In July, she was running three miles a day at a slow, steady clip; by mid-August, a brisk five-miler no longer made her feel like she was going to throw up or die of heatstroke. She ran a 10k race on Labor Day, finishing ninth in the Women Forty and Over category. In six months, she lost twenty pounds, streamlined her entire lower body, and realized, to her delight and amazement, that she looked thinner and healthier than she had in college, where she'd majored in Psychology and minored in Doritos. The only downside to this midlife physical transformation was that it made her that much more conscious of the absence of a man in her life—it seemed like such a waste, having a nice body again, and no one to appreciate it.

What the running mainly did, though—she could see it more clearly in retrospect than she'd been able to at the time—was provide her with a way of working through her anger and coming to some level of acceptance of the new regime. Because as much as she would have liked to stand up for what she believed in and resign in protest, where would she have been then? She was a divorced mother with two daughters who would soon be going to college, a tenured teacher with six years to go before she qualified for a full pension. It wouldn't be easy to find another district in the area willing to hire someone with her baggage. And besides, as Randall frequently reminded her, if she quit then *they* would win, the forces of shame and denial, the people who'd praise the Lord if they forced her out of the classroom and re-placed her with someone more compliant. Wouldn't it be better to stay put and see what happened? The Abstinence curriculum was a pilot program, part of a two-year study funded by a federal grant. When it ended, who knew what would take its place?

All of these arguments had seemed perfectly plausible to Ruth as she'd jogged around Stonewood Lake at dusk, or huffed and puffed down the bike path at the first light of dawn. But right now, looking out on a classful of ninth graders, she wondered if she'd been betrayed by the endorphins, because all she wanted to do was apologize to her students for letting them down, for allowing it to come to this.

She knew it was past time to get started, but she couldn't seem to locate her voice. The kids were watching her closely, their faces alert and curious, paying the kind of attention she would have killed for on any other day. In the back row, the minders were growing restless, ex-changing glances of puzzlement and concern. JoAnn leaned in close to Dr. Farmer and whispered something in his ear. Principal Venuti cleared his throat at high volume and made a spinning motion with his

index finger, signaling that it was time to get rolling. Ruth felt a dis-
gustingly fake smile—an adolescent reaction to social panic that she'd
never fully conquered—tugging at the corners of her mouth. It took
an effort of will for her to rein it in.

"Well," she finally managed to croak, in a voice she didn't recognize
as her own. "Here we are."

# Let's Find Out

IT WAS A LITTLE AFTER SIX ON FRIDAY EVENING, BUT ALREADY Bombay Palace was packed, the entrance overrun with cranky families who'd just been informed that they'd have to wait half an hour for a table at the town's only half-decent alternative to Applebee's. Tearing off a piece of alu paratha, Ruth registered a flicker of pleasure at her own free agent status. It was one of the few compensations of divorce, she thought, the one night a week when Frank took the girls and she was able to do what she wanted, no babysitter to pay, no one to report to when she got home. A perfect opportunity to be bad, if she'd had anyone to be bad with.

"Look on the bright side," Gregory told her. "At least you're practicing what you preach."

"I don't think it qualifies as abstinence if it's involuntary," Ruth told him. "It's just pathetic."

"And it's definitely not abstinence if a vibrator's involved," Randall added.

"You're right about that," she said. "The new curriculum clearly states that masturbation of any kind is strictly *verboten*. Apparently it's habit-forming and interferes with your schoolwork."

"Damn," said Gregory. "So that's why I didn't get into Harvard."

"Frankly," said Randall, "it's a miracle you got your real-estate license."

Gregory nodded. "I'm just glad I didn't have to take the test when I was fifteen."

"Believe me," said Ruth. "The kids didn't look too happy when I broke the news."

"I bet Homo Joe was pretty devastated, too," Randall observed. "What's he gonna do with that economy-size jar of Vaseline he carries around in his coat pocket?"

"Or that Burt Reynolds centerfold in his wallet?" said Gregory.

It was a running joke between Randall and Gregory that Principal Venuti was actually a closeted gay man—aka "Homo Joe"—who took extralong showers in the boys' locker room, kept a stash of pilfered jockstraps in his "Confidential" file cabinet, and was frequently seen dancing at The Manhole in tight jeans, a fishnet shirt, and a Prince Valiant wig. Whenever possible, a new perversion was added to the list.

"I really don't get the logic behind the whole abstinence thing," said Gregory. "I mean, I grew up being taught that premarital sex was wrong, and gay people were going straight to hell, and playing with yourself was a sin. And look how I turned out."

"Greg was wearing leather hot pants and a studded dog collar on the night we met," Randall told Ruth.

"I know," said Ruth. "You showed me the pictures."

"It was a Halloween party," Gregory explained. "And I'd just left the seminary. I was trying to make up for lost time."

"I'm not complaining." Randall reached across the table and gave his boyfriend's hand a furtive squeeze. "And I wouldn't say no to a reenactment later on."

"We can try," Gregory said skeptically. "But you'll need a crowbar to get my fat ass into those shorts."

"The collar will suffice," Randall assured him.

As she often did in their company, Ruth wondered how much of this banter was serious and how much was manufactured for her entertainment. Either way, dinner with Randall and Gregory was a lot livelier than the occasional girls' night out she shared with Donna DiNardo and Ellen Michaels, a longtime colleague who taught History. Defying the *Sex and the City* stereotype of randy, uninhibited single gals dishing colorful secrets to their friends, the three women rarely spoke about anything but work and movies. Ruth and Donna made a special effort to steer clear of the problematic realms of sex and romance, lest they trigger one of Ellen's weepy, chardonnay-fueled tirades against her ex-husband, Marty, a lawyer who'd run off with a much younger colleague and started a new family, leaving her all alone in a big empty house, her kids grown up and gone, nothing but the goddam TV for company, probably for the rest of her life.

Tonight, especially, Ruth was grateful to have such diverting companions. It had been a rough week, a sustained attack on her dignity and self-esteem. Here she was—a woman who had always prided herself on being a fighter—standing up day after day in her own classroom and, under the watchful eyes of her three "guest observers," betraying everything she'd ever stood for as a teacher, the values on which she'd built her entire career. She'd done what she could to let the kids know she wasn't buying what she was selling—grimacing, talking in a robotic voice, stressing as often as she could that the curriculum didn't necessarily reflect her personal opinion—but it didn't matter much. She still felt dirty at the end of each class, unable to meet her students' eyes as they filed out of the room.

"Abstinence is perfectly reasonable in theory," Gregory said. "It just doesn't work in practice. It's like dieting. You can go a day or two, maybe even a week. But eventually that pizza just smells too good."

"Just ask Father John," Randall said.

"Who's that?" asked Ruth.

"The priest who molested him." Randall looked at Gregory. "What were you, twelve?"

"Thirteen," said Gregory.

"What?" Ruth was taken aback. "You guys are kidding, right?"

Both men shook their heads.

"Really?" she said. "By a priest?"

"Finally." Randall pumped his fist in mock triumph. "A story we haven't told her."

"*Molested* is too strong a word," Gregory said. "I think it's more accurate to say it was consensual."

"Come on," Randall protested. "Nothing's consensual when you're thirteen."

"Not technically," Gregory conceded. "But I did enjoy it. And I certainly volunteered for more."

"That's putting it mildly," said Randall.

"Don't mind him," Gregory told Ruth. "He's just jealous."

Ruth nodded, trying to look as nonjudgmental as possible. No woman she knew would have admitted to enjoying sexual advances from an authority figure at thirteen, but she had come to believe that certain things really were different for men.

"He was a cute little altar boy," Randall said. "The whole thing was such a tawdry cliché."

Ruth had no trouble believing this. Even at thirty-eight, with his apple-cheeked face and lank, sandy hair, Gregory still looked like a member of the Vienna Boys' Choir, despite the weight he'd put on in the past couple of years. At thirteen, he must have been an angel.

"Father John was a sweet, mixed-up man." Gregory smiled wistfully at the memory. "He died of AIDS, but none of the parishioners would admit it. To this day, they still call it cancer."

"Thirteen's too young," Randall insisted. "I agree with the abstinence people on that."

"Maybe," said Gregory. "But the other kids had been calling me a fag since second grade."

"So?" Randall said. "What's that got to do with anything?"

"I don't know." Gregory looked thoughtful. "It was just kind of a relief to make it official."

"You were lonely, and he took advantage," Randall said. "You should at least be able to see it for what it was."

"It happened to me," Gregory snapped. "Not to you. So don't tell me what it was."

"I just don't think it's right," Randall muttered.

"I guess I wasn't as lucky as you." There was an edge in Gregory's voice that Ruth hadn't heard before. "I didn't meet Mr. Perfect on the first day of college and have a storybook romance."

"Honey, I'm not criticizing. I'm just trying to make a point." Randall turned to Ruth. "Don't you think thirteen's too young?"

"Everybody's different," Ruth said after a brief hesitation, reluctant to take sides in the dispute. "It's hard to generalize."

"That's too easy," Randall shot back. "You're a mother. Do you want your daughters having sex at thirteen?"

Ruth shrugged. "I hope they wait till they're in college. But a lot of people don't."

Gregory pounced. "Did you?"

Ruth poked at her sag paneer for a moment before answering.

"I had my first real boyfriend in college," she said. "There were a couple of weird experiences in high school, but I didn't really know how to process them."

Randall and Gregory traded prurient looks, allies again.

"Weird experiences," said Randall. "Now you've got our attention."

"Come on." Gregory made a coaxing motion with his hand. "Don't hold out on us."

"It was nothing," Ruth insisted. "Just, you know, the standard groping."

"The standard groping's always been good enough for me," Randall said.

"As opposed to the substandard?" Gregory inquired.

"Even that's better than nothing," Randall said with a laugh. "Who wants another Kingfisher?"

RUTH HAD trouble falling asleep. This was often the case when she'd had too much to drink, and she almost always had too much to drink when she hung out with Randall and Gregory. She'd gone to their house after the restaurant, ostensibly to watch a Margaret Cho video, but they'd gotten sidetracked. First they headed down to Gregory's basement studio to look at his latest work, an unusually large installation that placed several French Resistance Fighter GI Joes in a maze of soulless office cubicles, each doll staring at identical miniature computer screens displaying the smiling face of the late Pope John Paul II. Ruth was puzzled by the piece until Gregory explained that it was an allegory designed to illustrate the way that existentialism/atheism had lost ground to organized religion in recent years as a result of the widespread anxiety generated by the ever more intrusive presence of digital technology in our lives.

"Wow." Ruth was impressed. "You really packed a lot into it."

Gregory seemed pleased. "Art is all about compression."

"It took me three months to round up those action figures," Randall said, reminding them of his own contribution to the project. He wagged a finger at Gregory. "From now on you're going to have to start working with Barbies."

"Yeah, right," Gregory muttered, as if this quip had been intended seriously. "That'd be really original."

Randall smiled the way people do when they're hurt and trying not to show it, then herded them upstairs to try out a recipe for chocolate martinis that he'd cut out of last Sunday's paper.

The experiment was not a success. After a couple of sips, they dumped the vile concoction into the sink and switched to Manhattans, a much safer bet. While Randall mixed her drink, Ruth picked up a MotoPhoto envelope resting on the table and shuffled through the pictures, which documented the Massachusetts wedding of Dan and Jerry, two of Randall and Gregory's oldest friends. They made for a striking pair, one man tall and bald and amiable in a black tux, the other in white, bearded and stocky and a bit too intense. The two grooms danced cheek to cheek, fed each other cake, and posed with their elderly parents, who smiled gamely, if a bit uncomfortably, at the camera. Randall had found the ceremony to be incredibly moving—*like a dream,* he said—while Gregory took a darker view, knowing what he did about Dan and Jerry's troubled relationship.

"These guys break up every six months or so," he said. "They only get back together because they're so devoted to making each other unhappy."

Ruth laughed. "Sounds like a lot of couples I know."

"Dan and Jerry have every bit as much right to a bad marriage as anyone else," Randall said.

"People shouldn't get married just because they *can,*" Gregory said.

Randall glared at him, his face flushed from a combination of alcohol and anger.

"Everything doesn't have to be perfect, you know. You just have to love each other for better or worse."

Gregory turned to Ruth. "This is about us, you know. He's mad at me for not proposing."

"I'm not *mad* at you," Randall insisted. "I just can't figure out why you're so scared. We've been together for twelve years."

"I'm not scared," Gregory said. "I just don't see the point of getting engaged if we can't get married."

"We're making a commitment," Randall said. "Once it's legal, we'll be first in line."

"Let's cross that bridge when we get to it," Gregory said.

"Forget it." Randall's face tightened into an unconvincing smile. "It's really not worth fighting about."

"Who's fighting?" said Gregory. "We're having a calm discussion."

Randall drained his martini.

"Let's just watch the movie."

It was already after ten. Ruth tried to make a graceful exit, but Randall insisted she at least watch the first ten minutes, where Margaret did the hilarious imitation of her crazy Korean mother. She reluctantly agreed, but then got sucked in and stayed to the bitter end, by which point both her hosts had fallen asleep—Gregory dozing in an armchair, hands resting on his belly, and Randall snoring softly on the couch, his face naked, almost babyish, without his glasses. It didn't look to Ruth like anyone would be breaking out the dog collars anytime soon. She kissed them both good night and showed herself to the door.

RUTH MADE a point of sleeping in the nude when her daughters were out of the house. It was a simple indulgence, and, sadly enough, the erotic highlight of her week. This private ritual—shedding her clothes in the dark, slipping between the cool sheets, savoring the soft touch of cotton against her skin—had come to seem like a kind of foreplay, automatically nudging her toward that vibrant fantasy realm that, by default, was her sole source of sexual pleasure. And if these fantasies sometimes inspired her to break out the vibrator she kept hidden in a shoe box on a high shelf in her closet, well, so what? It was her body— her lean, muscular, lovely, unloved body—and didn't it deserve to feel good every once in a while, especially if there was no one around to overhear the humming of the busy little machine, or the grateful cries of a woman who had no one to thank but herself?

Tonight, though, her mind was elsewhere. She lay in the dark, exhausted and wired at the same time, her eyes wide open, the weight of solitude pressing down on her like a heavy blanket. She missed her daughters, wondered if the house would always feel this empty when they left for college, vast and unmoored, ready to lift away from its foundation like a hot-air balloon. She comforted herself with the thought that she still had seven years before Maggie graduated high school, long enough to make some changes. Maybe there'd be a man by then; maybe the exodus of the girls would feel more like a honeymoon than an abandonment, a transition from one rich phase of her life to the next.

Maybe.

Because it was just too creepy to consider the alternative: nothing changing at all, everything shrinking into the sad belated recognition that the best days had come and gone without her even realizing it. Ruth's mother had sounded this note a lot in the weeks before she died, a kind of desperate nostalgia for everything she hadn't appreciated when she'd had the chance.

"Remember that house in Manasquan?" she'd say, propped up in the hospital bed, clutching the "pain button" that allowed her to dispense her own morphine. "The one we rented in what . . . 1978? That was a fun vacation. You enjoyed that, right?"

"I did," Ruth would say, because it would have been cruel to remind her of the truth, which was that they'd all been disappointed by something they'd been dreaming about for years. The house they rented was small and smelled bad; the beach had been closed for two days because of medical waste that had washed ashore. But mainly, that vacation had just come too late. Ruth was a teenager by then, a claustrophobic adolescent trapped in close quarters with her family, just gritting her teeth and waiting for it to be over. The only good times she remembered involved sneaking out at night with her older sister and smoking cigarettes on the boardwalk.

"It was so lovely by the ocean," her mother whispered, though it seemed to Ruth that she'd spent most of the week inside that cramped bungalow, cooking and cleaning and watching TV, the exact same things she did at home. "Let's go there again sometime."

Ruth shut her eyes tight and rolled onto her side, feeling perilously close to crying. The night had taken a toll on her, all that bickering between Randall and Gregory. She'd suspected they were having problems for a while now—Randall had certainly hinted at this in various ways—but until tonight, she'd allowed herself to assume that it was nothing serious. Now, for the first time, she felt it necessary to consider the possibility that they might be headed for a breakup, and she was surprised by how much it disturbed her. She liked them both as individuals, but she liked them even more as a couple. Sometimes, when she tried to imagine her future and couldn't summon the image of a man who loved her, she found herself entertaining an alternative scenario, in which she and Randall and Gregory traveled the world together, a witty trio visiting interesting places and eating adventurous food, laughing everywhere they went. It was hard to trade this in for an imaginary future in which she'd have to deal with them separately— like a child of divorced parents—watching what she said, trying not to take sides, eventually having to meet their new boyfriends, all the while pining for the good old days.

Beneath this worry, though, something else was gnawing at her. One of the things she most valued about her friendship with the guys was how honest it was. It had occurred to her more than once in the past couple of years that Randall and Gregory were the only people who really knew her anymore, the only ones she could trust with her secrets. Among other things, she'd confided in them about her lackluster sex life with Frank, about the two men she'd slept with in the year after her divorce—the memorable one-night stand at the Teachers' Association Conference in Atlantic City, and the divorced computer guy who'd decided to move to North Carolina just when things were heating up between them—and about the dry spell she'd endured since then. They were good listeners, worldly yet easily shocked, hungry for details, curious and nonjudgmental at the same time, always happy to give advice, but only if it was requested. That was why she'd been so surprised to find herself lying to them at dinner when Gregory asked her if she'd waited until college to become sexually active. It would have been the perfect time—and a huge relief—to finally tell the truth.

Because the fact was, she'd never told anyone about Paul Caruso—

not her mother or sister, not her college roommate, none of her boyfriends, not her husband, not even the two therapists she'd seen.

And she really didn't know why. There was nothing particularly shameful about it. Just two bored teenagers exploring their sexuality together, a necessary passage from curiosity into experience. It happened every day.

*Or at least it used to,* she thought.

PAUL CARUSO was Ruth's next-door neighbor growing up, a fat kid two years ahead of her in school. Because he happened to be a cool guy and a talented musician, he had been spared some of the ritual humiliations visited upon the other "big boys" at Oakhurst Regional. Alone among this long-suffering cohort, Paul had avoided being saddled with a nickname like Wide Load or Truck or Blob or Blivet or Butterball or Lardass or Tiny or Two-Ton or Chubby Checker. He was just Paulie C., star trumpeter of the jazz ensemble and the marching band, an award-winning outfit renowned for its complicated routines and high-stepping military precision. People seeing a Wolverines' halftime show for the first time would invariably find their gazes drawn to the tubby kid with the gleaming horn and the dark hair spilling out from the ridiculous toy soldier hat with the too-tight chinstrap, and feel compelled to remark on his nimble footwork, the surprising grace he displayed for someone lugging around such a heavy burden.

In the spring of his senior year, Paul broke his ankle stepping off an escalator at the North Vista Mall. It was a freak accident; he said he put his foot down wrong and the bone just snapped like a pencil. With only a couple of months to go before graduation, he found himself hobbling around on crutches, the lower half of his right leg encased in a bulky plaster cast. He couldn't practice with the band, couldn't work the clutch on his Civic hatchback. His girlfriend, Missy Prince—a broad-shouldered softball pitcher widely considered the prettiest girl jock in the school—picked him up in the morning, but she had practice in the afternoon. Apparently, Paul's other friends were occupied as well, because he was soon reduced to taking the bus home from school, the transportation choice of very last resort for a senior.

Paul had been riding the bus for about a week when Ruth approached him on the sidewalk; he had just completed a laborious dismount from the vehicle, hopping on one foot with his crutches tucked under his arm, backpack in one hand and a trumpet case in the other. He gratefully accepted her offer of help, and the two of them set off on the slow trek to Peony Road, making stilted small talk about Ruth's sister, Mandy, who was nearing the end of her first year at Rutgers. She helped him up the steps to his front door—he used her shoulder for support, bearing down so hard she thought she might crumple like an aluminum can—then followed him inside, through the hall and into the kitchen, which seemed instantly familiar to her, despite the fact that she hadn't been there in years, not since she, Mandy, and Paul had played together as little kids. Everything was exactly the same as she remembered: the cushiony red benches of the breakfast nook, the toaster that accepted eight slices of bread, the needlepoint sampler over the stove that said, *Take All You Want, But Eat All You Take.*

"Here you go," she said, setting the backpack and trumpet down on the table.

"Thanks." Paul smiled, wiping the sweat from his forehead with a pale green dish towel. He seemed to be having a little trouble catching his breath. "Didn't know . . . how I was gonna . . . carry all that shit."

"No problem," said Ruth. "It was on my way."

He used his pinky and ring fingers to lift a few strands of hair from his forehead and tuck them behind his ear, an oddly girlish gesture that made Ruth suddenly conscious of the delicacy of his features— small nose, feathery eyelashes, the ghost of a narrower face encased in the flesh of a broader one.

"You, uh, want a sandwich or something?" he asked.

Ruth hesitated. The kitchen was dim and silent, and it was no longer possible to ignore the obvious fact that they were alone in the house. Mr. Caruso worked on the assembly line at the GM plant; Mrs. Caruso ran the office for Ruth's dentist. His brothers and sisters were older, living on their own.

"I don't think so," she said.

"We got roast beef, ham, turkey—"

"I'm not really hungry."

"You sure? How about a soda or something?"

"I better get home."

He gave her what Ruth later remembered as a searching look, focusing a whole new kind of attention on her, as if he'd suddenly realized that she'd grown up, and had become something more interesting than his next-door neighbor's little sister.

Embarrassed by his scrutiny, Ruth felt her eyes drift down over his soft belly and broad thighs before finally landing on his cast, which was almost completely covered with psychedelic graffiti. There were still a couple of empty spaces near the toe, and she wished she knew him well enough to fill them with her name and a brief, cheerful message. She gave an apologetic shrug.

"Lotta homework," she said.

THAT WAS an odd, unsettled spring for her, the first time she'd ever really been alone. Ever since Mandy left for college, Ruth had been sunk in something approaching a state of mourning. Her big sister was the one indispensable person in her life—ally, best friend, consoler, explainer of the world. They'd shared a bedroom for thirteen years, trading gossip, complaining about their parents, mumbling secrets to each other until they nodded off, then waking up together to the tinny music warbling out of the clock radio on the table between their beds. With Mandy away, the house seemed perpetually out-of-whack—distressingly tidy and much too quiet, as if something more than a single person had been subtracted from the whole.

It hadn't been so bad for the first couple of months. Mandy called most nights and came home every other weekend, full of fascinating new information and unusually strong opinions. But then, at Thanksgiving, she solemnly informed the family that she'd *fallen in love*—she delivered this announcement at the dinner table, with an air of self-importance that Ruth had found both thrilling and vaguely sickening— and since then, she hadn't come home at all, except for an obligatory couple of days at Christmas. Now Ruth considered herself lucky if she spoke to her sister once a week, and when she did, Mandy's mind was a thousand miles away; she couldn't even fake an interest in the details of Ruth's pathetic teen dramas. All she wanted to talk about was Desmond, the Irish grad student with the beautiful eyes and soulful voice, who had awakened her to the suffering and injustice of the world. They were planning on traveling to Nicaragua over the summer to see the Sandinista Revolution for themselves, to cut through the fog of lies and propaganda spewed out by the American government and its toadies in the media.

*Great,* thought Ruth. *And I'll be home with Mom and Dad, waitressing at the IHOP.*

It wasn't that Ruth had a bad relationship with her parents, at least not compared to a lot of kids she knew. They weren't especially strict or even normally vigilant; for the most part, they trusted her to make her own decisions about who she hung out with, where she went, and what time she came home. It probably helped that Ruth got good grades, didn't have a boyfriend, and rarely got invited to parties.

She had only one real problem with her parents, but it was a big one: they were just so *depressing.* With Mandy around, she had barely noticed. Now, though, Ruth had no choice but to observe her mother and father during their interminable, mostly silent family dinners, and wonder how it was possible that two reasonably attractive, reasonably intelligent people could sleep in the same bed and have so little interest in what the other was thinking or feeling. They rarely spoke a kind or curious word to each other, and hardly ever laughed when they were together. They did kiss good-bye in the morning, but the act seemed utterly mechanical, no more tender or meaningful than when her father patted his back pocket on the way out the door to make sure his wallet was there. They paid so little attention to each other that a stranger might have assumed they'd been randomly assigned to live together, roommates who wanted nothing more than to keep out of each other's way.

It hadn't always been like this, though. Ruth had the photographic evidence to prove it—wedding albums, honeymoon snapshots, happy family portraits from when she and her sister were little. In the old pictures, her mother and father smiled, they touched, they *looked* at each other. So what happened? Every now and then, when Ruth was alone with her mother, she tried to find out.

"Is something wrong? Are you and Dad mad at each other?"

"Not at all. Everything's fine."

"Fine? You never even *talk* to him."

"We talk all the time. We have a very good relationship."

Conversations like this made Ruth glad her mother had gone back to work full-time, which meant that she at least had a few hours to herself when she got home from school, some time to mellow out and do her homework in peace. It hadn't mattered so much in the fall, when Ruth had been a jayvee cheerleader, an activity that kept her busy in the afternoons and gave her a ready-made social life. But she'd hung up her pompoms at the end of football season—she just wasn't *peppy* enough—and immediately found herself exiled from the clique of pretty, popular girls she'd drifted into freshman year, coasting on the widespread misconception that she was a younger version of Mandy, who actually *was* a pretty and popular varsity cheerleader, though she now regretted it on feminist grounds.

All Ruth really knew as that fateful April cracked open was that she was living in a kind of limbo, a waiting period between what had happened before and what would happen next. Temporarily sisterless and friendless, she spent a lot of time in a state of vague anticipation, staring at the phone, willing it to ring, hoping to hear a friendly voice on the other end, a mystery boy who confessed that he'd been watching her and thinking about her, and wouldn't she like to put away her homework and maybe have a little fun?

SO IT was nice to suddenly have a regular date with Paul Caruso, even if it didn't amount to anything more than a fifteen-minute walk home from the bus stop. They hit it off right away, slipping easily past the awkwardness of the first day into a realm of relaxed intimacy that made her feel like they'd been friends for years instead of neighbors who'd barely acknowledged each other's existence until a few days ago.

He confided in her about his troubles with Missy, who'd become increasingly clingy as they approached the end of high school. They were heading to different colleges—she'd been recruited to play softball at the U. of Delaware; he was going to major in Music at William Paterson—and Paul had no illusions that they could survive as a couple beyond the end of summer. But Missy was adamant about committing to a long-distance relationship.

"It never works," he told her. "Have you ever heard of a case where it works?"

Ruth liked the serious way he asked these questions, as if she were a mature adult with a wide experience of the world, someone he could count on for good advice.

"It didn't work for my sister," she said. "And she and Rich were only an hour apart. I guess she just wanted to make a fresh start or something."

"That's kinda how I'm feeling," Paul admitted. "But I don't know how to say it. Missy's just so emotional these days. She cries over every little thing."

Ruth usually considered herself a compassionate person, but she found it impossible to scrape up any sympathy for Missy, who refused to say hi to her in the halls even though they'd spent several Saturday mornings together in the fall, sorting glass and metal at the Recycling Center. Ruth just hated that, the way someone could be so nice to you one day, then cut you dead the next.

"She's probably just scared," Ruth speculated. "About going away and everything."

"Personally, I can't wait. I mean, don't you think it gets a little *boring* around here?"

"A *little*?" she said, and he gave a knowing laugh that made her feel thrillingly conspiratorial, like the two of them knew something that crybaby Missy didn't.

Every day she followed him inside and set his backpack and trumpet down on the kitchen table, then suffered through an excruciating moment of suspense, waiting for him to ask if she'd like a sandwich or a soda, or even a glass of ice water, but he never did. It was as if he'd taken her refusal on the first day as a statement of principle, a philosophical objection to food and drink.

THE WEATHER turned warm at the end of April, a glorious stretch of perfect days—birdsong, blue sky, blossoms dropping from fruit trees in little blizzards of pink and green. If Ruth had owned a dog, she would've taken it for a walk, but instead she changed into terry-cloth gym shorts and a T-shirt, spread a beach towel out on the lawn of her backyard, and lay down on top of it, her face to the sun. She could hear the sound of Paul's trumpet wafting out from his bedroom window, quivering in the air above her. He was playing a jazzed-up version of "My Favorite Things," and she let herself imagine that he was watching her from his window, including her among the raindrops and roses and brown-paper packages.

Even at that age—especially at that age—Ruth wasn't in the habit of thinking of herself as beautiful. At best, she figured, she was a 6 on the 1–10 scale that lots of ugly, obnoxious boys were happy to use on girls, but wouldn't have dreamed of applying to themselves. She believed that she deserved an above-average score due to the fact that there was nothing obviously wrong with her—she had a decent body and an okay face, no weird moles or facial hair or skin problems, nothing disfigured or bizarrely out of proportion. On the other hand, she lacked any of the truly outstanding features that would have qualified for the top group—her boobs were little, her face "cute" rather than "pretty," her hair mousy and a bit limp. You developed a fairly realistic assessment of yourself growing up in the shadow of an older sister who'd been turning the heads of grown men since she was twelve. If Mandy had been out here in her string bikini—she was a devoted sun worshipper, always happy for an excuse to show some skin—Ruth would've made sure to stay far away, out of range of unkind comparisons. But today she was alone, without a doubt the prettiest girl in the yard, and she wished she'd been brave enough to wear a bathing suit or at least a tube top, to allow her body to be appreciated on its own modest terms.

She picked up the copy of *Even Cowgirls Get the Blues* that she'd checked out of the library on Paul's recommendation, and tried to get started. But it was hard to coax her mind into visualizing an imaginary reality when the one right in front of her was so vividly and insistently alive—the marshmallow clouds drifting overhead, the garden ducks pinwheeling their wooden wings in the breeze, the inchworm making its ticklish journey up her shin. At some point she realized that the music had stopped, and couldn't keep herself from casting an anxious glance at Paul's bedroom window. But all she saw was the sunlight reflecting off the glass, a blinding glare where his face would've been.

THE NEXT day they were careful with each other on the way home from school, less talkative than usual. They had already turned onto their block by the time Paul asked her if she was enjoying the Tom Robbins novel.

"I'm not really sure," she said. "I tried to read it yesterday, but I couldn't concentrate."

"Why not?"

"I don't know. I guess my mind was on other things."

"That's weird," he said. "I was trying to practice my trumpet and the same thing happened to me. Couldn't keep my mind on the music."

"Spring fever."

"Must be."

Her heart felt big and jumpy as she followed him into the kitchen, certain that they'd crossed a point of no return. She set his stuff on the table and turned to him with a solemn expression.

"So," she said.

"Yeah," he agreed.

She didn't really know where to go from here, how you got from the talking to the rest of it, and he seemed just as baffled as she was, though he had less excuse, being older and more experienced. They stared at each other until the silence got embarrassing. She addressed her next question to the floor.

"I guess you have to practice, huh?"

"An hour a day."

"You're really disciplined."

"What about you?" he asked. "Will you be out in the yard?"

"Probably." She hesitated for a moment, giving him one more chance to save her. "I guess I better go, huh?"

All he had to do was say, *No, don't go. Stay here with me for a while.* But he didn't say anything, didn't make the smallest gesture to stop her, which made it impossible for her to do anything but leave. She could feel the frustration in his eyes as she headed for the door. It was painful, like being trapped in a bad dream where all you had to do was say one thing, but you didn't know the words.

RUTH LAY down on her towel in a purple one-piece bathing suit and pretended to read. It was a kind of torture, knowing how close he was, how simple it would be if she could only find the courage to take matters into her own hands, to walk across the lawn and ring his doorbell.

He was playing his trumpet again, but it was just scales, no more songs that might be secret messages, and the mechanical up-and-down-and-up of it started to drive her a little crazy, as monotonous as a chain saw or an ice-cream-truck jingle. She rolled onto her stomach, sealed her ears with her index fingers, and forced herself to concentrate on the novel. The story was ridiculous—something about a girl with big thumbs and her friend named Bonanza Jellybean—and it suddenly seemed like Paul had made a fool of her, convincing her to lie outside in a bathing suit and read this stupid book for nothing.

For nothing.

She cried out in frustration and scrambled to her feet, leaving the towel and the book behind as she hurried across the lawn to her house. She had just reached the patio when she heard a window being raised. Paul poked his head outside, peering down at her from the second floor.

"Ruthie," he said. He'd never called her that before, and she felt a warm blush spreading across her face.

"Yeah?"

"The back door's open."

WHAT AMAZED her wasn't that she went to him, crossing the lawn in her bathing suit, letting herself in, and climbing the stairs to his bedroom. That part of it was a foregone conclusion, all she'd been waiting for since the first day they had walked home together. What amazed her was what she did when she got there.

It was mystifying, really. She was a month away from her sixteenth birthday, and still fairly innocent, at least compared to a lot of girls she knew. She'd played a few rounds of spin-the-bottle in junior high, and had kissed three different boys in her first two years of high school. The most recent one, Scott Molloy, had touched her breasts, but only briefly, and only through her bra.

Ruth really didn't know how to account for the recklessness—the complete absence of fear—that came over her the moment she stepped into his room. He just looked so harmless—so sweet and nervous—sitting on the bed, the trumpet resting on his bedside table next to a bag of Ruffles, his injured foot propped on a pillow. He started to say something complicated—it was part apology for keeping her waiting so long, mixed in with guilty mutterings about Missy—but she shushed him with a kiss and started fumbling with his belt. His mouth tasted like tuna on rye.

"Ruth?" His voice trembled slightly, as if she were about to burn him with a cigarette. "What are you doing?"

"Let's find out," she told him.

It had something to do with Mandy, Ruth understood that much, because she had the distinct impression that her sister was watching her, an invisible third person in the room, smiling with approval as she unzipped Paul's fly and tugged his pants down to his knees, nodding in encouragement as she peeled off her bathing suit and tossed it on the floor.

"Ruth?" Paul said again. "Are you sure—"

She pressed a finger to his lips as she climbed on top of him.

*Go ahead,* Mandy seemed to say. *Don't be afraid. It'll only hurt a little, and then it'll get better.*

"It's okay," she whispered, reaching down and guiding him inside. And it did hurt, a lot more than she'd expected, though she tried not to show it, still keenly aware of the sensation of being judged by her sister, of proving herself to a beloved teacher.

Because, of course, that was how Ruth had learned everything she knew, lying in bed at night, listening drowsy and aroused to Mandy's half-sheepish, half-triumphant confessions about what she had and hadn't done with this boy or that—the first time she made Billy Frelinghausen hard with her hand, the first time she used her mouth on Danny Wirth, the night she lost her virginity in Rich Lodi's parents' bedroom, with a gallery of family photos smiling down upon her.

*But this is different,* Ruth thought, as Paul released a series of astonished grunts beneath her. Mandy had been working up to that for years, taking things one step at a time, inching methodically toward the goal line. She'd had serious boyfriends since eighth grade, and had somehow managed to postpone sexual intercourse all the way to the end of high school, and to save herself for a boy she really believed she loved.

"Ho, God!" Paul shouted. He seemed to have overcome his doubts, and was bucking his hips wildly, almost like he was trying to throw her off the bed. "Holy shit!"

For as long as she could remember, Ruth had felt herself trailing far behind her sister, so far that she couldn't even see her anymore. But now, in a matter of just a few minutes, in a single giant leap forward, she'd gotten herself all caught up.

"Jesus." Paul stared at her in bewilderment when it was over. His face was slick with sweat, his hair plastered against his cheek. "I just thought we were gonna make out a little."

IT LASTED for a little over two weeks. There was a feverish quality to those stolen afternoons that Ruth had never forgotten, a hectic intensity that left her feeling exalted, set apart from the world.

They'd head straight to his bedroom after school, yank down the shades, and pick up right where they'd left off the day before. Because of his limited mobility, Paul spent most of this time flat on his back, with his shirt still on (he was shy about his body) and his pants down around his knees (it was a big production to get them off over the cast), staring up at Ruth with an expression of awestruck gratitude as she sat astride his waist, basking in his admiration. He couldn't believe his good luck, couldn't believe that something so miraculous had been made possible by a broken ankle.

"It seemed like such a drag at the time," he said. "But it turned out to be the best thing that ever happened to me."

"You mean it?"

"Nothing even comes close."

At four o'clock she'd kiss him good-bye and head home, her body ripe and sore and unfamiliar, a subject of constant fascination. Sometimes she'd shower, but usually not—it was exciting to possess a sexual aura, to move around inside the memory of what she'd just done, an outlaw in her own house. Schoolwork was out of the question, so she occupied herself by cooking dinner, singing along with the radio as she peeled the potatoes or tossed the salad. Even her mother, usually so dense and indifferent, noticed that something was afoot.

"You seem so cheerful lately," she said. "If I didn't know better, I might think someone had a boyfriend."

"Yeah, right." Ruth rolled her eyes.

"Pretty soon," her mother told her. "Just you wait."

IF SHE'D been a character in one of JoAnn Marlow's abstinence fables, Ruth thought, she would have paid dearly for that brief interlude of after-school pleasure, and spent the rest of her life enshrined in a cautionary anecdote: *Poor Ruth, who found out she was pregnant on her sixteenth birthday; Poor Ruth, who went blind from a rare venereal disease; Poor Ruth, who was exposed as the little slut she was, and driven out of her own high school. . . .*

And it could have happened, of course, at least the pregnancy. In all their time together, Paul had never once used a condom, and Ruth never asked him to; it just seemed out of the question somehow, too bald and practical, as if they were operating in the real world of choices and consequences, rather than this sealed-off dream capsule where you could do whatever you wanted and not worry about anything. Sexually transmitted diseases, on the other hand, were a nonissue; Paul turned out to be as inexperienced as she was, though his virginity was more a matter of his girlfriend's preference than his own.

*Missy won't do that,* was a constant refrain on those afternoons, a phrase that not only applied to actual sex, but to less momentous stuff like ear-licking, or finger-sucking, or letting Paul see what you looked like in just your underwear and socks. *She thinks it's gross.*

"Why don't you break up with her?" Ruth asked.

"I can't do it now," he explained. "Not this close to graduation."

SHE HAD only one bad memory from those days, but it had stuck with her over the years, its power undiminished by the passage of time. It happened on a warm evening near the end of school, a couple of weeks after Paul's cast came off and he was reclaimed by real life, Missy, and the marching band. Ruth was in the kitchen, helping her mother clean up after dinner when her father called from the living room.

"Hey, get a load of this."

What he wanted them to see was the white stretch limo parked in front of the Carusos'. A small crowd of curious neighbors had gathered around to admire the vehicle—it was gleaming in the dusk, giving off a soft shimmery luster—some of them chatting with the uniformed driver, others circling the car, peering into the windows and kicking the tires, as if they were thinking about buying one for themselves.

"Must be the prom," Ruth's mother said.

Ruth's father was a man who liked to know what was going on. Whenever an ambulance or fire truck appeared on Peony Road, no matter what time of day or night, he headed out to investigate, buttonholing as many bystanders and emergency workers as he could, then returning home with the bulletin: *Mrs. Rapinksi was short of breath, it was a grease fire in the oven, the old man felt dizzy.* Ruth wasn't surprised to see him putting on his shoes.

"This oughta be interesting," he said.

"Who's his date?" her mother asked. "Is it that big girl? The baseball player?"

"How should I know?" Ruth snapped.

Her parents headed outside, unable to resist the glamorous pull of prom night. Ruth stayed in, staring out the window, wishing she had the courage to return to the kitchen and continue loading the dishwasher but finding it impossible to turn away from the spectacle.

The limo driver—he was an older man with a carefully expressionless face—had just pulled out a handkerchief and begun rubbing at something on the windshield when the people around him began to clap, as if applauding his diligence. It took Ruth a moment to realize that Paul and Missy must have just emerged from the house, though she couldn't see them from where she stood. Even with her face pressed against the glass, her field of vision only encompassed the bottom half of the front lawn, where Paul's father and another man—a burly guy in a windbreaker who must have been Missy's dad—were kneeling and snapping flash pictures.

Onlookers shouted out jokey-sounding comments that Ruth couldn't quite make out; she saw her own mother and father laughing on the sidewalk. Finally, she couldn't take it anymore, the sense of being cut off from the action, of being stuck in here while it was all happening out there.

She headed for the front door, hesitating for a moment as she took stock of her unflattering outfit—baggy sweatpants and an old Southside Johnny T-shirt inherited from her sister—nothing you'd want to be seen wearing in public. She wondered if there was time to at least grab a jean jacket from her room or run a brush through her hair, but there wasn't.

She stepped onto her porch just in time to see Paul and Missy making their way toward the limo, where the driver was waiting, holding the back door open and extending an eloquent gesture of invitation with his free hand. They stopped by the curb, posing for one last photo, Paul bulky and imposing in his rented tux, Missy a bit awkward in a sleeveless orange dress with a poufy skirt, a tight bodice—an unwieldy corsage had been pinned directly over her left breast—and spaghetti straps that emphasized the powerful girth of her shoulders. Her blond French twist seemed strangely luminous, almost iridescent, as she kissed Paul on the cheek, straightened his bow tie, and then ducked into the car. He was just about to follow her when he turned suddenly, as if drawn by Ruth's gaze, and looked straight at her.

That moment of eye contact couldn't have lasted more than a second or two, just long enough for Ruth to see that he'd gotten a haircut—nothing drastic, just a trim of a couple inches all around—and to notice his peculiar expression, as if his face had gotten stuck halfway between a fake smile for the cameras and a mute apology to her.

Or maybe she was imagining the apology part, because what did he have to apologize for? Ruth wasn't his girlfriend, never had been. They'd just had some fun, and now it was over. She had no right to be jealous, no right to wish herself inside the limo in a pretty dress after having just been applauded by her neighbors, no right to call out and ask him to reconsider, to remember how he'd stroked her hair and told her that she was the kind of girl guys wrote love songs about.

He held his arms close to his body and shrugged, as if to say there was nothing he could do. She had the feeling he was about to say something, but the limo driver stepped in before he had the chance, placing his hand on Paul's shoulder and guiding him gently into the car. He was still looking at her as the door slammed shut, his face baffled and unhappy, then lost behind the tinted window.

# Who Do We Appreciate?

RUTH ARRIVED LATE AND MILDLY HUNGOVER FOR HER DAUGHTER'S soccer game on Saturday morning. Smiling queasily, she made her way down the sideline, nodding hello to the more punctual parents, many of whom she hadn't seen in quite a while. A few of the spectators were sitting in collapsible chairs, but most were on their feet, chatting in sociable clumps as they sipped from state-of-the-art, stainless-steel travel mugs, giving the whole scene the air of an outdoor cocktail party.

As usual, Ruth's ex-husband, Frank, had removed himself from the talkers, his attention focused solely on the game. He stood like the baseball player he'd once been—knees bent, hands resting on his thighs—observing the action with an expression of intense absorption that Ruth might have mistaken for disgust if she hadn't known him so well.

"Morning," she said, tugging gently on his sleeve. "How we doing?"

"Tied at two," he muttered, shooting her a reproachful glance. "First half's almost over. Maggie thought you forgot."

"I overslept."

"Ever hear of an alarm clock?"

"Didn't go off," she explained, leaving out the part about how she'd unplugged the thing in a fit of three-in-the-morning insomniac misery. Because, really, what was worse than lying wide-awake in the dark, watching your life drip away, one irreplaceable minute after another?

"Come on, blue!" Frank bellowed through the loudspeaker of his cupped hands. "Move the ball! You're dragging out there!"

Ruth squinted at the field, cursing herself for forgetting her sunglasses. She'd actually had them on the first time she left the house, but she'd decided to dart back inside for one final pit stop, knowing all too well that once she got to the game, her only alternative would be an off-kilter Port-A-Potty at the edge of the woods. She must have removed her shades to use the toilet—not that she couldn't pee perfectly well in the dark—because they were no longer on her face when she pulled into the gravel parking area at Shackamackan Park.

"Candace!" Frank had both hands above his head and was waving them like one of those guys with the sticks on the airport tarmac. "You're sweeper! Get back!"

Candace Roper, a very pretty girl whom Maggie had known since preschool, had drifted up near midfield, apparently unaware that one of her opponents—they wore shiny yellow jerseys with the word *Comets* emblazoned on the front—had slipped behind her and would have a clear path to the goal if her teammates could get her the ball. Candace glanced over her shoulder, clapped one hand over her mouth in guilty surprise, then scampered back into position.

"Jesus," he said. "We're sleepwalking out here."

"Where's Eliza?"

Frank jerked his thumb over his shoulder. Ruth turned to see her older daughter sitting at a picnic table beneath a fiery red maple that had already lost half its leaves. She was engrossed in a magazine, most likely a back issue of *O* or *Martha Stewart Living* that Frank's lady friend, Meredith, made a point of passing along, knowing how much she enjoyed them. Ruth waved and called out a greeting, but Eliza didn't notice—probably too busy boning up on recipes for low-fat crème brulée or color schemes to beat those stubborn winter blahs. Ruth watched her for a moment, struggling against the combination of exasperation and pity that Eliza so often provoked in her. She was four-teen going on forty, for God's sake. Wasn't it past time for a little ado-lescent rebellion?

"Come on, ref!" Frank slapped his thigh. "Open your eyes! She's throwing elbows!"

"Easy," Ruth warned him. Both her daughters had recently com-plained about their father's obnoxious behavior at soccer games. "You're not allowed to harass the referees."

"Number fourteen's going to hurt someone!" he continued, as if Ruth hadn't said a word. "She's playing like a thug!"

He yelled this loudly enough that the thug in question—a big, rosy-cheeked girl who wore her blond hair in Valkyrie-style braids—turned and gaped at him, her arms spread wide in a gesture of puzzled innocence.

"That's right, honey!" Frank jabbed an accusatory finger. "I'm watching you!"

"Enough," Ruth said. "She's just a kid."

She spoke more forcefully this time, and Frank actually listened. His expression turned sheepish, and he shook his head, as if trying to clear away the cobwebs.

"Sorry. Sometimes I get a little worked up."

"No kidding."

"It's crazy. These Bridgeton girls are a bunch of bruisers. What're they putting in the milk over there?"

It was true, Ruth realized. The Comets *were* unusually big for their age—aside from one nimble Asian girl, they looked like a tribe of Viking warrior maidens—and they played a tough physical game, lots of pushing and shoving and body-checking. But you had to give Mag-gie's team credit; what they lacked in size they made up for in quick-ness and skill, frequently beating their opponents to the ball and moving upfield in a rat-a-tat-tat series of pinpoint passes. If not for several spectacular but risky saves by the Comets' goalie, who had no qualms about coming way out of the net to challenge the shooter, Stonewood Heights would have held a commanding lead.

Ruth was especially impressed by her daughter's performance. Maggie had always been a natural athlete, but in the past she'd seemed oddly tentative in the field, too polite for her own good. If a girl on the other team wanted the ball badly enough, Maggie would just stand aside and let her have it. Today, though, she was playing with a competitive fire that took Ruth by surprise, a beady-eyed intensity uncannily similar to her father's. She was all over the field, leading the breaks on offense, helping out on defense, fighting fiercely for control of the ball. She talked a lot during the game, barking incomprehensible instructions to her teammates—she wore a mouthpiece to protect her orthodontia—who seemed to understand exactly what she wanted from them.

"Wow," said Ruth. "She's come a long way."

Frank nodded. "She's been like this all season."

UNTIL HER divorce, Ruth had been a dutiful soccer mom, surrendering countless Saturday mornings to the dubious pleasures of watching little kids kick a ball up and down a grassy field, often in unpleasant weather. Now that Frank had the girls on Saturday, though, he'd become point man for weekend sporting events, a piece of parental turf Ruth had surrendered without complaint. God knew she spent enough time ferrying the girls back and forth to various lessons, practices, and friends' houses during the rest of the week.

Besides, Frank enjoyed the games more than she did, especially once Maggie began qualifying for the stronger teams. In the past couple of years, he'd become her advisor, practice partner, and biggest fan; besides taking her to numerous high-school and college games, he supervised her development, enrolling her in instructional clinics and expensive summer programs (this past July, she'd spent two weeks at a sleepaway camp run by former members of the USA Women's National Team). Eliza—a lackluster athlete who'd quit sports as soon as she was given a choice—frequently complained about Frank's favoritism toward her little sister, how all he could talk about was Maggie, Maggie, Maggie, soccer, soccer, soccer.

The irony of this was not lost on Ruth, who remembered quite vividly just how disappointed Frank had been to have a second daughter, rather than a son he could "play ball with." He used this phrase all the time, as if male children existed for the sole purpose of playing ball with their fathers. He pressured Ruth to reconsider the two-child policy that had been in place since the beginning of their marriage, and changed his mind about going in for the vasectomy he'd agreed to get once they reached their quota.

In retrospect, Ruth could see that Maggie's birth had marked the beginning of the end of their marriage. Slowly but inexorably, Frank began drifting away. Without consulting her, he signed up for graduate courses in Education, and threw himself into his studies with an energy that would have seemed admirable under other circumstances, earning his Master's in Administration in only two years while holding down a full-time teaching job. Only his family life suffered, but Ruth understood that that was the whole point—he'd gone back to school precisely so he could get the hell out of that house full of females, away from the unendurable torment of not having a boy to play ball with.

But now he had a girl to play ball with, and everything was forgiven. Ruth didn't begrudge him the pleasure, or his closeness to Maggie, not anymore. As far as she was concerned, he was welcome to stand out in the rain and scream at the refs to his heart's content, as long as it allowed her to spend her Saturday mornings waking up slowly in a warm, quiet house. This privilege had seemed doubly luxurious during the dark days of last spring's Sex Ed scandal, when running the gauntlet of concerned soccer parents ranked somewhere beneath oral surgery on Ruth's list of Fun Things to Do.

Maggie had seemed perfectly fine with this parental division of labor until a couple of months ago, when she'd been chosen to play for the Stonewood Stars, the town's elite traveling team for girls eleven and under. It was a high honor, and it had made her happier than Ruth had ever seen her. She slept in her team jersey—royal blue with a white star over the heart—and wore it every day in the yard, where she spent an hour dribbling between cones and kicking the ball against the side of the garage. And every Friday, just before Frank came to take her and Eliza for the weekend, Maggie would remind Ruth about the game on Saturday, and beg her to please come and watch her play, and this week Ruth had finally run out of excuses.

THE SCORE was still tied at halftime, but the Stars seemed relaxed and silly on the sideline, as if they'd already won. Several players were fussing over a black Lab puppy with a purple bandana around its neck; three others were teaching a dance routine—it combined elements of the Macarena, the Swim, and the Bump—to their coaches, an incongruous pair who seemed genuinely interested in mastering the complicated sequence of moves. After a moment of uncertainty, Ruth recognized the bulkier of the two men as John Roper, Candace's dad, though he'd lost most of his hair and put on about fifty pounds since she'd first seen him dropping off his daughter at Little Learners seven years ago. She didn't know the other coach—he was younger, unexpectedly hippie-ish for Stonewood Heights, a small compact man whose dark hair could easily have been gathered into a respectable ponytail.

Oblivious to the festivities, Maggie sat on the grass nearby, caught up in conversation with her friend, Nadima, a Pakistani-American girl with huge brown eyes and disconcertingly skinny legs. Nadima was scowling thoughtfully, nodding the way you do when you want your friend to know that you understand what she's saying and sympathize with her position, even if you don't completely agree with her. Ruth approached cautiously, hoping she might be able to overhear a few scraps of their conversation—they looked so endearingly serious, like grown women discussing a complicated relationship or a thorny problem at work—but her cover was blown by Hannah Friedman, who glanced up while scratching the puppy's belly.

"Hi, Mrs. Maggie's mother!" she called out, in a loud, stagey voice. Unlike most of the girls on the team—they were eleven and under, after all—Hannah had already begun to develop real breasts and an annoying adolescent personality to go along with them.

"Hi," Ruth replied, uncomfortably aware of several faces turning in her direction at once. "You girls are doing great."

With a startled cry of delight, Maggie scrambled to her feet and rushed over to her mother, greeting her with a hug several orders of magnitude stronger than usual. Ruth squeezed back, feeling the clamminess of her daughter's skin through the mesh weave of her jersey.

"Mommy!" Maggie's voice sounded as theatrical as Hannah's, but her eyes were full of honest emotion. "Thanks for coming."

"Happy to be here," Ruth told her. "I'm sorry it took so long."

Maggie stepped back from the embrace, tugging at her uniform to get everything back in order. Ruth was unexpectedly moved by the sight of her, as if she were being offered a glimpse of two Maggies at once: the little girl she still was—a dirty-kneed tomboy straight out of Norman Rockwell—and the happy, confident young woman she was already on her way to becoming.

"Did you see when I scored?" she asked, kicking an imaginary ball. "The goalie dove, but it went right through her hands."

Ruth frowned an apology. "I'm sorry, honey, I got here a little late. But I can't believe how well you're playing. You're like the Energizer Bunny out there. I'm so proud of you."

"You should be," said a man's voice. "She's our spark plug."

Ruth turned and saw the long-haired coach approaching with a friendly expression and a slight bounce in his step, probably a by-product of the dance lesson.

"Can I interest you in an apple slice?" he asked, extending a Tupperware container. "The girls barely made a dent."

Maggie took one, but Ruth declined.

"You sure?" The coach looked a bit put out by her refusal. "They're nice and fresh. I squeeze lemon juice on 'em so they don't turn brown."

"Good thinking," said Ruth. "Can't go wrong with lemon juice."

Nodding as if she'd uttered a profound truth, the coach shifted the container to his left hand and extended his right.

"Tim Mason. I'm the fearless leader of this motley crew."

They shook. His hand was unusually large and a lot warmer than hers.

"I'm Ruth. Maggie's mother."

Keeping a firm grip on Ruth's hand, Tim Mason studied her face, as if she were a good friend he hadn't seen in a long time. Up close, he looked older than she'd expected, at least forty. Some gray hair. Crow's-feet. A certain wariness around the eyes.

"I've heard a lot about you," he said.

Ruth chuckled nervously, glad she'd taken the time to shower and put on makeup before leaving the house.

"Good things, I hope."

Tim Mason didn't answer, nor did he loosen his grip. He just kept staring at Ruth, the moment stretching out, the air smelling like apples.

"It means a lot to her that you're here," he said. "I know how much she's missed you."

When he released her hand, Ruth felt relieved and vaguely let down at the same time.

"Well, thanks for coaching," she said. "I know it's a big time commitment."

"I love it," he said, turning to Maggie and ruffling her hair. "We got a great buncha kids."

*   *   *

RUTH WASN'T sure why the brief encounter with Tim Mason had left her so flustered. It was nothing, really, just some innocuous small talk and a handshake that lasted a little too long with a guy she wasn't even sure she found all that attractive (he was handsome enough, but she always found something vaguely off-putting about long hair on a middle-aged man). And yet here she was, all hot and bothered at the beginning of the second half, staring right through the players on the field to the coach on the far sideline—he was holding a clipboard, banging it against his leg like a tambourine—unable to think of anything but the pressure of his palm against hers and the way time seemed to stop when he looked into her eyes.

It was embarrassing, she understood that, pining for your daughter's married soccer coach—oh, she'd checked for the ring; she always checked for the ring—possibly a new low. Not that it was her fault. This was the kind of thing that happened when you went without sex for too long. After a while, any scrap of male attention—a wry smile, a kind word, the faintest whiff of flirtation—was enough to create a full-blown disturbance in your love-starved brain. A guy says, "Excuse me" in the supermarket, well, he must be the One, your Last Chance for Happiness. Or barring that—because happiness was a pretty tall order—your last chance for a normally unhappy life where somebody at least touches you every week or two.

What made it more ridiculous was that it wasn't even midmorning yet, and Tim Mason was already her second Last Chance of the day. During the night, she'd gotten so worked up thinking about Paul Caruso and their long-lost interlude of secret passion—Hadn't they shared something special? Wasn't it a pity that they'd fallen out of touch?—that she'd done something she already regretted. Dragging herself out of bed at three-thirty in the morning, she'd logged on to Classmates.com and posted a query on the Oakhurst Regional High message board: "Does anyone know how to get in touch with Paul Caruso, class of '80? He was a trumpet player who lived on Peony Road."

What was that, six hours ago? And already, she'd dumped her old lover for a hippie soccer coach who would undoubtedly be replaced by the surly Russian guy with liquor on his breath who pumped her gas at the Hess station. Is this what it's going to be like for the rest of my life, Ruth wondered, one unrequited fantasy after another until I shrivel up and die?

SHE WAS rescued from this unrewarding line of inquiry by the sudden appearance at her side of Arlene Zabel, a striking woman of about fifty, whose daughter, Louisa, played goalie for the Stars. Arlene had long gray hair that only heightened your awareness of how youthful she looked otherwise—her body trim and girlish, her face lively and unlined.

"Ruth," she said. "It's been ages."

Ruth agreed that it had. Arlene gave her an approving once-over as they exchanged pleasantries.

"You look terrific. Did you lose weight?"

"I've been running," Ruth explained. "Mainly just to keep sane."

Arlene nodded sympathetically, as if she understood exactly why Ruth might have needed to take steps to preserve her sanity. She was a tax-attorney-turned-massage-therapist—a true renegade, given the narrow parameters of acceptable adult conduct in Stonewood Heights—and Ruth had always considered her a kindred spirit.

"I've been meaning to call you for months," Arlene said. "But you know how it is. Mel's been traveling for work, and I run around so much, I barely have time to breathe."

"That's okay," Ruth told her. "I've been pretty busy myself."

The falseness of the moment was painfully apparent to both of them. Four years ago, they'd been good friends. They had each other's families over for dinner, went on double dates with their husbands, took the kids to movies, museums, and amusement parks. But Frank had known Mel since high school, and it was tacitly understood by everyone involved that he would get custody of the Zabels after the divorce. Ruth and Arlene tried to sustain an independent friendship for a while, but it had petered out after a couple of melancholy coffee dates.

"It's a shame what they did to you," Arlene said. "You didn't deserve to be raked over the coals like that."

"Thanks." Ruth appreciated the sentiment, though she would have appreciated it a whole lot more a few months ago, back when the coals were still burning.

"I don't know where all these Bible Thumpers are coming from," Arlene said. "I mean, they didn't used to be so—uh-oh!"

Ruth looked up just in time to see one of the Comets steal the ball from Nadima and boot it upfield to the Asian girl. A roar of anticipation went up from the Bridgeton fans as their star offensive player dribbled past Hannah Friedman and broke for the net. Alone in the goal, Louisa Zabel seemed jittery, uncertain whether to hold her ground or rush forward and force a shot.

"Oh God," Arlene said, grabbing hold of Ruth's wrist.

The Asian girl had a wide-open shot from ten feet out, but she drilled the ball straight at Louisa, who swatted it away with her gloved hands, then dove for the rebound, curling her body around the ball before the shooter could follow up.

"Way to go, Lou-Lou!" Arlene screamed. "Get it out of there!"

Louisa leapt to her feet, sprinted forward, and flung the ball almost to midfield.

"Wow," said Ruth. "She's got quite an arm."

"This game's gonna give me a heart attack," Arlene said. "What was I saying?"

"The Bible Thumpers?"

"Ah, forget it." She waved her hand in disgust. "I'm sick of talking about it. The whole world's going nuts."

"It's the kids who are being cheated," Ruth pointed out. "You got a small group of fanatics telling everybody else what they can and can't do, what they should and shouldn't read or talk about. Where's it gonna end?"

"I wish it were a small group of fanatics. I'm starting to think there's more of them than us. I mean, they're running the country."

"It's only because they're louder. The people on our side aren't speaking out. It's like we're a bunch of wimps who don't believe in anything."

The Stars had a throw-in. Nadima raised the ball high over her head and heaved it into an empty space in the center of the field, a little bit ahead of one of her teammates—a quick, dark-haired girl Ruth had never seen before—who came streaking out of nowhere to meet it. Unfortunately, one of the Comets—Number 14, with the Wagnerian braids—arrived from the opposite direction at exactly the same time. It was a sickening thing to watch: the two players crashing into each other at full speed, both going down hard.

The bigger girl got up right away—she was crying and clutching her midsection—but Maggie's teammate remained motionless on the grass. Tim Mason and John Roper came running onto the field before the ref had even blown the whistle.

"Who got hurt?" Ruth asked.

"That's Abby, Tim's daughter." Arlene drew an anxious breath. "I hope she's okay. Last week, a girl from Willard Falls broke her collarbone. They had to take her away in an ambulance."

The players took a knee while the coaches attended to Abby. Tim Mason crouched at his daughter's side, his hand resting lightly on her shoulder. He addressed a worried comment to his assistant, who nodded grimly, and signaled to the ref. By this point, the Bridgeton coach had wandered onto the field to see if he could help.

"This is scary," Arlene said.

At almost the same moment, though, Tim's face broke into a dazzling smile of relief as Abby pushed herself into sitting position and held out a hand. In a single smooth motion, her father hoisted her up from the ground and cradled her in his arms. He asked a question; she nodded yes. The spectators applauded as they made their way slowly across the field, like an old-fashioned bride and groom.

"He seems like a nice guy," said Ruth.

"Who, Tim?"

"Yeah. I just met him a little while ago."

"He's good with the girls," Arlene said, a bit stiffly.

Ruth couldn't help herself. "I actually thought he was kinda cute. I mean, I know he's married and everything."

"You're joking, right?"

"He's a little short," Ruth conceded. "But he's got a good build."

Arlene hesitated for a moment, apparently trying to decide if Ruth was pulling her leg.

"You know he's one of them, right?"

"One of who?"

"That church. Tabernacle. Whatever you call it."

"Really? He doesn't seem the type."

"Ask him," Arlene said. "He'll be happy to tell you all about it."

"Oh, shit." Ruth laughed, remembering the way the coach had held her hand and stared into her eyes. He hadn't wanted her body. He'd wanted her soul. "I'm such an idiot."

Arlene patted her on the shoulder.

"We gotta find you a boyfriend."

This was no idle offer. It was Arlene who'd set Ruth up with Ray Mattingly, the divorced computer guy with whom she'd had her only serious relationship since Frank had moved out. Not that it was all that serious. They'd had a couple of bad dates, then a couple of good ones, then a lovely weekend together in the Poconos, on the way home from which he informed her that he was moving to the Research Triangle of North Carolina. He said he would've mentioned it earlier, but he hadn't wanted to spoil their trip.

"Any candidates?" Ruth asked.

"I'll give it some thought," Arlene promised.

The ball went out of bounds off the Comets, and the Stars called for subs. Maggie was one of three girls who came sprinting onto the field.

"Thank God," said Arlene. "Now maybe we can get some offense going. If we win today, we'll be tied for first place in Division B-3."

RUTH DIDN'T think of herself as the kind of person who cared deeply about the outcome of a game played by fifth graders—or the standings in Division B-3, whatever that was—but even she found it impossible not to get swept up in the excitement as the clock wound down, and every play became fraught with danger and possibility. You could see the tension on the faces of the spectators—they'd abandoned their conversations and drifted en masse toward the sideline, creating an irregular human fence around the field—as well as the players, who seemed to have moved beyond fatigue into the realm of pure adrenaline. Watching them, Ruth felt a sharp pang of envy, wishing she could be out there herself—hair pulled back, shin guards tucked under her knee socks, completely alive in her body, in the moment—wishing she'd grown up at a time when sports were a routine part of a girl's life. She would be a happier person now, she was pretty sure of it.

The momentum had taken a worrisome turn in the latter part of the second half. Now it was the Comets who dominated, mounting one offensive assault after another, getting off numerous solid shots on goal—including a penalty kick that ricocheted off the post—without managing to score. The Stars seemed intimidated, as if they'd given up trying to win and had decided that the best they could hope for was to run out the clock and escape with a tie.

"Come on, ladies!" Frank bellowed from down the sideline—Ruth had moved away from him in the second half, unable to cope with his enthusiasm—his voice so ragged with emotion that Ruth felt ashamed for both of them. It was simply beyond belief that she'd spent two hours with a man like that, let alone twelve years of her life. "Let's get some backbone!"

Smelling blood, but clearly frustrated at their inability to score, the Comets launched a furious last-ditch onslaught, bringing their two defenders way up past midfield to increase the pressure on the beleaguered Stars, who couldn't seem to clear the ball from out in front of their net no matter how hard they tried.

"Oh Jesus," Arlene groaned. "This is not good."

One of the Comets—a lanky girl with boyishly cropped blond hair—had an open shot that went wide. A few seconds later, the same girl dropped a beautiful corner kick right in front of the Stars' goal, but Louisa reacted quickly, snatching it up on one bounce. Without a second's hesitation, she charged forward and whizzed the ball downfield, toward the right sideline. At first it seemed to Ruth that she was throwing wildly, just trying to get the ball as far away as possible, but suddenly it became clear that it was a planned maneuver, because Maggie was already far upfield, moving at full tilt, as if she'd known where the ball was going to land before it had left Louisa's hand, long before the Comets even sensed the danger.

Maggie took control of the ball near midfield, with nothing but grass between her and the goal. It looked to Ruth like one of those scenarios from a wish-fulfillment dream—one player way out front, everyone else stampeding behind, unable to catch up. When it became clear that help would arrive too late, the Comets' goalie began moving away from the net, hoping to force a bad shot. Maggie just kept charging forward as if the goalie weren't even there, and it looked to Ruth for a second like another collision was inevitable.

"Shoot!" Frank was shouting. "Bang it in!"

But Maggie didn't shoot. With the goalie closing in on her at full speed, she kicked the ball sideways instead of straight ahead, a maneuver that made no sense to Ruth until she noticed that Candace Roper had also outrun the Comets' pursuit and was pulling up even with Maggie just in time to receive the unexpected pass.

Candace had a little trouble getting control of the ball, giving the goalie time to whirl and make a panicky sprint back to the net, but it was too late. By the time she got there, Candace's shot—a weak dribbler that would have been an easy save under other circumstances—had already trickled across the goal line.

IT WASN'T true, as certain people insisted in the weeks that followed, that Ruth had gone to Shackamackan Park that morning looking to cause trouble. In fact, trouble was the furthest thing from her mind as the ref blew the whistle to end the game, giving the Stars a hard-fought 3–2 victory.

"We did it!" Arlene cried, hugging Ruth and jumping up and down at the same time. "I can't believe we did it!"

"What a game," Ruth said. "The girls just didn't give up."

She was surprised at how exhilarated she felt—proud of Maggie, mainly, but also mysteriously validated as a parent—and these good feelings even spilled over onto Frank as he approached with a cockeyed grin on his face. He looked wired, the way he used to get when he stayed up all night writing a term paper.

"Can you believe your daughter?" he asked. "Is she amazing or what?"

Ruth was about to launch into her own rhapsody of agreement, but she checked herself when she saw that Eliza had wandered over from the picnic table to join them.

"You missed quite a game," Frank informed her.

She shrugged. "How'd Maggie do?"

"Good," Ruth said. "They won."

Eliza nodded, and Ruth could see the struggle it took for her to produce even a halfhearted smile.

"Cool," she said.

Ruth's heart went out to her. Eliza was going through a rough patch. The divorce had shaken her, the newspaper stories about her mother had mortified her, and puberty had knocked her for a loop. In three years, she'd gone from being an adorable little girl to being a chunky, strangely proportioned adolescent with greasy hair—it didn't matter how often she washed it—a perpetual squint, and a mouth that hung open in a look of constant bewilderment. Her grades were mediocre, and her best friend had dumped her for a more glamorous crowd.

"She did *good?*" Frank asked. "Are you kidding me? She kicked ass out there."

Eliza's only reaction was to tug her upper lip over her lower one, a strange habit she had developed in the past few months.

"Can we go now?" she asked her father. "I'm starving."

"We didn't really have time for breakfast this morning," Frank explained. "I promised the girls I'd take them to the diner after the game." He hesitated, glancing first at Eliza, then at Ruth. "You can come with us if you want."

Ruth was tempted—she would have liked to talk about the game with Maggie, and see what she could do to cheer Eliza up—but she and Frank had agreed to have as few "family" outings as possible, to avoid misleading the girls about the possibility of their getting back together.

"No thanks," she said. "I gotta go. I'm just gonna say good-bye to Maggie."

She kissed Eliza on the cheek, then headed across the field just as the Comets launched into their obligatory postgame cheer.

"Two, four, six, eight, who do we appreciate? Stonewood Heights, Stonewood Heights, yaaay . . ."

The Stars hadn't done their cheer yet; they were sitting cross-legged in a circle on the grass, holding hands, looking unexpectedly solemn as they listened to whatever it was Tim Mason and John Roper were telling them. The coaches were part of the group, and that just made it cuter—the two grown men holding hands with the complete lack of self-consciousness they'd displayed while dancing at halftime—until Ruth suddenly realized what they were doing, at which point it wasn't cute at all.

"Excuse me," she called, quickening her pace. "Just a minute!"

Several girls turned at the sound of her voice, including Maggie. Ruth caught the warning look in her daughter's eyes, the silent plea for her to just please keep out of this, but she didn't slow down.

Tim Mason ignored her approach. He kept his eyes on the ground and spoke in a low voice.

". . . and all the blessings He has bestowed upon us. Our parents, our families, all the material—"

"Hello?" Ruth interrupted. "You can't do this."

The coach stopped talking and looked up.

"This is ridiculous," Ruth continued. "These aren't your children."

The glance he returned wasn't defiant, but it was calm and unwavering.

"Join us," he said. "You're more than welcome."

"Maggie," Ruth said, her voice harsher than she meant it to be. "You get away from there."

"*Mom,*" said Maggie.

"Ruth," said John Roper. "Calm down."

Tim Mason looked at Maggie.

"She needs to hear this," he said. "So do you."

"You don't know me," Ruth told him. "Don't tell me what I need."

"You're no different from anyone else," he replied. "We all need the same thing."

Ruth was startled by the surge of anger that coursed through her body. It was as if everything she'd swallowed over the past six months—

the abuse, the insults, the humiliation—had gathered into a fiery ball that was rising up from her belly, into her throat. She grabbed Maggie by the arm, jerked her to her feet, and yanked her out of the circle.

"It's okay, Mom," Maggie whispered. "It's really okay."

The softness of her daughter's voice threw her for a second, and she wondered if she'd done the right thing. But she had, she knew she had. She took a deep breath and pointed her finger at the coach.

"I'll tell you what I need," she said. "I need you to stay away from my kid."

# PART TWO

# Hot Christian Sex

# Three-Legged Race

ABBY WAS QUIET IN THE CAR ON SUNDAY MORNING, AND AS USUAL, Tim wasn't sure what to make of her silence. Was she sad about leaving him for another week, or relieved to be getting back to her normal life, the big fancy house she shared with her mother, stepfather, and little brother? Or was she just lost in her own head, worrying about homework, some intrigue with her school friends that didn't concern him at all?

"You okay?"

"Yeah," she said, a little too quickly. "Why?"

"I don't know. You just seem a little subdued or something."

She insisted she was fine, leaving him to wonder if the sadness was all on his side, if he was simply fishing for a sign that she wanted to stay with him a little longer. He couldn't help feeling a pang of nostalgia for the child she used to be, the little girl whose moods were as obvious as the weather. In the past year, she'd gone all poker-faced on him, turning every interaction into a guessing game. It didn't help that Tim could never quite decide whether this awkwardness was just the normal weirdness of adolescence setting in or something more specific to the two of them.

"Oooh, look," she said, whipping her head around to follow the path of a sports car that blew past on Pembroke Boulevard. "That's an Audi TT. Those things are awesome."

Tim didn't reply. Since she'd started going to private school, Abby had developed what he thought was a dishearteningly well-informed enthusiasm for the finer things in life—plasma-screen TVs, Rolexes, designer handbags, iPods, cars that cost more than he made in a year—and he tried, without getting all self-righteous about it, to let her know that he wasn't as impressed as she was, though she didn't seem to care much about his opinion one way or the other.

"Maybe one of these days you can come to Sunday meeting with me," he ventured. "You know, just give it a try. See what you think."

"You'll have to talk to Mom."

They both knew what that meant. The custody agreement gave his ex-wife exclusive control over their daughter's educational and spiritual upbringing, and Allison categorically refused to let Abby set foot in the Tabernacle, which she referred to as "that Nuthouse." Tim understood all too well where she was coming from, and if he'd been coming from the same place, he would've felt exactly the same way. But that place just happened to be a swamp of vanity and self-delusion, and he prayed that Allison would find her way out of it someday, as unlikely as that seemed.

Not that he was losing any sleep over the state of his ex-wife's soul; she was an adult, responsible for her own life, both in this world and the next. But Abby was still a child, and Tim felt like a coward and a bad father, letting some family court judge stand between his daughter and God. It was crazy: he was allowed to be Abby's soccer coach, but was barred from guiding her in something way more important, the only thing that really mattered.

"So, uh, what are you going to do the rest of the day?"

"Chill out," she said. "Probably just IM for a while, then go to the mall."

Tim sighed in a way he instantly regretted, knowing it made him sound like a Goody Two-Shoes, Ned Flanders without the mustache.

"It's the Lord's Day, honey. You shouldn't spend it at the mall."

"We might go to the movies," she said. "I'm not really sure."

His sense of helplessness—of personal failure—intensified as he turned into Greenwillow Estates, a luxury development full of bloated McMansions, one monstrosity more gaudy and boastful than the next. His disgust at the sheer excess of the houses—what family actually *needed* six thousand square feet of living space?—was aggravated by a professional grievance. Tim was a mortgage broker, but somehow he never managed to connect with the kinds of clients who bought places like this. He just handled the little guys, people he met through church, mostly—hardworking, two-income families with shaky credit and not much in the way of savings, who could only qualify for high-interest, variable-rate loans that just barely got them inside a run-down ranch or a garrison colonial on a busy street or otherwise marginal neighborhood.

Driving past the vast, oddly immaculate lawns of Country Club Way—it was mid-October, and there was barely a fallen leaf in sight—he fantasized, as he did every week, about pulling a U-turn and heading straight to the Tabernacle. What a pleasure it would be, walking into church with his little girl at his side, the person he loved best in the world, to stand beside her as she listened to God's word, surrounded by the love that filled the humble space, all those joyful voices mingling together in song.

But it wasn't gonna happen. Abby's stepfather was a lawyer, and by all accounts a good one. As polite and friendly as Mitchell always was, Tim had no illusions about the consequences he'd suffer if he violated the custody agreement. Pastor Dennis would have encouraged him to go for it anyway—to stand up for what was right, and trust Jesus to take it from there—but Tim hadn't reached that level of faith yet. There was a special bond between him and Abby—he'd felt it the first time he saw her, just seconds after she'd slipped into the world—and it had survived all sorts of turmoil, those years when he'd disappeared into the wilderness and inflicted all sorts of suffering on the people he loved. He had a lot to make amends for, and couldn't bear the thought of spending a minute less with his daughter than he already did, let alone risking the possibility of being cut off from her altogether.

MITCHELL AND Allison lived in something called a Greek Revival colonial on Running Brook Terrace, a monumental brick house with a portico supported by fluted pillars. Pulling his Saturn into the triple-wide driveway, next to an impossibly lustrous black Lexus SUV, Tim let the engine idle as he turned to his daughter. It was a way of prolonging their time together, as if his custodial rights didn't officially come to an end until he shut off his ignition.

"My little girl," he said, running his hand over her sleek dark hair, so similar to his own. "You be good, okay?"

She stared back at him, her face blank and patient. After a long moment, she nodded.

"Okay, Dad."

He felt a fullness in his heart that was almost painful and wished he could think of something to say that would do it justice. But words like that were never there when he needed them.

"I'm gonna miss you, Ab."

She laughed sweetly—the first happy sound that had come out of her mouth all morning—and patted him on the knee.

"Dude," she said. "It's only a week."

ALLISON STOOD in the sunlit, two-story entrance foyer—it featured a glittering chandelier that could be raised and lowered by remote control—looking sweetly disheveled in a gold silk robe that Tim had never seen before, tied just loosely enough for him to get a tantalizing glimpse of the sheer black nightgown underneath. She hugged Abby, then invited him in for the ritual Sunday morning cup of coffee and parental debriefing. He could've begged off, of course, could've told her he was in a rush, had to get ready for church or whatever, but he never did. She was the mother of his child, a woman who'd stood by him for way longer than he deserved before finally throwing in the towel, and the least he could do was give her fifteen minutes a week of his time.

He just wished she would put some clothes on. Allison was a beautiful woman—even at forty, with twenty pounds of post-childbirth weight that looked like it was here to stay—and Tim had to force himself to keep his eyes where they belonged as he trailed her through the dining room to the entrance of the family room, where he paused to say hi to Mitchell and his two-year-old son, Logan, who were playing a wooden ring toss game that looked like it came from a catalogue that only sold toys made of natural materials by the finest Old World craftsmen.

"*Hola*," Mitchell called out. He was a baby-faced guy in his late thirties with curly hair and a doughy physique. "It's *Señor Tim*."

"*Hola* to you," Tim replied. "How's the little guy?"

Mitchell wrapped his thumb and forefinger around Logan's pudgy bicep.

"Strong like bull," he declared in a ridiculous Russian accent that elicited a hearty chuckle from the boy, who appeared to have been cloned from his father.

Abby peeled off to join her brother and stepfather, while Tim and Allison continued into the breakfast nook. It was possible, he thought, that there was an innocent explanation for the fact that his ex-wife was hardly ever decently dressed when he showed up on Sunday mornings— it was true that she'd never been shy about her body, and had enjoyed lounging around half-naked on weekends ever since he'd known her— but he couldn't help suspecting that she got some satisfaction from re-minding him of everything he'd thrown away, all the pleasures and privileges he'd surrendered for the simple, stupid reason that he liked getting high better than he liked being a husband and father.

If that was her strategy, it was working a little too well. Standing in the archway of the eerily spotless dream kitchen—it looked like a

movie set, not a place where actual people cooked actual food—
watching her pour his coffee, he couldn't help noticing how shame-
lessly short her robe was, not much longer than a miniskirt, which
made him wonder how much shorter than that her nightgown must
have been, which led, inevitably, to more specific thoughts about her
body, and the many ways she'd shared it with him over the years.
Mitchell must have felt like he'd died and gone to heaven, a nerdy intellectual property lawyer living in a house like this with a wife who
had a black strawberry tattooed on her ass—she'd gotten it back in the
mid-eighties, when it was still a little bit daring—and, unless things
had changed, an unusually strong sex drive. The whole deferred-
gratification thing had really paid off for the guy, and Tim couldn't
help envying him for his discipline and foresight.

THE BREAKFAST island was long and sleek, the countertop a thick
slab of polished blue granite with a weirdly deep sink at one end. Sitting across from him, Allison rearranged the lapels of her robe in a
gesture of belated modesty, as if it had just occurred to her what she
was wearing and who she was with.

"So how'd the game go yesterday?"

"We won. We're tied for first place in the division."

"Wow." She sounded impressed, though both of them knew she
couldn't have cared less. "How'd Abby do?"

"Great." He took a sip of coffee, a dark roast that Allison insisted was
way better than Starbucks, though Tim could never taste the difference.
"I did want to tell you, though—she got into a pretty bad collision near
the end of the game. She and this other girl crashed into each other at
full speed, and I think she was knocked out for a minute or two."

"Oh my God, did you—"

"Don't worry. Dr. Felder says she's fine, no sign of concussion or
anything. He says to just keep an eye on her, but he doesn't anticipate
any problems. You can give him a call if you want."

Tim had expected to be grilled for details—he knew she questioned the soundness of his parental judgments, a holdover from the days when her worries were more than justified—but his explanation seemed to satisfy her. She shook her head with what seemed like genuine empathy.

"That must have been scary for you."

"You have no idea."

"I'm glad it was you," she said, rolling her neck in a lazy circle. She'd recently begun putting blond highlights in her hair, and he liked the way they glinted against the darker gold of her robe. He'd always enjoyed her hair; she used to tease him with it when they were making love, sweeping it across his face and belly like a broom, and she never complained if he pulled it when they were playing rough. "I woulda had a heart attack."

The conversation flagged for a few seconds, just long enough for him to register the music playing in the background; it was the Dead, a live version of "Cassidy" he'd never heard before. He grunted with surprise.

"What's this, a bootleg?"

"One of those Dick's Picks," she said.

"Since when do you—?"

"I always liked them," she said, a bit defensively.

"News to me."

"I appreciated the music. I just didn't like all the drugs and craziness."

"Okay," he said. "Whatever you say."

She looked at him with what felt like real curiosity.

"You still into them?"

"Not so much. I'm trying to put all that behind me."

"Must be hard." She smiled sadly, acknowledging the depth of his sacrifice.

"A little easier every day."

"Good for you." She paused, letting Jerry finish a jazzy little run, that clean sunny sound no one else could duplicate. "So how's Carrie?"

"Fine." He didn't like discussing his wife with Allison, though she was more than happy to discuss her husband with him. "Same as always."

"Well, tell her I said hi."

Tim nodded, feeling momentarily disoriented. Sitting across from Allison in this gorgeous kitchen, listening to the Grateful Dead on Sunday morning, it was easy to believe that this was his life—*their* life—a new improved version of the one he'd screwed up so royally. Abby was with them, and Mitchell and Logan and Carrie were just people they knew, and not especially important ones. It was such a convincing sensation that he had to make a conscious effort to remind himself that losing that life, painful as it was, had been the best thing that had ever happened to him. God had a plan for him, and it involved something more important than a big house and a beautiful wife and a happy intact family. He slid off the stool and pressed his palm over the lid of his coffee mug.

"I better be going," he told her.

MOST OF the time, Tim felt pretty good about his new condo—it was a two-bedroom townhouse with wood floors, central air, a gas fireplace, and Corian countertops—but it always struck him as cramped and dingy after he returned from Greenwillow Estates. Everything was all squashed together—the closet-sized half bath a step away from the front door, the kitchen table wedged between the refrigerator and the dishwasher, forcing you to turn sideways when serving or cleaning up. The furniture, which was perfectly nice, and not cheap by any means, seemed common and nondescript, and even slightly tacky, in a way he couldn't put his finger on.

He had a similar reaction to Carrie, who was sitting on the living room couch, flipping through *Parade* magazine. With Allison fresh in his mind, she seemed paler and less vivid than usual, vaguely disappointing. He must have stared at her a moment too long, or with a little too much intensity, because she put down the magazine and looked up with a worried smile.

"Everything okay?"

"Fine."

"How's Abby's mom?" For some reason, Carrie insisted on referring to Allison in this way, and Tim could never quite decide if she meant it as a subtle dig or an expression of respect.

"Hard to say. I just stopped in for a minute or two."

She nodded, keeping her gaze trained on his face, as if awaiting instructions. Though she was already dressed for church, he knew she was expecting him to take her by the hand and lead her up to the bedroom, the way he did on most Sunday mornings, taking advantage of this brief interlude—their first free moment of the weekend—between dropping Abby off and heading to church.

But Tim just stood there, hands jammed into his pockets, reminding himself of the promise he'd made to Pastor Dennis after Wednesday Night Bible Study, not to touch his wife until he cleared his head and purified his heart. Because it was deceitful and disrespectful, making love to Carrie after being aroused by Allison, turning one woman into a substitute for another.

"You look upset," she said. "Can I make you some eggs or something?"

He shook his head, feeling a sudden wave of affection for her. Carrie was a sweet girl and wanted nothing except to make him happy. He stepped toward the couch and extended his hand, as if asking her to dance.

"Pray with me," he said. "Would you do that?"

TIM AND Carrie had been married for less than a year. Pastor Dennis had introduced them at a church picnic shortly after Tim had found his way to the Tabernacle and been reborn in Christ.

"There's someone I want you to meet," he said. "I think you'll like her."

Tim was pleasantly surprised when the Pastor led him over to the condiment table, where a folksingery blond was struggling with a big Costco bag of plastic forks, spoons, and knives that didn't seem to want to open. Unlike most of the single women who worshipped at the Tabernacle, she was young and reasonably cute, with long straight hair and startled-looking blue eyes. In the strong afternoon sunlight, Tim couldn't help noticing that her peasant blouse—a gauzy embroidered garment, the kind of thing pothead girls wore in the late seventies—was translucent enough that you didn't have to strain to see the outline of her bra underneath, which was about as much excitement as you could hope for at a gathering like this. Her breasts were plump and pillowy, not what he normally went for, but he had to make a conscious effort to stop staring at them. He wasn't proud of himself for behaving in such an ungodly way, but he'd been lusting after women since he was twelve, and it was turning out to be a harder habit to break than he'd expected.

Pastor Dennis relieved Carrie of the troublesome bag.

"You're fired," he told her. "Now get outta here. And take this guy with you, okay?"

Carrie smiled sheepishly at Tim, wiping the back of her hand across her sweaty forehead.

"Hey," she said. "You're the guitar player."

"Bass," he corrected her, momentarily distracted by Pastor Dennis, who was having no more luck with the bag than Carrie had. He was tugging at it with both hands, grimacing fiercely, like a man trying to rip a phone book in two.

"Gosh darn it," he muttered.

"That's really thick plastic," Carrie warned.

With one final heroic grunt, the Pastor tore the bag asunder, unleashing a mighty cascade of utensils all over the table, including a few knives that landed in a bowl of bean dip. Tim and Carrie tried to help him with the mess, but he shooed them away.

"I'm okay," he insisted. "You two go and get acquainted. I bet you have a lot in common."

THEY SAT in the shade, drinking lukewarm soda, watching the kids tie themselves together in preparation for a three-legged race. The Tabernacle was a relatively new church at that point—it had only been planted for two years, after Pastor Dennis and a handful of disaffected families had split off from the Living Waters Fellowship in Gifford Township, which he accused of being "a namby-pamby, touchy-feely bunch of mealymouthed hypocrites who loved their cable TV better than they loved Jesus Christ"—so there were only about a dozen contestants in the race, ranging in age from five or six to twelve or thirteen.

On the whole, Tim couldn't help thinking, they were an unprepossessing bunch, the boys scrawny and somber, the girls overdressed for such a hot day, visibly uncomfortable, nothing at all like the confident little jockettes Abby played soccer with. They stood at slouchy attention, nodding earnestly as Youth Pastor Eddie explained that sin was like a third leg, a foreign growth that hobbled us on our walk through life. If we could just cut ourselves loose from it, we'd run like the wind, with our Savior at our side.

It was an interesting metaphor, and it didn't seem to spoil anyone's enjoyment. When the first heat began, the little kids leapt forward, managing a few herky-jerky steps before squealing in alarm and toppling onto the grass with their partners. After a few seconds of hilarity, they untangled themselves, got up, and started over, dragging that extra limb around as best they could.

"You've had such an interesting life," Carrie told him. "I haven't done hardly anything."

As far as he could tell, she wasn't exaggerating. She was a twenty-four-year-old woman, raised in a strict evangelical home, who hadn't gone to college or even lived on her own. She rarely dated, had no close friends outside of church, and spent her days running the office of a Christian insurance agent who was a friend of the family. The way she described it, the only act of defiance she'd ever committed was to follow Pastor Dennis to the Tabernacle, against the wishes of her parents, who'd stayed behind at Living Waters. It made sense that she'd be intrigued by Tim's checkered past, especially the rock bands he'd played in when he was her age.

"That must have been incredible," she said, as if he'd told her that he'd climbed Mount Everest or fought in a war. "I can't even imagine."

"It seemed like fun at the time," he conceded. "But I was selfish. I hurt a lot of people."

"But now you're saved," she told him. "So it's okay."

For a second or two, he wasn't quite sure if she was putting him on. It happened a lot to him in his first few months at the Tabernacle, before he'd spent a lot of time with hard-core Christians. He'd gotten so used to hanging around with wiseasses, liars, and addicts that he was easily thrown off-balance when someone spoke to him in a forthright manner, without doubt or irony.

"It's wonderful," he said. "But I'm carrying a lot of guilt around."

He told her about Allison and Abby, and the regret he lived with every day.

"We lost a house," he said. "I put the mortgage payments up my nose."

"I'm a sinner, too," Carrie told him.

He nodded, understanding that her intentions were good, even if what she was saying was pure bullshit—Christian boilerplate designed to make people like him feel a little better, a little less alone.

"You don't look like a sinner," he told her, glancing toward the field, where the second heat had just begun. The eleven-year-old Rapp twins, Mark and Matthew, were running in perfect unison, sprinting way ahead of the pack, as if their third leg were the most natural thing in the world. Carrie laughed, a little more loudly than he expected, and touched him lightly on the forearm.

"Doesn't matter what you look like," she assured him. If he hadn't known better, he might've thought she was flirting with him. "Matters what you do."

THEY WERE thrown together a lot in the weeks that followed, way more than could have been accounted for by mere coincidence. Pastor Dennis would invite him to dinner, and Carrie would be there, too, along with a couple of ringers, so it didn't look too obvious. If he volunteered to paint the sanctuary on Saturday morning, it turned out that she'd signed up for the exact same shift. When he offered his Saturn to the Jesus Jam Festival car pool, she just happened to end up in his passenger seat. He understood exactly what was going on—there weren't a whole lot of singles in the Tabernacle, and Pastor Dennis regularly warned them of the dangers of dating nonbelievers—so he tried, as politely as he could, to let her know he wasn't interested.

The thing that baffled him was why a good Christian girl like Carrie would even *want* to get tangled up with a guy like him. Couldn't she see he was damaged goods—a divorced father, a recovering addict, a musician who could have qualified for his own episode of *Behind the Music,* if only anyone had ever heard of him?

The flip side of his inability to see what was in it for Carrie was an all-too-clear awareness of what *wasn't* in it for him. Because the sad fact was that, even now, after he'd accepted Jesus into his heart, turned his back on drugs and alcohol, and committed himself to walk in the light of the Lord, he still couldn't manage to get himself all that excited about good Christian girls. Certain kinds of toothpaste, it turned out, were harder to get back into the tube than others.

Partly it was just habit—at least he hoped it was. The women he'd gone for in the past, Allison included, had been smokers and drinkers and sexual troublemakers, bad girls in tight pants who let you take

Polaroids, and laughed about the time they gave that cute stranger a handjob on the Greyhound bus, because it was a long way from Harrisburg to New York, and what else were you going to do to pass the time? It wasn't that Tim wanted to be attracted to women like that, he just *was*, and it sometimes seemed to him that his sexuality had gotten so twisted over the years that he'd never be able to straighten it out.

The whole subject was so fraught and muddled that he didn't even know where to start when Pastor Dennis took him aside after Sunday worship, about a month after the picnic, and asked him why he was being so cool to Carrie, when she'd obviously developed a deep affection for him.

"I—I . . . don't know," he stammered. "I mean, she's a sweet girl and everything. But she's just so young. It's like we're living on different planets."

Pastor Dennis didn't seem too happy with this response.

"You both love Jesus," he said. "That sounds like the same planet to me."

THE PASTOR had a point, but it was a lot easier for Tim to mutter about the discrepancy in their ages than it was to tell him the truth, which was that he was involved in a strange and stupid affair with a married woman who was the complete antithesis of Carrie, and, sad to say, a lot more to his liking.

Deanna Phelan was an addiction counselor he'd met a few years earlier in what, for him, at least, turned out to be a spectacularly unsuccessful outpatient rehab program at St. Bartholomew's Hospital. She was his group leader, a cute, foul-mouthed woman who alluded frequently, and with great comic effect, to her own impressive history of chemical dependency and self-destructive behavior. She'd called a couple of times to check up on him after graduation, but he'd been too busy to call back; the day after completing the program, he'd done a triple back somersault off the wagon and embarked on the epic coke binge that ended his marriage and ultimately brought him face-to-face with his Savior.

He didn't see her again until shortly after he'd turned his life around at the Tabernacle, when they ran into each other at a Jiffy Lube on McLean Road. Tim was reading his Bible in the waiting area when she stepped in through the service bay door, talking on her cell phone so loudly and unself-consciously you would have thought she was alone in her own house.

"I'm not running a fucking restaurant, honey. You want something different, you can cook it yourself."

Her voice seemed instantly familiar—it had a ragged, slightly belligerent quality that made him look up in spite of himself—but it took him a few seconds to place her. She'd worn her hair in a long ponytail at the hospital; now it was as short as a boy's, giving her a pixieish look that went well with her lanky figure and tough-girl demeanor.

"Too bad, kiddo. You're stuck with the mother you got." She blew a raspberry into the phone. "I love you, too. Now go do your homework."

She flipped the phone shut and pounded her palm against the side of her head, as if trying to dislodge water from her ear.

"Teenagers," she told him, by way of explanation.

Tim smiled; her eyes widened in recognition.

"Holy shit," she said. "It's Mr. Deadhead."

Flattered to be remembered, he stood up and shook Deanna's hand. She gave him a careful once-over as they reintroduced themselves.

"You look a helluva lot better than the last time I saw you."

"I've been clean for a year," he told her, doing his best not to grin like a kid who'd gotten all A's on his report card.

"Good for you," she said. "Twelve-step?"

He showed her his Bible.

"Jesus."

A familiar look of disappointment passed across her face. People who weren't saved didn't want to hear you talk about Jesus. It made them uncomfortable, like you were bragging about a great party they hadn't been invited to, though of course they had.

"There's a lot of that going around these days," she said.

"I wasn't strong enough to do it on my own," he explained. "I needed His help."

She looked like she wanted to say something dismissive, but then thought better of it.

"Hey," she said, giving him a congratulatory squeeze on the shoulder. "Whatever works. Your wife must be thrilled."

Tim's face heated up, the way it always did when the subject of marital status arose.

"We, uh . . . we're not together anymore."

He gave her a capsule version of the saga, stressing that he didn't blame Allison for leaving him and insisting he was thrilled she'd landed on her feet so quickly, finding a man who could give her the kind of life she'd always dreamed about.

"I'm serious," he said, detecting a certain amount of skepticism in Deanna's nods. "The woman deserves a medal."

"You have a little girl, too, right?"

"Good memory. Only she's ten now, not so little. I'm playing catch-up. I feel like I missed so much of her childhood."

"It goes fast," she said. "Our boys are in high school now. They don't even know how to talk anymore. It's all just grunts."

The Jiffy Lube guy called out, "Blue Saturn," and Tim went to the register to pay. He stopped on his way out to say good-bye to Deanna.

"It's really good to see you," he said.

She slipped a business card into his shirt pocket.

"Drop me a line if you ever need to talk to someone," she said, surprising him with a hug that lingered longer than he expected. "I'm really proud of you, Tim."

* * *

HE STUCK the card in his wallet—it had Deanna's work phone number printed on the front and her e-mail address scribbled on the back—and told himself she hadn't meant anything in particular by giving it to him. She was just a friendly acquaintance, making the usual insincere offer to keep in touch. It was ridiculous to read any hidden meanings into it.

Except that he was lonely—he hadn't touched a woman in months—and as horny as a high-school sophomore. And a voice in his head—the worldly voice of the corrupt, selfish man he no longer wished to be—kept reminding him that grown women didn't slip their phone numbers into your pocket if they weren't interested in hooking up. It didn't matter if they were married or not. He'd been around the block enough to know that some people were more married than others.

Through sheer willpower, he managed to get through two weeks without contacting her, the business card burning a hole in his wallet the entire time. But then Pastor Dennis gave a sermon on the subject of "Temptation" that made him rethink his strategy.

"You know what temptation is?" he asked. "It's a fungus. It hides in the dark corners of the soul, those damp cracks and moist crevices we'd prefer not to think about. Well, I'll tell you what, people. You can't ignore temptation. Nuh-uh. That's how it thrives. You pretend it's not there, and pretty soon this tiny speck of mold turns into a giant poison mushroom with deep, twisted roots. Then see how easy it is to get rid of it! No, the thing to do with temptation is face it head-on at high noon! Right away! The second you realize it's there! Expose it to the fresh air and sunlight of Jesus Christ! Because you know what, friends? That slimy fungus can't stand the light of day! It just shrivels up and dies! Amen!"

After the sermon, Tim went home and wrote a long e-mail to Deanna, telling her all about the Tabernacle, what a beautiful positive force it had been in his life, and how compelled he was to share it with his friends. He didn't know where she stood on the subject of Jesus, but he thought it might be a good idea for her and her family to come visit on Sunday. It might be an especially powerful experience for her sons, who, as teenagers, were exposed to so many evils that they might not be morally equipped to face. He hoped she didn't mind his being so forward, but he believed that God had brought them back in touch for a reason.

"I know you're searching for something," he wrote. "We all are. I'm living proof of God's mercy. My only job is to praise Him and spread the word."

"Nice to hear from you," she wrote back. "I'm sorry to say that I'm not the least bit interested in your religion. But I'd love to meet you for a cup of coffee. Weekdays are good for me."

IN THE name of facing temptation, Tim met Deanna at Starbucks the following Thursday morning. She wore a skirt, high heels, and a shirt with a plunging neckline, and he couldn't keep from telling her how good she looked. Even as he paid the compliment, though, he berated himself for setting the wrong tone, which he'd hoped would be cordial but not flirtatious.

"Thanks," she said, nervously fiddling with a bead bracelet. "I'm glad you approve. I must've gone through six fucking outfits before settling on this one. It was hard, 'cause I wasn't really sure what kind of a date this was."

"It's not a date at all," he assured her. "It's just . . . you know, old friends meeting for coffee. Nothing datelike about it."

"Okay, good," she said. "I'm glad you cleared that up. We're old friends meeting for coffee."

And that's what it felt like for a while. They talked about kids and jobs and the challenge of staying sober, and swapped war stories from their druggie days. She gave him updates on some of the members of his group at St. Bartholomew's, including one guy who was in jail and another who died while driving drunk.

"That could've been me," he said. "I did so many stupid things back then. It was only by the grace of God that I didn't kill myself. Or someone else. You know why the judge ordered me into rehab that time?"

"Some kind of DUI, right?"

"It was after a gig. The guitar player was sleeping in the passenger seat, and I started driving the wrong way down the parkway. Not just driving, *speeding*. It was four in the morning, but there were a fair number of cars out there, and I thought *they* were the ones who were confused. I kept honking my horn and flashing my lights and screaming at those stupid idiots to get out of the way, and I guess that's what saved me. I musta drove a good five miles before the cops showed up. Apparently I was completely indignant when they put on the cuffs. I kept asking why they were picking on me and not those other crazy fools."

Deanna laughed and shook her head. Without warning, she moved her hand across the table and rested it on top of his. The gesture felt so natural and unpremeditated that he didn't think to resist.

"It's so good to see you," she said. "I know it's unprofessional to admit this, but I had quite a little crush on you back then."

"Huh," he said, flattered and alarmed at the same time. He slid his hand out from under hers. "I had no idea."

"Yeah. I wanted to ask you out, but you never returned my calls."

"Ask me out?" he said. "We were both married."

"I'm not saying it was a smart move." Her expression grew sheepish. He felt her foot rubbing against his ankle under the table. "I don't know. I kinda have a problem with monogamy sometimes. I mean, Jack's a great guy, but twenty years is a long time."

Tim listened to this confession with equal parts desire and dismay. This was exactly what he'd been afraid of. Or was it exactly what he'd been hoping for?

"Don't you get like that with food sometimes?" she asked. "You know, you love chicken, chicken's your favorite, you could eat chicken every day. And then one day it's like, *wham,* you don't even want to *look* at chicken."

"I—I'm fine with chicken," he said, moving his ankle away from her foot.

"I am, too," she said. "That was just a hypothetical."

Summoning a panicky sense of resolve, he drained the tepid dregs of his latte and jumped up as if he'd heard a gunshot.

"This was a real treat," he said. "But I gotta get back to work."

"Right now?"

"Yeah, I, uh—"

"Did I scare you?"

"Not at all. I have an appointment. I completely forgot about it."

"All right," she said, pursing her lips together in a sweet little pout. "Will you call me sometime?"

"Sure," he said, sticking out his hand as if concluding a business transaction. "Great seeing you."

"Same here," she said, mimicking his manly tone as they shook hands. "Great seeing you, too."


TIM KNEW he'd dodged a bullet, and swore to himself that he wouldn't let it happen again. Two days later, though, Deanna sent him an e-mail at work asking if he was busy that night. He replied that he had no plans. She asked if it would be okay if she dropped by his place for an hour or so. He saw a perfect opportunity for clearing the air between them.

"NO," he wrote. "IT WOULD NOT BE OKAY. PLEASE DON'T TEMPT ME LIKE THIS. THIS IS NOT HOW I WANT TO BE CONDUCTING MY LIFE!!!"

He pondered the words on the screen, feeling proud of himself for holding fast to his convictions. But even as he congratulated himself, he felt an exhilarating sensation of surrender spreading through his body. He had been strong for so long. And weakness was such a good old friend. He held down the backspace key until the screen was clear, then typed, "Sure, that would be great!!!"

He spent the rest of the day trying to talk himself out of what he'd just set in motion. He couldn't eat or concentrate on his work, just kept trying to think of strategies for keeping Deanna at bay. He could leave his apartment, or hide inside with the lights off. He could leave a note on the front door telling her to go away. But he was kidding himself. Eight o'clock found him showered and clean-shaven and trembling with excitement as he opened the door. She stepped inside, wearing sneakers, Lycra shorts, and a pink-and-purple sports bra. She kissed him hard, running her hand down his belly to his belt buckle.

"You better make me sweat," she told him. "I'm supposed to be at the gym."

THAT'S ALL the affair ever amounted to—a lot of e-mailing and an hour of illicit sex once or twice a week. And yet it seemed huge, casting a dark shadow on everything else in his life, including—especially—his personal relationship with Jesus. Because how could you love Him the way He deserved to be loved if you couldn't keep yourself from sinning, or worse, if you *looked forward* to sinning? And how could you praise Him the way He deserved to be praised when your heartfelt prayers for strength fell on deaf ears?

To his credit, Tim wasn't going down without a fight. Every time they were together, he swore to her that this was it, that as much he enjoyed her company, he could no longer continue living as a hypocrite, betraying the solemn promises he'd made to himself and to God. She acted like she believed him, nodding sorrowfully and telling him he had to do what he had to do, that she completely understood, and would miss him very much. But then, a few nights later, as if the conversation had never occurred, Deanna would show up unannounced at his doorstep in gym clothes, and the whole farce would repeat itself.

As the weeks went by, their encounters grew increasingly hostile. It seemed to him at times that she delighted in his weakness, deriving some perverse pleasure out of watching him crumble, as if his inability to control himself reflected well on her as a woman. But what really irritated him was the air of innocence that surrounded her, as if he were the only morally compromised person in the bed.

"What happens?" he asked her one night, as she was performing oral sex on him. "Do you go home and kiss your sons good night with that mouth?"

She looked up, more surprised than hurt.

"I brush my teeth first, if it makes you feel better. You think I should gargle, too?"

"I don't care what you do. I was just curious."

A few minutes later, when Tim was reciprocating, Deanna suddenly said, "I wonder what Jesus would do."

He raised his head. "What? What did you say?"

"I wonder if he was going down on me, would he do that swirly thing with his tongue? It's a pretty fancy move."

"Leave Him out of it, would you?"

"Do we have to?" she said. "You guys could double-team me."

That should have been the last straw. He should have gotten up, gathered her clothes, told her to please leave and never come back. But he just lowered his head and went back to work.

Later, when he tried to figure out why he let her get away with insulting the Lord like that, he came up with two explanations. The first, which made him feel a little bit better, wasn't so much an explanation as an acknowledgment of the fact that he'd asked for it, that she never would have said a word about Jesus if he hadn't provoked her by raising the subject of her sons. In this version of events, he let her off the hook out of guilt and an instinctive sense of fairness, knowing that he'd crossed the line of decency and that she deserved to retaliate.

The second explanation, on the other hand, didn't make him feel better at all. Because the more he thought about it, the more he could see that her mockery of his religious beliefs had excited him as much as it offended him, and that it had this effect precisely because part of him—the old Tim, the cynical addict who was hanging on for dear life—agreed with her, or was at least willing to consider the possibility that this Jesus kick had outlived its usefulness. Sure, it had been a great crutch, helping him to finally break his dependence on alcohol and drugs. But maybe that's all it was. Maybe now that he'd gotten himself clean, he could ditch Jesus and go back to his old ways, stop trying to live up to what was turning out to be a pretty damn rigorous code of conduct, a path so straight and narrow that a lonely forty-year-old man had to beat himself up every time he made love to a pretty woman who came to his door and offered herself to him with an open heart and no strings attached, the kind of windfall that at any other time in his life he would have celebrated as a miraculous gift from above.

WHO KNOWS how much longer it would have lasted, how much lower he would have sunk, if he hadn't been rescued by a knock on the door one Thursday night. It followed so swiftly upon Deanna's departure that Tim automatically assumed she'd come back to retrieve something she'd left behind, or to give him one last kiss, which was why he answered the door wearing only sky-blue boxers and a dopey grin that melted away at the sight of his visitor's grim face.

"Wow," he said. "I wasn't, uh . . ."

Pastor Dennis slipped past him without a word, pausing just inside the door to sniff at the air with canine concentration.

"Lovely," he said, and though Tim hadn't noticed it before, he suddenly became aware of the overpowering smell of sex in the apartment, as pervasive and unmistakable as the odor of frying garlic.

Without waiting for an invitation, Pastor Dennis crossed the room and sat down on the couch, as if this were a casual social visit. He was younger than Tim by almost ten years, a wiry guy with thinning blond hair, visible jaw muscles, and unfashionably large eyeglasses. In pressed khakis and a navy polo shirt, he looked exactly like what he used to be—a geek who sold computer equipment at Best Buy— before the Lord tapped him on the shoulder and entrusted him with a new set of responsibilities.

"Nice place you got here," he said, glancing around the sparsely furnished living room. "A real swinging bachelor pad."

"It's a dump," Tim told him. "But it's all I can afford right now."

He'd lived here a full year, but the TV was still resting on a milk crate. The hideous plaid couch and woven synthetic curtains had been left behind by the previous tenant, an elderly man who'd pleaded with Tim to adopt his two trembling, rheumy-eyed dachshunds—they weren't welcome in the assisted-living complex his kids were forcing him into—then called him "a heartless S.O.B." when he declined.

Pastor Dennis reached for the Bible Tim kept on the glass-topped coffee table, the one decent piece of furniture in the apartment— someone in Greenwillow Estates had put it out for trash, amazingly enough—and began flipping through the pages. It was something Tim had seen him do numerous times at Addicts 4 Christ meetings, and it rarely took him longer than a couple of seconds to locate something uncannily relevant to the situation at hand.

"Been studying the Good Book?" he inquired.

"Every day," Tim assured him. "First thing in the morning and right before bed."

"Impressive." The Pastor slammed the Bible shut and tossed it back onto the table with a carelessness Tim found disturbing. "Looks like you learned a lot."

Tim's face burned with shame. Despite his fig leaf of underwear, he felt naked and damned, like Adam standing before God with a fruity taste in his mouth.

"Maybe you read it more carefully than me," the Pastor continued. "I never came across the verse that said it was okay to entertain whores in your apartment."

"She's not a whore," Tim said. "Don't call her that."

"Whatever." The Pastor shrugged. "You never told me you had a girlfriend."

"She's not my girlfriend. She just . . . stops by once in a while."

"How convenient. You don't even have to buy her dinner?"

"Look," Tim muttered. "I'm sorry about this."

"She's cute," the Pastor said. "Have to give her that. I tried to talk to her, but she seemed to be in kind of a hurry. You think someone's waiting for her at home?"

Guilty as he was, Tim began to bristle at the interrogation. He was an adult, a divorced man who lived alone. He was entitled to a private life, just like anybody else.

"You know what?" he said. "I'm not proud of what I'm doing. But it's really none of your business."

"None of my business?" Pastor Dennis looked hurt. "You're one of my flock. I don't want you to get lost again."

"I'm not lost," Tim insisted. "I just get lonely sometimes. I'm only human, okay?"

The two men stared at each other for a long time before the Pastor finally nodded, conceding the point.

"Fine," he said. "Do what you want. But I don't want to see you in church this Sunday. Adulterers aren't welcome in the Tabernacle."

"What?" Tim was taken aback. "I can't come to church?"

"Not mine." Pastor Dennis rose from the couch. "Take your sin somewhere else. I'm not going to tolerate it."

"That's not fair. You can't just—"

"I'm sorry." Pastor Dennis's voice was flat and hard. "We're trying to set an example. You know that."

"Wait." Tim grabbed at the Pastor's arm as he headed for the door. "Don't do this to me."

"You're doing it to yourself." The Pastor's voice faltered, and Tim was startled to see him wipe a tear from his cheek. "I misjudged you. I thought you were one of my warriors."

"I'm doing my best," Tim protested.

"No," Pastor Dennis told him. "I refuse to believe that."

For a few seconds after the Pastor left, Tim stood stunned and angry in the middle of his living room. *Fuck you,* he thought. *And fuck your church, you sanctimonious asshole.* He should've known it wasn't going to work out. There were people who could live within the rules and people who couldn't, and he had always been one of the ones who couldn't. It didn't matter who was spouting them—parents, teachers, coaches, bosses, fellow musicians, women he was sleeping with, and now a minister. It had been crazy for him to imagine that it could have been otherwise.

But then it hit him. *No,* he thought. *No way. This can't be happening.* It was impossible, intolerable, at this point in his life, to just be left with *this*—lousy job, cruddy apartment, the wasteland of the TV and the computer, the emptiness relieved only by Saturdays with Abby and a visit from Deanna once or twice a week. Sure, there were other churches, churches where the busybody Pastor wouldn't make a house call to tell you you were going to hell, and wouldn't cry if you disappointed him. But what would be the point of belonging to one of them?

He was out the door and running barefoot across the still-warm slate of the walkway before he remembered that he wasn't really dressed for it. Luckily, Hillside Gardens wasn't the liveliest of places at this time of night. He made it all the way to the parking lot without encountering a neighbor, and saw to his immense relief that Pastor Dennis was standing by the trunk of his Corolla, head bowed in prayer.

"Wait," Tim called out. "We gotta talk."

He slowed to a walk as he crossed the nubbly blacktop, trying to catch his breath and compose his thoughts. Before he could speak, though, Pastor Dennis opened his arms and began walking toward him.

"Hallelujah," he said.

Tim was a little self-conscious at first, embracing another man in a public place while wearing so little clothing, but the embarrassment passed quickly. He closed his eyes and let himself be held.

"I'm right here," the Pastor whispered, pressing Tim's head softly against his bony shoulder. "I'm not going anywhere."

IN AN effort to get right with God after this fiasco, Tim began attending one-on-one prayer and counseling sessions with Pastor Dennis, in addition to his weekly Men's Bible Study and Addicts 4 Christ meetings. The Pastor believed that Tim needed to look deep inside his heart and decide once and for all if he was with Jesus or against Him. He also believed it would be an excellent idea if Tim asked a certain young Christian woman on a date.

"Just take her to the movies," he said. "If you don't get along, I'll never mention it again."

Tim agreed, more out of guilt than enthusiasm, and had a better time than he'd expected (they went to *Spider-Man 2*, and to the Rustic Barn Diner afterward). Carrie was easygoing and surprisingly non-judgmental. She asked a lot of questions about his life, and he answered them as fully as he could, at one point giving her a detailed explanation of the differences between freebasing and smoking crack that she seemed to find fascinating. At the end of the night, he walked her to the front door of her parents' house to say good night. He thought about kissing her, but played it safe by sticking out his hand. She giggled and pecked him on the cheek.

"I had fun," she said.

They went to *King Arthur* the following Friday, then took a long walk around Blue Lake after Sunday meeting. It was a spectacular day, and he could feel her exerting a subtle gravitational pull, drawing him slowly but irresistibly into her orbit. Halfway around the lake, he worked up the courage to take her hand. She let out another nervous giggle as their fingers intertwined.

There were more movies as the summer slipped away, a couple of dinners, a day trip down the shore, some sweet kisses. But it wasn't like falling in love, at least not as Tim had experienced it in the past. No physical fireworks or emotional roller coasters, just a calm feeling of acceptance, a surrender to something so obvious it quickly came to seem inevitable. By late September, they'd begun tiptoeing around the subject of marriage.

Not that he was without the occasional misgiving. Unlike most of the women he'd been attracted to over the years, Carrie wasn't much of a conversationalist; sometimes they had trouble finding things to talk about besides themselves and the Tabernacle. And then there were those jarring moments when she drew a blank on what for him was a shockingly obvious reference—Muddy Waters, R. Crumb, Agent 99. Trivia mostly, but he never failed to suffer a jolt of deep disappointment when it happened, a sense that the distance between them was vaster and more unbridgeable than he'd realized.

In mid-October, Carrie's parents invited him over for dinner. Mr. and Mrs. Frischknecht were stern, solemn people, old enough to be Carrie's grandparents. They'd lived overseas for many years, working as missionaries in places like Bolivia and South Korea, but had returned to America in the late seventies, when Mrs. Frischknecht began suffering from debilitating migraines. Carrie had arrived a few years later, long after her parents had resigned themselves to a barren marriage.

The Frischknechts were polite to Tim, but clearly wary. He did his best to put them at ease, speaking truthfully about the troubles in his life, and the astonishing transformation he'd gone through since accepting Jesus. He told them about Abby, too, what a good student and talented athlete she was, wanting them to know that he was a dedicated father, while not sugarcoating the fact that he came with baggage.

"She's a good kid," he said. "This year she's gonna be Hermione for Halloween. You know, the smart girl from *Harry Potter*?"

Mr. and Mrs. Frischknecht regarded him with studied blankness, and Tim realized that he'd said something wrong.

"I-I guess you guys aren't big on the Harry Potter stuff. I mean, I know it's full of witches and magic and that kind of thing, but the kids really love it."

Mr. Frischknecht nodded curtly and returned to his meal. Carrie looked at Tim.

"We don't celebrate Halloween," she told him.

"You don't?"

She shook her head.

"Not even when you were little?"

"It's not a Christian holiday," Mrs. Frischknecht interjected.

"I don't care to see a child dressed as the Devil," Mr. Frischknecht added. "That I don't find amusing."

"Hmm," said Tim. "I hadn't really thought about it like that."

Mr. Frischknecht explained that some churches had begun using Halloween for the purposes of Christian outreach—they set up truly creepy haunted houses that taught kids about sin and hell.

"You get them good and scared to death," he said. "And then they're ready to hear about the alternative."

"There might be one in the area," Mrs. Frischknecht told him. "Maybe you could take your daughter."

On the way home that night, it occurred to Tim that he and Carrie had effectively grown up in different countries. At first this seemed depressing to him, but after a while he came to realize that it was helpful to think about their relationship in this way, and even oddly comforting.

If she'd been a Japanese or Turkish woman, say, he wouldn't have expected her to know who Bad Company was, or to laugh at a passing mention of the Coneheads. He would have either explained the reference or told her that it wasn't important enough to worry about. But he wouldn't have been annoyed or troubled by her ignorance of something she had no reason to know about in the first place. And he wouldn't have been surprised to hear that she'd never dressed up for Halloween or gone trick-or-treating with her friends.

It wasn't like he was one of those losers sending away for a mail-order bride because he couldn't get an American woman to give him the time of day. Not at all: *he* was the immigrant, a tourist who'd gone to a foreign country, met a local woman, and decided to stay. The point wasn't to make her more like him, to fill her head with the same crap that cluttered his own; it was just the opposite—for him to become more like her, to leave the old country behind so he could create a newer, better version of himself. It was in this spirit of adventure and self-renewal that, a few days later, Tim asked Carrie to be his wife.

THEY WERE married in a simple Christian ceremony at the Tabernacle, with Abby and the rest of Tim's bewildered family looking on. The uneventful buffet reception at the VFW hall—no drinking, dancing, or secular music—couldn't have been more different than the debacle that followed his first wedding, at which he'd gotten falling-down drunk, mashed the ceremonial piece of cake into his bride's face, insulted her father, and had to be dumped into the limo at the end of the night by a couple of groomsmen who were only slightly less tanked than he was. He couldn't remember anything after that, but had no reason to doubt Allison's claim that the marriage wasn't consummated until the following afternoon.

This time the festivities were over by nine. The newlyweds waved good-bye to their guests and walked hand in hand to Tim's Saturn, which he'd gotten washed and detailed for the occasion. Carrie's billowy gown seemed comically enormous inside the car; Tim had to tunnel beneath the fabric to release the emergency brake. He kissed her before starting the car.

"How ya doin'?" he asked.

"Pretty good." She gave him a sweet, slightly distracted smile. "I had a nice time."

He snuck a sidelong glance at her as they pulled out of the parking lot. She was sitting up straight in the passenger seat, hands folded in her lap, her face calm and watchful. If she was worried about the next phase of their wedding night, she wasn't letting on.

"I'm glad Abby was there," he said. "I think she really enjoyed it."

"She's so cute," said Carrie. "I just wish she'd warm up to me."

"She will. She just needs to get to know you."

"I hope so."

It was true that his daughter had been a bit standoffish—Tim had to coax her into giving the bride a good night hug—but that was to be expected. Abby and Carrie had only met a few times before tonight, and neither of them seemed to have any idea of how to communicate with the other. Tim blamed most of this awkwardness on Allison, who had poisoned Abby's mind about the Tabernacle and the people who worshipped there, and a little bit on Carrie herself, who seemed not to realize that the onus was on the adult to initiate and sustain a conversation with a child. And it certainly hadn't helped to have his family looking so grim and shell-shocked during the ceremony, and refusing to mingle with the church people at the reception. The sole exception was his father, a retired storm-window salesman who packed a flask in one pocket, a travel-sized bottle of Scope in the other, and prided himself on his ability to "get along with everyone."

"At least my dad had a good time," he pointed out.

"He's funny," Carrie observed. "He reminds me of you."

If Allison had heard this, she would've cracked up. For years, Tim had told her she had permission to shoot him if he started acting like his father.

"He's attentive to young women," Tim said. "I'll give him that."

Carrie patted him on the knee.

"Your poor mother, though. She looked like she was at a funeral."

Tim had considered it a triumph just to have his mother show up. She was bitterly opposed to the marriage and had been threatening to boycott the wedding from the day it had been announced.

"I'm sorry." Tim squeezed her hand. "She did the best she could."

"She tried," Carrie conceded. "She told me I was beautiful."

TWO DAYS earlier, at Pastor Dennis's urging, Tim had gone to his parents' house for dinner, hoping to make one last-ditch effort to change his mother's mind. Late in the evening, after the dessert plates had been put away and his father had gone to bed, he sat across from her at the kitchen table, and listened yet again to her case against the marriage, impressed by what a forceful and articulate speaker she had become. She'd been a pushover when he was younger, a sad, frightened woman willing to believe whatever outrageous lie he told her if it meant she could continue to pretend that everything was okay, that her favorite son didn't have a drug problem—the pot belonged to a friend, someone must have slipped LSD into his drink, he honestly knew nothing about the TV and stereo system that had disappeared from the rec room while his parents were away at the family reunion. But years of disappointment and Al-Anon had toughened her up, giving her a clear-eyed, slightly cynical view of his behavior, and a vocabulary with which to express it.

"You've got an addictive personality," she said. "And I'm worried that you're using Jesus as a substitute for drugs, like methadone or something. And that's great for now. But eventually you're going to have to face the world on your own two feet."

"I understand what you're saying, Mom. But Jesus isn't some kind of means to an end. He's real. And I know what He wants from me."

His mother grimaced. "Please don't talk to me about Jesus. I feel like I don't know you anymore."

Tim had to bite his tongue to keep from reminding her that she called herself a Presbyterian and allegedly believed in Jesus herself. But they'd had this argument before—she insisted that his Jesus and her Jesus were two totally different things—and there was no reason to rehash it now.

"I want you to know me," he said. "I want to love and honor you for who you are, and I want you to do the same for me."

"I do love you. That's why I'm telling you this is a bad idea."

"How about if I beg?" he said, making a puppy-dog face. "Would that work?"

Her expression didn't soften. "You hardly know this girl. You said so yourself."

"Maybe that's a good thing," he pointed out. "Allison and I were together for five years before we got married. We knew everything about each other. And look how that turned out."

"Don't give me that crap," she said. "You and Allison were perfect together. You never should have let her go."

"I didn't *let* her go. She went on her own."

"No, honey." His mother shook her head, as if she pitied him. "You *made* her go."

"Whatever," Tim said. "She's gone now, and I'm getting married on Saturday. You just have to accept that."

"I'd be fine with it if I thought it would make you happy. Do you really think it will?"

"I don't know. I'm leaving it in God's hands."

"That's a pretty big risk." His mother looked straight at him, and he could feel her pleading with him at a level deeper than words. "Why can't you postpone the wedding for six months or a year, make sure you know what you're getting into?"

This was a question Tim had asked himself numerous times in recent weeks; it was also something he'd discussed in a premarital counseling session, when Pastor Dennis first raised the possibility of waiving the usual waiting period for couples who wanted to get married in the Tabernacle. The Pastor firmly believed that it was time for Tim to remove himself from the temptations of bachelorhood, to stop questioning himself and his commitment to Jesus, to bind himself to someone who shared his faith and his priorities, and to get on with his life as a husband, father, and servant of the Lord. He cited 1 Corinthians 7: 1-2: "It is good for a man not to marry. But since there is so much immorality, each man should have his own wife, and each woman her own husband."

It was a weird verse, Tim thought, encouraging marriage not as a good thing in itself, but simply as the best of bad alternatives. Hardly the stuff of love songs. And yet, like a lot of stuff in the Bible, it possessed a kind of hardheaded wisdom that resonated with his experience of the world and his circumstances at the present moment. From a Christian perspective, to be a forty-year-old bachelor was simply not a spiritually viable condition.

"The wedding's not gonna be postponed, Ma. And it'll break my heart if you're not there."

His mother let out a defeated breath and slumped back in her chair. She gave him a tired smile that made her look like an old woman.

"It's late," she said. "And I haven't been sleeping very well."

"Dad still snoring?"

She laughed. "You wouldn't believe the noises that come out of that man."

"Why don't you kick him out? Send him to the guest room?"

"I tried that," she said, a bit sheepishly. "Got kinda lonely."

She walked him to the door and gave him the usual motherly peck on the cheek. But then, instead of letting go, she hugged him with all her strength, as if Tim were leaving on a long trip, and she wasn't sure when she might see him again.

* * *

CARRIE SPENT a long time in the bathroom on their wedding night, so long that he started to worry.

"You okay?" he called out.

"Just a minute," she replied.

He couldn't blame her for being nervous; he was suffering from a mild case of butterflies himself. Now that they were alone, the minutia of planning and the excitement of the big day behind them, the enormity of what they'd done had finally begun to settle over him. It's one thing to take a leap of faith, he thought, and another thing to hit the ground.

"Anything I can do?" he said.

"Not right now."

He wasn't sure if it helped or hurt to have this thick cloud of sexual suspense hanging over everything, like it was 1955 all over again. He hadn't been this jittery about getting laid since junior year of high school, when Jenny Rego invited him over on a Friday night, told him that her parents were out of town, and instructed him to bring pot and protection.

Even in his wild days, Tim hadn't exactly been a Don Juan, but he was a relatively good-looking musician, and there always seemed to be women around who found him charming, especially the ones who shared his enthusiasm for controlled substances. On more than one occasion he'd lived out the rock star fantasy of waking up next to a girl whose name he didn't know, or at least couldn't remember.

But he'd been a gentleman with Carrie, and he didn't regret it. Somehow they'd gotten through their entire courtship without doing anything more than making out like teenagers, even though they could have slipped over to his apartment at any time. After their engagement, Carrie had even hinted a couple of times that she wouldn't object, but he didn't take her up on it. They'd both signed contracts with the

Tabernacle pledging to refrain from premarital relations, and he was determined not to start things off on the wrong foot.

In addition to not having sex, they'd also managed not to talk about it very much, aside from repeatedly telling each other how much they were looking forward to living together as man and wife. Partly, Tim thought, this was because it was hard for two people whose histories were so different to talk about sex in the abstract, and partly it was because Carrie became visibly embarrassed whenever the subject came up. He just assumed they'd jump in and figure things out as they went along.

But maybe they should have discussed their fears and expectations in greater detail, he thought, when Carrie finally emerged from the hotel bathroom. Wearing a satiny white nightgown that was a gift from her mother, she looked like an old-fashioned pinup girl—curvy and soft and heartbreakingly young—and he would have been thrilled to lie down with her on the conjugal bed, if only her face hadn't been so pale and terrified, her eyes so raw and puffy from crying.

"Honey," he said. "What is it?"

She tried to tell him, but the words wouldn't come. After two or three false starts, she shook her head in frustration and burst into tears. He took her in his arms and held her until she calmed down. He whispered that it was okay to be afraid, that it was natural to be nervous before your first time. He promised to be gentle, or, if she preferred, they could just go to sleep and try again in the morning, that is, if she felt up to it.

"It's not—" she began, but couldn't complete the sentence.

"Not what?"

She took a big breath and made a visible effort to get hold of herself.

"My first time," she said.

Tim was startled, but tried not to show it.

"That's okay," he told her. "It's not mine, either."

She laughed through her tears. He got her a glass of water.

"Should we talk about it?" he asked.

"I've wanted to," she explained. "It's just hard."

She sat beside him on the edge of the bed. In a quiet, quivery voice she told him about the spiritual crisis she'd suffered when she was nineteen, after the death of her grandmother. She lost her faith and ran away from home.

"Where'd you go?"

"Buncha places."

"On your own?"

"Sometimes," she said, unable to meet his eyes. "Not always."

"You met a guy?"

She bit her lip and nodded.

"It's okay," he said. "That was a long time ago. It's over and done with."

"It wasn't just one," she said.

"One, two, whatever. Doesn't matter."

She didn't respond. He started to get a little worried.

"Just out of curiosity," he said. "How many guys are we talking about?"

"A lot," she said. "Eight, maybe nine. I lost count."

"Really? How long were you gone?"

"Couple months."

"Wow. You kept yourself busy."

"I strayed," she said, finally working up the nerve to look into his eyes. "I went a little crazy."

IN A funny way, Carrie's confession served to correct an imbalance in their relationship that had nagged at him from the beginning, liberating them both from the rigid script in which he was forced to play the chastened older man seeking redemption from the saintly young girl. It also relieved some of the sexual pressure he'd been feeling in anticipation of the Big Night. He'd never understood the fetish some guys seemed to have for sleeping with virgins. The two times he'd done it—once in high school, the other in college—the experience had been painful for the girls and not much fun for him; it was a weight off his shoulders to know that there would be no deflowering taking place that night in the Honeymoon Suite.

And the sex turned out to be fine, not nearly as delicate or somber an operation as he'd feared. Carrie was enthusiastic enough, if a bit on the quiet side—Tim liked to hear women purr and moan and talk dirty—but somehow completely herself. He looked down at one point and noticed an expression on her face—eyes squeezed shut, a small private smile playing at the corners of her mouth—that he'd seen numerous times at Sunday meeting, when she raised her arms aloft and swayed to the music. When it was over, she laid her head on his chest and let out a sweet sigh.

"Oh Lord," she said. "I am so happy to be out of that house."

CARRIE WAS, in many ways, an ideal Christian wife—modest, affectionate, sincerely devoted to his happiness. Tim knew how lucky he was to have found her, so he was baffled by the doubts and second thoughts that began plaguing him almost from the moment they moved into their first apartment, the upstairs unit of a two-family on Baxter Street.

He had a few specific complaints. Carrie wasn't much of a cook—because of her father's stomach problems, her family had shunned any spices more exotic than salt and pepper—and Tim found himself mildly depressed by a steady diet of overcooked meat and potatoes. It also bugged him how little interest she had in politics or current events. He made an effort one morning to get her up to speed on the deteriorating situation in Iraq, but he could tell from the glazed look in her eyes once he began tossing around words like *Sunni* and *Shiite* that it wasn't going to stick.

And Carrie's inability to connect with his daughter was an ongoing source of irritation. Tim normally thought of Abby as a sweet kid, but something about her new stepmother brought out the spoiled brat in her, an eye-rolling snottiness that had only gotten worse despite his repeated requests for her to show a little respect. Carrie responded by hiding her hurt feelings behind a wall of unconvincing endearments and smothering solicitude—*What can I get for you, sweetie? Honey, do you need more light?*—that grated on Tim as badly as it did on Abby.

Ultimately, though, these were all minor grievances, the inevitable little letdowns that marked the transition between the honeymoon and *till death do us part.* The thing that really bothered him was bigger and more elusive, but it got closer to the heart of their relationship, his nagging suspicion that some vital ingredient was missing from their marriage.

*They never argued.*

Carrie was the most agreeable person he'd ever met. Whatever he wanted was fine with her. He controlled the finances, chose the shows they watched on TV, and told her what they would do on the weekends. She followed his instructions happily, without resentment or hesitation, in accordance with the passage from Ephesians, a framed version of which they had received as a wedding gift from Pastor Dennis, and was now hanging on their bedroom wall: "For the husband is the head of the wife, even as Christ is the head of the church. Therefore, as the church is subject unto Christ, so the wives to their own husbands in everything."

He realized that a lot of guys would have envied him; in some ways, it was like living in an *I Dream of Jeannie* fantasy world. All he could figure was that the years he'd spent with Allison—a moody, demanding woman in the best of times—had warped his view of marriage, made him think of it not as a loving partnership but as an exhausting struggle for the upper hand, relieved by occasional bouts of angry, exhilarating sex. Whatever the reason, he was finding it a bit boring, getting his way all the time, never having to wheedle, compromise, or even engage in the most mundane sort of marital horse-trading. It just seemed a little too easy.

He felt this keenly in the bedroom. Unlike Allison, who was a master of withholding sex—she got real pleasure out of making him beg—Carrie never, ever said no. Their entire love life happened on his timetable, according to his whims. He told her when to take off her nightgown, when to roll onto her stomach, when to use her mouth. It was a powerful feeling at first, to have an obedient young woman so completely at his disposal.

But it got old fast. There was never any resistance, but there was never any suspense, either. Carrie didn't say no, but she never initiated sex, either, never snuck up on him from behind while he was washing dishes and reached around for his dick, the way Allison had done on a couple of memorable occasions. She wouldn't have dreamed of waking him in the morning by lowering her nipple into his half-open mouth, or coming home from the video store with *Naughty Neighbors 2* instead of *Apollo 13* (not that this would have done him any good, now that he'd sworn off porn).

He wondered sometimes if he should talk to her about this, but he wasn't quite sure how to go about it. It seemed like it would kind of defeat the purpose, telling someone to please be more spontaneous, and then providing them with detailed instructions for how to go about it.

PASTOR DENNIS must have sensed something was amiss, because he took Tim aside a few months after the wedding and asked, in a slightly ominous voice, how he and Carrie were making out.

"Fine," said Tim. "No complaints."

The Pastor lowered his voice. "What about your love life? Everything working the way it's supposed to?"

Tim hesitated. This wasn't really anyone's business but his and Carrie's.

"Not bad," he said. "Still gettin' acquainted."

Pastor Dennis pondered this for a moment.

"You know what? I think it would be a good idea if my wife had a chat with your wife."

"That's okay," Tim told him. "It's really not necessary."

"Nothing too heavy," the Pastor assured him. "Just a little girl talk."

The Pastor's wife, Emily—a plump, almost alarmingly upbeat woman—dropped by the apartment one Saturday while Tim and Abby were at a soccer game. She brought along a book called *Hot Christian Sex: The Godly Way to Spice Up Your Marriage*.

"She said we should read this," Carrie informed him in bed that night. "It supposedly worked wonders for her and Pastor Dennis."

Considering the somewhat puritanical character of the Tabernacle, the book turned out to be surprisingly racy. The authors, the Rev. Mark D. Finster and his wife, Barbara G. Finster, proclaimed the good news right in the Introduction: "For a Christian married couple, sex is nothing less than a form of worship, a celebration of your love for one another and a glorification of the Heavenly Father who brought you together. So of course God wants you to have better sex! And He wants you to have more of it than you ever had before, in positions you probably didn't even know existed, with stronger orgasms than you believed were possible!"

Tim was particularly intrigued by Chapter Five, "Is This Okay?" in which the Finsters gave an itemized list of just about every conceivable sexual act—including a few that were unfamiliar to him—along with a thumbs-up or thumbs-down, depending upon whether the practice in question was expressly forbidden by Scripture.

According to the Finsters, sex between married Christians was a lot more freewheeling than Tim had realized. Prostitution, adultery, threesomes, orgies, bestiality—basically anything involving a person or animal outside of the marriage—were off-limits, but beyond that there was considerable leeway. Masturbation was fine (especially if the nonmasturbating partner got to watch), as was role playing, just as long as the couple was married within the fantasy scenario, a requirement that struck Tim as a little unwieldy: *Okay, you're the nurse and I'm the patient . . . and, uh, we got married right before my hernia operation.* The Finsters saw no biblical reason why a husband shouldn't take nude pictures of his wife, or vice versa, just as long as no one else laid eyes on them, and they couldn't locate anything in the Scriptures that conveyed explicit disapproval of light bondage and/or consensual S&M. Ditto for cross-dressing. Even anal sex, which Tim had assumed fell under the *verboten* category of "sodomy," turned out to be okay for heterosexual married couples; only homosexual men were barred from backdoor intercourse, which struck Tim as a little unfair, but he wasn't the one making the rules. The authors did express a certain amount of ambivalence about "so-called rim jobs"—they didn't believe in pussyfooting around with euphemisms—but their objections were more bacterial than religious.

The Finsters were generally gung ho about sexy lingerie—the Reverend rhapsodized a couple of times about the sight of Barbara G. in a garter belt and silk stockings—but they warned their readers to be wary of purchasing these items through secular catalogues and websites. The sight of glamorous models in skimpy, deliberately provocative outfits tended to produce sinful feelings of lust in the men who viewed them, while also inspiring unfair comparisons between their wives and the emaciated, surgically enhanced women in the photos. As an alternative, the Finsters recommended a handful of Christian websites that sold lingerie without the assistance of models. Tim showed the list to Carrie.

"What do you think? Should we order a few things?"

"Sure," she said. "If that's what you want."

FOR A while, at least, the book administered a welcome jolt of electricity to their marital bed. Tim ordered a see-through teddy for Carrie, some thigh-high stockings, and even a crotchless mesh bodysuit that rendered her mute with embarrassment (he finally just told her to take it off and toss it in the garbage). For some reason she was less freaked out by the merry widow, and girlishly happy to don the French maid costume, as if it were payback for all the Halloweens she'd been deprived of as a child. The element of dress-up freed them both somehow, made it a bit easier to try out some of the "Fun Activities" outlined in Chapter Seven, "Steamin' Up the Sheets."

It would have been great, except that Tim found himself thinking more and more frequently of Allison—she was a total Victoria's Secret junkie—and the sexy outfits she'd surprised him with back in the day. On a few occasions, he succumbed to the temptation of ordering more or less identical items for Carrie—camouflage thong and tank top, pleated Catholic schoolgirl skirt, lacy red peekaboo bra and matching tap pants—and then attempting to re-create memorable scenarios from his first marriage.

It never really worked, though. Whatever she wore, and however he asked her to behave, Carrie always remained stubbornly herself— sweet, compliant, eager to please. She would talk dirty if he insisted, but her vocabulary was severely limited, and she never managed to put any conviction behind the words. The one time he spanked her was a disappointment as well. No matter how hard he tried, he couldn't make himself believe, even for a minute or two, that she was a naughty girl who deserved correction. And she didn't say *Ouch* the way Allison did, as if she were secretly enjoying the punishment. Carrie just said it like it hurt.

Despite these setbacks, they kept at it, working doggedly through the summer and into the fall to claim their portion of hot Christian sex. Carrie never complained, but recently he'd begun sensing a certain weariness setting in, a desire to just do her part and get it over with. Tim's own enthusiasm was flagging, too; for the first time in his life, he began suffering from an intermittent failure to perform, a dismal turn of events that made both of them feel inadequate.

There were nights when he felt so trapped that the only thing he could do was get in his car and drive aimlessly around Stonewood Heights, listening to one of the three Grateful Dead CDs—*American Beauty, Workingman's Dead,* and a bootleg of a show in Buffalo from the summer of 1988—he hadn't been able to part with, despite his assurances to Pastor Dennis that he'd cut his ties, not only with the people he'd gotten drunk and high with in the past but with all the books and music and clothes connected to that dark chapter of the past. And if that wasn't bad enough, he sometimes found himself driving repeatedly past certain bars, thinking of how pleasant it would be just to pop in and have a beer, less for the beer than for the company, and the darkness, and the music—the relief of finally being back home among his own kind. He'd been down this road before, of course, and knew with grim precision what sort of danger he was in.

HE WAS so downhearted about the whole situation that he didn't bother to conceal the truth when Pastor Dennis walked him out to his car after last week's Wednesday Night Bible Study and asked how things were going with him and Carrie.

"So-so," said Tim. "We're kinda treading water right now."

"I was wondering," the Pastor said. "I sort of figured she might be pregnant by now."

"We're not quite ready," said Tim. "You know, money-wise. Buying the townhouse pretty much wiped out our savings."

"You know how I feel about waiting," the Pastor reminded him. "You just gotta jump in."

"She's young. We've got a lot of time."

"What about that book my wife gave you? Did it help?"

"A little." Tim gave a puzzled shrug. "I don't know. I've just been feeling . . . kinda confused lately."

They were standing in the nearly empty parking lot of the Tabernacle. The night was cool and breezy; papery leaves skittered across the blacktop. The Pastor leaned forward, studying Tim a little more closely.

"Confused? In what way?"

"It's weird." Tim paused, taking a moment to wipe an inappropriate smile off his face. "I don't know why, but I've been, uh, having a lot of feelings for my ex-wife lately. Sexual feelings. It's kinda messed me up with Carrie."

"Your ex-wife is remarrried," Pastor Dennis reminded him. "She's moved on. So have you."

"I know." Tim's voice was barely louder than a murmur. "But some of the time . . . I mean, I'm not proud of this, but some of the time it's like I'm using Carrie as a substitute. Like I'm with her, but I'm kind of letting myself pretend she's Allison."

Even in the darkness, Tim could see the Pastor's eyes go cold.

"You're pathetic," he said.

"I know," said Tim. "But what am I supposed to do?"

"Fix yourself," the Pastor told him. "Ask God to help."

"I've tried that."

Pastor Dennis looked up at the sky, as if seeking advice. The moon was bright, three-quarters full, its bottom edge obscured by a raggedy cloud.

"Try a little harder," he said, bringing his gaze back to earth. "In the meantime, keep your unclean hands off your wife. She deserves better."

Tim hung his head. The Pastor sighed. He sounded beleaguered, like a guy who could use a stiff drink.

"You made promises, Tim. It's time to start keeping them."

TIM KNEW exactly what he was supposed to do that Sunday morning as he and Carrie knelt together on the living room rug. According to Pastor Dennis, there was an accepted procedure—it was drawn from I Corinthians 7—by which a husband notified his wife that he would be abstaining from sexual relations with her for a defined period until he purged himself of the lust that was preventing him from being the kind of husband God wanted him to be. Luckily, the husband was under no obligation to inform his wife about the specifics of his sinful desire; all he had to do was reassure her that he was working on the problem and that things would soon return to normal.

Tim smiled at Carrie and took her hands in his. She smiled back, her face sweet and trusting, as always, but shadowed by a watchful anxiety that hadn't been there on the day Pastor Dennis had brought them together at the church picnic. She still looked terribly young, but there was no denying that marriage had changed her.

"Lord Jesus," he said, "sometimes we're not as strong as You want us to be."

Carrie nodded in agreement, but Tim could see the way her body tensed, as if she were bracing herself for bad news. He wondered sometimes if she wished they'd never met, wished that God had saved her for a younger, kinder, less demanding man, a husband who didn't come burdened with a snotty daughter, an ex-wife he couldn't seem to get out of his head, and such puzzling sexual needs.

"That's why we need Your help," he said.

"We all do," Carrie said in a soft voice, and Tim couldn't tell if this was part of the prayer, or if she was speaking directly to him. "It's nothing to be ashamed of."

Tim turned his gaze to the ceiling. He understood perfectly well that the throat-clearing was over, and that the moment had come to level with his wife. He even had his lines memorized. He was supposed to look her in the eyes and say, *Carrie, I've made a decision.*

She wouldn't cry, he thought. She'd bear the news like a trouper. But she'd worry, he thought, and probably blame herself for having done something wrong, even though she'd never done anything wrong. Not to him, and probably not to anyone. The whole mess was his fault, and it seemed heartless to make her suffer for it. It took an effort of will for him to restore eye contact with his wife.

"Oh, Lord," he said. "I am so grateful to you for bringing this wonderful woman into my life. You know I'm not worthy."

Carrie shook her head no, but he could see how pleased she was. Tim leaned forward and kissed her on the forehead.

"Do me a favor," he prayed. "Help me to love her the way she deserves."

# Praise Team

TIM AND CARRIE ARRIVED FORTY-FIVE MINUTES EARLY FOR SUN-
day meeting. The lot was nearly empty, but they parked several rows
back from the main entrance, leaving the closer-in spaces for old
people, families with small kids, and anyone else who had a hard time
getting around.

Despite its impressive-sounding name, the Tabernacle wasn't a
grand religious edifice, a marble-and-stained-glass monument to the
glory of God. It was, in fact, a bland commercial building, a two-
thousand-square-foot storefront—it had been a Fashion Bug in its previous incarnation—in Griswold Commons, a once-thriving outdoor
mall that had fallen on hard times since the glittering Stonewood Arcadia Retail & Entertainment Center had opened less than a mile
away, on a stretch of land along the railroad tracks that had formerly
been home to a chemical plant, a cardboard box factory, and a manu-
facturer of inflatable pool toys.

Considering that the Tabernacle's attendance and revenue had
more than doubled over the past year, Pastor Dennis could probably
have afforded a move to classier digs—the local archdiocese was ac-
tively seeking evangelical tenants for some of its recently mothballed
facilities—but he showed no interest in relocating. Aside from the thrill
of preaching to a packed house every week, the Pastor appreciated the

ample parking—only a couple of the neighboring stores were open on Sunday morning—and the fact that curious passersby and nervous first-timers could watch the service through the plate-glass window before making the momentous decision to step inside. He also liked the symbolism of a church in the mall—one more Temple of Greed reclaimed for the Lord—and did his best to exploit the possibilities it offered for creative proselytizing. This morning, for example, there was a bright orange banner taped across the front window.

"PUT SATAN OUT OF BUSINESS!" it said. "DON'T MISS OUR BIG SAVINGS!"

BEYOND ALL the practical advantages of the current location, though, Tim and the rest of the congregation knew that Pastor Dennis had a more personal reason for staying put: he believed Griswold Commons was sacred ground. It was here, just a few short years ago, that he'd first heard the call of the Lord and begun his career as a preacher.

He'd told the story in a sermon delivered during one of Tim's first visits to the Tabernacle, and referred to it frequently in the months that followed, always striking the same note of quiet wonderment at the fact of having been struck down on the Road to Damascus.

The way he described it, he was a lost soul at the time, a man in his late twenties with a low-paying job, living in the basement of his mother's house. It was especially embarrassing because he'd been a boy of great promise, the salutatorian of his high-school class, winner of a partial scholarship to the prestigious Rensselaer Polytechnic Institute.

But something had gone wrong when he got to college. Almost immediately, a darkness settled over him. He felt foggy and tired all the time; he slept badly and couldn't concentrate on his schoolwork. The doctors called it depression, but that didn't seem right. Depression comes from inside you; this had come from outside, like someone had dropped a heavy blanket over his head.

He lived beneath this blanket for ten long years, working part-time when he could, taking a class here and there. He had few friends and suffered from a debilitating loneliness that could only be soothed, temporarily, by pornography or violent video games.

Not long after his twenty-eighth birthday, for reasons no one could explain, he began to feel a little better. He took a full-time job in the computer department of the old Best Buy in Griswold Commons (the store had since relocated to the Arcadia Center), where he impressed his supervisors with his positive attitude, technical know-how, and strong communications skills. There was talk about management opportunities, a long-term future with the company.

And the cool thing was, he liked Best Buy; he felt at home there. It was a privilege to be surrounded by all these amazing products—big-screen TVs, audio components galore, wafer-thin laptops with ultrafast processors, pocket-sized digital cameras, rack upon rack of movies, music, and video games—the accumulated bounty of the world's high-tech wizardry. It was, he often thought, like working in a Museum of Wonders.

At least that was how he felt for about six months, until the old man showed up late one Saturday afternoon, a burly white-haired guy in a shabby suit, gimping around on a bum leg. He came hobbling up to Dennis with a sly smile on his face, as if they were pals from way back when.

"There he is," the old man said. "Just the kid I've been looking for."

"Can I help you?" Dennis asked.

The old man held out a fat paperback.

"The boss told me to give this to you."

Dennis accepted the book, surprised to see that it was a Bible.

"This is from Kenny?"

Kenny was the Assistant Manager on duty, a middle-aged frat boy who always headed straight to a bar when he was finished with work. Dennis had tagged along a couple of times, but once he had a few drinks in him, all Kenny wanted to talk about was how he loved women with

huge bottoms, the bigger the better. He could hold forth on the subject for hours.

"I told you," the old man said. "It's from the boss."

"You mean Phil?" Phil was the weekday manager, Kenny's direct
superior.

"It's not from Phil," the old man scoffed. "Phil's not the boss."

By this point, Dennis was losing his patience.

"I'm a little busy right now. Is this some kind of joke?"

The old man looked offended.

"I traveled a long way to bring this to you. Believe me, I would've
been happy to stay home."

"I think you got the wrong guy," Dennis told him.

"That's not possible," the old man replied.

"But I don't want a Bible."

"That's not my problem. I just said I'd deliver it. What happens after that is your business."

The old man gave him a searching look, then turned and walked
away, moving at a pretty good clip for a guy whose right foot never
quite made it off the floor. Dennis would have followed him—he still
wanted to clarify this issue about the boss—but he was waylaid by an
imperious young woman carrying a handwritten list of questions entitled, "Wireless Networking Problems/Solutions."

Dennis wasn't sure what to do about the Bible. He didn't want to
take it home, but he didn't feel right throwing it away. In the end, he
just stuck it on a cluttered shelf beneath the Computer Information
desk and forgot all about it.

But the Bible didn't forget him, though it took him a while to realize it. All he really knew at the time was that the store suddenly began
to feel strange. He'd always thought of it as a humming hive of useful
machines and ingenious works of art, but now it struck him as soulless, vaguely malignant. The customers didn't seem excited so much as
dazed, pod people hypnotized by flickering images, stupefied by all

that shiny metal and molded plastic. Sometimes, walking down the DVD aisle, he was almost certain he could smell something putrid, as if rotting flesh were hidden inside those elegant little boxes with pictures of handsome men and beautiful women on the front. He'd watch kids trying out video games on the in-store consoles and have to suppress an urge to rip the controllers out of their hands and scream for them to run for their lives. On more than one occasion, he found himself on his knees in the employee restroom, puking up his guts, although he didn't feel the least bit sick.

He wondered if he was losing his mind, if he was going to have another episode like the one that had knocked him for a loop in college, but this seemed different. Back then he'd felt thickheaded, two beats behind the rest of the world, but this time around he was lucid, hyperaware. It was the store that was messed up, not him; he was sure of it.

He thought seriously about quitting to preserve his sanity, but he didn't want to alarm his mother. She was so thrilled to have him working, to be able to believe that her son had recovered, that everything would be all right. He didn't want to take that away from her, to do something that would make her frightened again.

One busy Thursday night, he crouched down below the Computer Information desk to get a manual for a Handheld Organizer when his eyes landed on the Bible the old man had given him. What he saw struck him with amazement. The book was glowing like a beacon, pulsing with energy, calling out to him. All at once, as if the knowledge had been poured into him like a fiery liquid, he understood who the Boss was, and what he was required to do.

"Oh Lord," he said, placing his hand on the book. "You found me."

His own memory of what happened after that was dim and fragmentary—all he really knew was that the Spirit had entered his heart and irrevocably transformed him—but he'd been able to reconstruct much of it from the police report, conversations with sympathetic eyewitnesses, and the amateur video taken near the end of the incident.

By all accounts, he had emerged wild-eyed from below the counter, holding the Bible aloft with both hands, and babbling in a language that had never before been heard in Best Buy. He stepped out from behind the desk, knocked a flat-screen monitor to the floor, and proceeded to kick over a display of knockoff MP3 players.

The Spirit was still overflowing from his mouth, though a few people claimed that there was intelligible speech mixed in with the divine gibberish, warnings to specific customers to turn a blind eye to the sinful works of man and fix their gazes on the Lord.

Dennis was not a big man, and he had never done much exercise, but the Spirit made him strong. He tossed all-in-one printers through the air like they were empty boxes, toppled a shelf of home-theater components, scattered CDs like playing cards. A couple of his fellow employees tried to stop him, but they were too weak. A gaggle of customers—some moved by his passion, others excited by the possibility of violence—began to follow him as he made his way, inevitably, it seemed, to the back of the store, where he planted himself in front of a three-thousand-dollar, sixty-one-inch, wide-screen flat-panel plasma TV that was playing *Lara Croft: Tomb Raider.*

"Whore!" he shouted. "Abomination!"

There was some uncertainty about where the boombox came from, whether he'd picked it up on the way or someone had handed it to him just then, but there was no dispute about the fact that he raised the sleek black tube overhead—it was a JVC with built-in subwoofers—and hurled it at the screen, causing Angelina Jolie to disintegrate in a rain of shattered glass. Screams of protest and cheers of approval mingled as Dennis fell to his knees and called out to God.

Some witnesses believed he was about to demolish a second TV, but he never got the chance; two security guards jumped him from behind and began attacking him with fists and billy clubs, delivering a savage and prolonged beating that was captured by a customer on a display model camcorder. Tim remembered seeing the grainy video on the TV news—he was going through his divorce at the time and was a long way from God—and thinking, "Big deal, the jerk had it coming to him," which he later realized, with a feeling of deep shame, was exactly what lots of "good" people must have thought two thousand years ago, watching a half-dead man getting whipped by soldiers as he dragged a wooden cross up a hill in the desert.

INSIDE, THE Tabernacle didn't look like much: a big open room with a low ceiling, white walls, and gray industrial carpeting. Two smaller areas—the lobby and the Young Apostles' room—were carved out of the larger space by temporary office partitions. Tim said good-bye to Carrie just inside the main entrance—she was on the Loaves and Fishes Committee, which served refreshments in the lobby—and continued into the Sanctuary.

It was quiet in there, a field of empty white folding chairs, and Tim paused at the back of the room, as he did every week, to savor this moment of homecoming. No matter what else was going on in his life—how distracted he was by problems with Abby, Carrie, or Allison—he never failed to be cleansed and lifted up by these first few breaths of sanctified air. He could feel God's presence surrounding him, a calm but still mighty benevolence radiating down from the ceiling and up from the floor, and his heart swelled with a mingled sense of awe and gratitude and humble pride that a man such as himself could have his own small part to play in the ceremony that was about to unfold.

He headed down the center aisle toward the altar, a low wooden platform that also served as bandstand for the Praise Team. His fellow musicians were already onstage, tweaking their amps and instruments and glancing over the set list, professionally oblivious to the Prayer Squad meeting taking place directly in front of them. About a dozen church members were swarming around Alice Palmiero, a mother of two not much older than Tim, who'd recently been diagnosed with ovarian cancer. It looked from the outside like a loving rugby scrum, hunched bodies pressing close together, hands wrapped around shoulders and resting on backs, a low murmur of supplication rising from the group. Tim knew what it was like to be at the center of all that powerful energy—the Prayer Squad had taken up the cause of his sobriety shortly after he'd accepted Jesus—and he hoped Alice was drawing the same comfort and reassurance he had from the knowledge that he wasn't alone in his trials, that good people wanted him to get better, and wanted the Lord to know it.

A little off to the right of the prayer huddle, Youth Pastor Eddie and Elise Kim were standing with their arms outstretched, their ecstatic faces tilted toward the ceiling. Tim wasn't sure if they were satellites of the larger group or bystanders with a separate agenda. He slipped between them as unobtrusively as he could and stepped onto the stage, nodding hello to Bill Spooner, the lead guitarist and bandleader, who was down on his knees fiddling with his pedalboard, an elaborate miniature city of metal boxes and multicolored wires.

"Brother Mason." He spoke softly, acknowledging Tim's arrival with a sardonic salute. "Rock on."

"Amen," Tim muttered in reply. "Turn it up to eleven."

FOR TIM, Sunday worship was an easy gig; all he had to do was tune up, plug in, and play. His Fender Jazz Bass and Peavey amp were already up on stage, right where he'd left them last week, and the week before that. He didn't bother taking them home anymore.

Unlike a couple of guys from the Praise Team—Bill fronted a popular oldies band called Gary and the Graybeards, and the drummer, Ben Malinowski, played in a jazz trio that had a regular Saturday night booking at the Red Roof Inn in Gifford Township—Tim no longer had a musical life outside the Tabernacle. That world was just too fraught with temptation. He wasn't the kind of reformed alcoholic who could spend the night in a bar drinking nothing but Diet Coke, nor was he the kind of reformed pothead who'd have an easy time passing a joint to the next guy without taking a toke for himself, or the kind of responsible married man who remembered to mention the existence of his wife the instant a pretty woman started flirting with him. He wished it were otherwise, but he'd never figured out a way to separate the rock 'n' roll from the sex, drugs, and booze that always seemed to come along with it, the good and the bad tied up in a thrilling, sloppy, ultimately toxic package. He remembered laughing about Little Richard years ago, thinking how pathetic it was for a performer of that stature to have found it necessary to denounce "the Devil's music," but he'd reluctantly come to accept the possibility that Mr. Tutti Frutti had a point.

Which was sad, because Tim loved to rock, and knew how good he was at it. A bass player who could sing harmony, he'd been recruited by all sorts of bands over the years—Southern Rock, New Wave, blues, punk, rockabilly, funk—and still got calls from musicians who knew of him by reputation or remembered him from shows stretching all the way back to the mid-eighties, and he always had to fight down a surge of excitement before regretfully declining their invitations to audition.

Luckily, Bill Spooner had remembered him, too; they'd played a lot of the same clubs in the early nineties, back when Tim was in a grunge band called Placenta, and Bill was the main songwriter and lead shredder for Killing Spree, a locally famous death metal trio that had released a couple of well-received albums on an indie label out of New Brunswick. Bill had called out of the blue a year and a half ago to ask if Tim could bail him out for a single gig on Sunday morning.

"It's at my church," he said. "Just four songs. I can teach 'em to you in half an hour."

"You go to church?" It didn't even occur to Tim to hide his amusement. Killing Spree had done the whole Slayer trip—studded bracelets, gratuitous references to Satan, pictures of dead animals projected onto a screen behind the band—without offering the slightest hint that they might just be kidding around.

"Dude," he said. "This church saved my life. You know, after Jill died. I was in a dark place."

"Jill died?" Tim felt like an idiot. "I didn't know that. I'm really sorry."

Bill and Jill had been a famous rock 'n' roll couple back in the day. Black leather, tattoos, hair hanging in their faces. They went everywhere on Bill's Harley, wore matching fringe jackets with the Killing Spree logo on the back, a skeleton with a cigarette in its mouth, blasting away on a tommy gun.

"Three years ago," Bill said. "We were living out in Pennsylvania. She was having a baby, and something went wrong. They saved the little one, but not her. Can you imagine? The guy I was, with a dead wife and a newborn baby to take care of?"

"Not really," Tim said.

"I came home to live with my parents." He gave a soft laugh of amazement. "Man, I was a mess. Then this guy invited me to his church."

"And now you're inviting me," Tim said.

"You don't have to believe," Bill assured him. "You just gotta play a couple of songs. And besides, it's all the donuts you can eat."

"What the hell," Tim had said. "I'm not doing anything on Sunday."

TIM AND Bill went out to the lobby after sound check to grab a cup of coffee. It was just starting to fill up, and there was a cheerful cocktail party vibe in the air, lots of hugs, handshakes, and *how are you*'s. Ever since his first visit to the Tabernacle, Tim had been struck by the warmth and fellowship he found there; almost without exception the church members were kind and openhearted, nothing like the grim Puritans he'd expected. It had been the same with the punks and

Deadheads he'd known in his wilder days: despite their fearsome reputations in the outside world, they usually turned out to be surprisingly normal once you got to know them.

Carrie was standing behind the snack table, trying to console Evelyn Braithwaite, who'd lost a son in Iraq a year ago, but was still mourning as if it had happened last week. Tim raised an eyebrow in commiseration as he passed—Carrie had complained more than once about what a trial it was, having to listen to Evelyn recount the same half dozen memories of Jason every week—and she replied with an inconspicuous flutter of her fingers, as if she were typing a brief message on an invisible keyboard.

Bill's wife, Ellie, arrived just as they were finishing their donuts, a big-boned, flustered-looking redhead with a three-month-old baby cradled in her arms, and her four-year-old stepdaughter in tow. Little Gillian was a delicate, slightly unnerving child, eerily reminiscent of her late mother, a black-haired waif with pouty lips and an expression of lofty disdain for the world. Tim felt a small shock of recognition every time he saw her, a window into a crazier time, drugs and motorcycles and shrieking feedback from a Marshall stack, glassy-eyed chicks with white makeup and black lips.

Bill hurried over to greet his family, lifting Gillian into his arms, then planting a hard, lingering kiss on Ellie's mouth. Maybe it was just for show—Tim didn't always trust married couples who carried on like teenagers—but it didn't look that way. Bill was at peace with his new life, liberated from the past. He didn't seem to mind that he'd lost his hair and put on weight, or traded in his biker's vest for an outlandish Hawaiian shirt with hot dogs and hamburgers printed on it, just like he didn't seem to mind that Ellie couldn't hold a candle to Jill; he accepted his second wife the way he accepted Jesus—unquestioningly, with delight and gratitude for the gift he'd been given, and no apparent desire to look back. It must have helped that Jill was dead, Tim thought. Maybe Bill wouldn't have found it so easy if he had to see her every week with another man and remember what they'd been to each other.

Bill kissed Gillian on the forehead and set her back down on the floor. Then Ellie handed him the baby, and his face lit up with happiness. Tim didn't feel jealous so much as guilty; he still insisted on wearing a condom with Carrie, postponing the child he knew she desperately wanted. He told her it was because he wanted to save some money, get them on their feet financially so she could afford to stay at home with the baby, but that was only part of it. Something else was holding him back, a stubborn reluctance to take that final irrevocable step, to create a new family that would forever supersede the old one.

His eyes strayed back to Carrie, who still hadn't managed to extricate herself from the conversation with Evelyn. It wasn't much of a conversation, really—Evelyn did all the talking; Carrie just nodded or shook her head, occasionally touching the older woman on the arm. Even so, Tim could see how intently Carrie was focused on her, and how comforted Evelyn was to be enveloped in the cocoon of her sympathetic attention. He felt a surge of respect and affection for his wife; she was a good woman, and he was a fool for letting himself lose sight of it. He made up his mind to join her, to take some of the burden of consoling Evelyn off her shoulders, but he received a hard slap on the back before he'd managed to take the first step in her direction.

"Hey, coach!"

Tim turned to see his friend John Roper, a man of alarming girth, looming over him with a big Sunday morning grin on his face. Tim returned the smile, momentarily startled—he reacted the same way every week—by the sight of his assistant coach in a suit and tie. Until a few months ago, Tim had only ever seen him in sweats.

"How's Abby?" John inquired.

"Okay. A little woozy last night, but she felt fine this morning."

"Praise God." John stepped toward Tim, spreading his arms wide. "Gimme a hug."

With a reluctance he hoped he managed to conceal, Tim submitted to the larger man's embrace. It wasn't that he was squeamish about hugging other guys—it was standard practice at the Tabernacle—but as a smallish man, he found it embarrassing to be crushed in the arms of a big lug like John, a former offensive tackle at Montclair State who had to outweigh him by a hundred pounds. It made him feel childish, like a little boy who needed to drink more milk.

John kept his arms wrapped tightly around Tim well after the two men had exchanged the obligatory three thumps on the back. These ex-tralong hugs were a habit of John's, his way of saying thanks. It was Tim who'd invited him to the Tabernacle over the summer—he'd seen an opening after a conversation in which John had complained about middle-of-the-night panic attacks, a dizzying sense of peering down into an endless void—and Tim who'd acted as his spiritual guide and sponsor in the subsequent months, much as Bill Spooner had done for him. Pastor Dennis called it the Rescue Chain: I save you, you save the next guy, and he'll save someone else.

"That was an awesome game yesterday," John said, giving Tim a final, anaconda-like squeeze before letting go. "I'm still on cloud nine."

"Well, we've got this one to thank." Tim nodded at John's daughter, Candace, who was standing next to her father, nervously plucking at the Livestrong bracelet on her left wrist. "That was an amazing goal. I can't believe how fast you got upfield."

Candace blushed; she was a lovely girl with the long neck and regal bearing of a ballerina. Tim caught himself gazing at her with a little too much interest—she wasn't even twelve, for Pete's sake—and hastily shifted his attention back to her father, who wasn't nearly so pleasant to look at.

"She almost flubbed it," John said with an affectionate chuckle. "For a second there, I didn't think the ball had enough juice to make it across the goal line."

He reached out to muss his daughter's hair, but she swatted his hand away.

"*Daddy.*"

John drew back in mock surrender.

"Sorry." He rolled his eyes for Tim's benefit. "I keep forgetting. The hair's off-limits."

Tim shook his head in parental solidarity. He wondered if it was weird for John, watching his little girl grow into such a striking young woman, a long-legged blonde who, within a year or two, wouldn't be able to walk down the street without causing a physical disturbance in every man and teenage boy within a hundred-yard radius. It wasn't nearly so complicated for Tim, at least not yet. Unlike Candace, Abby still seemed a long way from puberty, even if she was disconcertingly adolescent in some of her behaviors and attitudes.

"I'll tell you what," Tim said. "By that point, I didn't really care if we won or lost. I was just so proud of the girls for not giving up."

John's face grew solemn. He dropped a beefy hand on Tim's shoulder.

"That was a gutsy thing you did after the game."

"It was no big deal," Tim muttered.

"Yes, it was," John insisted. He spoke softly, looking Tim straight in the eye. "It was a very big deal. You stood up for the Lord, and I want to thank you for it."

PLAYING MUSIC was a bit like making love, Tim thought, as the Praise Team launched into "Marvelous," the upbeat kickoff to their three-song opening set. Sometimes you were right there in the thick of it, completely at one with your partner, your entire being submerged in the act. Other times you were oddly detached, floating above yourself, watching with mild interest as you phoned it in, thinking how you were overdue for an oil change, or wondering when it was, exactly, that you'd lost your taste for chunky peanut butter.

Today, he could tell, was going to be one of those half-there days. His fingers were hitting the right notes, and his voice felt strong as he leaned into the mic, smiling at the lead singer, Verna Deaver, as they harmonized on the chorus:

> *The Lord has done this,*
> *And it's fabulous,*
> *Miraculous,*
> *Wonderful.*
> *The Lord has done this,*
> *And it's marvelous*
> *In our eyes!*

But his mind was far away, drifting insistently back to the prayer at the end of yesterday's soccer game, the nagging sense—only compounded by John's praise—that he'd done something foolish, or at least gotten himself into something a little messier than he'd bargained for.

He'd never asked the team to pray with him before, had never even considered it a possibility. But it had been an emotional game, and when the girls gathered around for the final cheer, a feeling of such love came over him—all those sweet, flushed, youthful faces gazing up at him—that he spoke from the heart, without premeditation.

"Let's hold hands," he'd said, "and give thanks to God."

None of them complained or even hesitated; they didn't seem to feel threatened, or even the least bit uncomfortable about what he'd asked them to do. They linked hands and sat down on the grass as naturally as if they prayed together every day. It wasn't until Maggie's mother came running up with that look of horror on her face that it occurred to Tim that he might have overstepped his bounds.

He'd known she was there, of course. They'd met at halftime, and had a nice chat—she was friendlier than he'd expected, with a surprisingly girlish laugh—so he had no excuse for not anticipating her reaction. In fact, he wouldn't have blamed her for thinking he'd orchestrated the whole incident simply to antagonize her.

But the truth was, he'd forgotten all about Ruth Ramsey by then. The latter part of the second half—everything after Abby got knocked out—had been a blur to him. He'd been so terrified to see his daughter lying motionless on the grass—there was one nauseating moment when she'd honestly looked dead to him—and so overcome with relief when she finally opened her eyes, that he still wasn't thinking straight when Maggie's mother showed up and started screaming.

He'd tried to calm her down, but she wouldn't listen. She just yanked her daughter away from the team, with all the other girls watching, and told him that her child's days on the Stars were over. Maggie burst into tears when she heard this—she was a tough little girl, and he remembered thinking she cried like a boy, angrily, like she'd been betrayed by her body—and that was the thing he couldn't get out of his head.

He wasn't sorry about saying the prayer, and he certainly wasn't sorry about offending someone like Ruth Ramsey, but he was deeply sorry about putting Maggie in that awful position, embarrassing her in front of her teammates, taking what should have been a nice moment for all of them and turning it into something ugly and confusing.

And now he was going to have to apologize to Maggie's mother, as much as he hated the idea. Because he'd be heartbroken if Maggie left the team, and not just because she was his best player. He'd be heartbroken because she was a great kid who loved the game, and because she shouldn't have to stop playing it because of a dispute between adults, something that didn't involve her at all.

TIM STARTED to perk up a bit on "Jerusalem," the final song of the opening set. He could tell from the moment Verna Deaver hit the first note that autopilot wasn't going to cut it; he'd have to step up his game if he didn't want to get left behind.

"My soul is weary," she called out, the richness of her voice frayed by a ragged edge of grievance. "And my body is tired!"

Tim and Bill Spooner supplied the baritone response.

"Goin' up to Jerusalem."

"But my faith is burning with a heavenly fire!"

"Goin' up to Jerusalem."

A large black woman of indeterminate age, Verna was the newest member of the Praise Team. Tim didn't know much about her, except that she worked at the KFC on Route 23, seemed to be raising a couple of grandchildren on her own, and suffered from some kind of chronic foot ailment that forced her to rehearse while sitting in a chair. On Sunday mornings, though, she always stood straight and proud at the microphone, waving her arms and swaying gently from side to side, as if God had granted her a temporary waiver for the relief of pain.

There weren't a whole lot of black people who belonged to the Tabernacle—even by the most generous standard, Stonewood Heights could not be considered a diverse community—but their number had been increasing steadily over the past year, as word had spread throughout the surrounding area of Pastor Dennis's charismatic leadership and uncompromising denunciations of immorality.

Verna had been among the first wave of African-Americans to join the church, a core group of a dozen or so mostly older women who'd arrived last winter, around the time Pastor Dennis began appearing on a weekly cable access TV show called *The Good Seed.* Tim had a vivid memory of the first time he'd seen her, because she'd been accompanied by a gorgeous young woman with dreadlocks, high cheekbones, and almond-shaped eyes—she wore a tight skirt and shiny knee-high boots—who didn't return the following week, or ever again, though Tim still hadn't stopped looking for her.

Verna asked to audition for the Praise Team in late spring. The guys were skeptical at first; she had no previous experience as a singer and didn't seem like she'd fit in very easily with a group of veteran musicians who'd been playing in rock bands since they were teenagers. But these objections disappeared by the time she finished the first verse of "Amazing Grace"—it was instantly clear that Verna was a natural, endowed with a big expressive voice and an instinctive sense of how to use it. There was none of the stumbling you expected at an audition, the newcomer following the band instead of leading it. Verna just stepped in and took over, and no one begrudged it for a second.

"Let the first be last and the last be first, uh-huh!"

"Goin' up to Jerusalem."

"Help me, Lord! Lift me up now!"

"Goin' up to Jerusalem."

Over the summer, the Praise Team had undergone a major transformation, changing from an ensemble of equals—up to that point, Bill, Tim, and the keyboard player, Gary Rawson, had traded off on the lead-singing responsibilities—to a backing group for a virtuoso vocalist. Or, as Bill liked to say, "We used to be Crosby, Stills, Nash & Young; now we're Big Brother and the Holding Company."

"My feet are sore! But I got to keep on walking!"

"Goin' up to Jerusalem!"

"Oh, Lord! I'm right here at your side!"

"Goin' up to Jerusalem."

During the same period, their repertoire had shifted slowly but decisively away from the slightly bland pop/rock that had been their default mode toward more traditional gospel music, which was what Verna sang best. The longtime church members had been mystified at first, especially by the ecstatic improvisational runs built into the end of the songs, during which Verna sometimes worked herself up into quite a lather, clutching her head and punching herself repeatedly in the leg as she testified, but lately they'd come around. In the past few weeks, the worshippers had begun clapping along with the music, making a tentative but still joyful noise that was new to the Tabernacle, and surely pleasing to God.

THERE WAS no applause when the song finally ended, nothing to suggest that anything in the way of a performance had occurred. The musicians just put down their instruments—Tim and Bill each took one of Verna's arms as she stepped down from the stage, breathing hard, her eyes wild and unfocused—and took their seats among the worshippers.

For Tim, this was one of the most satisfying moments of the service, the one that captured what it meant to be a Christian. It wasn't a question of Us and Them—the band set apart from the audience, the special people lording it over the drones—they were all one, the believers, the people of the Tabernacle.

For as long as he could remember, Tim had been drawn to this feeling of community; it was something he'd sought, at very different points in his life, from both punk rock and the Grateful Dead, and in each case, for a little while, he'd found what he was looking for. But it hadn't lasted, and in any case, the communities in which he'd claimed membership were disappointingly narrow and homogenous compared to this one. The punks and the Deadheads were overwhelmingly white, suburban, and young; almost everyone wore similar clothes and hairstyles, and had had more or less the same experience of the world. Not like here, where you saw grandmothers and little kids, people in wheelchairs, whole families, interracial couples, immigrants who barely spoke a word of English, college teachers, twelve steppers, cancer patients who'd lost their hair, lonely people who didn't have a friend in the world until they stepped through the door of the Tabernacle.

Tim nodded at the familiar faces and patted a couple of acquaintances on the shoulder as he made his way to the empty aisle seat next to Carrie, who was watching him with the usual mixture of affection and worry. She squeezed his hand and gave him a quick smile before turning her attention back to the podium, clearly curious, as he was, about who would be delivering this morning's sermon.

Tim wasn't sure why, but Pastor Dennis had been cutting down on his preaching this fall, and not because he was sick or out of town. For three out of the past four weeks, guest speakers—a missionary who'd worked among the poor in Guatemala, a nurse who spoke about Christianity and medical ethics, and an ex-gay man who'd renounced his homosexuality and was now a married father of two—had addressed the congregation while Pastor Dennis listened intently from the cheap seats.

This phenomenon had caused a great deal of discussion among the people of the Tabernacle, who couldn't help speculating about the reasons behind the Pastor's uncharacteristic retreat from the spotlight. Was he feeling burnt-out? Was he worried that the church had become a "Cult of Personality," as a disgruntled letter writer had charged in the *Bulletin-Chronicle*? Or was there some broader, subtler purpose behind his choices that would gradually make itself known over the next month or two? While different people gravitated toward different explanations, there was a near-unanimous feeling among the congregation that the guest speakers had not been very good, despite their interesting life experiences. It was one thing to talk about yourself; Pastor Dennis had the rarer talent of inspiring others, using his words to connect with his listeners and draw them closer to God.

The ex-gay man—he introduced himself simply as "Troy"—was the most problematic speaker for Tim, and not only because there didn't seem to be anything "ex" about him. Tim understood that it was unfair to stereotype, but he was pretty sure he could recognize a gay guy when he saw one. It wasn't just Troy's effeminate voice, or his exaggerated gestures, or his suspiciously buff body, or even the flirtatious way he put his hands on his hips, cocked his head to one side, and said, "People, I am sooo not proud of my behavior." Any one of those things could have been pure coincidence, but taken together, the whole package just seemed to scream, "I'm still gay!" Tim wondered how Mrs. Troy managed to convince herself that everything was on the up-and-up when she stood before him in a filmy negligee and saw the look of profound indifference on his face, unless she happened to be a recovering lesbian herself, in which case she was probably more relieved than anything else.

Most of the time, Tim did his best to be a good Christian and toe the biblical line, but no matter how hard he tried, he couldn't get himself all worked up about the sin of homosexuality. It just didn't seem that bad to him, certainly not worth banishing someone to hell for, and probably not worth all the time and energy Pastor Dennis and lots of other people spent obsessing about it, especially since Jesus didn't have a single word to say on the subject in the Gospels.

It seemed like a glaring omission, considering that Jesus had a fair amount to say on other points of sexual morality, including one that was particularly inconvenient for Tim: "Anyone who divorces his wife and marries another woman commits adultery." You couldn't get much clearer than that, and yet Pastor Dennis hadn't objected to Tim's marriage to Carrie, far from it. He'd just let the whole remarriage-adultery thing slide, tempering God's harsh law with a dose of human compassion. Tim couldn't help feeling like gay people deserved a similar break, a recognition that a choice between a life of sin and a life of celibacy was no choice at all.

IT WAS amusing for Tim to find himself so squarely in the camp of sexual tolerance because it was a long way from where he'd started out. He'd been a teenager in the late seventies, part of the last generation of American boys who could say the word "fag" with an air of innocence, without it even occurring to them that someone somewhere might have a right to be offended. The mere thought of two men getting it on was enough to send him and his buddies into paroxysms of disgust. At the same time, they joked about it constantly; it was the rare conversation that ended without the ritual invitation to "suck my dick." They devoted lots of fevered speculation to the nightmare of prison rape, especially the variety in which a large black man claimed you as his steady girlfriend.

His homophobia survived intact through a good part of college—Stockton State in the early eighties was no hotbed of progressive thinking—until he met Scott D'Alerio. This was in the spring of his junior year, at a time when Tim had stopped going to classes and pretty much resigned himself to flunking out. Scott was his neighbor, a stoner goofball with long hair and a mellow personality; he wore a black watch cap indoors and out, twelve months a year, and hosted a late-night jazz fusion show on the college radio station. They ran into each other all the time around the apartment complex—Scott seemed to have as few academic obligations as Tim—and gradually fell into the habit of hanging out together in the afternoons, smoking dope and listening to music at Scott's place.

One day, out of the blue, Scott put his hand on Tim's leg and asked if he could suck him off. Tim sat up in stoned bewilderment—he'd been sprawled on the couch, contemplating the monstrous genius of the Mahavishnu Orchestra—his mind lagging a second or two behind the action.

"Dude," he spluttered. "What did you just say?"

Scott was kneeling on the rug, gazing up at Tim, his face bold and vulnerable at the same time.

"I asked if I could suck you off."

A dopey, one-syllable laugh escaped from Tim's mouth.

"That's not funny."

"I'm not joking," Scott assured him. He had these long pretty eyelashes that Tim had never noticed before. "Nobody else has to know."

"You're wasted. You don't know what you're saying."

"It's just a blowjob," Scott replied, in a weirdly peevish tone. "Just close your eyes and pretend I'm a girl."

Tim grabbed his weed and rolling papers off the coffee table and stood up.

"Dude," he said. "I better go. You're freaking me out."

"Oh shit." Scott clapped his hand against his forehead and started moaning. "Fuck. I'm really sorry."

Tim took a couple of uncertain steps toward the door.

"Don't go," Scott called after him.

"I think I better," Tim replied.

"Come on," Scott pleaded. "Don't do this to me."

Tim wasn't sure what made him turn around. Maybe the shakiness in Scott's voice. Maybe just an unwillingness to be the kind of person who walks out on a friend when he's begging you to stay.

*"Please."* Scott sounded like he was on the verge of tears. "I really didn't mean to offend you."

"It's okay," Tim told him. "I'm not offended."

He was surprised to hear himself say this, and even more surprised to realize it was true. He was shocked and embarrassed for both of them, but he wasn't angry.

"It's just—" Scott stood up. He tried to smile but it didn't really work. "I've been thinking about you a lot. Like all the time. Sometimes, I don't know, sometimes I think I'm in love with you."

"I didn't even know you were gay."

"I don't wanna be," Scott assured him. "I just fucking am."

They went into the kitchen, drank a couple of beers, and talked for a long time. Scott said he'd known the truth about himself since he was a little kid, though he'd resisted it as best he could. He'd even had a couple of girlfriends in high school, but it was all for show, like acting in a play. He said he'd never had a real boyfriend, but that he went to bars sometimes, places where straight-looking college guys were pretty popular. When Tim finally left, they assured each other that everything was cool between them, that they were still friends, and that they'd go on as if the whole episode had never happened.

It didn't work out that way, of course. They tried hanging out a handful of times after that, but there was always a thick cloud of awkwardness following them around, a troubling new set of possibilities in the air. In the past they'd sat together for long periods of time without talking, content to be stoned and grooving on the music—at least that was how it seemed to Tim—but now they felt compelled to break the silence with lame stabs at conversation, each one trying to make sure that the other was okay, wasn't feeling self-conscious or uncomfortable. After a while, it just got easier to make excuses. Tim started playing a lot of ultimate Frisbee; Scott suddenly had a shitload to do at the radio station.

Tim dropped out of school at the end of the summer, and never saw Scott again. But he thought about him a lot in the years that followed, whenever anyone made a fag joke or said that gay men deserved to get AIDS. Sometimes, if the circumstances were right, Tim would challenge the speaker, ask if he—in Tim's experience, it was always a he—had any friends who were gay. Almost always, the guy would say no.

"Wait till you do," Tim would tell him. "That's when you'll realize what an asshole you used to be."

PASTOR DENNIS normally began the sermon right after the Praise Team vacated the stage, but this morning there was some sort of holdup. After two or three minutes of staring at the empty podium, people began checking their watches and glancing around uncertainly, wondering if somebody should do something, or at least make an announcement.

The audible sigh of relief that greeted the Pastor's sudden arrival— he came hustling down the center aisle just as Youth Pastor Eddie was shuffling onto the stage with a grim expression on his face—quickly dissolved into murmurs of confusion and concern at his disheveled appearance. Instead of the neatly pressed khakis and light blue polo shirt that had been his preaching uniform for as long as Tim had been coming to the Tabernacle, he was wearing a rumpled, ill-fitting gray suit with a torn sleeve. His striped tie was loosened and askew, his shirttail partially untucked; he could have been a businessman slinking back to his hotel after a night of hard carousing in a strange city. The fact that he was limping slightly and cupping his hand over his right eye only added another layer of mystery to an already unsettling situation.

The two Pastors embraced on the stage. After a brief whispered conversation, Youth Pastor Eddie retreated to his seat, while Pastor Dennis took his accustomed place behind the microphone.

"You'll have to excuse me," he said. "I didn't get to sleep last night. I was at a wedding, and there was a lot of drinking going on."

He took his hand away from his eye, revealing a hideous green-and-purple shiner in full bloom.

"As you might suspect, this was not a Christian wedding. Oh, don't get me wrong—if you asked the people there if they believed in Jesus, most of them would have said yes. But you and I understand that they only say that because they don't *know* Jesus, not like we do. In fact, they wouldn't recognize our Lord if he rang their doorbell, wearing his dazzling white robes—you know, the clothes the Gospel of Mark describes as being 'whiter than anyone in the world could bleach them.' He could introduce himself as the Son of God, and explain that He'd died for their sins, and these *Christians* would just slam the door in His face and go right back to watching *Desperate Housewives.*

"So what was *I* doing there, you might ask? The easy answer is that I had no choice. The bride was my wife's cousin, and she'd asked Emily to be one of her bridesmaids. So I went to the wedding with my wife, because we were invited. But the better answer is that I belonged there, among those drunken fools and faithless believers. This is exactly what Jesus told the Pharisees when they demanded to know why a holy man would stoop to break bread with sinners: 'It is not the healthy who need a doctor, but the sick.'

"Just so you understand the situation, I should explain that the wedding party got to sit at a big long table in the front of the banquet hall. That's where Emily was, which meant I was flying solo. It turned out there were a fair number of unattached men at the wedding, enough that we actually got assigned a table of our own, stuck way in the back of the hall, by the kitchen. The stag table, that's what the guys were calling it.

"My tablemates were just regular guys—one was an electrician, another sold cell phones, a couple worked with computers. All they really had in common was that they all liked sports and they all had come to the wedding with the goal of getting as drunk as possible. And I'll tell you what, they succeeded. By the time dinner was served, a couple of my companions were already pretty intoxicated, and the others were well on their way. So maybe it's not too surprising that they started discussing strip clubs right there at the wedding reception, though I have to admit I was taken aback, not having realized that this was an acceptable subject for conversation at the dinner table. Nobody seemed to think there was anything shameful about it—far from it. My tablemates weren't ashamed! They were proud of themselves! They were so macho, so sophisticated, such men of the world!

"You wouldn't think it could get much worse than that, right? But there was this one loudmouth at the table—Jay was his name—who couldn't stop talking about Jenna Jameson. Now it's my hope that most of you have never even heard of Jenna Jameson, and if that's the case, I'm sorry to be the one bringing her to your attention. Suffice it to say that Jenna Jameson is the biggest whore in the world, and that she gets paid very well for her services. And this pathetic man couldn't shut up about her. 'I love Jenna,' he said. 'She's the only girl for me.'

"Now, you can imagine how I felt about this vile nonsense, but I held my tongue, for as Jesus said, 'I did not come to judge the world.'

But Jay must have sensed that I was withholding myself from the conversation, and it made him nervous. After a while, he turned to me, and said, 'So, uh, Denny, you a big Jenna fan?'

"I told Jay I was happily married to a flesh-and-blood woman, and that I loved her with all my heart. 'Think about it,' I said. 'What possible use could I have for a pig like Jenna Jameson?'

"Well, the other guys seemed to think this was hilarious, as if it were a sissy thing for a man to say he loved his wife more than some piece of trash from a dirty movie. 'Who is this jerk?' one of them asked another. I took the opportunity to tell them that I was a man of God, and that I preached the Gospel of Jesus Christ to anyone who would listen. And these idiots laughed even louder. Except for one thing. I noticed that Jay wasn't laughing. He was staring at me with this angry, wounded expression, like I'd just insulted him.

"After dinner the dancing started up, and I would have been more than happy to shake the dust of that wedding off my feet. But I sat tight and bided my time. And when Jay got up to go to the men's room, I followed him in. When he was in no position to run away, I stepped up beside him, and said, 'Jenna Jameson doesn't love you, but I know someone who does.'

"Jay told me he was in no mood for my Christian garbage, though, believe me, he used a stronger word than garbage. He even went so far as to suggest that I was gay. Can you imagine?"

Pastor Dennis paused, allowing the absurdity of this charge to sink in with the congregation. Tim couldn't help chuckling, along with several other people around him.

"I assured him there was not a homosexual bone in my body," the Pastor continued, "and that if there was, I wouldn't hesitate to pluck it out, as the Lord commands. But he didn't believe me. 'If you're not gay,' he said, 'why did you follow me into the men's room?'

" 'Because I care about you,' I told him. 'Because I don't want you to burn in hell.'

"He didn't like that one bit, and I can't say I blame him. His voice got all whiny, like I'd hurt his feelings. 'Why would you say something like that? Here I am at my friend's wedding, minding my own business, and you come into the bathroom to tell me that I'm going to hell? It's just rude, that's what it is.'

" 'I only say it because it's true,' I explained. 'And because I have some good news for you.'

"He walked away from me, shaking his head and muttering under his breath. I followed him to the sink. 'I can see you're in pain,' I told him. 'You hate yourself, and you hate your life. But it doesn't have to be this way.'

"Well, Jay lost his temper. He grabbed me by the shirt and slammed me up against the wall. 'I'll tell you who's gonna be in pain,' he said.

"I told him that hell was a place of eternal torment. 'Think about that,' I said. 'The fire never goes out. You will just suffer and suffer and suffer.' He screamed at me to shut up. I told him that the worst day of his life would be a picnic compared to one second in the lake of fire. And that's when he hit me."

Pastor Dennis reached up, gently probing the lurid flesh around his eye.

"It was a pretty good shot, too, definitely the best punch I've taken since I've started spreading the Word of God. But I'll say this for Jay, he felt terrible about what he'd done. Before I could even offer to let him hit me again, he started apologizing. I told him that it was okay, that people who loved Jesus had been beaten and cursed and spit upon for two thousand years, and that we welcomed the punishment. And I quoted: 'Blessed are those who are persecuted because of righteousness, for theirs is the Kingdom of Heaven.' Jay got a bag of ice for me from the kitchen, and we went outside and had a good long talk. I told him about my life, and he told me about his. We got to know each other pretty well. And when the sun rose this morning, we were on our knees in the empty parking lot of the Pinehurst Manor.

That's why I was a little late for our meeting today. And that's why I stand before you right now, and say, 'Rejoice with me, for I have found my lost sheep.' "

Pastor Dennis peered out at the worshippers.

"Jay, my friend, will you come up here?"

Tim turned, along with the rest of the congregation, and saw a prematurely balding guy in a suit as rumpled as the Pastor's rise from a chair in the back row. Jay was younger than Tim had pictured him, in his late twenties at the most, a broad-shouldered ex-jock with a weak chin and a big belly. It was easy to imagine him sprawled on a couch in his boxers, staring slack-jawed at Jenna Jameson.

Tears were streaming down his cheeks as he made his way toward the altar, but he was smiling like a bride, nodding and saying thanks to all the well-wishers who were reaching out and touching him as he passed, offering their congratulations. Tim recognized the complicated emotion on his face. It was joy, the sudden knowledge that you have a chance to start over and do better, to salvage some hope and meaning from a life you thought you'd screwed up beyond repair. He leaned into the aisle and held out his hand so Jay could high-five him as he passed.

# PART THREE

# Coach Tim's God

# So Be It

LIKE ANY SEX EDUCATOR WORTH HER SALT, RUTH WAS A BIG FAN of latex condoms. They were cheap, effective, easy to use, and widely available. In terms of the misery they'd spared humanity over the years—the unwanted pregnancies, the horrible diseases, the disrupted young lives—she would have happily placed the humble rubber right up there beside antibiotics and childhood vaccines in the pantheon of Public Health Marvels of the Modern World. For the average high-school student, moreover, condoms *were* birth control—there was really no viable alternative. Ruth used to joke, in simpler times, that the entire ninth-grade Sex Ed curriculum could be reduced to three words: *Condoms, Condoms, Condoms!*

Which was why it was so galling to be "teaching" today's prepack-aged lesson, whose misleading and dangerous title she'd scribbled on the blackboard at the beginning of class with a shaky, self-loathing hand: "THERE IS NO SUCH THING AS SAFE SEX." Well, of course there wasn't, not if you defined safety as the impossibility of anything bad ever happening to anyone. There was no such thing as risk-free automobile travel, either, but we didn't teach our kids to stay out of cars. We taught them defensive driving skills and told them a mil-lion times to wear their seat belts, because driving was an important part of life, and everyone needed to learn how to do it as safely as possible.

"The lesson plan calls for another role-playing exercise," Ruth announced. "Any volunteers?"

To no one's surprise, Dan Hayes's and Courtney Brenner's hands shot into the air. The class had done four of these skits in the past week, and Dan and Courtney had played the young lovers in all of them.

"How about someone new? Someone who hasn't had a chance yet?"

Ruth wasn't optimistic about this request; she had learned long ago that role playing and Sex Education didn't mix that well. Most teenagers were hesitant to get up in front of their peers and enact scenarios that were either painfully close to their real lives or even more painfully distant. The ones who enjoyed it tended to be experienced thespians like Dan or shameless exhibitionists like Courtney.

"Come on, guys. This is a class. We all need to participate." Ruth let several seconds go by, but no one took the bait. "All right, I guess it's time for another episode of the Dan and Courtney Show."

The two stars rose from their seats and headed to the front of the room, happily acknowledging the applause of their classmates, which, for the most part, wasn't meant sarcastically. Aside from being thankful to Dan and Courtney for letting the rest of them off the hook, the other kids seemed genuinely entertained by their performances, and Ruth could at least see why they felt this way, even if she didn't completely share the sentiment. As annoying as they could be, Dan and Courtney did have an odd, counterintuitive chemistry, and they threw themselves into their roles with an enthusiasm and lack of self-consciousness that was highly unusual in high-school freshmen.

Dan was small for his age, barely pubescent, a skinny, big-headed kid with a strangely commanding personality. He'd been acting since elementary school, not only in local and regional theater, but also on TV commercials. Ruth had seen him in an ad for the Olive Garden, shoveling a gigantic forkful of spaghetti into his mouth while a jolly waiter looked on, clapping a hand to his cheek in astonishment, and in a spot for State Farm, in which he bounced on a trampoline in slow motion while his ersatz parents gazed at him with loving expressions, happy to know his future was secure.

Courtney was at least at head taller than her partner, and looked to be about a decade older, a young girl endowed with a woman's body and an unnerving aura of sexual confidence. Her outfits just managed to obey the letter of the school dress code while violating its spirit at every turn; things she wore had a peculiar way of slipping down or creeping up or popping open. Ruth often saw her in the hall with older boys, junior and senior football players mostly, and it was the jocks who looked starstruck and grateful for the company, not Courtney.

"All right." Ruth smiled wanly, trying to ignore the familiar heaviness in her chest. "Let me give you the setup. Courtney, you're Gina, and Dan, you're Ethan, and you two—"

"Wait," said Courtney. "Could I be Heather instead?"

"There is no Heather," Ruth told her. "The girl's name is Gina."

Courtney frowned. "Could I change it to Heather? I really don't like the name Gina."

"This is role playing," Ruth reminded her. "It's pretend."

"I'm just not comfortable being Gina."

"Fine, whatever. It doesn't really matter."

"It matters to me," Courtney insisted. "I totally prefer Heather."

"Could I be Skip?" Dan inquired. "I mean, if she gets to change her name—"

"Skip?" Courtney scoffed. "What kinda stupid name is that?"

"It's cool," Dan replied, but with less self-assurance than usual. "He's like this laid-back preppy dude."

"That's pathetic," Courtney informed him. "Nobody's named Skip."

As she said this, Courtney absentmindedly lifted the hem of her shirt above her navel, revealing a taut expanse of youthful midriff. The whole class seemed to freeze for a moment as she languorously rubbed her belly, like an old man who'd just eaten a big meal.

"Skip's a good name," she declared, pulling her shirt back into place. "For a dog!"

"Woof!" Blake Vizzoni called out from the back of the room. His lackeys responded with the usual chorus of servile chuckles.

"That's enough," Ruth told them. She turned back to Dan and Courtney. "Okay, so you're Skip and Heather, two sixteen-year-olds who've been going steady for a year. It's after school, and you're alone in the rec room, with no adult supervision."

"My house or hers?" asked Dan.

"Does it matter?"

"Kind of," he said. "I like to be clear on the details."

"Let's just say it's Skip's house, okay? You guys are making out, and it's getting hot and heavy. This is something that's happened once or twice before, but you've managed to stop yourselves before things got out of hand. But today something's different. Today, Skip's got a condom in his wallet."

Ruth was finished, but the actors just kept staring at her, as if awaiting further instruction. After a moment, she realized what she'd forgotten—it was something Dan insisted on—and halfheartedly clapped her hands.

"Action."

The word was barely out of her mouth when the young lovers flung their arms around each other and began making out in a disturbingly realistic manner, with Dan all the way up on his tippytoes, his neck cranked back at an uncomfortable angle. Ruth didn't think they were using their tongues, but it was hard to be sure—the way Courtney was stooping, her hair formed a kind of curtain around their faces. Meanwhile, Dan's hands were roaming freely up and down the length of her back, making occasional forays into the northern precincts of the butt region, eliciting whoops of delight and cries of "Go for it!" from the peanut gallery, which couldn't have been what JoAnn Marlow had in mind when she designed the exercise.

Happy as she was to see the new curriculum subverted in any and every way, Ruth also knew better than to assume that what happened in her classroom would stay in her classroom. She was particularly concerned about the loyalties of one student, a watchful girl named Robin LeFebvre, whose family supposedly belonged to the Tabernacle (Ruth had made inquiries). Robin took copious notes from one end of class to the other—she was scribbling away right now, her face pale and visibly shocked by the spectacle Dan and Courtney were making of themselves—and Ruth had a sneaking suspicion that she wasn't doing it just to get a good grade on the end-of-unit test.

"All right," she called out. "That's enough. We get the point. Let's move on."

With what appeared to be genuine reluctance, Courtney unscrewed her face from Dan's. She was blushing as she fixed her hair and tugged her clothes back into place; her voice was ragged, slightly breathless.

"Oh my God, Skip. You make me so hot. I just want to . . . you know . . ."

"What, Heather?" Dan spoke in a stage whisper that was clearly audible throughout the room. "I make you want to what?"

"To do it, Skip. To go all the way. Because I really, really love you."

"I love you, too," said Dan. "Now take off your pants."

Courtney bit her lip in consternation, waiting for the laughter to die down.

"I want to take off my pants," she said. "Oh God, Skip, you don't know how badly I want to. But I'm scared."

"Of what?"

"You know. We've talked about this before. I'm scared of getting pregnant, or catching a disease."

"Well, have no fear." With a magician's flourish, Dan pulled an imaginary wallet out of his pocket and mimed the act of withdrawing a condom from the billfold. "I came prepared."

"Oh my God." Courtney's eyes got big. "Is that what I think it is?"

"It's foolproof," he told her. "I guarantee you won't get pregnant, and you won't catch any diseases. Not that I have any diseases."

Courtney took her chin in hand and thought this over for a moment. Then her face broke into a big smile.

"Awesome!" she said. "Let's get busy!"

There was a moment of startled silence in the classroom, followed by a sudden uproar. Half of the audience shouted its approval, while the other half howled in protest. A normally well-behaved boy named Donald Swift fell out of his chair and began banging his fist repeatedly against the floor to express his otherwise inexpressible delight.

"People!" Ruth called out. "Come on, now. Pipe down! Donald, get back in your seat. This isn't kindergarten."

Donald sheepishly complied. Shaking her head in weary exasperation, Ruth turned to Courtney, preparing to admonish her for ruining the exercise. But she checked herself when she saw the look of innocent confusion on the girl's face.

"I don't get it," Courtney said. "Why's that so funny?"

"I think you misunderstood," Ruth told her. "Heather's not supposed to say yes. She's supposed to forcefully rebut Skip's claim that condoms provide foolproof protection against pregnancy and disease."

"They don't?" Courtney looked alarmed. "I thought they did."

"Not foolproof," Ruth informed her. "Didn't you read the assignment?"

"I meant to. I was kinda busy last night."

Ruth asked if anyone could help her out. Vik Ramachandran raised his hand.

"Heather could tell Skip that condoms don't protect against certain STDs, like HPV, which can cause genital warts."

Several people groaned, and a few others made the retching sound that was the customary response to any mention of this particular affliction.

"Fair enough," Ruth said. "You're absolutely right that condoms don't prevent transmission of HPV, though they do a good job preventing a number of other STDs, including gonorrhea, chlamydia, and HIV. Anyone else? What else could Heather tell Skip about condoms?"

"She could talk about failure rates," Marsha Gewirtz suggested. "Didn't the handout say that they have a 36 percent failure rate? So that's like a one-in-three chance that Heather could get pregnant, even if Skip uses a condom, right?"

Ruth winced. "I know that's what the handout said, but that's a pretty dubious number. First of all, I've never seen another study that even comes close to 25 percent, and I've seen a couple that put failure rates as low as 3 percent. The usual number is somewhere around 10 percent, but you have to understand that that's an *annual* rate, meaning that over the course of one full year, 10 percent of the couples using only condoms for their birth control might expect to have an unwanted pregnancy. The failure rate for any individual act of intercourse would of course be much, much lower."

"What about on the test?" asked Susan Chang. "Do we say 36 percent failure, or 10 percent?"

"For this curriculum, I guess we're required to say thirty-six," Ruth told her. "But I do want you to be aware that that's not a universally accepted number. If you're looking for a more credible source of information about birth control, I suggest you check out the website for Planned Parenthood." Ruth turned back to the actors. "All right, guys. Are we ready for Take Two?"

"It's too late," a lunkhead named Mike Petoski called out. "Skip already creamed his pants."

This witticism inspired great mirth in the back two rows of the classroom, and a good deal of eye-rolling closer to the front.

"Enough," Ruth snapped. "If you can't control yourself, I'm going to have to ask you to leave."

"That's what *she* said," Blake Vizzoni muttered.

Ruth decided to ignore him. She was just about to say *Action* when she noticed Robin LeFebvre's hand in the air.

"Yes, Robin?"

"I didn't hear you before." Robin kept her eyes glued on her notebook as she spoke. "What was the name of the website you mentioned?"

"Plannedparenthood.org," Ruth replied. "All one word, no punctuation. Planned Parenthood is a highly respected national organization with a long history of defending women's reproductive freedom. They're an excellent resource for anyone who needs information about contraception or sexual health in general."

Robin's pen raced across the page with impressive speed. It looked like she was taking dictation, trying to record every word Ruth said for posterity, or at least the next school board meeting.

"Am I talking too fast?" Ruth asked her. "Do you want me to repeat anything?"

Robin looked up. She was a pretty girl, if you could get past the dowdy clothes and the scraped-back ponytail. But there was no sign of friendliness in her face, not the slightest effort to disguise the loathing she felt for her teacher.

"That's okay," she said. "I think I got the important stuff."

IT WAS a rainy afternoon, the low gray sky pressing down on the world like the lid of a box. A gusty wind scoured the treetops, stripping away the foliage with merciless efficiency. Fumbling for her car keys in the school parking lot at the end of the day, Ruth caught herself glancing anxiously over her shoulder as though it were late at night on a deserted street.

*It's the goddam Christians,* she thought, ducking into her car and pulling the door shut behind her. *They won't leave me alone.*

She knew she'd crossed a dangerous line in fourth-period Health, openly challenging the Wise Choices curriculum, encouraging the kids to seek out more reliable sources of information. There would be a price to pay down the road—probably sooner rather than later—she had no illusion about that. But what was the alternative? To just stand there like a good little zombie and let the half-truths and outright lies—36 percent failure rate!—pass by without a peep of protest?

*I'm done doing their dirty work,* Ruth thought, flicking her wipers to peel away the wet leaves plastered to her windshield like souvenirs in a child's scrapbook. *They're gonna have to do it themselves from now on.*

In a way, she was grateful to Maggie's coach for making the situation so clear. Until she'd seen those girls, those beautiful young athletes, sitting on the grass in the sunshine, being coerced by adults they trusted into praying to the God of Jerry Falwell and Pat Robertson and the Republican Party—the God of War and Abstinence and Shame and Willful Ignorance, the God Who Loved Everyone Except the Homosexuals, Who Sent Good People to Hell if They Didn't Believe in Him, and Let Murderers and Child Rapists into Heaven if They Did, the God Who Made Women as an Afterthought, and Then Cursed Them with the Pain of Childbirth, the God Who Would Have Never Let Girls Play Soccer in the First Place if It Had Been up to Him—until then, she'd allowed herself to succumb to the comforting fiction that her quarrel with the Bible Thumpers was confined to the classroom, to a political dispute about what got taught or didn't get taught to other people's children. But now she understood that she'd been fooling herself. This wasn't just professional; it was personal. They'd already messed with her job, and now they were coming for her kids.

THE FULL extent of the threat hadn't become clear until Saturday evening, when Frank brought the girls home, and Ruth tried to engage them in a conversation about what had happened that morning on the soccer field. At the time, she'd been most concerned with explaining her position to Maggie, but she wasn't unhappy to see Eliza follow her little sister into the kitchen and take a seat at the table. Eliza still hadn't fully recovered from her mother's fifteen minutes of infamy last spring, and it seemed like a good idea to prepare her for the possibility that things could get ugly again, which was something Ruth hoped to avoid, but couldn't rule out.

"Who wants hot chocolate?" she asked brightly. "It got kinda chilly out."

Both girls shook their heads.

"So." Ruth smiled stiffly, settling into her chair. "You guys have a good day?"

"Okay," Eliza muttered.

Maggie just shrugged, fixing Ruth with a frosty stare. On normal Saturdays she showered and changed at her father's, but tonight she was still wearing her rumpled, grass-stained soccer uniform like a reproach, letting Ruth know that she hadn't been forgiven.

"Look," Ruth told her. "I know you think I overreacted this morning."

This was an understatement. Maggie had been stunned by her mother's intervention in the postgame prayer, and had only managed to stammer a couple of mild objections as Ruth forcibly separated her from her teammates and marched her off the field. It wasn't until they reached the parking area that Maggie found her voice, but by that point she was a complete wreck, sobbing furiously and calling Ruth an asshole over and over again, a word that Ruth had never heard her use before. Maggie also repeated the phrases *You're insane* and *I hate you* several times, in response to her mother's increasingly flustered attempts to defend what she'd done. Though she believed she deserved an apology, Ruth had decided to let the matter slide; she didn't think there was a whole lot to be gained from rehashing statements her child had made in anger and probably regretted.

"I admit that I may not have handled the situation as well as I could have," she said. "Maybe it would have been smarter if I'd taken your coach aside and spoken to him in a less confrontational manner. But that doesn't change the fact that he was doing something he wasn't supposed to do, and that I intend to make sure he doesn't do it again."

Maggie pushed out her bottom lip and scowled, a look that, for all its attempted ferocity, just made Ruth want to hug her. It was the exact same face Maggie had made as a tiny baby, when she was working herself up to a good cry.

"Why are you doing this to me?" she demanded. "Coach Tim wasn't doing anything wrong. He was just thanking God for all our blessings and saying how happy he was that no one got hurt. I don't see what's so bad about that."

Ruth didn't know where to start.

*"Thanking God?"* she spluttered. "He's a soccer coach, not a minister."

"So what? You don't have to be a minister to believe in God."

"First of all, honey, not everyone believes in the same God. There are Jewish girls on your team, and Nadima, is she—?"

"Muslim," replied Maggie. "But not strict."

"See, you've got Jewish girls, a Muslim girl—"

"Atheists," Eliza piped in. Until that moment, Ruth hadn't even known if she'd been paying attention to the conversation, she'd been so completely absorbed in the origami box she was constructing out of a sheet of notepaper.

"That's right," Ruth agreed. "Atheists and agnostics, too. Not everyone believes in the same God, and some people don't believe in God at all. And other people aren't sure what they believe. But you know what? Even if every girl on your team belonged to the same church, the coach still doesn't have the right to say a prayer with them. The soccer team is a town organization. I'm sure they taught you about the separation of Church and State in Social Studies."

Maggie looked puzzled. "You said it's the town, not the state."

"The State just means the government. Town, state, federal, it doesn't matter. The government can't promote a specific religion."

"My soccer team's part of the government?"

"It's a town-sponsored league," Ruth said, worried that the discussion was drifting into a swamp of technicalities. "Plus you were playing in a county park."

Maggie seemed momentarily stymied by the legal argument, but she quickly regrouped.

"Well, I still don't see why you had to yell at Coach Tim like that. You looked like such a weirdo. Your voice got all high and shaky." Maggie flailed her hands around her head like she was being attacked by a swarm of bees, and screeched, *"Stop that praying or I'll call the police!"*

Eliza snickered, and Ruth shot her a dirty look. It was not a pleasant thing to be mocked by your children, especially when you were trying to protect them.

"I was upset, honey. After what those nuts did to me last year, maybe you can understand why I'm not willing to give them the benefit of the doubt. And I didn't threaten to call the police, by the way."

"Whatever," Maggie conceded. "But just so you know, I'm not quitting the team. I don't care what you say, and Dad agrees with me. He's the one who signed my permission slip."

Ruth had to make an effort not to say something nasty. It drove her crazy when Frank pulled the old Divide and Conquer. At the same time, she sincerely regretted suggesting to the coach that Maggie wouldn't be allowed to play on the Stars anymore. She'd spoken out of anger, without thinking things through, and now she found herself in a no-win situation—either compromise herself publicly or turn her family life into a living hell.

"I didn't say *you* had to quit," she explained, refining her position on the fly. "All I want is a guarantee that your coach will behave appropriately in the future. And if he can't do that, then I think *he's* the one who should quit."

"Coach Tim can't quit," Maggie said in a trembling voice. "He's the best coach I ever had. All the girls would hate me."

"I don't think so," Ruth replied. "Some of them might be happy about it. But if it's a choice between doing the right thing and being popular, we've gotta do the right thing."

"But we're tied for first place. We need him."

"Mr. Roper could take over, couldn't he?"

"He's part of the church, too."

"Really?"

"That's what Candace says."

Ruth was startled by this, though she realized that she shouldn't have been. John had been part of the prayer circle that morning, even if he hadn't been speaking. She'd just assumed that he'd gotten sucked in like everyone else. Back when she'd known him, he'd been a hard-charging, hard-drinking guy with some sort of high-powered financial job, not her idea of a born-again. It was like living in a horror movie, she thought, *The Invasion of the Body Snatchers* or something. You never knew who they were going to get to next.

"I'm sure you'd find somebody," Ruth said. "Your father would be happy to coach the last few games. He knows a lot about soccer."

"Please," Maggie said softly. "Just mind your own business."

"This *is* my business," Ruth said. "Your coach has no right to make you pray to a God you don't believe in."

Eliza snickered. "You mean a God *you* don't believe in."

"That's right. I don't believe in Coach Tim's God, and I don't think your sister does, either." Ruth turned to Maggie, suddenly worried that Eliza knew something that she didn't. "You don't, do you?"

"I dunno," Maggie said. "Nobody ever taught me about it."

"Well, I do," Eliza said. "I believe in Coach Tim's God."

"No, you don't," Ruth snapped.

"Do you think I'm an idiot?" Eliza shot back. There was a whitehead at the corner of her left nostril that Ruth had to restrain herself from popping.

"No," Ruth assured her. "And I don't think you're a born-again, fundamentalist, evangelical, nutjob Christian, either. Because that's what he is."

"I believe in God." Eliza spoke slowly and calmly, locking eyes with her mother. "And I believe that Jesus is His only son, and that He died on the cross for my sins."

Maggie was staring at her sister, clearly startled by this news. Ruth's immediate impulse was to try to convince herself that Eliza wasn't serious, that she was just crying out for attention, but it didn't work. There was something in her face and voice—the eerie serenity of the believer—that couldn't be denied.

"Since when?" she asked.

"A few months," Eliza said. "I've been talking to this girl in my class."

"What girl? Do I know her?"

"Grace Park. She just moved here last year. I met her in Homework Club."

"I'd like to meet her sometime."

"Her family wants me to come to church with them."

Ruth groaned. "Not the Tabernacle?"

Eliza shook her head. "It's called Living Waters Fellowship. In Gifford."

Ruth closed her eyes, trying to get her bearings, to react to this like a good parent, to not do anything that would open a bigger rift between herself and Eliza than there already was.

"Do you really want to go?"

Eliza nodded. "I was scared to tell you."

Ruth reached across the table and took her daughter's hand. It was

dry and rough—just like her father's—despite Ruth's frequent reminders to use lotion.

"You shouldn't be scared to tell me anything. I need to know what's
going on in your life."

Eliza seemed suspicious, but she didn't withdraw her hand.

"So I can go?"

"I guess. If you really want to."

"You're not mad?"

"I'm not *mad*," Ruth told her. "I just don't see what you need Jesus
for."

Eliza smiled sadly and shook her head, like she pitied anyone
who had to ask.

"He loves me," she said.

THE STONEWOOD Medical Group had its offices on the third floor of
the Healing Arts Complex, a squat four-story building with dark mir-
rored windows that seemed to have been plunked down by mistake on
a grim stretch of Hawkins Road otherwise dominated by auto body
shops and small manufacturing facilities with mysterious names: Dia-
mond Catalysis, Universal Recoil, Northeastern SaniSys, Zip Global
Force. Ruth had only been inside the H.A.C. once before, when Maggie had gotten a plantar's wart dug out by an insensitive podiatrist she
still referred to as Dr. Ouchenberg.

The receptionist informed her that Dr. Kamal was running a little
late. Ruth took a seat in the waiting area, picked up a *People* magazine,
and pretended to be unperturbed by the elderly woman three seats away
who appeared to be on the verge of coughing up a hairball. During a
moment of inadvertent eye contact, the woman smiled gamely and assured Ruth that she wasn't contagious. Ruth thanked her for the information and returned to her article detailing the collapse of Jessica
Simpson's storybook marriage. She found it hard to focus; her thoughts
kept drifting to her mother, who had spent a lot of time alone in doctor's

waiting rooms during the last year of her life and was always happy to engage a total stranger in small talk. Ruth looked up from the magazine.

"Nasty out today, isn't it?"

The woman held up her index finger while another fit of coughing ran its course. Grimacing an apology, she wiped at the corners of her mouth with a Kleenex and took a sip from a water bottle that she carried in a foam holster suspended from a strap around her neck.

"I don't mind the rain," she said. "It's the snow I hate."

"I hear you," said Ruth. "It's okay when it falls, but then it sticks around."

The woman pressed her fist against her mouth and cleared her throat for a long time, as if she were about to begin an oration. When her voice finally emerged, however, it was small and raspy, barely audible.

"My daughter's in California. I'm going there for Christmas."

"That sounds nice."

"I have two grandchildren. A girl who's eight and a boy who's three."

"Three? I bet he's a cutie."

"A holy terror. But I love him to death."

Ruth was about to ask the boy's name when a violent bout of wheezing made the woman bend forward at the waist. She had just straightened up and taken a couple of deep ragged breaths when a nurse poked her head into the waiting area.

"Mrs. Ramsey? We're ready for you."

Ruth stood up, smiling regretfully at her companion.

"It was good talking to you."

The woman squeezed out an uncomfortable smile as she massaged her collarbone.

"Tomorrow's going to be sunny," she said. "Much nicer than today."

THE NURSE led Ruth into an examination room, told her the doctor would be right with her, then promptly departed. After a moment's hesitation—there was a chair by the computer, but it seemed presumptuous to sit in it—Ruth hoisted herself up on the exam table, wondering if Dr. Kamal had somehow misunderstood the purpose of her visit.

Her first impulse was to be amused by this possibility, but it got less and less funny the longer she waited in that cramped, antiseptic space, with nothing to look at but a couple of badly illustrated pamphlets on managing diabetes and hypertension. Her own doctor at least kept a stack of ancient magazines lying around in case of emergency.

The worst part of it was that Ruth hadn't even wanted to talk to Dr. Kamal on the phone, let alone visit him here. He was clearly a very busy man—Ruth had somehow managed never to meet or even lay eyes on him, despite the fact that their daughters had been friends since first grade—and she would have been much happier just to work everything out with his wife.

All she'd been doing on Sunday afternoon was calling the parents of Maggie's teammates to discuss what had happened at the game and feel them out about the possibility of cosigning the letter of complaint she planned on drafting to Bill Derzarian, the Director of the Stonewood Heights Youth Soccer Association. Like the Zabels and the Friedmans, the Kamals seemed like natural allies in this particular fight.

As she expected, Nafisa Kamal answered the phone. Ruth didn't consider her a friend, exactly, but they were on good terms. They'd shared dozens of perfectly pleasant front-door chats while picking up or dropping off their daughters at each other's houses over the years, as well as the occasional cup of tea, and Ruth had always found her to be excellent company—warm and friendly, with a sweet accent and a quick laugh. But something happened when Ruth mentioned the prayer at the soccer game.

"I'm sorry." Nafisa's voice turned suddenly formal, a bit chilly. "On this matter, you must talk to my husband."

Ruth was startled. Nafisa was a sophisticated, highly educated

woman—she'd come to America as a graduate student in Biology—
who drove a Mercedes and always dressed like she'd just returned
from a shopping spree in Paris. She drank wine, wore lots of makeup,
and told funny stories at her husband's expense. She'd never said anything to suggest that she was in the habit of deferring to him in any
traditional way.

"Uh, okay," said Ruth. "Is he there?"

"I'm afraid Hussein is working this weekend."

"Can you give me his number?"

Nafisa hesitated. "I'll let him know you called."

Ruth went for a run late in the day, and when she returned, there was
a message on her machine from "Heidi at the Medical Associates,"
telling her that Dr. Kamal would be happy to see her at his office at 4:30
on Monday afternoon.

"MRS. RAMSEY." The doctor's smile was cool and guarded as he
stepped into the examination room at five minutes to five. "Sorry to
keep you waiting."

He was lanky and unexpectedly boyish, not at all what Ruth had
expected from Maggie's descriptions of Nadima's strict father, the hu-
morless taskmaster who drilled his children on their math and spelling
homework at the dinner table and timed their piano practice with a
stopwatch.

"It's nice to finally meet you." Ruth slid off the table to shake his
just washed and imperfectly dried hand. "I'm sorry to bother you at
work."

"No need to apologize." Dr. Kamal's accent was less pronounced
than his wife's, but he spoke rapidly, running the phrase together as if
it were a single word. "It was at my suggestion. Now tell me what I can
do for you."

Ruth hesitated, uncertain how to proceed. She felt herself at a subtle
disadvantage, and had to make a conscious effort not to assume the

attitude of a supplicant, a patient, or a saleswoman who had only the most tenuous claim on the important man's time. *I'm a friend of the family,* she reminded herself. *I'm doing him a favor.*

"I'm very fond of Nadima," she told him. "She's such a lovely girl. I'm sure you're very proud of her."

"We're proud of both our daughters," the doctor allowed.

"She's such a good athlete, too. All the girls are. I hadn't seen them play this season, but I was at the game on Saturday, and I was amazed at how good they've gotten."

Dr. Kamal smiled uncomfortably. "So I'm told. Unfortunately, I have an unbreakable tennis date on Saturday mornings." The doctor turned sideways—he had remarkably slender hips for a grown man—and performed a graceful forehand smash with an imaginary racquet in support of this assertion. "But I'm told that next year the girls will play in the afternoon, so I'll finally get a chance to see if the hype is justified."

"It's no hype," Ruth assured him. "I really envy them. When I was growing up, girls didn't play sports the way they do now."

Dr. Kamal pondered Ruth for a moment. He had the same bruised eyes and delicate features as Nadima, the same expression of gentle, slightly wary intelligence.

"Where I grew up, girls couldn't wear short pants."

Ruth nodded, doing her best to maintain a politely neutral expression. It wasn't easy; very few things pissed her off more than the treatment of women in the Muslim world, the drapes and the veils, the pathological fear of their sexuality, the way they were considered property by their fathers, brothers, and husbands, who in certain places would prefer that they die rather than be examined and treated by a male doctor.

"Did you come here for college?" she asked.

"Twenty years ago," he said. "The University of Pennsylvania. The coed bathrooms came as quite a shock. I still haven't fully recovered."

Ruth laughed, though she had a feeling the doctor wasn't really joking. An awkward silence followed, and she knew that the time had come to make her plea. Before she could formulate an opening statement, though, Dr. Kamal fixed her with a reproachful look.

"I must tell you, Mrs. Ramsey, that you upset my wife a great deal with your phone call yesterday."

"Upset her? What do you mean?"

"You have to understand. We come from a place where religion is taken very seriously. We made a choice to get away from that."

"That's why I thought you'd want to know what happened at the game," Ruth explained. "Fanatics are fanatics. It doesn't matter what religion they follow."

Dr. Kamal shook his head. "If what I'm told is correct, all this man did was say a brief prayer. I don't think it warrants a big hullabaloo."

"He's a soccer coach. He has no right to force the girls to say a Christian prayer."

"Nadima assures me she wasn't forced to say anything against her will."

"Maybe not directly," Ruth conceded. "But Coach Tim's an adult they respect, and he's taking advantage of his position to proselytize these impressionable kids. I don't think it's right."

"I don't like it, either," Dr. Kamal told her. "But it seems like an isolated episode that didn't do any harm."

"The one thing it's not," Ruth assured him, "is isolated. The Christian Right is taking over this entire country. Pretty soon our kids are going to be praying in school and reading the book of Genesis in Biology class."

Dr. Kamal didn't argue with her. Instead, he turned and walked to the sink, where he washed his hands with a thoroughness that struck Ruth as excessive, and possibly even a bit ostentatious.

"Do you know what my name is?" he inquired, pulling a paper towel from the dispenser. "My first name?"

"It's Hussein, isn't it?"

The doctor smiled sadly. "If you don't mind, Mrs. Ramsey, I think my family and I will sit this one out."

THE SIGHT of the chicken breasts in the refrigerator made Ruth unexpectedly angry. Sometimes it seemed like that was all they ever ate anymore. Maggie hated fish and every vegetable except lettuce and frozen peas, Eliza objected to red meat on ethical grounds (Ruth wasn't sure why her moral qualms didn't extend to poultry, and she didn't plan on asking), and both girls objected bitterly if their mother tried to make a main course out of soup or chili. So aside from the occasional lasagna or take-out pizza, that pretty much left chicken. And since the girls didn't like dark meat or any inconvenient reminders that their dinner had once been a living thing, "chicken" actually meant skinless, boneless breasts, which Ruth served with rice or potatoes or pasta on the side, followed by a green salad with Paul Newman dressing. Even Paul Newman was starting to get on her nerves, the smug way he grinned at her from the bottle, as if he knew all too well that he was the only man at the dinner table.

Tonight was lemon-pepper marinade, a recipe she got from a book called *500 More Ways to Cook Chicken*, which might more accurately have been entitled *It Doesn't Matter How You Dress It Up, It's Still the Same Crap as Last Night*, or *Eat Chicken Till You Die*. Because there were nights when that was what it felt like, like you were just some stupid animal, put on earth to eat a few hundred—a few thousand?— animals who were even stupider than you were, then disappear without a trace.

If nothing else, she did enjoy pounding the chicken with a wooden mallet, taking some of her frustration with Dr. Kamal out on the innocent cutlets. And it wasn't just the doctor who'd let her down. None of the other parents whose support she'd been banking on had stepped up and offered to sign her letter of protest, not even Hannah Friedman's father, Matt, an environmental lawyer who had a Darwin Fish and a "Don't Blame Me—I Voted for Kerry" sticker on his Audi. By way of an excuse, he told Ruth that he didn't want to make any trouble for Tim Mason, whom he described, to her surprise, as a recovering addict who'd done an amazing job getting his life back together in the past couple of years.

"I'm telling you, Ruth. You gotta give credit where credit's due. These Christians turn a lot of lives around. From what I hear, Tim was a complete wreck before he found Jesus. His ex-wife wouldn't even allow their daughter to get in the car with him."

"How do you know all this?"

"A partner in my firm married the ex-wife. He told me the whole saga."

"That's great," Ruth said. "I'm glad he's cleaned up his act. But that doesn't give him the right to do what he did."

Matt sighed. "I know. And I'm gonna send him an e-mail about the praying business. But this whole official letter of complaint thing sounds pretty harsh. There's only a couple of weeks left in the season. It might not be such a bad idea to just let it slide."

"I'm not gonna let it slide, Matt. I've let too much slide already."

"Come on, Ruth. They say 'under God' every day in the Pledge of Allegiance, and I don't hear you screaming about that."

"Maybe I should start," she shot back. "Maybe you should, too."

"Maybe," Matt conceded. "But I still think you should give the guy a break."

At least Matt Friedman had a decent humanitarian reason for turning Ruth down; Mel Zabel was just being a self-serving coward. Despite the fact that Arlene was a hundred percent on Ruth's side, Mel had convinced his wife to keep their name off the letter out of fear that it would jeopardize their daughter's position on the top team.

"He doesn't want us to be involved," Arlene reported sheepishly. "He says the bigwigs in the Soccer Association have long memories.

If we rock the boat this year, we shouldn't be surprised if Louisa's back on the B team next year."

"Louisa's too good," Ruth said. "They wouldn't drop her to the B team."

"I know," Arlene said, "but everything's so competitive these days. I'm sure there are a lot of girls on the B team just as good as she is."

Ruth tried to argue that there were more important things than a spot on the A team, and Arlene agreed in principle.

"I'm with you in spirit. But I promised Mel I wouldn't sign the letter."

"I guess I'm on my own then."

"I'm sorry, Ruth. I wish I could help."

*Fine,* Ruth thought, as her mallet thudded into the rubbery meat, which she'd wrapped in plastic to prevent any salmonella-laden flecks from splattering around her kitchen. *If that's how it's gonna be, then so be it.*

It didn't help that Maggie was out in the yard in her Stars jersey, kicking the ball against the side of the garage. Ruth could see her out the window, a skinny girl standing out in the rain, her legs bare, her hair straggling down across her angry, determined face as she blasted one kick after another off the clapboards, trapping the ball on the rebound, then booting it again, alternating legs the way they'd taught her at All-Star Soccer Camp last summer. She usually kicked into a net, but today it seemed like she wanted to make as much noise as possible, to remind her mother of how much she loved the game and how hard she worked at it.

*You're gonna hate me,* Ruth thought, listening to the ball thunk against the wall a split second after her mallet thudded into the chicken, the two sounds creating a strangely conversational rhythm, as if she and Maggie were talking to each other through the glass.

*Thunk!*

*Thud!*
*Thunk!*
*Thud!*
*Thunk!*

She must have gotten a little carried away, because there was a strange expression on Eliza's face as she entered the kitchen, carrying the paperback Bible that Ruth hadn't even known she owned until yesterday. She must have kept it hidden in a drawer or under a mattress, the way Ruth and Mandy had hidden books like *The Godfather* and *The Happy Hooker.*

"Mom," she said. "Are you okay?"

"Fine," Ruth told her. "Why?"

"I don't know. You're just kinda whalin' on that meat."

Ruth looked down, and what she saw wasn't pretty. The plastic wrap had begun to shred under her repeated blows, and the chicken wasn't so much flat as traumatized, mangled in places, and fraying unpleasantly at the edges. Ruth wiped her forearm across her sweaty brow and smiled at her daughter.

"Just tenderizing," she said. "I do it all the time."

# Yusuf Islam

RUTH HAD EXPECTED TO SIT DOWN AND BANG OUT HER FORMAL letter of complaint in a matter of minutes. It seemed like a simple, straightforward proposition: *Coach Mason violated Article X, Section Y of the Soccer Association Guidelines—i.e., "Coaches are not permitted to inflict their religious beliefs on their players"—and should therefore be punished for this infraction.*

There was only one problem: no such rule existed. She scoured the *Stonewood Heights Youth Soccer Association Handbook*—it was available as a .pdf download at SHYSA.org—and couldn't find a single reference to religion in the entire twenty-two-page document. Even the surprisingly detailed *Coach's Code of Conduct* was mute on the subject. There were paragraphs devoted to the coach's responsibility for civil behavior on the sidelines ("SHYSA has zero tolerance for verbal abuse or second-guessing of referees"), for ensuring that each player got a roughly equal amount of time on the field, for taking care that players weren't exposed to severe or dangerous weather conditions, and for providing a smoke-free youth soccer experience for the children of Stonewood Heights. A whole page was devoted to the issue of sexual abuse—Ruth was pleased to learn that coaches had to submit to a background check, and impressed by the Association's stern and highly specific set of prohibitions, issued under the bold heading, YOU MUST NOT:

- Allow or engage in inappropriate or intrusive touching of any kind (Examples: Don't "help" a child change clothes, or even tuck in a child's jersey. Refrain from delivering "congratulatory" pats on a child's buttocks)

- Make sexually suggestive remarks to a child, even in jest

- Take children, other than your own offspring, alone on car journeys, no matter how short

- Engage in roughhousing or sexually provocative play with a child

As thoughtful and thorough as the drafters of the *Handbook* had been in most matters, it had obviously not occurred to them that a coach might take it upon himself to lead his team in organized prayer. The closest Ruth could come to the kind of rule she was looking for was an ambiguously worded catchall provision: "The coach must confine him/herself to the technical realm and only provide athletic instruction."

Though this guideline could reasonably be construed as barring coaches from discussing subjects other than soccer with their players, Ruth found it way too vague for her purposes, and completely unrealistic. Was the coach not supposed to comment on the weather, or tell the kids a silly joke, or ask how someone had enjoyed their trip to Disney World? Strictly speaking, all these things were as far outside the boundaries of soccer instruction as The Lord's Prayer. If Tim Mason was guilty of breaking this rule, so was every other coach in the league. Besides, it seemed like a depressing anticlimax, writing a letter full of moral indignation, only to accuse someone of "not confining himself to the technical realm."

As a result of this confusion, Ruth made several false starts on the letter on Monday night. Some of the early drafts were too emotional, verging on melodramatic ("I was flabbergasted. This was not the Stonewood Heights I knew, or the America I loved."); others got bogged down in unnecessary detail ("I believe that Assistant Coach Roper was sitting on Coach Mason's right, though it's possible that I've gotten the mental image reversed, and that he, Mr. Roper, was actually on the left."); still others strayed into such deep legal water that Ruth quickly found she was in over her head ("I am, of course, not an attorney, but it seems like simple common sense to assume that if it's unconstitutional for public-school teachers to lead their students in prayer, then surely the Establishment Clause of the First Amendment is equally violated when a youth soccer coach, who can be viewed, in a certain sense, as a sort of volunteer teacher, engages in a similarly religious exercise in a public forum, in this case a county park.").

It wasn't until she hit upon the tactic of putting Maggie front and center that things began to fall into place:

. . . My daughter loves playing for the Stonewood Stars, and has enjoyed participating in youth soccer since the age of five. She participates because she loves the game and wants to compete at a high level while honing her athletic skills, improving her fitness, and enjoying the camaraderie of belonging to a team. She does not, however, play soccer for the purpose of receiving religious instruction. That is what churches and synagogues and mosques are for. I don't know what the Association's policy on coach-sponsored prayer is (there doesn't seem to be any spelled out in your Handbook), but it seems clear to me that organized prayer at a soccer game falls far outside the purview of the SHYSA mission statement, which, as you know, proclaims the admirable goal of "teaching the game of soccer to the youth of Stonewood Heights in a way that encourages healthy competition, good sportsmanship, physical fitness, and above all, fun."

I don't, for the life of me, see how Christian prayer fits into this. If I'm wrong, please let me know. If, however, you agree with my opinion that Coach Mason has egregiously overstepped the bounds of appropriate conduct, then I would like to know, as soon as possible, what disciplinary action SHYSA plans to take against him before I consider any and all steps (including seeking advice from legal counsel) I might take to ensure that my daughter and her teammates are not exposed to this sort of behavior again.

Once she found her footing, the writing flowed quickly. She began what turned out to be the final version of the letter right after dinner on Tuesday evening and finished it shortly before her unofficial deadline of eight o'clock, the time when Tim Mason said he would be stopping by to discuss the matter with her in person.

HE'D CALLED on Monday afternoon, around the time Ruth was meeting with Dr. Kamal, but she hadn't gotten the message until several hours later, when she was tucking Maggie into bed.

"Sweetie," she said, laying her hand softly on her daughter's shoulder. "Sleep well, okay?"

Maggie's only reply was a halfhearted, mildly hostile shrug. Ruth couldn't help but be impressed—Maggie had managed to last two full days without uttering an unnecessary word in her presence. She'd answer a direct question if she had to, using monosyllables or grunts if possible, but other than that she was implementing the silent treatment with monklike discipline.

"I love you," Ruth told her. "I know it may not seem that way sometimes."

Maggie didn't exactly flinch when her mother's lips brushed against her forehead, but she did tense up ever so slightly, as if she were receiving an injection and trying to be stoic about it. Then she pulled her stuffed owl, Morton, tightly to her chest and rolled onto her side to face the wall.

"I once went a whole week without talking to Grandma," Ruth said, her eyes straying to the poster on Maggie's closet door, Mia Hamm looking cute and boyishly fierce in her white uniform, two fists clenched above her head, the crowd a pixilated blur behind her. "My senior year of high school. I can't even remember what we were fighting about. It seems so silly now."

Ruth pulled the chain on the bedside lamp and stretched herself out on the narrow twin bed. It was an old habit, only recently broken—for the first nine years of her life, Maggie hadn't been able to fall asleep without one of her parents lying beside her. On a lot of those nights, Ruth had dozed off herself, lulled by the sound of her daughter's breathing, only to wake at one or two in the morning, cold and disoriented, still in her clothes. More often than she would have liked to admit, the journey across the hall to her own room seemed too arduous, so she just wriggled under the covers, snuggling up against Maggie's warm little body.

"I used to get so furious with your grandmother," she continued. "I thought she was too nice. She always smiled and pretended everything was fine, even when it wasn't. It was like she lived in a world where it was illegal to complain. Sometimes I would get frustrated and say really terrible things to her. And you know what she used to tell me?"

Maggie didn't reply, but Ruth responded as if she had.

"She told me I'd miss her when she was gone."

Ruth stopped the story there, leaving out the part that suddenly seemed most important, and sad beyond words, which was that she used to swear to herself, *No, I won't. I won't miss you a bit.* At least she'd never said it out loud, not that she could remember, anyway. But she wished she could apologize to her mother for even thinking it.

"Mom?" Maggie said, after a minute. She sounded wide-awake.

"Yes, honey?"

"Coach Tim called after school. He said he needs to talk to you."

"After school?" Ruth was puzzled. "Why didn't you tell me before?"

"I don't know." Maggie let a couple of seconds go by. "I just didn't want you to be mean to him."

AFTER SEALING the letter in a stamped envelope, Ruth still had fifteen minutes to spare before Coach Tim was scheduled to arrive, most of which she spent trying to resist a powerful urge to change her clothes and put on some makeup. She'd gone for a run that afternoon—three laps around Stonewood Lake, four and a half miles total—and was wearing her usual postshower ensemble of Adidas warm-up pants and a hooded cotton sweatshirt, not dowdy, exactly, but hardly flattering.

It would have been easy enough to run upstairs and throw on a pair of jeans and a casual shirt—the fitted maroon top with the scoop neck always looked good—maybe a bit of lipstick and a quick touch-up around the eyes, but she was disgusted with herself for even considering it. This wasn't a date, it was a negotiation—possibly even a confrontation—with a man who had abused his authority and driven a wedge between herself and her daughters, a man about whom she had just composed an impassioned letter of grievance. What did she care if a man like that thought she was pretty, or at least reasonably attractive for her age?

And yet, she couldn't help being aware of a strange undercurrent of schoolgirlish anticipation about his visit, the sense of being on the verge of something unusual and exciting. After all, when was the last time a good-looking man—at least a good-looking man who wasn't gay or to whom she hadn't once been unhappily married—had shown up on her doorstep, even on an errand as unpromising as this one? What harm would it do to brush her hair and hide the shadows under her eyes?

*My God,* she thought. *I'm pathetic. I'd probably put on a skirt and heels for Dick Cheney.*

If there was one thing that rankled about being a woman, it was this conviction, drummed into your head before you had a chance to defend yourself, that it was your job—your *obligation*—to always look your best, even in situations when you had no logical reason to care. The truly courageous feminists, Ruth had long believed, weren't the sexy ones like Gloria Steinem, but those combative women like Andrea Dworkin who made a point of embracing a kind of defiant frumpiness—ugliness, even—as an announcement to the world that they were through living as ornaments, subordinating their own comfort and selfhood to the remorseless demands of the male gaze.

*Jesus,* she thought. *It's just a pair of jeans.*

Finally, with only a couple of minutes to spare, Ruth gave in and hurried upstairs, as she'd known she would all along. She compromised to the extent that she rejected the maroon top—it really was the kind of thing you'd wear on a date—in favor of a stretchy gray T-shirt beneath a cropped black cardigan. She dabbed on a tiny bit of eye makeup, but skipped the lipstick.

*It's not for him,* she reminded herself. *It's for me. So I won't be at a disadvantage.*

LATER, AFTER Tim left, she realized—though maybe it was less a matter of realizing than of being able to admit it to herself—that she'd secretly been hoping to find herself enmeshed in one of those corny "opposites attract" narratives that were so appealing to writers of sitcoms and romantic comedies. The formula was simple: you brought together a man and a woman who held wildly divergent worldviews—an idealistic doctor, say, and an ambulance-chasing lawyer—and waited for them to realize that their witty intellectual combat was nothing but a smoke screen, kicked up to conceal the inconvenient and increasingly obvious fact that they were desperate to hop into bed with each other.

Luckily for Ruth, this ridiculous fantasy crumbled immediately upon contact with reality. The visibly uncomfortable man who stepped into her house a few minutes after eight was barely recognizable to her as the scruffy hipster coach she'd been so taken with on Saturday morning, and completely unsuitable for even the most outlandish romantic scenario. In his Dockers and button-down Oxford shirt, his long dark hair strangled into an ill-considered ponytail with the aid of some kind of gel or pomade, this cleaned-up version of Tim Mason looked shifty and a little too slick for his own good, like a small-time criminal whose lawyer had instructed him to wear something nice for the judge.

"Mrs. Ramsey," he said, without looking her in the eye or offering his hand. "I won't take up a lot of your time."

"Don't worry about that," she told him, withholding the ritual invitation to call her by her first name. "I really think we need to talk. Can I get you some coffee or tea or something?"

She could see that his first impulse was to refuse, but for some reason he checked it.

"Coffee's okay, if it's no trouble."

"Decaf?"

"Regular, if you got it."

"You're lucky," she said. "If I drink coffee at night, I'm wide-awake at three in the morning, ready to start the day."

He stared at her with such a pained expression that she had to stop and review the conversation to make sure she hadn't said anything inadvertently offensive. But then it occurred to her that it didn't really matter what she said. It was just being here, under these circumstances, that was making him look so miserable.

*He hates me,* she thought, but instead of being offended, she just felt sorry for him, which was probably a bad idea, given the hard line she was determined to take on the prayer issue.

COACH TIM followed her into the kitchen and took a seat at the table while Ruth attended to the coffee. Unfazed by the buzz saw shriek of the grinder, he picked up the Bible that Eliza had ostentatiously left propped against the wire basket full of apples, kiwis, and grapefruits—if he was surprised to see it there he didn't let on—and began flipping through the pages.

"That's my older daughter's," Ruth explained, banging the heel of her palm against the bottom of the grinder. "She's very interested in Jesus these days."

"Good for her." He spoke distractedly, his eyes fixed on the book, expressing no more enthusiasm than if she'd told him Eliza was taking Spanish or had signed up for swimming lessons. After a moment, though, he looked up. "Wish I could say the same about my own kid."

"She doesn't go to church with you?"

"Abby lives with her mother," he said. "My ex-wife. I don't have a whole lot of say in how she's brought up."

"That must be hard," Ruth said, glancing over her shoulder as she extracted a box of Lemon Zinger from the high shelf of the cabinet. "I'm divorced, too. You know Frank, right? Maggie's father?"

"Oh, I know Frank," Tim assured her. "I probably get ten e-mails a week from him. He's very generous with the coaching advice. And the, uh, constructive criticism."

Ruth felt strangely embarrassed, as if Frank were still her husband.

"Just ignore him," she said. "He can't help himself."

"He's not an easy guy to ignore."

"Sometimes you have to insult him," Ruth explained. "That was my preferred method."

"I'll have to give that a try." Tim put down the Bible and turned his attention to the coffeemaker, which was hissing and groaning on the countertop as if it were about to explode, but not producing a whole lot of coffee. "Something wrong with that thing?"

"I don't know. It used to work a lot faster."

"You probably just need to clean it. You're supposed to run vinegar through the machine a couple times a year."

"I used to do that," she said, though what she really meant was that Frank had. "I never really noticed a difference afterward, except the house smelled bad."

"Minerals collect inside," he said, making a fist to illustrate this process. She noticed again how big Tim's hands were, at least compared to the rest of his body. "It gets all gunked up in there, like plaque on your arteries."

The teakettle whistled meekly—there was something wrong with the hinged cap on the spout—as if reluctant to interrupt the conversation. Snatching it off the stove, Ruth set it down on a trivet bearing the inscription, *Come live with me, and be my love.* Both the kettle and the trivet had been wedding presents, and should have been replaced a long time ago.

"You gotta use the white vinegar," he added. "My ex-wife used balsamic once, and it was a disaster."

Ruth laughed as she poured boiling water into her mug.

"You're pretty big on the household hints, aren't you?"

He eyed her warily, uncertain if he were being mocked.

"What do you mean?"

"At the game on Saturday you were bragging about how you put lemon juice on apple slices."

"I wouldn't call it bragging," he said, sounding slightly miffed. "It's just, the kids won't eat the apples if they're brown."

"Whatever. You seemed pretty proud of yourself." Ruth jerked the tea bag up and down, not really sure if this sped the steeping process. She wouldn't have been surprised if Coach Tim had a theory on this as well. "Maybe you should get yourself a newspaper column. Call it Tips from Tim. Like Hints from Heloise. Except you're a guy, which might make it more interesting to your readers since it's mostly women who care about that stuff."

He looked puzzled, as if he couldn't understand what she was up to, blathering away about whatever popped into her head, as if this were just a friendly social visit. Ruth couldn't help wondering the same thing herself, and the only thought she could muster in her own defense was that it was hard to maintain an attitude of frosty politeness toward someone who was sitting in your kitchen, offering helpful advice about your appliances. Not to mention the subtle hangdog vibe Tim was giving off, which was making her feel weirdly self-conscious, like it was her responsibility to cheer him up.

She brought him his coffee and sat down at the other end of the table, letting a few seconds go by as a signal that it was time to get down to business. But instead of clearing her throat and telling him how concerned she was about what had happened after the game, she took a sip of tea, and said, "So, did you play soccer in high school?"

"Not seriously. Where I grew up, the soccer players were mainly these Italian guys fresh off the boat, Angelo and Mario and Guido, and the Schiavoni brothers. The American guys played football."

"You don't look like a football player."

"I wasn't. I devoted my teenage years to getting stoned and learning to play 'Stairway to Heaven.'"

"Hey," she said. "I think we knew each other."

"Then I apologize," he replied. "Because I probably wasn't very nice to you."

Ruth laughed, but she found herself mildly annoyed by the condescension implicit in the joke, the assumption that he'd been a little too cool for the kind of girl she'd been back in the day. Of course, what really bothered her was the knowledge that he was probably right.

"What, were you some kind of big ladies' man in high school?"

He bobbed his head noncommitally, as if to say that this was a complicated question deserving of a thoughtful answer.

"Not at first. I was a skinny kid with a bad complexion. But I joined a band my junior year. We called ourselves Circuit Breaker for a while. Then we changed it to Balin Son of Dwalin."

"That's a terrible name."

"We liked it," he said. "It was some kind of Tolkien thing."

"Balin Son of Dwalin? Why not Big Buncha Dorks?"

"Go ahead and mock," he said. "But we were pretty popular. Lots of female fans."

"Groupies?"

"Kind of, yeah."

"In high school?"

"You must be about my age," he said.

"I'm forty-one."

She expected him to be startled by this revelation, but he just nodded, as if he'd figured as much.

"I'm a year older," he said. "So you remember what it was like. Sometimes I think about what kids were doing back then, and I can't believe it really happened. I mean, I'd hate to think of my daughter growing up the way I did."

"It's a different world," Ruth agreed. "But we didn't turn out so bad."

Chuckling, Tim reached for a kiwi.

"I don't know about that," he said, pondering the hairy fruit with skeptical concentration, as if he'd never encountered one before. "Some of us got pretty screwed up."

Ruth wasn't sure if he was taking a swipe at her or just making a general statement about their generation.

"You think it's better now?"

"I do," he said, returning the kiwi to the basket. "At least for me it is."

"So what happened to the band? Did Balin Son of Dwalin survive high school?"

"Not really." He shook his head, as if he hadn't thought about this stuff in a long time. "The singer and the lead guitarist had a fight over a girl. It was like a bad divorce. The guitar player got custody of the drummer, and the singer got me. Jerry and I stayed together for eight years, played in five different bands. We even put out a couple of records in our early twenties."

"Anything I might have heard?"

"I doubt it. We called ourselves The Freebies. There were a couple college stations that played our stuff."

"You must've been pretty serious."

"Jerry more than me," he said. "He really wanted it, and he had the talent. He kept changing and trying new things, and I kinda went along for the ride."

"So what happened to him? Did he make it big?"

Tim looked at the table.

"He died when we were twenty-five. Choked on his own vomit. Just like Jimi Hendrix, that's what we used to tell ourselves. As if that made it okay."

"That's terrible."

"Coulda been me," he said. "I was just as messed up as he was."

Tim fell into a momentary funk, rubbing his index finger in a circle on the tabletop, as if trying to erase a stain, and Ruth couldn't help feeling like she was getting a glimpse of the beaten-down guy Matt Friedman had described, the recovering addict who couldn't even be trusted to drive his daughter home from school.

"But you changed," she reminded him. "You turned your life around."

He looked up in surprise.

"It took a long time. I wish I could have those years back."

A funny thought occurred to Ruth.

"You know who you're like?" she said. "Yusuf Islam."

His response was a blank stare.

"You know, Cat Stevens. He became a Muslim and changed his name to Yusuf Islam."

"I'm not a Muslim."

"I don't mean that. I just mean you're a musician who rejected the rock 'n' roll life and found happiness in religion."

He made a face. "I wouldn't exactly call Cat Stevens rock 'n' roll."

"You know what I mean. Besides, 'Peace Train' was kinda a rock song, right?"

"I guess, but—"

Before he could finish the thought, Tim's face broke into a peculiar grin, so radiant and unexpected that Ruth felt momentarily cheated

when she realized it hadn't been meant for her, but for Maggie, who
had materialized behind her in the doorway, dressed in pajama bottoms and her soccer jersey.

"Hi, Monkey," he told her.

"Hello, Turnip."

"Honey," Ruth said wearily. She'd specifically asked her daughters
to stay upstairs while she and Coach Tim had their conference.

Maggie shrugged. "I just wanted to say hi."

"Well, you said it."

Maggie bowed to her mother, hands pressed to her forehead in
prayer position.

"Yes, master." She straightened up and flashed a conspiratorial grin
at the coach. "Practice on Thursday?"

"You bet."

"Regular time?"

"Yup." Tim waved good-bye. "Now get outta here. Your mom and I
need to talk."

THE ATMOSPHERE seemed to thicken around them after Maggie's departure. Ruth sighed, and Tim nodded, acknowledging the suddenly
obvious fact that the time for small talk had expired.

"So," he said. "I guess we have a problem."

Ruth had spent the last three days preparing for this exact moment—
nursing her grievance against Coach Tim, sharing it with other parents,
setting it down on paper—but now that she had a chance to say it to his
face, she didn't quite know where or how to begin. It seemed beside the
point somehow, as if the man in her kitchen bore only a tangential relationship to the man she'd been complaining about.

"I'm a little curious," she said. "Why do you call her 'Monkey'?"

"It's just a nickname. She likes to climb trees, and Monkey sounds a
little like Maggie. I do it for all the kids. Nadima's Nomad, and Candace
is Caddyshack."

"And you're Turnip?"

"I prefer 'Coach Turnip,' but yeah. And I got off easy. They call John Roper 'Mullet.'"

"Ouch."

The coach grinned. "Candace showed some of the girls his high-school yearbook. Class of '85. Apparently he had an unfortunate haircut."

"Girls that age can be a little mean."

"Nah, it's just fooling around. They're good kids. Maggie especially. You're lucky to have a daughter like that. You've done a great job raising her."

Ruth felt a surge of gratitude that took her by surprise. She tried hard to be a good parent, but she didn't often get credit for it. It was hard enough just being divorced; to be a divorced Sex Education teacher who'd been publicly accused of immorality made you a bad mother by definition, or at least it had begun to seem that way.

"Thank you," she said. "That's nice of you to say."

"Look," he said. "I know you're upset about Saturday, and I don't really blame you."

"You don't?"

"Believe me," he said. "I didn't mean to offend anyone, or make you feel uncomfortable. I have no interest in shoving my faith down anyone's throat."

"Then why'd you do it?"

"I got carried away," he explained. "Abby got hurt, and the game was so amazing, I just kind of lost track of where I was. You have to understand, for me praying is like breathing. It's just something I do."

He sounded sincere, but Ruth didn't want to let him off the hook so easily.

"That's fine, as long as you realize that not everybody believes the same thing as you. You've got Jewish girls on that team, a Muslim—"

"I'm well aware of that. A couple of the other parents have already spoken to me about it." He paused unhappily. "They said you were maybe planning to write to the Soccer Association?"

"I was thinking about it," Ruth admitted.

"I hope you won't," he said. "I made a mistake, and I apologize. I promise it's not gonna happen again."

"You mean that?"

His eyes made a silent plea for mercy.

"I love coaching this team," he said. "I don't know what I'd do if they took it away from me."

ALL IN all, Ruth thought as she slipped her nightgown over her head, the meeting had gone surprisingly well. Coach Tim had turned out to be so much more reasonable than she'd expected, a lot less rigid and confrontational than the other Tabernacle people she'd tangled with in the past.

It must have been his background that set him apart, the hard living he'd done before he found Jesus. She had known a couple of other recovering addicts and AA types over the years, and to one degree or another, they'd all displayed the same vulnerability and melancholy self-awareness as he had, the same refusal to judge other people or condemn them for their shortcomings. It made perfect sense to her that people who'd hit bottom would be attracted to Christianity and find solace in its message of forgiveness, the idea that it didn't matter how badly you'd screwed up your life, there was always another chance to start over and get things right. Where she always came up short was in figuring out how that part of the religion coexisted with the sanctimonious and intolerant part, the angry, Goody Two-Shoes Christianity that was always gleefully damning people to hell and turning its believers into hypocrites. All she could figure was that Coach Tim just ignored that stuff and took what he needed to keep himself going.

She fell into bed feeling happier than she'd been in a long time. It was just such a relief to know that she wasn't going to have to gird herself for a bitter public fight, expose herself once again to the anger and ridicule of her neighbors, or get maneuvered into a corner where she had no choice except to betray her principles or break her daughter's heart. She hadn't fully understood how heavily the burden had been weighing on her until it had been removed.

On top of the relief, though, she felt a sense of giddy possibility that had nothing to do with Coach Tim or her kids or the normal parameters of her life, and everything to do with the strange thing that had happened just a few minutes after he'd left. She was in her study, ripping up the letter she'd written to the Soccer Association, when the phone rang. Her first thought was that it must be Tim, calling from his car with something he'd forgotten to tell her—the image was startlingly clear in her mind, for some reason—but the voice on the other end belonged to a different man.

"Ruth?" he said. "Is that Ruth?"

"This is Ruth," she said. "Who's that?"

"Don't I sound familiar?"

"I don't think so."

"You do. Your voice is exactly the same."

"Is this some kind of joke?" she said. "Because if it is, I really don't have the time."

"It's Paul," he said. "Paul Caruso. Your old next-door neighbor."

"Paul? Oh my God."

"So Ruth," he said. "I heard you were looking for me."

SHE WOKE the next morning with her high spirits intact, amazed by the sudden change in her fortunes. It was weird to remember how bad she'd felt just twelve hours ago—besieged and heavyhearted and alone—and how little it had taken to turn things around.

She and Paul hadn't talked for long. He explained that an old buddy of his, Artie Lembach, a trombone player in the marching band, had seen Ruth's posting on the Classmates.com bulletin board and passed along the information.

"I couldn't believe it," he said. "It's gotta be what, twenty-something years?"

Embarrassed, Ruth started muttering untruthfully about how she'd decided to reconnect with lots of different people from her past, as if to suggest that he was no one special, just a small part of a much bigger group.

"I was so excited to get Artie's e-mail," he said, lowering his voice to an intimate register. "Because, Ruth, I think about you a lot."

"Really?" She felt a warm surge of blood moving into her face and was glad he wasn't there to see it.

"Yeah," he said. "I mean, sometimes you don't realize it when things are happening, but then when you look back . . ."

He let the statement hang there, and she didn't ask him to complete it. Instead she changed the subject to him, asking where he lived, and what he did for work, and whether he was married. He said he'd been in Connecticut for the past ten years, working in the high-tech field. As for his marriage, it was a long, complicated story, one he'd be happy to tell her if she was free for dinner over the coming weekend.

"This weekend?" she said. "You mean three days from now?"

"I'm in the city on business," he said. "I can easily make it out to where you live. How about Friday night?"

"Okay," she said. "Sure. I don't have any plans I can't change."

"Excellent," he said. "It'll be great to catch up with you."

And just like that she had a date, her first in a long, long time. And not a blind date, either, but something better, a date with a man she already knew, a boy she'd grown up with, and, more to the point, her first lover. She'd read a couple of articles recently about couples reconnecting at high-school reunions, rekindling romances from their youth. The thing everybody mentioned was how strong those old bonds remained despite the passage of time, how meaningful a shared history could be. Over and over, people talked about picking up right where they'd left off, not miss-ing a beat, as if the intervening decades had never happened.

Sensing that she was getting carried away, she did her best to put the brakes on. After all, she hadn't seen Paul Caruso in a long time. For all she knew, he was bald and weighed 350 pounds. Plus, she realized, he had never really answered her simple question about whether he was married, which struck her as a bit worrisome. On the other hand, people who were happily married didn't tell you it was "a long, compli-cated story," so she felt fairly optimistic on that count.

*Ruth, I think about you a lot.*

The whole thing was just so sappy and romantic and out of the blue, she couldn't wait to tell Randall all about it. She got to school a few minutes early, and was rushing down the hall with a latte in each hand, whistling the chorus of "Peace Train"—the song had been stuck in her head all morning—when Joe Venuti popped out of his office and planted himself directly in her path. He looked the way he always did in the morning, like he'd been up half the night sweating on the toilet.

"Excuse me," she said, trying to veer past him on the right.

"Ruth," he said, blocking her way with an outstretched arm, "I need to talk to you."

"Can it wait?" she said, gesturing at him with the coffee cups. "My hands are full."

"Not really," he said.

On a normal day, Ruth would've told him that she was busy just then and would be happy to talk to him during one of her free peri-ods, but she was feeling a little too cheerful to make a fuss, so she sighed and followed him into his office. If she'd been thinking a little more clearly, she wouldn't have been so surprised to find JoAnn Mar-low and Superintendent Farmer inside, scowling at her and shaking their heads, and she certainly wouldn't have blurted out, "Hey, guys!" in such an excited, high-pitched tone of voice, as if she were thrilled to death to have been invited to this particular party.

# God's Warrior

TIM KNEW IT WAS A BAD IDEA TO STOP AT THE BAR ON THE WAY back from Ruth Ramsey's. It just seemed like a better idea than going home to Carrie just then, and not much worse than what he'd been doing for the past half hour anyway, which was driving aimlessly around Stonewood Heights listening to *Workingman's Dead,* thinking about how much better it would be to kill an hour or two in a bar than it would be to go home to Carrie.

He must have orbited the Homestead Lounge four or five times—this was after casing and rejecting the Evergreen Tavern and the Brew-Ha-Ha, both of which were much too conspicuously situated on Central Avenue in the heart of downtown—before working up the nerve to pull into the parking lot, conveniently tucked away in the rear of the building, which meant that he at least wouldn't have to worry about Pastor Dennis or anyone else from the Tabernacle driving by at exactly the wrong moment and wondering if that was Tim Mason they just saw going into that gin mill, 'cause it sure looked like him.

Even so, he felt shaky and exposed—but also oddly joyful, like a convict tiptoeing away from prison—as he crossed the patch of cracked blacktop that separated his car from the back entrance, his heart hammering against his rib cage the way it always did at moments like this, the blood roaring so loudly in his ears that it drowned out the panicky whimpers of his conscience. It was one of those things that hadn't changed with age: he'd felt just like this at sixteen, buying a bag of pot in the high-school bathroom, and at twenty-one, ducking into XXX World, the sleazy "Adults Only Boutique" out on Route 27. The same heady mixture of exhilaration and dread had raced through his veins at thirty-two, the first time he'd cheated on Allison, and again two and a half years ago, when he shook off a host of doubts, and stepped through the doors of the Tabernacle, a sinner hoping to be cleansed. It was impressive in its way, this lifelong ability to forge ahead in spite of his better judgment, to wade into one sticky situation after another with his eyes wide open.

Inside the Homestead, he hesitated for a few seconds at the end of a short entranceway, grappling with a sharp sense of disappointment. When he'd seen the old-fashioned neon-martini-glass-sign from Lorimer Road, he'd imagined a dim, smoky bar, the kind of place where a man could skulk anonymously in a corner, nursing his shame to a sound track of Sinatra and George Jones. But that, he realized, was the movies; this was Stonewood Heights on a Tuesday night. The place was bizarrely well lit, the air disconcertingly fresh—the statewide smoking ban had been in place for over a year—and there wasn't a jukebox in sight, just a half dozen TVs strategically deployed throughout the room, all of them playing ESPN with the sound off. A handful of patrons were stationed at the bar—one youngish guy in a suit was tapping away at his laptop—and a few others were shooting pool, and damn if every last one of them didn't swivel their heads more or less in unison and stare at Tim with the same look of hungry welcome in their eyes, as if maybe he was gonna be the one to finally liven things up a bit around here.

"Come on in," the bartender called out. He was a chunky, friendly-looking guy with a goatee and a green-and-white-striped apron tied around his waist. "We don't bite."

Tim returned the smile and took a couple of steps forward, into the light and back in time, before suddenly remembering who he was, whirling around, and fleeing for his life.

CARRIE WAS in bed when he got home, watching Nancy Grace on the little TV on top of her dresser, a guilty pleasure she only indulged in when he was out of the house. Tim couldn't figure it: wars, elections, and natural disasters barely made a blip on his wife's radar screen, but if someone killed a family member, or a pretty teenager went missing on a tropical island, she was all over the case like Encyclopedia Brown, spending hours listening to windbag legal experts split hairs about a defense motion to limit discovery, or the significance of the fact that authorities were still calling the husband a "person of interest" rather than a "suspect."

Tim didn't say a word or even raise an eyebrow, but Carrie grabbed the remote and turned off the TV the moment he entered the bedroom, before Nancy could finish explaining just how sickened and offended she was by this latest outrage against common sense and human decency.

"You didn't have to do that," he said.

"That's okay. I know you don't like her."

"Really, Carrie. Watch whatever you want."

She shook her head dismissively.

"I wasn't even paying attention."

"Whatever," he muttered, unbuttoning his shirt. "Just don't feel like you have to do it on my account."

"I'd rather talk to you anyway," she said. "We've hardly seen each other all day."

This was true, though not unusual. Carrie started work an hour earlier than he did, so they rarely spent more than a few minutes with each other at the breakfast table, and dinner was equally dicey; they only managed a real sit-down-and-talk meal a couple times a week, on those evenings when Tim wasn't working late, and neither of them had to rush off to Bible Study, soccer practice, band rehearsal, or a small group meeting.

He pulled the change out of his pocket and dumped it into a glass jar on his dresser. When the jar got full, he gave it to Abby; there was usually close to thirty dollars in there by that point, a windfall that used to be a lot more exciting to her when she was younger, before her mother married a rich lawyer. Now it was just a habit, more money she took for granted. He turned to Carrie.

"Did you see the sandwich I left you in the fridge?"

"Yeah, thanks."

"Sorry about the onions. I told the guy twice not to put them on."

"That's all right," she assured him. "I just picked 'em off."

She kept her eyes on him as he undressed, but as far as he could tell, it wasn't for the purpose of admiring the relative flatness of his belly, or marveling at the way his middle-aged butt continued to resist the relentless claims that gravity made on flesh. Nor was she gazing at him with the kind of critical eye he sometimes turned on her, issuing mental demerits for the stubble on her legs, or the ominous plumpness of her upper arms, which were going to be a problem down the road if she wasn't careful. It seemed to Tim that she barely noticed his body at all; she was just trying to get a reading on his mood, so she could adjust her own behavior accordingly. What she didn't seem to understand was that her constant scrutiny *affected* his mood, made him annoyed with her and vaguely ashamed of himself, implying as it did that he was a sullen, difficult guy who needed to be humored and coddled for the sake of domestic tranquility.

"So how was the group," he asked. "Good turnout?"

"The usual. We barely got to discuss the reading, though. We spent most of the night trying to cheer up Patty DiMarco."

"Her mother?"

"The doctors thought she was responding to the medication, but she's right back where she started."

"Poor Patty." He tossed his dirty clothes in the hamper. "As if she didn't have enough troubles."

"What about you?" Carrie asked. "Everything go okay?"

"I think so," he said, stepping into a pair of plaid pajama bottoms. "I had to eat a little crow, but it wasn't as bad as I thought."

She pondered him for a moment, smiling thoughtfully.

"C'mere," she said. "Let me give you a back rub."

"That's okay." He still hadn't gotten around to notifying her of his decision to put their sex life on hold for the time being. "It's kinda late."

"It's no trouble." She pursed her lips, a pouty little girl. "You seem tense."

"Really, Carrie. I'm fine."

She threw off the covers and stood up. She was wearing a sleeveless white undershirt of his, tight enough to emphasize the fullness of her breasts, and a pair of tattered maroon gym shorts, also his. It was a cute look for her, much better than the long-sleeved flannel nightgowns that he'd found so depressing the first few months of their marriage.

"Come on." She took him by the arm. "It'll feel good."

"Carrie, please."

"Let's go." She spoke firmly, a nurse addressing a skittish patient. "Lie down."

Tim was about to protest again, but he was distracted by the sight of her nipples pressing against the flimsy ribbed cotton of the undershirt.

"All right." He sighed. "But just a quick one."

He lay facedown on the bed—the sheets were still warm and fragrant from her body—feeling both annoyed and excited. A soft grunt escaped from his lips as she sat down on top of him, straddling his hips with her knees and settling the bulk of her weight directly on his ass.

A full chapter in *Hot Christian Sex* was devoted to "The Loving Art of Marital Massage," and Carrie had clearly given it some study. Her early efforts had been timid and ineffectual, but recently she'd become bolder and more proficient, kneading and mashing his muscles with gratifying savagery.

"Oh yeah," he croaked. "Right there. Little higher."

"I can't believe how tight you are. It feels like a bunch of tennis balls under your skin."

She took her time—Carrie was nothing if not patient—moving methodically down his back, karate-chopping his shoulder blades, digging her thumbs into the knotty channel along his spine. Ripples of calm spread through his body, filling the empty spaces where the tension had been. Sensing his relaxation, she lowered her mouth to his ear.

"I was worried about you," she whispered. "I expected you home a long time ago."

"I was just driving around," he explained. "Trying to clear my head."

Her voice was warm in his ear.

"Is everything okay? You haven't seemed like yourself lately."

Tim felt a momentary urge to open up to her about his stubborn feelings for Allison, his close call at the Homestead, the sense he sometimes had that Jesus was losing interest in him, or vice versa, but it seemed like a shame, getting into a serious talk right now, when he was finally feeling loose and even a bit cheerful, so he clenched his butt cheeks and bucked his hips, not quite hard enough to knock her off-balance. She giggled and slapped his thigh.

"Bad boy."

He did it again, and she laughed even harder. It was almost sad how easy it was to please her, like she was a little kid who just wanted a playmate. He bucked a third time, and she let out a whoop.

"Yee ha!" she said. "Ride 'em, cowboy!"

AS USUAL, Carrie fell asleep right after they finished making love, while Tim remained wide-awake beside her in the dark. Allison used to complain about the speed with which he dozed off after sex (at least on those nights when he wasn't all coked up); she was one of those women who believed that a heart-to-heart postcoital conversation was as essential a part of the experience as a cigarette in an old movie, as necessary on the back end as foreplay was on the front. Tim, on the other hand, didn't mind at all now that the roles were reversed. As comforting as it was to have Carrie curled up beside him, making the soft strangling noise that was the closest she ever came to snoring, it was a relief not to have to talk, to be able to follow his thoughts wherever they felt like drifting.

Not that they were drifting all that far. His mind remained pretty firmly anchored on those few bewildering seconds he'd spent inside the Homestead Lounge, peering dumbly over the lip of the abyss, as if he didn't know exactly what kind of misery was down there at the bottom, as if he hadn't spent the last three years of his life dragging himself out of it.

Something had made him turn away before it was too late, but what? It would have been nice to say that Jesus had come to his rescue, or that he'd heard Pastor Dennis's voice crying out to him, but the more he thought about it, the more it seemed like pure chance. If the bar had been darker, or a good song had been playing, or a pretty woman had been sitting next to an empty stool, the night might have gone in a completely different direction.

*Where were You, Lord?* he wondered. *Why didn't You stop me?*

He knew what Pastor Dennis would have said. He would've said that Jesus had better things to do—sinners to save, sick children to heal, a world of hurt in desperate need of His love. He didn't need to be wasting His time telling people things they already knew, or helping them do things they were fully capable of doing on their own. And if a man like Tim—a warrior for Christ—wasn't strong enough to keep himself out of bars, then maybe he'd never accepted Jesus into his heart in the first place.

*But I did,* Tim thought. *And You helped me. Don't give up on me now.*

He would've been a little less freaked out if he'd had a clearer sense of what had brought him to the Homestead. It seemed obvious to him that Ruth Ramsey was at least partly responsible, but it was hard to say why. He'd said good-bye to her feeling pretty good about their meeting. He'd accomplished what he'd set out to do—she'd accepted his apology and assured him that she wasn't going to make any kind of official fuss to the Soccer Association—without experiencing any embarrassment or unpleasantness. She hadn't insulted him, or made him grovel, or taken any cheap shots at his religion, with the possible exception of that one weird comment about Cat Stevens, and even that made a certain kind of sense once she explained it.

On the contrary, she'd been polite and friendly, and he'd enjoyed her company, though not in the way he'd feared. He arrived at the house with his guard up, remembering how attractive she'd seemed at the soccer game, but now he had to wonder if that wasn't some kind of illusion created by the sun and the blue sky, combined with the aura of scandal that trailed her wherever she went (the one other time Tim had seen her, she'd been standing before a school board meeting, issuing a grim, clearly coerced apology for making inappropriate sexual comments in the classroom). During their brief conversation at halftime, he'd been struck, not only by the weathered prettiness of her face and the surprising litheness of her figure—if he wasn't mistaken, she'd looked a bit dumpier in the auditorium—but by something stubbornly girlish in her demeanor, a combination of feistiness and shyness that he'd found instantly appealing, and that only made it that much more mortifying when she started screaming at him at the end of the game.

At her house, though, she seemed older and more ordinary, a forty-year-old woman with tired eyes and a melancholy smile, hardly the formidable opponent he'd expected. She didn't express any anger toward him, just treated the whole prayer thing like an afterthought, nothing either one of them needed to worry about, and he was happy enough to follow her lead, to be absolved from the responsibility of having to defend what he'd done, or tell her what he knew to be true, which was that she needed Jesus just as much as he did, and that Maggie did, too. Because, really, who was he to dictate how anybody else should live their life, especially when he was a guest in her house, asking for a favor, and she'd been so nice to him?

Pastor Dennis would have seen the work of the Devil in that, and maybe he had a point; after all, how could you be tempted into betraying the Lord with your silence if you felt scared or repulsed by the tempter? All Tim really knew was that the moment he left her house, he found himself overcome by a strange sensation of emptiness and defeat, or maybe just loneliness, a feeling deep in his heart that what he needed more than anything else was some good music, a stiff drink, and a little more time away from his wife.

HE STILL felt a bit rattled at work the next morning—jittery and furtive and antisocial—though none of his colleagues seemed to notice anything amiss. They were used to Tim's keeping to himself in the morning, heading straight to his cubicle and getting a jump on his e-mail while the rest of them made a slower transition into the workday, analyzing last night's episode of *Lost*, or catching up on the latest escapades of Aimee, the hot twenty-three-year-old loan processor whose complicated love life was the source of enormous vicarious pleasure to the mostly female staff of Loanergy Home Finance.

"So it's back on with me and Vinnie," she announced, ostensibly addressing Rita Mangiaro, but speaking loudly enough for everyone to hear. "We went out for a drink last night, like just to talk, right? And sure enough, I woke up in his bed this morning. I'm like, *Hello, Aimee? You are such a slut!*"

"You did not!" Rita gasped. She was the office's top producer by a long shot, a retired teacher who got tons of referrals from her former students at Bridgeton High. Sitting next to her all day, Tim never failed to be both amazed and irritated by her inexhaustible appetite for gossip and idle chatter, which somehow didn't interfere with her ability to make four times as many loans as he did.

Aimee gave one of her patented what's-a-girl-to-do shrugs. She was a round-faced, voluptuous blonde with a salon tan, stiletto heels, and a cheerfully ditzy personality. She would've been a textbook bimbo, except for the fact that she also happened to be the best processor Tim had ever worked with, a fastidious, punctual, almost pathologically organized master of complicated paperwork who had saved his and everyone else's bacon ten times over. The whole office would have fallen apart without her.

"It was crazy," she admitted, with a rueful mixture of pride and embarrassment in her voice. "And then I had to get up and do the walk of shame, right past his mother. I'm like, *Hi, Mrs. Ruffo, long time no see.*"

"Ouch," said Kelly Willard, a single woman a few years older than Tim who was always going on adventure vacations to places like Tanzania and Chichén Itzá, then complaining that she hadn't enjoyed herself. "Why didn't you just go to your own apartment?"

"His was closer," Aimee explained. "We were kind of in a rush. And I definitely wasn't planning on spending the night."

"I'm sure his mom was thrilled to see you," said Rita.

"Totally," Aimee agreed. "I'm like her most favorite person in the world."

Even Tim had to laugh at that. Without really trying—the office

had an open floor plan, so it was hard not to overhear—he'd been following the saga closely enough to know that Mrs. Ruffo hadn't been
particularly fond of Aimee even before Vinnie, a short-tempered
bodybuilder, had gotten himself arrested for assaulting Gary Wilkin-
son, the married real-estate agent she'd been seeing on the side. According to Aimee, Gary had been unaware of Vinnie's existence, so he
didn't know enough to be alarmed rather than creeped out when this
angry muscle-bound dude approached him in the locker room of the
Ultra-Body Health and Racquet Club and asked if he wanted to see a
picture of his girlfriend.

"Uh, sure," Gary said, thinking it impolite to refuse. "I guess."

Vinnie produced what was described in the police blotter as an "intimate Polaroid snapshot of a mutual acquaintance," then gave Gary a
couple of seconds to study it before punching him in the face. He
squeezed in a couple more shots before being restrained by three bystanders in various states of undress, including an off-duty cop in a
jockstrap. In the end, Vinnie pled guilty, and Gary's wife filed for divorce.

"Was this a fluke?" Shelley Margulies asked. Too-frequent Botox
treatments had left her with a single expression, an all-purpose grimace of unpleasant surprise. "Or are you guys really back together?"

"I don't know," Aimee replied. "We've been through this so many
times, I'm kind of scared to say yes. But I really think we've grown a
lot in the past few months."

"The thing I'm wondering," Rita said, "is what he's gonna do about
that tattoo."

Tim had actually been wondering the same thing. After their most
recent breakup, Vinnie had gone through a Billy Bob Thornton–style
crisis that he'd resolved by modifying the "Aimee" tattoo on his mas-
sive left bicep so it now read, "Aimee = Bitch." Tim knew this because
he'd been present the day Vinnie barged into the office to display his
revenge to its victim.

"I told him he could keep it." Aimee smiled, tickled by her own magnanimity. "I'm the first to admit that I deserve it. And you know what else? It kind of turned me on to see it there. Plus, it's really nice work."

Like a lot of people her age, Aimee was a tattoo aficionado. She had four of them herself, including one she'd gotten just a couple of months ago, placed so low on her back that she'd had to undo her pants so her office mates could admire it.

"Tim," she'd said, right before the big unveiling, "you may want to turn away."

Tim's coworkers knew he was a born-again Christian and a recovering addict; he'd told them early on, as Pastor Dennis had advised, and kept a Bible and a book of Devotions on his desk in case anyone forgot, along with a Gospel-Verse-a-Day calendar that Carrie had gotten him for Christmas. Today's selection was Mark 9:50: "Salt is good, but if it loses its saltiness, how can you make it salty again? Have salt in yourselves and be at peace with one another."

"Thanks," he'd told Aimee. "I'll cover my eyes."

Although Pastor Dennis frequently warned his flock to expect persecution and/or mockery as Christians in the secular workplace, this hadn't been Tim's experience at Loanergy. At worst, he suffered from a mild, intermittent sense of apartness, as if there were an invisible wall separating him from the rest of the office. If anything, his coworkers treated him with a little more solicitude than necessary, apologizing for using profanity in his presence, or telling him to plug his ears while they discussed *The Da Vinci Code* or one of Aimee's drunken hookups. He sometimes had the feeling that they enjoyed having him around to shock, and he did his best to play the role assigned to him, though it wasn't always easy to pretend to be scandalized by the revelation that drunken young women sometimes had sex they regretted, or that a fellow loan officer who happened to be a grandmother might call a double-crossing client a "shithead."

*Come on,* he occasionally found himself thinking. *If you're gonna sin, at least do something interesting.*

Though he had to admit, he did like Aimee's tattoo. He'd meant to turn away, but there was something riveting about the sight of an attractive young woman unbuttoning her pants in the middle of an office. She only tugged them down a couple of inches in the back, just far enough to reveal the sweet slope of her hips, the triangle of a pink cotton thong, and three fairly large Chinese characters, which she said stood for Strength, Loyalty, and Perseverance. He didn't look for long—just enough to admire the thickness, precision, and startling blackness of the calligraphy, and to trade an appreciative glance with Antonio Morris, the only other male witness—but it was apparently long enough for the image to sear itself permanently into his brain, so he could conjure it at will in those odd moments when something like that came in handy.

HE LEFT the office around eleven for his twelve o'clock lunch with George Dykstra of DBH Design & Build, one of the bigger residential developers in the area. It was an important meeting for him, a rare face-to-face with a serious player in the industry, and he thought it would be a good idea to take a little walk beforehand, to clear his head and think about how he wanted to present himself.

As ironic as it was for someone with his abysmal credit history to be working as a loan officer, Tim enjoyed his job and considered himself pretty good at it. He'd gotten into the business four years earlier, after building the kind of spotty résumé that might have been expected from a musician with two years of college and a problem with substance abuse: a little temping here, some construction work there, a failed attempt at running his own landscaping business, followed by a hodgepodge of retail and restaurant jobs, and capped off by a three-year stint as an agent for Lucky Rent-A-Car, during the sober, responsible period that followed Abby's birth. It wasn't a terrible gig, and he drew frequent praise from his superiors for his ability to calm irate customers. There was talk about a possible promotion to Assistant Manager, but it died down around the time he returned to his true vocation of snorting coke, at which point the job stopped looking like a stepping-stone to better things and revealed itself to be a deeply annoying distraction from the serious business of getting high and fully deserving of the contempt with which he began to treat it.

Divorced and precariously sober at the age of thirty-seven, he was searching for a new career path when he came across the classified ad in the *Bulletin-Chronicle*—"Mortgage Professional, Experience Preferred, Will Train"—and decided that he had nothing to lose by applying. His timing couldn't have been better: shockingly low interest rates had triggered a tsunami of residential refinancing, and warm bodies were needed throughout the industry to perform the humble but nonetheless critical work of matching eager borrowers with appropriate (or at least willing) lenders.

Within a week he was on the phone, identifying himself to prospective clients—their names and numbers had been purchased from a telemarketer—as a representative of the Dream House Mortgage Company, a start-up run by three former frat brothers in their mid-twenties who didn't seem to notice, or at least weren't overly concerned about, the hard-to-explain gaps in Tim's employment history. His "training" consisted of a quick lesson on how to read a rate sheet and price a loan, a one-day seminar at the Warrenton Marriott, and whatever on-the-fly advice he could grab from his bosses, who didn't spend as much time in the office as he might have expected.

For two full years, Tim stayed afloat doing one ReFi after another. With rates hovering around 5 percent, the decision was a no-brainer for most homeowners. All you had to do was lay out the facts, no arm-twisting necessary. You felt like you were doing your clients a favor, arranging things so they had hundreds more dollars in their pocket every month, while making a nice little commission in the process. It was one of those rare situations in life where everyone came out a winner.

Dream House went out of business around the time rates began creeping up—one of the partners moved to Florida, and another decided to go to physical therapy school—and Tim made the jump to Loanergy, a more established firm, signing on as "Senior Mortgage Consultant." With the ReFi market losing steam, he had no choice but to shift his focus to purchases, transactions that were more satisfying on a personal level—he got to work much more closely with his clients—but also fraught with pressure and the potential for bad feelings. Deals fell apart all the time, due to unpredictable contingencies, rigid deadlines, and the sometimes unreasonable demands of lawyers, sellers' agents, and lenders, not to mention good old human error (Tim learned the hard way what happened when you failed to lock in a good rate the day before the Chairman of the Federal Reserve made a big announcement). But deals got made all the time as well—the papers got signed, the checks got written, the property changed hands. His income varied widely from month to month, but on the whole he was doing better than he'd imagined possible when he'd started.

About six months ago, though, after years of booming, the real-estate market went flat. Houses sat all spring and summer with FOR SALE signs planted in their front yards. The buyers disappeared. Ever since he'd started at Loanergy, he'd gotten most of his leads through the Tabernacle—Pastor Dennis encouraged his flock to do business with other believers whenever possible—but it was just too small a niche to keep him going. Feeling the need to branch out, he got new business cards, did some mass mailings, even started buying lists from telemarketers again. He tried making inroads into some of the other evangelical churches in the area, but it turned out that Pete Gorman of Faith Financial had them pretty well locked up.

With the slow winter season looming, Tim had come to see the situation as urgent, if not dire. He still had some savings, and Carrie had a steady job. Allison and Mitchell were rolling in money, so he figured no one would begrudge him a missed child support payment or two if he explained his situation. But that was just the short term. Taking the long view, it was clear that the profession was about to undergo a contraction, and that a fair number of people weren't going to survive. Tim was determined not to be among those left behind. It wasn't just that he liked his job; he *needed* it. Because he could imagine all too well what it would feel like to wake up in the morning with nowhere to go, the whole day stretching empty in front of him, and the Devil hovering at his shoulder, whispering all sorts of suggestions as to how a guy like Tim might want to fill it.

THE HOSTESS at Cosmo's Diner directed him to a window booth where a barrel-chested guy dressed like a construction worker was squinting at *The Wall Street Journal* through a pair of half-frame glasses perched on the tip of his nose. It took Tim a second or two to connect this formidable figure with George Dykstra, the sunburned goofball in board shorts and wraparound shades he'd met a couple of months ago at an instructional clinic for youth soccer coaches.

"Hey," said Tim. "Sorry to keep you waiting."

George waved off the apology and folded up his paper.

"You're not late," he grunted, gripping the edge of the table and beginning the arduous process of extricating himself from the booth, which clearly hadn't been designed to accommodate torsos of unusual girth. "I was early."

George led Tim through an elaborate series of greetings—handshake, back slap, manly hug, hair tousle—before sucking in his gut and wedging himself back into his seat. As Tim followed suit, George drew his attention to the young, olive-skinned waitress in tight black pants filling water glasses at a nearby table. He admired her for a moment, then leaned forward with a confidential air.

"I'm telling you, Timmy. I don't know who does the hiring around here, but I'd like to write him a thank-you note."

"She's a nice-looking girl," Tim observed.

"I think she's Greek. Cute little accent." George's eyes narrowed with calculation. "Wonder if Cosmo's slipping her the old souvlaki. I wouldn't put it past the bastard. Bring 'em in on the boat, ship 'em out when you get bored. Pretty good deal, eh?"

Tim replied with a noncommittal bob of the head, doing his best to maintain a neutral expression. George removed his reading glasses and tucked them in his shirt pocket. Deprived of their senatorial gravity, his face looked shrewd and boyish, suddenly familiar.

"I'm just curious," he said. "You ever fuck a Bulgarian?"

"Not that I know of," said Tim.

George nodded slowly, as if pondering a subject of great complexity.

"Only reason I ask, I dated this crazy chick for a while before I got married. Yanka. That was her actual name if you can believe it." He gave a nostalgic chuckle. "Total nympho. Used to claw at my back and thrash her head around like she was having a fit. Loud, too. Touch her in the right place, and she'd scream like the Russians were invading. I could never tell if it was just her, or something they put in the water over there."

Tim forced a smile, thinking that it would be a good idea to find some gentle way of cluing George in to the fact that he was a Christian. They'd spent a whole morning together at the coaches' clinic, but the subject of faith hadn't come up, and George had clearly developed a mistaken impression of what kind of guy he was. It would spare them both some awkwardness if he came clean, but how to do it without casting a chill over the meeting was a thornier question. Sometimes the wiser course was just to let things unfold naturally and wait for the right opening to present itself.

"It's nice to see you," he said, hoping to steer the conversation in a healthier direction. "I really appreciate you meeting with me."

George was staring at the waitress again, his gaze so insistent that she put down the pitcher and asked if he needed something. He grinned and shook his head, then turned back to Tim.

"Sorry I had to cancel on you last week. We had a big disaster out at Fox Hollow. Whole shipment of granite countertops came in, and they were all too big. Had to send 'em all back to the quarry. Now my tile guys gotta sit around for two weeks with their thumbs up their asses while the counters get recut. That job's been one headache after another."

"I hear it's a pretty big development."

"Twenty units. Almost all presold, thank God. Just got in under the wire. I know some guys who are all set to break ground on big projects next spring, and believe me, they're all shitting their pants. Nobody's buying jack."

"It's a tough market. I'm feeling it on my end, that's for sure."

"You wanna know who's really fucked? My cousin Billy. Asshole bought himself a Hummer dealership. Try selling a fucking Hummer these days. I warned him, but he's a stubborn little prick. Serves him right."

"It's a weird time, all right. Kinda scary."

After the waitress took their orders, George excused himself to go to the restroom. Tim took advantage of his absence to remind himself of his strategy for this meeting, which wasn't to whine about hard times but to sell himself as an experienced, up-and-coming, can-do loan officer with a solid client base, someone a guy like George Dykstra could be proud to be in business with. Not that he was expecting much, at least not right off the bat; he understood all too well that a high-volume developer like DBH probably had long-standing relationships with a whole stable of mortgage brokers. All he really wanted was a foot in the door, a chance to prove himself, to show that he could play with the big boys.

"Damn," George said, as he squeezed back into the booth. "Those

fucking mochaccinos are worse than beer. I'm pissing every ten minutes."

Tim sat up straight, preparing to make his pitch, but a strange feeling of self-consciousness came over him before he could begin. The
moment seemed wrong somehow, but he couldn't tell if this was an
accurate reading of the situation or just an excuse for avoiding the unpleasantness of asking a favor from a person who wasn't really even a
friend. He turned to look out the window, as if the answer might be
found in the passing traffic on River Street.

"How's your team doing?" George asked.

"Not bad," Tim replied, feeling simultaneously relieved and disappointed to be let off the hook. "We had a rocky start, but we're finishing strong. As of this week, we're tied for first in our division."

"Lucky bastard." George looked dejected. "We did just the
opposite—started out like gangbusters, then we fell apart. It's gotta be
my fault, but I can't figure out what I'm doing wrong."

"There's only so much you can do," Tim reminded him. "You gotta
work with the players you got."

"I got the players," George insisted. "At least on paper. But some of
these kids, they got attitude problems. The other team scores one lousy
goal, and they just give up. *We stink, we never win, can we just go home?*
It drives me crazy."

"I'm lucky that way. I'm coaching the A team, and my girls are totally motivated. They hustle, they come to practice on time, they cheer
each other on, they give a hundred percent every game. I really couldn't
ask for a better bunch."

When George's cell phone rang, it played the theme from *Rocky*.
He withdrew it from the leather holster attached to his belt, checked
the caller ID, and muttered something under his breath.

"Lemme put this thing on vibrate," he said, pressing some buttons
and setting the phone on the table. "You know who my biggest problem is? George, Jr. Last year, I swear, he was incredible. Leading scorer

on the team, Charlie Hustle. His coach loved him, said he woulda been happy to have a whole team of little Georgies. Now this year, it's like he can barely drag his ass up and down the field. I don't know, maybe he's depressed or something. But he sure looks happy enough when he's banging away on that goddam Xbox."

"It's tough with your own kid," Tim agreed. "My daughter's not playing up to her potential, either. I try to talk to her about it, she just tunes me out."

"You gotta be careful, though," George reminded him. "You know, not to be too hard on 'em. The other parents are quick to say you're favoring your own kid, but if you ask me, the problem is just the opposite. Another kid screws up, I'm Mr. Cool. *No problem, Eddie, don't sweat it.* But my own kid makes a mistake, I'm like, *No dessert tonight, you little shit!*"

Their burgers arrived, and Tim sensed another opportunity to nudge the conversation back to real estate. But again he hesitated—it was hard to have a serious conversation with your mouth full—and George was more than happy to pick up the slack by asking if Tim knew any good throw-in plays he could teach his kids. Tim borrowed a pen from the waitress and diagrammed his favorite maneuver on the back of a place mat. Studying the X's and O's, George was surprised to see that Tim utilized a two-two-one formation, which led to a fairly involved discussion of its strengths and weaknesses vis-à-vis the more standard three-two configuration, a subject Tim had given a fair amount of thought over the summer.

"I wouldn't say that one's inherently better than the other," he explained. "My system puts a lot of pressure on the midfielders, so you gotta be pretty careful about who you put there."

"You know what?" George said. "It wouldn't matter what kind of setup I ran if I could use this kid Matt as my goalie all the time, but his parents won't let me. They want him out on the—"

George's phone went off again, buzzing so vigorously that it began skittering across the tabletop. He shot Tim a quick grimace of apology before snatching it up.

"Yeah?" He listened for a second, then let out an exasperated sigh. "Ah, shit. All right, I'll be there in twenty minutes. Half hour, tops."

He snapped the phone shut and shook his head.

"Sorry to cut this short, but I gotta run. Another mess at the job site."

George wolfed down the rest of his burger, then paid the bill on the way out, insisting on picking up the tab. Feeling like an idiot for blowing his big chance, Tim trailed him out of the diner and through the parking lot, the bigger man moving so quickly it felt like he was about to break into a run any second.

"All right," George said, stopping in front of a behemoth SUV. "It was good talking to you."

"Same here," Tim told him, nodding a little longer than necessary, as if it were the moment of truth at the end of a first date. "Thanks for lunch."

"No problem. Thanks for letting me pick your brain. I'm definitely gonna try that throw-in."

"I hope it works for you. I've had really good luck with it."

George clicked the remote and the locks of his Navigator opened with a solid *ka-chunk*. He reached for the door handle, but then thought better of it and turned around.

"Oh, hey, I almost forgot. Me and some buddies have this poker game, every other Tuesday. We're looking for a new guy. You interested?"

"Poker?" Tim said, blindsided by the invitation.

"They're good guys," George assured him. "Couple contractors I work with, a real-estate guy, my brother-in-law, and my stupid cousin Billy. The stakes aren't too high. It's more about drinking a few beers and shooting the shit. I think you'd fit right in. And you'd make some great contacts for work, tell you that."

Tim stared at the ground. He knew what to do, because they'd talked a lot about how to handle moments like this at his Addicts 4 Christ meetings. If the other person was a friend, you could just remind them that you'd dedicated your life to Jesus and made a sacred commitment to steer clear of temptation. In the event the other person was unfamiliar with your religious beliefs, you could keep it simple. *Just say, 'No thank you,'* Pastor Dennis had advised. *Say you're busy that night and leave it at that.* But when Tim looked up and saw George smiling at him, he found to his surprise that it was impossible not to smile back.

"I've been known to play a little poker," he said.

# A Big Day for the Lord

NORMALLY, ON GAME DAYS, TIM WAS JUMPING OUT OF HIS SKIN TO get going. He'd wake up long before the alarm and chug several cups of coffee, but after that he was useless—couldn't eat breakfast, couldn't read the paper, couldn't manage a conversation with Carrie, couldn't do anything but glance obsessively at the clock until it was time to pick up Abby and head for the field.

Today, though, for the first time since he could remember, he was dragging. The weatherman had predicted a 50 percent chance of showers, and Tim spent a good part of the morning gazing morosely out his kitchen window, hoping the rain would start early enough and be heavy enough to wash out the Stars' eleven o'clock match against the Gifford Bandits. It wasn't the game itself he was hoping to avoid—the Bandits were one of the weaker teams in the league, an easy tune-up before next week's make-or-break showdown with the Green Valley Raiders—it was the decision he was going to have to make when it was over.

Until he went to Bible Study on Thursday night, the situation had seemed clear enough. He'd made a promise to Ruth Ramsey, and he intended to keep it. He wasn't sorry he'd led the team in prayer last week—it was his fervent hope that he'd planted a seed in some of the girls' hearts (his own daughter's especially) that would blossom in due time—but he understood it as a one-shot deal, a spontaneous act of worship he'd be a fool to repeat, at least if he wanted to keep on coaching.

FOUR YEARS ago, when he'd checked the box on Abby's registration form, volunteering his services as assistant coach, Tim barely knew the difference between a direct and an indirect kick. All he'd wanted at the time was a way to stay involved in his daughter's life after the divorce, to prove that he could be something more than the loser her mom had kicked out of the house.

In what he later came to recognize as a stroke of genuine good luck, he was assigned that first season to help out on a U-8 team led by Sam "Corny" Hayes, the founder and elder statesman of SHYSA, a visionary who'd climbed aboard the youth soccer bandwagon way back in the late 1970s, when most Americans still viewed the sport with suspicion, if not outright contempt, as a pastime fit only for sissies and Europeans. Corny was a crusty old guy, a retired pipe fitter given to dark mutterings about the goddam rich people who were ruining his town, but he loved coaching and had vowed to keep doing it until the undertaker made him stop. For whatever reason—maybe because Tim obviously wasn't one of those goddam rich people—Corny took a liking to his new assistant and went out of his way to teach him to think like a soccer coach. They got in the habit of heading to Victor's Luncheonette after every game—in those days, Abby went straight home with her mother—and conducting detailed postmortems on the day's action, evaluating the performances of individual players and strategizing about the lineup combinations that would maximize their strengths and neutralize their weaknesses.

Tim assisted another veteran coach on Abby's U-9 team, and was entrusted with his first head-coaching assignment the following year, when he took charge of the U-10 Sharks. Despite his inexperience, the team did remarkably well, coming in second in the C Division with a solid eight-and-four record. Even so, Tim had been taken aback when

Bill Derzarian called last August to let him know he'd been chosen to be head coach of the Stars.

"The A team?" Tim said. "Are you sure you want to do that? There have to be a lot of other guys way more qualified than me."

"That's not what Corny says. And I'm telling you, Tim, we got a lot of great feedback on you from the parents. They really like your enthusiasm, the way you run your team."

"Wow. I really don't know what to say. I'm honored."

"You've proven yourself," Bill assured him. "You have our complete confidence."

TIM HAD come close to skipping Bible Study altogether, partly because he hadn't finished the reading—they were making their way through the two books of Samuel, and it was tough going—but mainly because he was ashamed of himself. At the end of every session, Pastor Dennis set aside time for a "spiritual gut check," in which each participant was invited to give an account of his successes and failures in leading a godly life during the previous week. Tim did his best to be honest—what was the point otherwise?—and he was painfully aware that his recent behavior didn't make for a very uplifting picture: he'd gone into a bar for the first time in years; he'd had sex with his wife, contrary to the Pastor's explicit instructions; and, on top of everything else, he seemed to have joined a poker game.

The meeting was held at Bill Spooner's house, a small Cape Cod near Shackamackan Park. Tim arrived a half hour late, not because anything had detained him but because he kept pulling up at the curb behind John Roper's Odyssey, losing his nerve, then driving off again, only to come back and do the same thing a few minutes later.

Pastor Dennis was reading about Goliath when Tim stepped sheepishly into the tiny living room, barely large enough to contain a couch and a recliner, let alone the kitchen chairs that had been dragged in to accommodate the extra guests. All the usual suspects were present—Bill,

John, Andy McNulty, Jonathan Kim, Steve Zelchuk, and Marty Materia—as well as one familiar-looking stranger Tim took a moment to recognize as Jay, the Jenna Jameson fan.

A notorious stickler for punctuality, Pastor Dennis stopped midsentence and looked up from his Bible. Fixing Tim with a gaze of unnerving intensity, he raised his right hand and unfurled a stern finger of accusation. At least it felt like an accusation—when you knew you were guilty, lots of things felt like that—until the Pastor's face opened into a smile full of warmth and affirmation.

"A righteous man walks among us," he said, much to Tim's surprise. "And we know from Scripture that 'the prayer of a righteous man is powerful and effective.'"

ONE BENEFIT of his dawdling was that his daughter was waiting on the front stoop in her uniform when he pulled into the driveway. Usually, no matter how he timed his departure, he managed to show up at her house a few minutes early and had to suffer through an awkward round of small talk with Mitchell while Allison flounced around in a skimpy nightgown, trying to locate Abby's shin guards or electric toothbrush.

"You're late," Abby said, hugging him at the foot of the wide granite steps. "What happened?"

"Nothing. I'm just moving a little slow this morning."

"Mom thought maybe you forgot."

"Yeah, right. Like I'm gonna forget a game."

Abby nodded. "That's what I said."

She headed to the car, but Tim hesitated for a moment, not quite sure if he needed to check in with Allison before he left. It seemed a little rude, driving off without even sticking his head in the door to say hello. On the other hand, it would've been nice to escape without his regular fix of misery, one more depressing reminder of how well she was doing without him.

Before he could make up his mind, she came hurrying out of the house, looking both flustered—she was carrying Logan like a football in one arm and clutching Abby's overnight bag with the other hand—and unusually modest, in a knee-length robe over cotton pajamas.

"Wait!" she called out, as if he were driving away instead of standing a few feet in front of her. "Abby forgot her stuff."

She made her way down the steps and handed him the bag.

"I told her four times: *Don't forget your stuff, don't forget your stuff*. Of course she forgot her stuff." She flipped Logan into an upright position with a nonchalance that verged on carelessness, her face scrunching into a familiar expression of distaste. "Ugh. He's a stinky boy. Second time this morning."

Logan smiled proudly. Even with a dirty diaper, he was a happy camper, a plump wide-eyed cherub with a headful of chaotic ringlets, the kind of kid who got treated like a celebrity by the old ladies at the supermarket. Tim was fond of him, despite his uncanny resemblance to his father.

"Mr. Logan," he said. "How's the big guy?"

"Teem!" he exclaimed. "Abby Dad!"

Tim poked a finger into Logan's doughy belly and smiled at Allison.

"You want me to change him?"

Allison kissed her stinky boy on the forehead.

"Abby Dad a silly man."

"I don't mind," he insisted. "I've never had a problem with that."

"You don't realize what you're dealing with. He's not a sweet little baby anymore. He eats what you eat."

"It has been a while," Tim conceded. The fumes had just begun wafting into his airspace, and they were bracing. "I guess you forget."

"Don't worry," she said, a hint of gloating in her voice. "Your turn's coming. Then you can tell me how much fun it is."

"I don't know. We're not even sure if we want kids."

She tilted her head in surprise.

"I'm sure Carrie does."

Tim didn't reply. Allison pondered him for a moment. She seemed on the verge of asking him a question, but instead she lifted Logan into the air, brought his padded butt close to her nose, and gave a cautious sniff.

"Wow," she said, with a small shiver of amazement. "What the heck is in there?"

AFTER CALLING Tim a righteous man, Pastor Dennis rose and embraced him.

"You did a beautiful thing," he said.

"Who, me?" Tim glanced anxiously around the room, more bewildered than relieved. "What'd I do?"

The men of the Tabernacle laughed, as though charmed by his modesty.

"I told them about Saturday," John Roper explained. He was leaning forward on the couch, sandwiched between Jonathan Kim and Andy McNulty, but eclipsing the two smaller men with his bulk. "What you did after the game."

Pastor Dennis turned to Jay, the new guy.

"If you want to know what our church is all about, I couldn't give you a better example. This isn't some once-a-week-sit-on-your-butt-and-praise-Jesus sort of operation. It's a twenty-four/seven ministry, and its purpose is to find new ways to inject our faith into every aspect of our lives."

Jay nodded thoughtfully, as though he were beginning to get the picture. Pastor Dennis sat back down, and Tim made his way to an empty chair next to Marty Materia, who clapped him on the shoulder and whispered, "Way to go."

"I'll tell you something," Pastor Dennis went on, still directing his comments to Jay. "What we do isn't easy. It's hard not to get lazy and forget our purpose. It's tempting to turn on the cruise control and let the car drive itself for a while."

Pastor Dennis looked at the floor and shook his head.

"I'm talking from experience. I haven't really discussed this with anyone but God and my wife, but these past few months, I've been a little lost. Don't get me wrong—we're growing, picking up lots of new members, but it was starting to feel like we were going soft like all these other so-called Christian churches. I mean, the reason we're doing so well is because we made waves—we shook things up in this town and convinced maybe 2 percent of the people to really look at the way they were living; and then we showed them that there's a better way in Christ.

"But I've known for a long time that we needed some new tactics, a way to get through to the 98 percent of the people who've been tuning us out. But for some reason I was stumped. The Lord just wasn't telling me what to do. I thought He'd abandoned me, but I see now that He was just instructing me to be patient, to wait for one of my warriors to step up and relieve me of my burden. Because this church isn't about me, it's about us. What we can do together to be instruments of God's will.

"So I want you all to think about the example Tim has set for us. If you coach a Little League team, or a soccer team, or Pop Warner football, or whatever, that's great—now you know what to do. And if you don't coach, think about signing up, because it's a wonderful opportunity to bring the Good News of Jesus Christ to the children of your community, the ones whose parents won't let them hear it because they're the ones who need it most. And if the powers that be don't like it, if they want to stop good Christian citizens from saying a simple prayer at a youth sporting event, I say bring it on. That's a fight we want to be having."

Pastor Dennis turned to Tim.

"Thank you," he said. "You're an inspiration to everyone in this room."

Tim shifted uncomfortably in his chair.

"It really wasn't a big deal," he explained.

"Don't listen to him," Pastor Dennis told Jay. "Any time a man sticks his neck out for the Lord, trust me, that is a *very* big deal."

ABBY COULDN'T understand why Tim didn't have satellite radio in his car. As she frequently pointed out, her mother had XM in her Volvo and her stepdad had Sirius in his Lexus, and both services had top-forty channels way cooler than the crappy FM station she was forced to listen to in the Saturn now that Tim had banned her iPod (he'd gotten sick of waiting for her to remove the earbuds every time he asked a question). Even so, her scorn for the idiot deejays and the tacky commercials didn't stop her from turning on WRZO before they were even out of the driveway, cranking up the volume and singing along with the soulless ballad that came blasting out of his tinny sound system.

Tim made an effort to humor her—he hated being maneuvered into the role of Uptight Dad—but he couldn't help sensing something slightly hostile in the way she closed her eyes and swayed in her seat, a deliberate attempt to shut him out, or at least keep the conversation to a minimum. They hadn't seen each other in a week; it wouldn't kill her to talk to him for a few minutes. He waited for the song to end, then lowered the volume. Abby opened her mouth to protest, then decided to let it go.

"So," he said. "How was school this week?"

"All right."

"Anything interesting happen?"

"Not really."

"Anything funny?"

"It was just school, Dad."

They enacted this tooth-pulling ritual every week without a whole lot of variation. He'd hoped things would improve when she moved to the front seat—she'd only gotten the pediatrician's okay a month ago—but having her right next to him only made him that much more aware of how little they had to talk about. These rides had been a lot easier last year, when a couple of her teammates carpooled with them—Tim had found it both amusing and instructive to listen to the three girls squeezed together in the backseat, laughing and gossiping the whole way—but neither Natalie nor Jess had qualified for the A team. Tim still missed those girls, Natalie in particular, a sweet goofy kid who would sometimes forget where she was and start turning cartwheels on the soccer field, and who thought it was hilarious to call him "Coachie-Poo."

"Take any tests?" The only thing worse than interrogating her like this was sitting in silence, waiting for her to volunteer some information about her life.

"Just math."

"How'd you do?"

"Eighty-seven."

"That's pretty good."

"My teacher's kind of mean, though."

"Don't tell me. Ms. Holly, right?"

"She's Social Studies. Mrs. Harris is Math."

"Harris, that's right. I got them confused."

Tim always felt himself at a disadvantage, discussing school with Abby. The decision to enroll her at Elmwood Academy had been made without his participation; he'd only been notified after the fact. Even now, her second year there, he still hadn't visited the campus or met any of her teachers. All he really knew was that Elmwood had a stellar reputation—"nurturing but academically challenging," was the word on the street—and cost nearly as much as a top-notch private college.

"They both start with H," Abby conceded. "But Holly's young and nice and Harris is old and crabby."

"I'll try to remember that."

"You better." There was a note of affectionate teasing in her voice
that cheered him up a bit. "There's gonna be a quiz."

"You still like English best?"

"It's not called English. It's Language Arts."

"Back in my day, we called it English."

"When was that, the Middle Ages?"

"Ha-ha. So what are you studying in Language Arts?"

"We're doing a unit on biography. This week we wrote an essay on
the Man I Admire Most."

"Man?" Tim was surprised. From what he'd heard Elmwood was a
pretty PC place. "Not *person*?"

"We did the Woman I Admire Most two weeks ago."

"Oh. Who'd you choose for that?"

She hesitated.

"Mom."

He nodded, taking this in.

"Hey, that's great. Did, uh, everyone pick a parent or grandparent?"

"Not everyone. This one girl did Condoleezza Rice."

"So what did you say about your mother?"

"I don't know." Abby sounded irritated, like he'd asked an unfair
question. "Just, you know, how nice she is."

Tim didn't press for details. He could easily imagine Abby's portrait
of a noble single mother who goes back to work full-time after her irre-
sponsible husband falls apart and the bank takes their house away.
Times are hard, but she keeps her spirits up, never complains, not even
about the shabby apartment that's the only place she can afford, or the
pathetic Mercury Tracer that keeps breaking down on her. The story
comes complete with a Cinderella ending: the woman goes on a blind
date with a friend of a friend, a wealthy lawyer who falls in love with
her at first sight, then whisks her and her child away to a suburban
castle where they live affluently ever after.

"What about the man?" he asked, as if he were simply curious, as if he weren't already imagining a piece of wide-lined paper, and a young girl's careful cursive: *My parents are divorced, but my Dad is a huge presence in my life. He coaches my soccer team, and all the girls love him.* "Who'd you pick for that?"

Abby looked slightly mortified. She wasn't always the most perceptive kid in the world, but even she seemed to have realized that the conversation had taken a problematic turn.

"It was stupid," she said. "I couldn't really think of anyone. I just, like, picked someone at random."

A horrible thought came to Tim: *My stepdad is the greatest guy. He's really fun and knows more than anyone else in the world about patents and trademarks.*

"I guess that means you didn't write about me," he said, hoping to defuse the tension with a joke, but not managing to sound as playful as he'd intended.

Abby turned her head, suddenly fascinated by the red brick buildings of downtown Gifford. He wondered if it was possible, if she really did admire Mitchell more than him. It was true that she spent way more time with her stepdad, and he bought her everything she wanted. But he wasn't her father. That had to count for something.

"If you really want to know," she said, "I wrote about Donald Trump."

Tim's immediate sense of relief only lasted a second or two.

"*Donald Trump?* Are you kidding me?"

"He's cool," she said.

"He's not *cool*, Abby. Trust me on this one."

"Yah-huh," she insisted. "He's totally cool on *The Apprentice*."

"I can't believe Donald Trump is your hero."

"I didn't say he was my hero. I just said I admire him."

"For what?"

"Come on, Dad. Everybody admires him. He's got a skyscraper, a private jet, a casino, and his own TV show. He can do whatever he wants."

"That just means he's rich. It doesn't mean he's a good person."

"You're just jealous."

"I'm not jealous of Donald Trump."

"You have to admit," she said, "it'd be pretty cool to have a private jet."

"I'm sure it would," he agreed, as they pulled into the SUV-choked parking lot of Gifford Memorial Park, a six-field complex that would have been a prime soccer venue if not for the goose shit the kids were always slipping on. "I'd get one if I had a bigger garage."

BECAUSE THERE were never enough playing fields to go around, the Stars had to wait for a Boys U-10 game to finish before they could begin warming up. Some coaches focused on stretching and others on passing drills, but Tim liked to get in the goal and have the girls shoot on him at point-blank range. It was a good way for him to interact with his players, to see who was psyched and who might be needing a little extra motivation, which he liked to dispense in the form of some good-natured trash talk.

Tim felt his spirits lift a little as the balls began whizzing in his direction, concentrating his mind on the here and now. *We're here to play soccer,* he reminded himself. *Just like any other week.*

"Whoa, Slinky!" he wailed, slapping down a cannon blast from Sara D'Angelo. "Take it easy on an old man."

"Come on, Hangman!" he shouted at Hannah Friedman. "My grandma coulda stopped that, and she's been dead for fifteen years!"

"Bring it on, Monkey!" he told Maggie Ramsey, who seemed a little more tentative than usual, as if the memory of last week's shame hadn't completely worn off. "Show me the Big Foot!"

Maggie smiled at him—at least he thought it was a smile; the mouth-guard made it hard to say for sure—and began dribbling toward the right corner of the goal. Tim came charging out, modeling the aggressive goal-tending techniques he'd been working on with Louisa Zabel, but Maggie surprised him with a tricky stepover turn, suddenly reversing course to the left. Scrambling back into position, he dove for the shot, but it sailed past his outstretched fingers and into the net.

"There you go!" he gasped, pushing himself up from the grass and resting for a moment on all fours. He'd hit the ground harder than he'd anticipated and was having a little trouble catching his breath. "Just like that in the game, all right?"

He stood up gingerly, rubbing at his rib cage. At his age, he really didn't need to be diving for saves, but he couldn't help himself. Unlike most of his fellow coaches, he hadn't been a jock in his younger days, hadn't gotten the sports out of his system when he was supposed to. For guys like Jerry Writzker of Bridgeton, who'd been the starting point guard on his college basketball team, or Mike Albers of Green Valley, a highly ranked over-forty marathon runner, supervising a team of eleven-year-old girls must have been small potatoes, but for Tim it was a big deal, a weekly blast of adrenaline.

"Your turn, Nomad!" He bounced on the balls of his feet, shifting his weight from side to side. "Don't hold back. See if you can take my head off!"

JOHN AND Candace Roper didn't show up until a couple of minutes before the opening whistle, after the ref had completed his pregame shin guard and jewelry inspection, and Tim had selected his starting lineup. This wasn't unusual; with three soccer-age kids, John spent his Saturday mornings rushing maniacally from one field to the next, driving like he had a freshly harvested liver packed in a cooler on the front seat.

"Praise God," he said, embracing Tim with disconcerting fervor on the sidelines. "Today's a big day for the Lord."

"They're all big days," Tim replied. He extricated himself from the hug and looked at Candace. He could've sworn she'd grown a couple of inches since yesterday's practice. "When we sub, I want you in at midfield."

"Midfield?" she groaned. "Can't I be forward?"

"Maybe second half."

Turning away from the Ropers, Tim clapped his hands sharply and repeatedly until he had the attention of the whole team. It was no small feat, getting a gaggle of fifth-grade girls to stop talking among themselves.

"All right, guys! No overconfidence today. Let's get focused and play our game. We pass, we hustle, we anticipate, and we stick to our positions, okay?"

"We need this one!" John chimed in over his shoulder. "Let's play strong, just like last week!"

There was a moment of confusion as the players took the field, when the opposing coach—a cheerfully nerdy guy who wore a Bandits jersey with the words SOCCER DUDE emblazoned on the back—suddenly realized that he didn't have a shirt for his goalie.

"I left it in the car," he explained. "It's been one of those mornings."

Tim offered to loan him a couple of practice pinneys, but the guy begged the indulgence of the referee to make a quick trip to the parking lot.

"I'll run," he promised. "It'll take two minutes, tops."

Uncertain how to proceed, the ref—a nervous high-school kid with spiky hair frosted at the tips—deferred to Tim. A lot of other coaches would've made a fuss, but he didn't think it was worth arguing about.

"Whatever." He shrugged. "I guess we can wait."

John shook his head as Soccer Dude set off across the field in the direction of the parking lot, which had to be a couple hundred yards away.

"What a space cadet," he muttered. "No wonder they're two and six."

Tim thought about calling the girls back to the sidelines for a last-minute strategy session, but instead directed them to take a knee and sit tight. He really needed to talk to John and wasn't sure when he'd get another chance.

"Listen—" he began, but John cut him off before he could go any further.

"Oh, hey, I talked to Marty last night. We're all set for the Faith Keepers conference on Friday night."

Tim was startled by this, but tried not to show it. The Bible Study guys had arranged this outing months ago, but it had always seemed way off in the future.

"*This* Friday?"

"Yeah. You didn't know?"

"Kinda snuck up on me."

"We talked about it at Bill's the other night," John told him. "Maybe it was before you got there."

"It's bad timing," Tim pointed out. "I hate to reschedule practice before the biggest game of the season."

"Don't worry about that. The girls don't care what day they practice."

"Some of 'em might not be able to make it. They have a lot of commitments."

"We have commitments, too," John reminded him.

Tim glanced at the dull gray sky looming over the field.

"I know. I'm not complaining."

John squinted in the direction of the parking lot. The Bandits' coach was jogging toward them at a pretty good clip, a mesh equipment bag slung over his shoulder. Tim knew he couldn't wait any longer.

"Listen, John, I know what the Pastor said the other night, but I'm just not feeling right about praying today. A couple of the parents complained to me last week. They don't think it's fair."

John took this news more calmly than Tim expected.

"I disagree," he said. "What's unfair is depriving these kids of the only thing that's gonna save them."

"It's not just the parents," Tim continued. "It's the Soccer Association. If they hear about it, we're up the creek."

The coach was on the field now, tugging a garish orange-and-yellow jersey over his goalie's head. The other players rose and began drifting back to their positions. John placed his hand on Tim's shoulder.

"I don't blame you," he said. "Jesus didn't want the cup, either."

Soccer Dude came jogging back to the sidelines, clutching his side and breathing raggedly.

"Thanks, guys." He jerked his thumb over his shoulder. "That's her lucky jersey. She's kinda superstitious about it."

"No problem," Tim told him.

The ref set the ball down at midfield and raised his right hand. Tim looked at John.

"Jesus took the cup," he said quietly.

"He had to," John replied, as the whistle sounded to begin play. "It was His Father's will."

AS HEAD coach, Tim was responsible for keeping track of the big picture. He had to spread his awareness over the entire field, to make sure his players were where they needed to be at any given moment, and to communicate with them simply and effectively from the sidelines—directing this one to move up, that one to protect the weak side, alerting the girls to threats and opportunities before they materialized—while at the same time managing his subs, calculating who to put where, and when to make the changes.

It was a tall order, but he handled it pretty well, at least when Abby was out of the lineup. When she was playing, he often found it difficult to maintain his focus, to resist the temptation of thinking like a father instead of a coach. As soon as Abby stepped onto the field, his range of vision narrowed, his gaze drawn as if by magnetism to wherever she happened to be, regardless of her proximity to the ball, the game as a whole overshadowed by the riveting spectacle of his daughter in motion. He had to make a conscious effort to tear his eyes away from her, to look around and see what the rest of his team was up to.

He wasn't sure why it mattered so much to him, why he felt such a thrill when Abby made a good pass or beat an opponent to the ball, or why all the air went out of him when she screwed up. Part of it was pride, he supposed, the simple selfish desire to see your own kid succeed, to prove herself better than—or at least equal to—other people's kids. But it went deeper than that, down to something more primal. Because there were moments on Saturday mornings—amazing moments in which his mind and her body were in perfect synch— when he felt such an intimate connection with his child it was almost like they were one person. Just as often, though, in those bad-dream interludes when she flubbed an easy scoring opportunity, or stood frozen in place while an opponent dribbled around her, what he glimpsed was the impossible distance between them, a gulf that he feared would grow wider with each passing day and year of their lives, and it was this sense of hopeless separation that made him clutch his head, and cry out, "Oh, Abby!" with such anguish that John sometimes felt the need to pat him on the shoulder and tell him to take it easy.

It didn't help that she was such an erratic player. On her good days, his daughter was a valuable member of the team, maybe not a star—she lacked Nadima's nimble footwork, Sara's intimidating power, Maggie's competitive fire—but a solid and reliable performer, speedy enough to be an offensive factor, and surprisingly tenacious on defense, considering her waiflike proportions. On her off days, though, she seemed like an entirely different kid—sluggish, uncertain, emotionally disconnected from the action—as if soccer were just one more boring obligation in her overscheduled life. Weirdly, Tim could never judge her mood from talking to her in the car. He had to wait until the game started to see which Abby he was dealing with.

Today looked to be a good day, though he couldn't quite decide if this was because she'd come to play or because the Bandits were so outclassed that it didn't really matter. The Stars asserted their dominance from the outset, moving upfield at will against their smaller, slower opponents—oddly, many of the Gifford girls were short and stocky, not the best build for soccer—and getting off several quick shots on goal before the Bandits had even managed to move the ball across midfield.

A fairly predictable rhythm developed in the opening minutes of the game. The Stars would attack, and the Bandits would somehow manage to beat them back. But Tim's girls were relentless; before the defense could catch its breath, they'd return for another try. Pretty soon the Bandits began to panic. They gave up any pretense of strategy or deliberation and just booted the ball randomly downfield to clear it away from their goal. Tim waved his sweeper up toward midfield to increase the pressure.

"They're gonna crack," he told John. "It's only a matter of time."

After making a nice diving save on Hannah Friedman, the Bandits' goalie tried to punt the ball—she had a weak throwing arm—but it squibbed off the side of her foot, bouncing erratically toward the far sideline. Abby got to it first, but instead of passing right away—her usual impulse on offense—she took a moment to settle the ball and scan the field. Then, to Tim's surprise and delight, she began moving toward the goal, something he'd been urging her to do all season. Without any hesitation or windup, she blasted a high, hard shot that sizzled past two defenders before bouncing off the goalie's arm. As luck would have it, the ball landed right in front of Maggie Ramsey, who was perfectly positioned to bang in the rebound.

"Bingo!" John raised his hands overhead like a football ref. "Yeah, baby!"

Tim called for subs—no one ever complained about being taken out right after a goal—stepping onto the field to slap hands with his starters as they came charging off, sweaty and exultant. He could hear Frank Ramsey bellowing his approval from the far sideline—"Yo, Maggs, way to be there!"—and double-checked to see if he could spot Ruth standing among the spectators. It seemed odd for her not to be here, after raising such a big stink about last week's prayer, but some people were like that—big on the bluster, weak on the follow-up.

*Or,* he thought, with a bitterness that caught him by surprise, *maybe she has something better to do.*

TIM HAD actually stopped by Ruth's house the night before, ostensibly to drop off a sweatshirt Maggie had left at practice. Even at the time, he understood that this was just a pretext. Girls forgot water bottles and articles of clothing on a regular basis, and he'd never before felt the need to hand-deliver these items to their rightful owners. He was their coach, not the UPS man.

Although he was pretty sure he had an ulterior motive, he wasn't completely clear about what it was. It would have been nice to believe he was acting as a responsible adult—a gentleman, even—going out of his way to level with Ruth, to let her know that his situation had grown more complicated since they'd last spoken, giving her one last chance to remind him of the bargain they'd made, and what a disappointment he'd be if he reneged on it. But if that was the case—if everything was completely aboveboard—then there was no reason to hide behind Maggie's sweatshirt. He only needed the sweatshirt if something murkier and less respectable were afoot—if, for example, he were a married man in no particular hurry to get home to his wife, looking for an excuse to pay a visit to a divorcee whose kids, he happened to know for a fact, spent Friday nights at their father's condo.

It must have been this lingering uncertainty about the propriety of his errand that kept Tim trapped in his car for such a long time after he'd pulled up in front of her house. She seemed to be home: the downstairs was lit up, the windows glowing warmly in the bluish twilight. The porch light was shining as well, almost as if she'd been expecting him. He could easily picture himself walking up the steps and ringing the bell, but at that point his imagination faltered. Did he greet her solemnly and inform her that they needed to talk? Or did he just hand over the sweatshirt with a sheepish grin and wait for her to invite him inside?

He'd been thinking about her a lot over the past couple of days, so much that it had begun to make him nervous. Not with lust—he knew what lust was, and this wasn't that—but with a kind of hopeful curiosity, a sense that they had more to say to each other. He would've liked to know a little more about Ruth's marriage, how she'd hooked up with a blowhard like Frank Ramsey, and at what point she realized it was a mistake. And why had she kept his last name even after the divorce? She didn't seem the type. That was all he really wanted—a chance to sit down with her at the kitchen table and resume the conversation they'd started on Tuesday night.

Was that so bad?

AT ONE of the first Bible Study sessions Tim had attended after joining the Tabernacle, Pastor Dennis had proposed a simple test the men could use in case they found themselves in what they believed to be a morally ambiguous situation, and weren't sure how to handle it.

"All you have to do," he told them, "is to imagine Jesus standing right beside you, and then ask yourself, *Would my Companion be proud of me right now? Or would He be ashamed?* And you know what? Ninety-nine point nine percent of the time, if you have to ask the question, you already know the answer. You need to turn around and get yourself out of there!"

Over the past couple of years, Tim had applied this test on a number of occasions, and for a while, at least, it had worked pretty much the way the Pastor had predicted. Tim's Companion had been highly observant and easily alarmed. Lately, though, He seemed to be slacking off a bit, or at least becoming more tolerant of human weakness. Tim knew this wasn't quite right—in the Gospels, the Son of God was often angry and harshly judgmental, despite His injunction against mortals passing judgment on one another—but there were times when the Jesus by his side seemed no more helpful than one of his old stoner buddies from high school, the kind of guy who'd watch you screwing up, then just chuckle and say, *Wow, dude, I can't believe you did that.*

In thorny cases such as this one, the verdict usually seemed a lot clearer if he imagined Pastor Dennis looking on instead of Jesus. As far as the Pastor was concerned, it wouldn't have made one bit of difference if Tim had come here to return a sweatshirt, or to have a serious conversation with Ruth about prayer, or to sweet-talk her into bed. No matter how you sliced it, the bottom line didn't change: Tim was a married man and a Christian, and he belonged at home with his Christian wife. He needed to turn around and get out of there!

And that's what he was about to do—at least he was thinking about moving in that general direction—when Ruth stepped out of her house and began heading straight down the cement path toward his car, peering quizzically into his passenger window as she approached. There was nothing for him to do but unbuckle his seat belt and get out, as if he'd just pulled up a couple of seconds ago, and hadn't sat through five repeats of "Uncle John's Band," trying to talk himself into leaving.

"Tim?" she said, sounding a bit flustered. "Is that you?"

"Maggie forgot this," he explained, holding up the sweatshirt as he circled his car to join her on the sidewalk.

"Oh, thanks," Ruth said, accepting the garment with a certain amount of reluctance. "You didn't need to come all the way out here. You could've just given it back to her tomorrow."

"It's no trouble," he insisted. "I just thought she might need it to-night."

"She's not even here. The girls spend Friday night with my ex-husband."

"I didn't realize," Tim said. "Sorry to bother you."

"It's no bother." She glanced back at her house. "I'd invite you in, but . . ."

Her voice trailed off, as if she didn't know how to complete the sentence.

"That's okay," he assured her. "I better get going."

Ruth laughed nervously. Tim was surprised to feel her hand resting lightly on his forearm.

"I'm going on a date," she confided, her face close enough to his that he could smell wine on her breath. "First one in a long, long time."

"Wow." Tim tried to ignore a pang of jealousy that made no sense. "That's exciting."

"Can I ask you something?" She sounded a bit embarrassed. "I kinda need a second opinion."

She tossed him the sweatshirt and took a couple of steps back toward her house, where the light was a little better.

"Do I look okay?" she asked, turning in a slow circle. "I tried on six different outfits, and they all felt wrong."

"You look fine," he said.

"Really?" Maybe it was the light, but her face looked younger than he remembered it, touchingly girlish. "Just give me your honest opinion."

Tim didn't need to study her, but he did it anyway, just to make her feel better. She was wearing a belted leather jacket over a tweedy skirt, black tights, and high shiny boots. Her hair was loose, and she tucked a strand of it behind her ear, watching him closely.

"My honest opinion?" he said. "You got nothing to worry about."

* * *

THE RAIN held off until midway through the second half. Just seconds after Tim felt the first fat droplet strike his face, the sky seemed to burst open like a water balloon. The players ignored it at first, running doggedly through the downpour as umbrellas blossomed up and down the far sideline and subs scrambled for their soggy fleeces, but before long they were glancing plaintively at their coaches, hoping for a reprieve.

Tim didn't blame them. The game was a blowout, either nine or ten to one; he'd stopped keeping score early in the second half, after the Stars had scored for the seventh time, and the Bandits' goalkeeper left the field in tears. In an effort to show a little mercy, he'd instructed his team to pass the ball at least three times before shooting, and to be sure to use their nondominant foot when doing so, but even that didn't stop the bleeding. He'd gone so far as to consider an out-and-out moratorium on scoring, but had decided against it on the grounds that it was more insulting to stop trying than it was to beat your opponent by twenty goals.

With less than fifteen minutes to play, Tim had no objection to calling the game on account of bad weather—it would still count as a victory for the Stars in the Division standings—but the Bandits' coach wouldn't go for it. He insisted that his girls soldier on to the bitter end, apparently to teach them some sort of lesson about perseverance in the face of adversity.

Tim was annoyed at first—it was a cold November rain, and he had no hat or umbrella—but the longer the girls slogged on, the more he began to think Soccer Dude had a point. An oddly festive mood took hold in the last few minutes of the game, once the players realized they were thoroughly drenched and might as well make the best of it.

A broad shallow puddle had formed in a badly trampled patch of earth around midfield, and the ball kept getting stuck there. One of the Bandits lost her balance trying to kick it out, and ended up sitting on her butt in the dirty water with a comically forlorn expression on her face, a mishap some of the other girls seemed to find inspirational. Before long, players were finding all kinds of excuses to slip and fall in the muck. And then they dispensed with the excuses and just went for it. The moment the ref blew the final whistle, both teams converged in the center of the field and began stomping around, laughing and splashing one another, completing the transformation from game to party.

Standing next to John on the sideline, Tim hoisted the collar of his jacket up over his head and laughed as one girl after another ran squealing and flailing through the puddle, many of them so mud-splattered it was hard to tell which team they were on.

"I've got half a mind to join them," he said, but John didn't seem to hear. Tim turned to say it again, but then fell silent at the sight of his assistant coach.

John had his arms out and his wet stricken face turned to the sky, his expression frozen somewhere between joy and terror as he stepped onto the field. His lips were moving as he made his way slowly toward the girls, but Tim couldn't hear a word he was saying.

# Refresher

ROGER, A SIXTYISH GYM TEACHER WITH AN IRON GRAY CREW CUT, smiled at his fellow miscreants as he smeared cream cheese on a rubbery bagel.

"Hey," he said, sounding suspiciously cheerful for someone attending an abstinence refresher course at eight o'clock on Saturday morning. "It's just like *The Breakfast Club*, except they actually provide breakfast."

Ruth didn't know for a fact that Roger was a gym teacher, but it seemed like a safe bet, given that he was wearing those high-waisted polyester shorts favored by coaches of a certain age and a T-shirt that read PROPERTY OF WEST HIGHLAND EAGLES.

C. J., the mannish lesbian standing next to Ruth, gave an appreciative snort. (Ruth didn't know for a fact that C. J. was a lesbian, but she had yet to meet a straight woman who thought it was a good idea to dress like the lead singer in Sha Na Na.)

"Yeah," C. J. said, eyeing the meager spread of coffee, juice, and supermarket baked goods that had been laid out for them. "You get treated real nice here. Just stay away from the Kool-Aid."

There were four of them in all—Roger, C. J., Ruth, and Trisha, an earnest young woman who'd brought along her own supply of herbal tea bags—standing around a folding table in the regional headquarters of Wise Choices for Teens in downtown Lakeview, an hour's drive from Stonewood Heights. The other tenants in the brick office building included a dentist, a test-prep service, and a company called Home Surveillance Solutions.

"I don't know what you're talking about," Roger told C. J. "I drank the Kool-Aid and it had no effect on me whatsoever. I just happen to firmly believe that sex is bad and my penis is an instrument of the Devil." He paused, looking momentarily puzzled. "No, wait, it's my wife who thinks that."

"Well, she's at least half-right," C. J. quipped, tearing open a packet of Sweet 'N Low.

Trisha sipped her Wellness Tea and studied the poster pinned to the wall above the copy machine. It showed a horrified college boy backing out of a dorm room, trying to escape the clutches of a seductively dressed, otherwise lovely coed who had "HIV+" stamped on her forehead in bold black letters. *If Only It Were This Easy*, declared the headline at the top of the poster. A smaller caption at the bottom read, *Abstinence: Because You Never Really Know.*

"This place gives me the creeps," she muttered.

"What did you do?" C. J. asked her.

Trisha turned away from the poster. She was a short, plump woman with straight dark hair and a pretty mouth. If not for her serious-intellectual eyeglasses, she could have easily been mistaken for a college student herself.

"I admitted to my students that I masturbate," she said, sounding mortified and defiant at the same time. "It wasn't like it was part of the lesson plan or anything. We were just talking in a general way, and I said that most people probably did at one time or another in their lives, and that it was nothing to be ashamed about. And then this boy asked me point-blank if I had ever done it myself."

"Oops," said Roger.

"I know." Trisha's face flushed pink with astonishing rapidity. "I should've just told him it was none of his business, but it seemed cowardly to evade the question. I mean, I tell them all the time that I want my classroom to be a safe place where people can talk openly about every aspect of sexuality and ask any question they want."

"And look where it got you," C. J. said. "What about you, Ruth?"

"My story's not so interesting," Ruth told her. "I just lost my head and suggested that there might be some problems with our handouts from the Jerry Falwell Institute of Disinformation."

"Hear, hear," said Roger.

"I'm a repeat offender," C. J. volunteered. "They made me come last spring for the same reason I'm here now. Because I don't care what the goddam curriculum says, abstinence until marriage can't possibly apply to gay and lesbian people until we're allowed to get married. Sentencing someone to life without sex is a cruel and unusual punishment."

"Tell that to my wife," said Roger.

"Ba-dum-bum," said C. J. "And I thought Rodney Dangerfield was dead."

"What about you?" Trish asked Roger. She seemed to have relaxed a bit now that her secret was out. "What's your sin?"

Roger shook his head.

"I'd rather not talk about it."

"That's not fair," C. J. told him. "We all fessed up."

"Whatever," Roger said. "If you really want to know, I showed my kids a *Playboy* centerfold. Miss April, 1973."

"Why'd you do that?" Ruth asked, genuinely curious.

"It was stupid," he said. "I was just trying to make a point about fake tits."

C. J. looked bewildered. "What's that got to do with the curriculum?"

Roger cupped his hands beneath his pectorals and gently lifted up.

"I just like 'em natural," he said.

Ruth and Trisha exchanged queasy glances.

"It's something I feel strongly about," Roger explained. "Don't even
get me started."

JOANN MARLOW was her usual perky, overdressed self, as if she
couldn't imagine a better way to kick off the weekend than to throw
on a tailored silk blouse, a tasteful string of pearls, and three coats of
makeup before heading over to the office to knock some sense into a
bunch of reprobate Sex Education teachers.

"Good morning!" she said, once they'd all taken their places around
the big table in the conference room. "It's nice to see you all!"

JoAnn flashed a brilliant smile at her captive audience and didn't seem
the least bit put out when it wasn't returned. She took a sip of coffee
from a to-go cup—Starbucks, Ruth noted, not the cheap stuff they
brewed for the inmates—and drummed her polished fingernails on the
tabletop.

"Before we start, just let me say that I'm well aware of the fact that
these special Saturday reinforcement sessions aren't very popular. Some
of the teachers who've been invited here in the past have been pretty vo-
cal about that on their evaluation sheets. Some have said they felt they
were being punished. Others have used words like 'indoctrination' and
'total waste of time.' Maybe some of you share these sentiments. If
that's the case, all I can tell you is, get over it."

JoAnn rolled her chair away from the table and stood up. She
wasn't particularly tall, but there was something elegant and powerful
in the way she carried herself, a quality of absolute confidence that
Ruth couldn't help envying, even though it was completely foreign to
her and deeply off-putting.

"The first thing you need to remind yourselves," JoAnn continued,
"is that you're here for a simple reason. You did something wrong.
Maybe it was an honest mistake, maybe it wasn't. I can't look into your
hearts, and I don't know that I'd want to if I could. At the very least, I

think it's safe to say that everyone here this morning is having a little trouble adjusting to a new way of thinking. And I want to help you fix that."

She strode over to the whiteboard and wrote the words "GREAT OPPORTUNITY" in squeaky red marker.

"So instead of feeling sorry for yourselves and resentful of me," she said, "I think you'd all be better served by adjusting your attitudes right now, before we start. As hard as it might be for some of you to believe, this is a great opportunity for all of us to reconnect with our shared goal, which is to teach the Wise Choices curriculum to our students as enthusiastically and effectively as possible."

"Yez, boss," Roger muttered under his breath. "I sho is enthusiastic."

C. J. covered her mouth with one hand in an unsuccessful attempt to stifle her amusement. Ruth and Trisha stared at the table.

"Go ahead and laugh," JoAnn said. "But I guarantee your local school board doesn't see abstinence as a laughing matter. That's why they've adopted our curriculum, and that's why they expect you to present it to your students in good faith, without additions, caveats, or sarcastic commentary. And if you can't do that, you should think about resigning or requesting some form of reassignment before you end up facing more serious disciplinary action."

JoAnn turned back to the board, wrote the word "PARTNERS" in very large letters, and underlined it three times.

"All I'm asking this morning is for you to make a small leap of faith. Just this once, and just as a kind of experiment, could we try to think of ourselves as partners instead of adversaries? If we approach this morning's activities in the right spirit, then maybe we can make the first small step on the road to establishing a relationship of trust and mutual cooperation. Because the fact is, whether we like it or not, we're in this together."

None of the teachers nodded, but none of them protested, either, and that seemed to be good enough for JoAnn.

"Great," she said. "What I'd like to do is start with some autobiographical writing."

RUTH STARED at her exam book and tried yet again to focus her thoughts. So far the only words she'd written were a restatement of the assignment JoAnn had given them before stepping out of the room: "A Sexual Encounter I Regret." By now, enough time had passed that this simple phrase had become the center of an elaborate solar system of doodled objects—stars and crescent moons and sinuous vines, a palm tree and a pair of sexy lips, the Eiffel Tower and a fish wearing sunglasses, the planet Saturn with a large tulip sprouting from its surface.

Writing had never come easily to Ruth in the best of circumstances, and this morning's circumstances didn't even qualify as half-decent. She was tired from a night of fitful sleep, cranky about missing Maggie's soccer game, and deeply suspicious of JoAnn's motives in choosing this particular subject—she'd said she was "looking for common ground" with the teachers, but Ruth was pretty sure she was just trolling for more horror stories to inflict on impressionable adolescents. It didn't help that all three of her colleagues were scribbling away like honor students, C. J. and Trisha unburdening themselves with grim diligence, Roger looking oddly exhilarated, chuckling and shaking his head fondly at the sights on memory lane. On top of everything else, Ruth suddenly realized that she was extremely hungry, a condition she deduced from the fact that she was drawing an excessively detailed picture of a donut with sprinkles on it, floating like the sun above the Eiffel Tower and shooting quivery rays of deliciousness into the sky.

It wasn't that she was stumped for something to write about. Like anyone else her age, Ruth had committed her share of youthful and not-so-youthful indiscretions. There were a couple of tipsy one-nighters in college she would have taken back if she could, as well as an ill-considered fling with a married, much older grad-school professor that had fizzled after a lackluster session on his office couch. And she certainly regretted her weekend in the Poconos with Ray Mattingly—not because it had gone badly, but because it had gone so well, and because she'd humiliated herself by weeping inconsolably when he broke the news that he was moving.

And then, of course, there was Frank. They'd had some good times early in the marriage—a nice honeymoon in Tortola, lazy Saturday mornings in their first apartment on Hillcrest—and brought two beautiful children into the world, but from where she sat now, it was hard to feel anything but sorry about that whole misguided era of her life. They'd stayed married for at least four years after they both knew it was over, and during that time, they continued to sleep together out of some pathetic combination of need, habit, and wishful thinking. If she counted all that, then she had no choice but to admit that she regretted most of the sex she'd ever had, and thinking that way made her even more depressed than she'd been when she woke up in the morning, with last night's date still fresh in her memory.

SHE HAD set out from her house on Friday night with two condoms in her purse and a totally open mind. She wasn't exactly *planning* on sleeping with Paul Caruso, but she certainly wasn't ruling out the possibility in advance, or looking for reasons to say no. At her age, in the midst of a two-year dry spell, there wasn't a whole lot to be gained from playing hard to get, or from asking more from the world than the world was prepared to offer. Because most of the time, as Ruth well knew, it wasn't offering anything at all.

And besides, she and Paul were already lovers. It didn't matter that it had happened more than half a lifetime ago, so far back in the past that she couldn't even picture him clearly anymore. Once you'd broken through that invisible barrier that separates one person from another, you were connected forever, whether you liked it or not. She felt this even with Frank sometimes, an undercurrent between their bodies that didn't seem to care about—or even acknowledge—the fact that they were divorced, or that she thanked God on a daily basis that she no longer had to wake up next to him in the morning, no longer had to see him brushing his teeth in his underwear, staring soulfully into the bathroom mirror.

She and Paul had arranged to meet at Ferraro's, a homey Italian place in Bridgeton that Randall and Gregory had recommended. Ruth braced herself as she entered for that moment of unpleasant surprise she remembered so well from her twentieth reunion—the gasp of disbelief she had to swallow over and over again as she looked down at the name tag and back up at the face—but the shock she felt upon seeing Paul was a different thing entirely.

If it took her a few seconds to recognize him, it wasn't because time had done its usual number on him—quite the contrary. He looked good, way better than she'd let herself imagine in her most optimistic fantasy. He'd cut his hair, of course—no man his age wore it long and parted in the middle anymore—but that wasn't what threw her off, nor was it his expensive suit, or the fact that he had acquired one of those deep, even tans that didn't look like it came from spending a lot of time in the sun.

Sometimes, in magazine ads for weight-loss products, you can see a continuity between the obese person who used to wear those gigantic blue jeans and the skinny grinning individual who displays the gargantuan empty pants to an admiring world. Other times, though, the transformation is so complete that you're tempted to wonder if Before and After are even the same person.

That's the way it was with Paul. Ruth had come here to meet the grown-up fat kid of her memories—the sweet vulnerable teenager with a can of Pringles in one hand and a trumpet in the other, the boy who'd taught her that you didn't have to fit the world's definition of "perfect" to be loved—and she wasn't quite sure what to make of the studly businessman sipping a glass of red wine at the bar, exuding an air of masculine self-possession she would have found very attractive if this were a blind date, if he'd been anyone else in the world.

Suddenly aware of her scrutiny, Paul spun on his stool and met her gaze, his face breaking into a broad smile that didn't betray a hint of the ambivalence she was directing at him. If he noticed this discrepancy, though, he didn't let on as he slid off his seat and began moving toward her, opening his arms as he approached, gathering her against his disconcertingly flat body, squeezing her tight and letting out the kind of soft groan you're allowed to make when you're hugging someone who's heard you make sounds like that before.

"Ruth," he said. "Wow."

He let go of her and took a step back, smiling at her with a kind of awestruck disbelief as his eyes roamed up and down her body.

"Holy shit," he said. "Guess you're not my little neighbor anymore."

C. J. VOLUNTEERED to be the first reader.

"Ever since I've been aware of myself as a sexual being," she began, "I've known that I am a lover of women."

"Me, too," Roger chuckled, but C. J. silenced him with an imperious glare and resumed her narrative.

"When I was a teenager, this knowledge frightened me, implying as it did a lonely outcast life, lived on the fringes of quote unquote normal society. Growing up in small-town, Red State America in the 1970s, I was as yet unaware that there were vibrant communities of women just like me—supportive, loving, beautiful, strong dykes of every race, creed, and color—and even if I had, I'm not sure that I would have had the courage to imagine myself living among them.

"All I really did in high school was muddle through, biding my time until I could sneak off to college and figure out who I was without my parents, siblings, neighbors, and everyone else I knew looking over my shoulder, ready to mock and ostracize me for any deviation from the so-called norm. Scoff if you must, but even today, in this supposedly enlightened country, there are places where it isn't safe to be a gay teen—not just physically, but mentally, spiritually—"

JoAnn tapped the table. "We get your point, C. J. Could we just skip ahead to the part where you're actually responding to the assignment?"

"I'm sorry," C. J. said, in a voice oozing with insincere apology. "Am I making you uncomfortable?"

"Not at all," JoAnn replied. "I'd just appreciate it if you picked up the pace. I'd like to give everyone else a chance."

"Fine." C. J. flipped forward a couple of pages, squinting to find her place. "Okay . . . here it is . . . So what's a confused young dyke to do when a boy asks her to the prom? All I can tell you is that I found it very difficult to say no. I had four close girlfriends at the time, and they all had dates. Plus, they were all going to Lori Welker's lake house after the prom, and I didn't want to miss out. It was our senior year, and they were my whole life, those girls. You can probably imagine how happy my mother was. Her butch little girl, dressing up like a princess on the big night. She put makeup on me and stuffed me into a frilly dress. I felt sick about it, sick and dishonest, but there I was.

"My date was a boy named Donnie, and he wasn't so bad. He didn't care about me one way or the other, he just wanted to be part of the fun. One thing we had in common, we both liked our Southern Comfort, and we both liked to dance when we were drunk. So the prom itself was actually a pretty cool experience.

"The after-party was when things got weird. We hung out as a group for a while, but then the couples started to drift off, one by one, looking for private places. And finally, it was just me and Donnie, and we were trashed."

C. J. paused to gather her courage.

"You ask me why I let him have sex with me, and I guess I could hide behind that as an excuse, say I was just too drunk to resist, and maybe there's a little truth in that, but only a little. I think deep down I was just praying that I would like it, that Donnie would do what the prom and the rest of my life hadn't—turn me into a good little straight girl like everyone else.

"I guess you want to know what it was like for me. It was disgusting, and painful, and humiliating. Sobering, too. If there was one last shred of doubt in my mind that I was queer, Donnie Bolger's penis knocked it right out of me on prom night."

C. J. smiled sadly, running her fingers through her slicked-back hair.

"As everyone here has probably guessed, I'm not a big fan of abstinence. I believe that we human beings have been put on this earth to love and worship one another to the best of our abilities and inclinations, regardless of our sexual orientation or marital status. But I will say this—for as long as I live, I'll think back to that awful night in 1979 and wish to God I had abstained. Thank you."

PAUL SEEMED a little more familiar to her once they sat down and began to talk. Even as a child he'd spoken slowly and with unusual precision, as if he'd gone to broadcasting school, and the sound of his voice made her feel a little more certain that the boy she'd spent those wild afternoons with a quarter of a century ago was still hiding out somewhere inside the body of this handsome stranger.

"You look great," he said, once they'd gotten through the obligatory small talk about traffic and the perils of MapQuest. "You haven't changed a bit."

"Everyone tells me that," she replied. "I guess it's the upside to having gray hair and wrinkles when you're a teenager."

Paul grinned. There was some loose skin around his collar that was the only physical trace she could find of his former self.

"Touché," he said. "You were always funny. I remember that."

Ruth was surprised by this—humor didn't often get included in the inventory of her virtues—but let it pass unchallenged.

"Can I ask you something?" she said.

"Sure."

There were a hundred ways to phrase the question, some kinder than others. Ruth chose the direct route.

"What happened? You're a completely different person."

Paul shrugged. "I got tired of being fat. I decided to make some changes."

"When?"

"Ten years ago. After Missy and I got divorced."

Ruth nodded sympathetically, trying not to reveal any pleasure or excessive interest in this revelation.

"I didn't know you two had gotten married."

"I knew it was a disaster when I was walking down the aisle. But it was like I had to do it, like it was in the script."

"Been there," she said.

"We have two kids," he said. "So that kinda complicated things."

Ruth resisted the urge to tell him about her own situation and what a hard road it was for a single mom. They'd have time for that later.

"So did you start going to the gym or something?"

"Exercise was part of it. But mainly I just had to learn to discipline my eating. Do you remember how much food there was in my house?"

"It seemed like a lot," Ruth conceded.

"All we ever did was eat. The whole family. I asked my mom about it a few years ago, and she pretended not to know what I was talking about. I mean, we had *two* spare refrigerators in the basement, and both of them were always full."

"But you got married," she pointed out. "You weren't living in your parents' house anymore."

"Overeating was a habit, and Missy aided and abetted it. But when my marriage finally ended, I just kinda woke up and realized I'd been given a second chance, and could live my life the way I wanted to. I lost 120 pounds in two years, and I've kept it off."

"Wow. That can't be easy."

Paul ran his hand slowly down the front of his shirt, as if he were trying to iron out the wrinkles.

"It's actually not that hard," he said. "Because I really like who I am now. I go to the gym sometimes, and I see this dude in the mirror, and I'm like, *Hey, who's that good-looking guy? I wish I could be like him.* And then I realize it's me."

"THANK YOU, C. J.," JoAnn said. "That was a very interesting piece. I think you put your finger on a couple of really important issues that some of us might want to address in the classroom. One is the link between alcohol abuse and self-destructive sexual behavior, and the other is prom-night peer pressure. A couple of schools I know have gone so far as to set up sobriety checkpoints at their proms, complete with Breathalyzers and police officers, and I think your essay goes a long way in showing why that might not be such a bad idea."

"That wasn't my point at all," C. J. protested. "What I object to is the mandatory heterosexuality at the prom, all those smug straight people rubbing it in everyone else's face. That's what led to my self-destructive behavior."

"One thing the rest of you might want to consider," JoAnn continued, as if C. J. hadn't spoken, "is encouraging parents in your communities to sponsor chaperoned after-parties in their homes. If you go to our website, you'll find a list of recommended group activities that'll help keep the kids out of trouble and restore some of the lost innocence back to prom night."

"Nude Twister," muttered Roger.

JoAnn stared at him in disbelief.

"How *old* are you?" she asked.

"Old enough not to give a crap," he replied.

"Ugh." Jo Ann grimaced, as if she'd just swallowed something unpleasant. "I can't believe they let you teach children."

"Not only that," Roger told her. "They gave me tenure."

"I feel sorry for your students," JoAnn said. She looked like she was about to say something more, but decided it wasn't worth the trouble. "Let's just move on. Trisha, would you like to go next?"

With obvious trepidation, Trisha glanced down at her composition.

"It's kind of embarrassing," she said.

"That's all right," JoAnn said. "We're not here to judge you. We just want to hear what you have to say."

"I'm really ashamed of myself," Trisha murmured.

"Excellent," JoAnn said. "Why don't you tell us about it."

EVER SINCE kindergarten, Trisha had been best friends with a girl named Eve, and right from the start, Trisha had been the dominant figure in the duo. She was the smart one, the athletic one, and later, the pretty one. Eve was the admirer; it was her job to stand loyally by Trisha's side, marveling at her friend's many gifts and talents, and broadcasting them to the wider world.

The interesting thing about this dynamic was that it somehow survived long after it had any basis in reality. Midway through high school, soon after the fog of puberty had lifted, it became painfully clear to Trisha that her sidekick was actually prettier, smarter, and more athletic than she was. Oddly, Eve seemed unaware that the ground beneath their relationship had shifted. She continued to defer to Trisha and sing her praises as if nothing had changed, as if they were still second graders hanging upside down on the monkey bars.

Trisha treasured the friendship as they grew into adulthood, but she was also troubled by it. She kept waiting for the long-overdue day of reckoning, when Eve finally saw her for the weak, underachieving loser she really was and began to treat her accordingly. But it never came, not even after Eve got admitted to a better college and had a string of boyfriends way cooler and kinder and better-looking than any of the jerks Trisha went out with.

Two years ago, Eve got engaged to Thad, a handsome investment banker with a passion for rock climbing, a sport, it turned out, for which she had an uncanny knack. Every weekend, they'd head off to the mountains to test themselves against a new rock face, each more challenging than the last. Trisha was mired in grad school at the time, miserably single, and the thought of Eve's happiness filled her with bitter envy. It sometimes seemed to her that they'd traded lives, that Eve had somehow ended up with rewards that rightfully belonged to Trisha.

A few months before their wedding, Thad and Eve invited a bunch of their friends to Thad's uncle's summer house in the Shawangunk Mountains of Upstate New York. All weekend long, Trisha watched the happy couple interact with an emotion so strong it could only be called hatred. Thad was gorgeous—lean and muscular with close-cropped blond hair and an air of quiet intelligence—and he couldn't take his eyes off Eve, who seemed to have acquired a new summer wardrobe—skirts and sundresses and halter tops—every item of which fit perfectly, and called attention to the loveliness of her limbs, the grace of her smallest gestures.

All the guests left on Sunday afternoon except Trisha, who was getting a ride home from her hosts on Monday morning (her car, a crappy Dodge Neon, needed a new transmission that she couldn't afford). They'd rented *Vertigo,* but Eve pled exhaustion around nine o'clock, saying she couldn't keep her eyes open another minute. When Thad offered to join her, she insisted that he and Trisha go ahead and watch without her.

"I don't want to spoil your guys' night," she said.

They cued up the movie shortly after Eve went upstairs. Trisha made herself comfortable on the couch while Thad took a seat on the floor. *Vertigo* was one of Trisha's favorite films, but she could barely follow the action, so distracted was she by Thad's magnetic physical presence, the soft fuzz of his hair, the taut muscles of his legs stretched out in front of him, his shins nicked and bruised and battered by the rocks, the little grunts of surprise he made as the story unfolded.

At some point, Thad shifted position so that his back rested against the bottom of the couch, his right shoulder just a few tantalizing inches away from her right foot. It was so easy to extend her leg, she barely realized she was doing it until she felt her big toe brush against his T-shirt. He moved away from the touch in a reflex of politeness, but then settled back into it, exerting a slight counterpressure so she'd know it wasn't an accident.

They sat like that for a long time. Trisha's heart was racing; it took all the concentration she could muster to slow down her raggedy breathing, to keep herself from panting. Finally, she worked up the courage to move her foot even closer, until her instep was pressing against the top of his arm. She moved it back and forth against the soft cotton, an awkward but tender caress. He turned slowly, smiling over his shoulder. She smiled back.

Thad's expression grew solemn. With an odd courtliness, he cupped his hand under her calf, lifted her heel off the couch, and planted a tender kiss on the sole of her foot. She giggled in surprise, then let out a soft moan of encouragement as his lips proceeded to her ankle. He paused there, glancing uncertainly toward the ceiling. Trisha followed his gaze, thinking of her lucky friend, asleep and clueless upstairs.

"Keep going," she whispered, and he did as he was told.

PAUL BARELY touched his gnocchi, but he seemed very enthusiastic about the wine.

"I'm really glad you posted that message," he said. "I don't think I'd have the guts to do something like that."

"I don't know what got into me," Ruth confessed. "I couldn't sleep one night, and for some reason I started thinking about you and me, and what happened back then. . . ."

"That was a crazy time," he said. "I had that broken leg and things were all messed up between me and Missy. You were a real bright spot. You saved that whole spring for me."

Paul poured more wine for both of them, finishing off the bottle. Ruth was already feeling a nice warm glow from her first two glasses, a mingled sense of nostalgia and anticipation. *I was a bright spot,* she thought.

"You still play the trumpet?" she asked.

Paul made a sad face.

"Haven't touched it since sophomore year of college. I thought I would major in music, but I ended up switching to computer science. Best decision I ever made."

"You were a good musician. I liked listening to you practice."

"Maybe I'll take it up again sometime," he said without conviction. "What about you? You said you were a teacher, right?"

"High school," she said. "Sex Education."

"Yeah, right." He seemed to find this amusing. "That's a good one."

"I'm serious," she told him.

He couldn't quite manage to wipe the smirk off his face.

"Scout's honor?"

"Why's that so funny?"

"I don't know," he said. "It just seems kind of weird, considering, you know, what you were like as a teenager."

"What do you mean?" Ruth said, feeling slightly miffed. "I was a perfectly normal teenager."

"You seemed kinda wild."

"I wasn't wild. Not even close."

"I mean, you were just a sophomore, right? You know, when we—"

"That was a one-shot deal," she told him. "You were the first and only guy I had sex with in high school. I didn't have another boyfriend until college."

"Really? You were a virgin?"

"I'm sure I told you."

"You did," he said. "I just didn't believe you."


JOANN STARED at Trisha with a look that teetered between pity and contempt.

"Eeew," she said. "I can't believe you had sex with your best friend's fiancé. While she was in the house."

"It was just that once," Trisha explained in self-defense. "It never happened again."

"Personally," Roger interjected, "I can't believe he kissed your foot. That's what's really gross."

"It was clean," Trisha informed him. "I'm pretty careful about that."

"The foot's a powerful erogenous zone," C. J. declared. "Anyone who denies that is missing out on one of life's great pleasures."

"Right," said Roger. "And I know some African tribesmen who say the same thing about sautéed monkey brains."

"Who knows?" said C. J. "They might be delicious. You never know until you try."

"Point taken," Roger said. "Whatever floats your boat."

JoAnn ignored this sidebar, still staring doggedly at Trisha.

"Did you tell Eve what you'd done?" she inquired.

"I meant to," Trisha confessed. "But it was so close to the wedding, and I was Maid of Honor. It just seemed awkward."

"I hope you're kidding me," JoAnn said. "I hope you didn't stand up at the altar next to the woman you betrayed."

"There wasn't an altar," Trisha told her. "The ceremony was in a French restaurant."

"You were the Maid of Dishonor," Roger said with a chuckle, giving Trisha a friendly pat on the shoulder.

"That was my punishment," she said, her voice trembling slightly. "To know that I'd been a terrible friend."

"What about Thad?" Ruth asked. "Did you ever talk to him about it?"

"Just that night," Trisha replied. "We made a pact to forget what we'd done, to pretend it never happened. And that's pretty much what we did, except that every now and then, when I'm over their house and Eve leaves the room, he'll give me this weird little smile. Sometimes he winks. It's horrible."

"I think you should tell her," C. J. said. "You've got to clear the air. She shouldn't stay married to a creep like that. Let her get out now, before they have kids and everything gets complicated."

Trisha winced. "It's too late. Eve's pregnant. She asked me to be the godmother."

"Yuck," JoAnn said. "I can't listen to this. Who wants to go next?"

"Me," Roger said. "Unless Ruth wants to."

"That's okay," Ruth told him. "I can wait."

"Fine," JoAnn said, with an audible lack of enthusiasm. "Let's hear from Roger."

Roger looked around the table, smiling at each member of his audience, making a preliminary claim on their goodwill. After clearing his throat and cracking his knuckles, he picked up the composition book and began to read.

"Anyone who has given any thought to the matter will understand that the difference between fifteen and sixteen is hard to pinpoint with the naked eye. I have known fourteen-year-olds who look like they're twenty, and seventeen-year-olds who could pass for twelve. Yet for the legal system, the distinction between fifteen and sixteen is crucial and enormous, and woe to the man who finds himself on the wrong side of that line. I accept this—many laws, such as speed limits, rely on arbitrary numbers, and we all do our best to obey them. But who's really to blame when a teenager claims to be an age she isn't? The deceiver or the deceived? Roberta was a camp coun—"

"You know what?" JoAnn said, raising her voice above Roger's. "Why don't you just stop there?"

Roger looked up from the page, puzzled and clearly annoyed.

"But I just started," he said.

"That's all right," JoAnn told him. "I think we've all had enough of you for today." She turned to Ruth. "Let's just hear from our final reader, and then we'll take the multiple-choice quiz."

"Do I really have to do this?" Ruth asked.

"Everyone else went," JoAnn reminded her.

"Not me," Roger said. "I was censored."

"That wasn't censorship," JoAnn informed him. "That was self-defense."

"I'm just not comfortable with this," Ruth explained.

"It can't be any worse than what I said," Trisha told her.

"No one's judging anyone," C. J. said. "We're just sharing our experiences."

"I felt like people were judging *me,*" Trisha said. "I sensed a lot of disapproval in the room."

"What did you expect?" JoAnn asked her. "A pat on the back?"

"I respect everyone else for volunteering," Ruth said. "But I'd really like to take a pass."

"Do what you have to," JoAnn told her. "But I think you should be aware of the fact that I'm evaluating you on participation, not just attendance. If you don't participate, you'll just have to come back next month."

"That's not fair," Ruth said.

"Just read the damn thing already," Roger told her. "You could've been finished by now."


THEY'D AGREED to share the tiramisu, but Paul didn't even bother to pick up his spoon.

"This is really good," she told him. "You should at least try some."

"That's okay. I'm stuffed."

"Stuffed? You barely touched your dinner."

"Something happened to my metabolism when I lost the weight.

I'm just not hungry anymore. I think it's actually more of a psychological than a physical thing."

Ruth wondered if he had some kind of eating disorder but decided to keep it to herself.

"So how come you haven't gotten remarried?" she asked. "You've been divorced for a long time."

"I don't know." He picked up his wineglass, realized it was empty, then put it back down. "Maybe I'm just having too much fun being single. I travel a lot for work, and I meet a lot of women. I'd hate to have to hide out in my hotel room all night, or feel guilty about flirting with some pretty sales rep at a bar."

"Just flirting? Or is that a euphemism?"

"I go with the flow," he explained, with just a trace of smugness. "If something's meant to happen it will. If not, that's cool, too."

Ruth hadn't spent time in hotel bars, and didn't know a whole lot about the sexual habits of business travelers, but it was easy to imagine Paul doing well in that setting. He was a fit, handsome, soft-spoken man with a nice tan and an inspiring story to tell, a cut above the aging frat boys who'd be his main competition.

"But what about when you're home?" she said. "Don't you get lonely?"

He seemed surprised by the question.

"Not really. I work long hours. I go to the gym. I see my kids on the weekend. Most of the time I'm so busy I don't even think about it."

"I have days like that," she said. "But sometimes I get depressed. Usually at night, when I'm alone in bed. It's like, why are all these other people able to find love, and I'm not? Is there something wrong with me?"

"Don't bring love into it," he said, smiling as though he were making a little joke. "That just confuses the issue."

Ruth wasn't sure what he meant, but she smiled back at him anyway. He glanced at their waitress, who was taking orders at a nearby table.

"More wine? Or should I get the check?"

"Whatever," she said. "I'm ready when you are."

She felt his leg brush against hers under the table.

"I'm ready now," he told her.

"I'VE MADE a few mistakes in my life," Ruth began. "Some of them have involved sex, and at least a couple have been pretty big."

She'd experienced a sudden breakthrough near the end of the writing session, and had composed her entire statement in a five-minute burst of inspiration. At the time, she'd felt as though she were articulating something true and important, but now that she was speaking them out loud, her words seemed vaguely embarrassing to her. They even looked childish on the page, no more substantial than the doodled universe floating above them.

"It would be all too easy to pick one of these errors and tell you what I should have done differently, and how much better my life would be if I'd been mature and responsible enough not to have made it. But I'm not sure I believe that. I think it would be more accurate to say that we *are* our mistakes, or at least that they're an essential part of our identities. When we disavow our mistakes, aren't we also disavowing ourselves, saying that we wish we were someone else?

"I'm halfway through my life, and as far as I can tell, the real lesson of the past isn't that I made some mistakes, it's that I didn't make nearly enough of them. I doubt I'll be lying on my deathbed in forty or fifty years, congratulating myself on the fact that I never had sex in an airplane with a handsome Italian businessman, or patting myself on the back for all those years of involuntary celibacy I endured after my divorce. If recent experience is any guide, I'll probably be lying in that hospital bed with my body full of tubes, sneaking glances at the handsome young doctor, wishing that I hadn't been such a coward. Wishing I'd taken more risks, made more mistakes, and accumulated more regrets. Just wishing I'd lived when I had the chance."

* * *

THEY WENT back to Paul's hotel room and began to kiss, experimentally at first, and then with more conviction. After a while, he slid his hand down her back and onto her skirt.

"You always had a nice ass," he told her.

"It's not what it used to be," she warned him.

"Feels okay to me," he said, punctuating this assessment with a gentle squeeze. "If you take your clothes off, I'll be happy to perform a more thorough examination."

If there was anything in the world Ruth wanted less at that moment than a thorough examination of her ass, she wasn't sure what it might be.

"I'll take your word for it," she told him.

He kissed his way down her neck to the opening of her blouse and began undoing the buttons, revealing her lacy black bra.

"Mmm," he said. "Look at that."

She placed her hand on top of his.

"Not yet. I'm feeling a little shy."

Paul didn't argue. He stepped away from her, looking directly into her eyes, and unthreaded his tie.

"It's okay. I'll go first."

With the teasing patience of a stripper, he unbuttoned his shirt. His chest was bronzed and nearly hairless, his belly startlingly flat. He checked for her reaction.

"You look good," she told him.

"It's amazing." He gazed affectionately down the length of his torso. "I can see my feet."

He sat on the edge of the bed and pulled off his socks and shoes. Then he undid his pants.

"Don't be surprised if it looks a little bigger than it used to," he said in a matter-of-fact voice. "It's not actually bigger, but the proportions in that area are different now. I think what it was, my belly actually used to make it look smaller than it really is."

"Makes sense," she said.

Wearing only boxers, he lay down on the bed and smiled up at her, hands cupped behind his head.

"Why don't you take your clothes off and join me?"

"In a minute," she said. "I'm not quite ready yet."

Paul slid his hand inside the waistband of his shorts and began stroking himself.

"You're a sexy woman," he said. "It really turns me on to have you watching me."

"I'm glad," she replied.

He wriggled out of his boxers and tossed them on the floor near her feet.

"Your turn," he said.

Ruth wasn't sure what was holding her back. In theory, this was what she'd come here for. But for some reason she couldn't move.

"Something wrong?" he asked. "Am I freaking you out?"

"It's not you," she assured him. "I just haven't been with anyone for a long time."

He nodded thoughtfully and sat up.

"We don't have to fuck," he said. "You could just go down on me if you want. You were always great at that."

"I was fifteen," she told him. "I didn't have a clue."

"Coulda fooled me," he said, scooching back to the edge of the mattress. "I thought you were amazing."

Ruth hesitated for a moment before kneeling at his feet. It felt like the least she could do.

"Sweetheart," he whispered.

The night had been interesting. It had been a pleasure to reconnect with Paul after all these years, to find him physically transformed and happier than ever. She was touched by how fondly he remembered their time together, and flattered by the fact that he still wanted her.

"Oh, Ruthie," he said, running his fingers through her hair. "I've been waiting for this."

Paul's penis was hard, just a few inches from her mouth, and it did seem bigger than she remembered. It was a very inconvenient time for her to be thinking about Tim Mason, and the way he'd looked at her earlier in the evening, after she twirled around for him on the sidewalk in front of her house. The twilight had been fading, and there was some distance between them, but his face seemed oddly vivid as he studied her, full of pain and longing.

*Do I look okay?*

Her question had seemed innocent enough at the time—part curiosity, part harmless flirtation—but it had been a physical shock to receive the answer, to register the full unspoken force of his approval, a jolt to her system from which she still hadn't recovered. She would've given a lot to still be standing with Tim on that dark quiet street, instead of kneeling here on the coarse hotel carpet, thinking how unhappy Paul was going to be in a second or two, when she stood up and told him that she'd made a mistake and needed to go home.

# Two Tims

FRANK DROPPED THE GIRLS OFF AROUND EIGHT O'CLOCK ON SAT-
urday evening, and Ruth sensed something was up the moment they
walked in the door. Normally, Maggie was bubbly and affectionate after
a night away from home, eager to talk about her game and find out what
her mother had done all day, while Eliza skulked in the background,
rarely volunteering more than a few grudging monosyllables before dis-
appearing into her room. Tonight, though, the dynamic was reversed.

"Mom," Eliza said, stepping forward and greeting Ruth with a suspiciously emphatic hug. "How *are* you?"

"Fine." Ruth smiled quizzically at Maggie, who was still hanging
back near the doorway, clutching a plastic trash bag full of muddy
soccer clothes, shin guards, and cleats. "Everything okay?"

"Great." Eliza let go of Ruth and folded her arms across her chest in
a pretty good impersonation of one adult leveling with another. "But
the three of us need to talk."

"Fine," Ruth said, glancing again at Maggie. "Let's talk."

The girls dropped their backpacks on the floor and headed straight
to the kitchen table, as if the Saturday night family conference were a
regularly scheduled event. Ruth followed, resisting the urge to offer a
snack or try to engage them in small talk. They had something serious
to say, and she wanted to honor it with her full attention.

"Mom," Eliza began, "you know how I'm going to church tomorrow with the Parks?"

Ruth had to make an effort not to roll her eyes. Going to church with the Parks was the only thing Eliza had talked about all week.

"I'm well aware of it, honey. They're coming at eight thirty, right?"

"Right." Eliza glanced at her sister. "Maggie wants to come, too."

"She does?" Ruth turned to Maggie, struggling to maintain a neutral expression. "Is this true?"

"Yes," Maggie said, and Ruth could hear the courage it took for her to utter this one simple word.

*Jesus,* she thought, *am I that terrifying?*

"Was this your sister's idea?" Ruth spoke carefully, hoping to sound curious rather than upset.

"No way," said Eliza.

"I asked *her,*" Maggie explained.

"But why? You never had any interest in church before."

With the tip of her right index finger, Maggie carefully traced the outline of her splayed left hand on the table, like a kindergartner drawing a turkey. Her voice was barely a whisper.

"I want to know Jesus."

"Oh, come on," Ruth groaned. "Not you, too."

Maggie looked up. Her voice was stronger now.

"I felt Him. After the game. When we said our prayer."

*"What?"* Ruth felt like she'd been sucker punched. "Who said a prayer?"

"The team. Just like last week. Some of the Gifford players joined us."

"Was Coach Tim part of this?"

Maggie nodded. "Coach John, too."

Ruth couldn't believe it. While she'd been at the refresher course, thinking tender thoughts about Tim, he'd been on the field, stabbing her in the back.

*Some Christian,* she thought.

"A few of the girls wouldn't do it," Maggie added. "Nadima and Louisa and a couple of others. They didn't kneel down or anything."

"They did the right thing," Ruth told her. "You know how I feel about that praying."

"I know," Maggie said. "But I wanted to."

"Why? You don't believe in Jesus."

"How do you know?" Eliza broke in. "Don't tell her what she believes."

Ruth shut her eyes. When she opened them, both girls were staring at her with fierce expressions. In a funny way, she was proud of them.

"Jeez," she said with a dark chuckle. "Couldn't you just get piercings like everybody else?"

"Yuck," said Maggie.

"So can she go?" Eliza demanded.

Ruth raised her hands in a gesture of surrender.

"If she wants. I'm not gonna say no."

"Great." Eliza stood up. "I have to call Grace."

Maggie and Ruth sat in silence for a few seconds after Eliza left. Ruth wanted to say something calm and encouraging, but she couldn't think of anything.

"Mom," Maggie said. "Do I have to wear a dress tomorrow?"

"Wear what you want," Ruth told her. "I don't think Jesus cares one way or the other."

ELIZA APPARENTLY had a different opinion about the Savior's fashion preferences, because the girls came down on Sunday morning looking like they were heading to a school dance. Not only were they both wearing skirts and tights, they'd also acquired elegant new hairstyles— Maggie's woven into a tight French braid, Eliza's piled high on her head, held in place by a tortoiseshell clamp. Ruth hadn't seen them this dressed up since they were flower girls at their cousin Melissa's wedding four years ago.

"You look pretty," she told them.

Maggie smiled shyly and touched the back of her head. "Eliza did my braid. You like it?"

"I love it. You should wear it like that to school sometime."

"We wanted to do each other's nails," Eliza added. "But we ran out of time."

Ruth was touched to see them bonding like this. She'd been troubled for a long time by their lack of interest in each other, so different from the intense, conspiratorial relationship she'd shared with her own sister. Ruth and Mandy had spent their adolescence hiding from their parents, listening to music in candlelit rooms, telling secrets, plotting their jailbreaks. Every transgression Ruth committed in high school, she'd understood herself to be hurrying down a glamorous trail Mandy had blazed specifically for her, trying to catch up to her big sister so that one day the two of them could walk together as equals. There was nothing like that kind of intimacy between Eliza and Maggie, who mostly treated each other with a polite indifference that occasionally flared into outright hostility. Ruth just wished they'd found something besides a visit to the Living Waters Fellowship to bring them together.

"So can I make you guys some breakfast?"

"We don't have time," Eliza told her. "Grace said they have donuts and stuff at the church."

"Yum." Maggie licked her lips and rubbed her hands together, as if trying to remind her mother that she was still just a little kid. "Donuts."

"Let me get you some cereal, just in case. It won't take long."

Eliza shook her head, inspecting Ruth with an unhappy expression. "Mom," she said. "Could you put some real clothes on?"

Ruth was startled by this question. She was wearing sweatpants and a long-sleeved T-shirt—a souvenir from her first 10k race—her usual weekend loungewear.

"Why? I'm not going anywhere."

"You're gonna meet Mr. and Mrs. Park like *that*?"

"Ugh," said Ruth. "I have to meet them?"

"Grace said they wanted to say hello. They figured you might be a little nervous about this."

Ruth would have liked to say *too bad,* the Parks would just have to accept her as she was, but, in reality, she had no more enthusiasm for the idea of meeting strangers dressed like this than her daughters did. She just hadn't thought it through, hadn't accepted the situation enough to foresee that the Parks might not just pull up in front of the house and honk the horn, the way soccer parents did when they were carpooling to practice.

"All right," Ruth said. "Let me go change. It'll only take a minute."

Eliza smiled gratefully.

"Mom?" Maggie added. "Could you maybe brush your hair, too?"

RUTH GOT herself spruced up as best she could in the short time available, but ended up feeling like she shouldn't have bothered. Grace's mother, Esther Park, was such a stunningly attractive woman—small-boned, well dressed, effortlessly radiant—that Ruth felt instantly and hopelessly drab by comparison, as though she might just as well have been wearing soup-stained pajamas.

"Good morning," Esther said, shaking Ruth's suddenly enormous hand with great vigor. She wore her hair in a shoulder-length bob, one side of it falling gracefully across her cheek. "It's such a privilege for us to take your children to worship with us. You've given us a wonderful gift."

"Thank you for offering," Ruth said. "I'm glad our kids have become such good friends."

"I am, too." Esther's teardrop face crinkled with delight as she glanced at her daughter, a solidly built girl just an inch or two shorter than she was, with a bigger bust. Grace smiled back, her mouth busy with orthodontia. "We just moved here from Chicago a few months ago, and it takes a while to get acclimated."

"Chicago," Ruth repeated, feeling a bit foolish. Somehow she'd gotten the impression that the Parks were newly arrived from Korea. "I didn't know you were from Chicago."

"The Windy City," Mr. Park said, by way of confirmation. He was a boyish-looking man with a high shiny forehead, dressed in a dark suit and an open-collared white shirt. "Ever been there?"

"Just once," Ruth said. "Quite a while ago. I had a nice time."

"We didn't live in the city proper," Esther explained. "We had a place in Evanston. That's where Henry grew up."

"But we like it here in Stonewood Heights," he assured her. "It's got a real small-town feel to it. Almost Midwestern."

"It's got its good points," Ruth allowed.

"Grace says you're a teacher."

"That's right," Ruth said. "In the high school. I'm not sure it's the brightest idea to teach in the town where you live, but that's how it worked out."

"What subject?"

Ruth felt her daughters watching her, silently pleading.

"Health," she said, to their obvious relief.

Henry smiled politely but didn't follow up.

"It must be hard," Esther observed. "Working full-time and caring for your children." She didn't say *without a husband,* but Ruth heard the words nonetheless.

"Sometimes," she said. "It's not so bad now that they're older. Besides, I always wanted to work. I'm not sure what I'd do with myself at home all day."

"You keep busy," Esther told her. "I used to be a biomedical researcher before Grace was born. I did a lot of work on autoimmune disorders. But once I quit I never really looked back. Lately, I've been playing a lot of tennis."

Henry took an expensive-looking digital camera out of his pocket and asked Eliza and Maggie if they'd mind posing for some pictures with Grace.

"This is a momentous occasion," he said. "I'd like to record it for posterity."

In the first couple of photos, the three girls stood smiling in front of the couch, arms around each others' shoulders. Grace was dressed just like Eliza and Maggie—dark skirt and tights, light-colored blouse—and seeing them all in a row like that, Ruth suddenly realized that they'd co-ordinated their wardrobes over the phone last night, the way she and her high-school friends used to agree to wear their tightest designer jeans on Fridays.

"Let's get a couple of Maggie kneeling in front," Henry suggested. "Big girls, you each put a hand on her shoulder."

When they were finished with that series, Henry asked the girls if they'd mind heading out to the front lawn for a few more shots, con-sidering that it was such a lovely fall day. The girls were more than happy to oblige, and Henry herded them out the front door, leaving Esther and Ruth alone in the living room. It all happened so smoothly that it took Ruth a couple of seconds to realize that she'd been set up.

"Your daughters are lovely people," Esther observed, with an incon-gruous note of sadness in her voice.

"Thank you," Ruth replied. "Grace seems sweet."

Esther laid a nearly weightless hand on Ruth's shoulder.

"Why don't you come with us?" she said. "It's good to keep the family together."

"No thanks." Ruth smiled over her irritation. "I think I'll just stay here and read the paper."

"It's a very low-key service," Esther informed her. "And very non-judgmental. Nobody cares if you're single or divorced. And the ser-mons are really good. Thought-provoking, but not too heavy. The Reverend's got a real sense of humor."

"It's nice of you to offer," Ruth said, "but I'm not the least bit interested."

Esther's face betrayed a fleeting hint of distaste.

"Are you sure? Won't it be lonely for you, all by yourself on Sunday morning?"

"I'll be fine," Ruth assured her. "But thanks for asking."

THE THREE giggling girls piled into the backseat of the Parks' Volvo wagon. Watching them drive away, Ruth couldn't help thinking, just for a second, that maybe she should've accepted Esther's invitation, because at least then she would've been with her kids, and not just standing here stupidly on her front porch, *all by herself on Sunday morning,* waving good-bye to a carload of people who weren't even looking at her, wondering what the hell she was supposed to do until they came back.

She went inside and lay down on the couch, knowing even as she did so that it was a bad idea, that this was one of those days when the couch should be avoided at all costs. The newspaper was sitting on the coffee table, a fat slab of distraction wrapped inside a blue plastic bag, but she couldn't seem to make herself sit up and get it.

*Come on,* she thought. *You can't just lie here.*

She knew what she was supposed to do. She'd checked her e-mail last night, and had found messages from Arlene Zabel and Matt Friedman, informing her of what had happened at the game and offering to add their names to her letter of complaint to the Soccer Association. Both of them said they felt betrayed by Coach Tim, who had verbally assured them that there would be no more prayers on the playing field.

"I gave him the benefit of the doubt," Matt wrote, "and he took full advantage."

"I don't care what my husband thinks," Arlene declared. "This has gone far enough. It's time to make a stand."

On some level, Ruth understood this development as good news.

She had allies now and could no longer be written off as an isolated crank. She could just print out another copy of the letter, send it off to Matt and Arlene, and then to Bill Derzarian, and wait for the war to start. But for some reason, all the fire had gone out of her. She no longer felt any anger toward Tim Mason, only a kind of wounded bewilderment.

All she really wanted was a chance to talk to him, to have him explain why he'd taken the trouble to visit her twice last week and make her like him so much—and why, for that matter, he'd looked at her so hungrily on Friday night—if all he was going to do was break his word and leave them both right back where they'd started.

As she pondered this it occurred to her that it was almost like there were Two Tims: Silky-Hair Tim and Greasy-Hair Tim. Silky-Hair Tim was charming and honest, a decent guy with a complicated history and fuck-up tendencies, who was trying his best to do right by everyone. Greasy-Hair Tim was a liar and a manipulator, a smooth talker who couldn't be trusted and was only out for himself. This theory didn't make sense on a literal level—his hair had been greased back on Wednesday night, when he'd behaved like his silky-haired alter ego—but it was such a good metaphor for his duplicitous behavior that she decided to call Randall and tell him about it.

She owed him a call anyway. Randall had left a message on Friday night, checking to see how her date had gone, and she still hadn't gotten back to him. It wasn't embarrassment that was holding her back—he was the kind of friend with whom she'd happily share an embarrassing anecdote—so much as it was uncertainty about how to tell the story. To make him understand why she'd walked out on Paul, she'd have to describe her recent interactions with Tim, and she hadn't known how to do that in a way that would make sense to herself, let alone to Randall. But now that she'd developed the theory of the Two Tims, she thought she might be able to explain it in a way that was amusing as well as true, or at least true enough to get away with.

She was a little nervous about calling so early on Sunday morning, but Randall and Gregory were already out. Either that or they were still in bed—drinking coffee, maybe, or making love—and happily ignoring the ringing phone. *Good for them,* Ruth thought. Nothing brings a couple closer than ignoring a summons from the outside world.

"Hi, guys," she told the machine. "It's me, just checking in after my not-so-big date. Call me when you get a chance."

Ruth thought it would probably be a good idea to put on some coffee, but instead she lay back down on the couch and closed her eyes. She wasn't planning on napping, or even "resting her eyes," as her father used to put it, but she must have drifted off because the next thing she knew the doorbell was ringing, and she was sitting up, blinking in confusion, and mumbling things like, "Whuh? All right. Okay. I'm coming."

The clock on her VCR said it was only 9:37, way too early for it to be the girls, unless one of them had gotten cold feet and asked to be taken home. She trudged over to the door with a sticky mouth and that sense of muddleheaded urgency that comes with not being fully awake, and pulled it open. She felt oddly unsurprised to see Greasy-Hair Tim standing on her welcome mat, muttering about how he needed to have a word with her, and very surprised indeed by just how good it felt to slap him across the face.

"WHOA!" TIM raised both hands in front of his face in a cringing attitude of self-defense. "Take it easy!"

In reality, he didn't mind the slap, which he thought he probably deserved. It didn't hurt too bad—all that remained after the initial shock was a tingly sensation where her hand had been—and it seemed to take some of the edge off her anger.

"I'm sorry," Ruth said, touching her own cheek as if in sympathy. "I shouldn't have done that. But you lied to me."

He nodded contritely, though he couldn't help feeling like the word "lie" was stronger than the circumstances warranted.

"I'm sorry about the misunderstanding," he told her.

"*Misunderstanding?*" She laughed bitterly. "That's a good one. I guess I misunderstood you to be an honest person."

Tim found himself gazing contemplatively at his fingernails. He'd done this all his life, when he was forced to account for something stupid or hurtful or selfish that he'd done.

"I meant to give you a heads-up," he said. "That's why I came here the other night."

"So why didn't you?"

"You didn't give me a chance."

"I'm not a mind reader, Tim. How could I give you a chance if I didn't know you needed one?"

"I get your point," he said. "I could've handled this a lot better."

"Yeah. You could've told the truth."

He made himself meet her eyes. Ever since he could remember, women had been looking at him with this same baffled, disappointed expression.

"Look, Ruth, I don't blame you for being pissed, and if you want me to go, I'll go. But if you want to talk, I'll be happy to tell you my side of the story. I doubt it'll make you feel any better, but at least you'll know where I'm coming from."

"Believe me," she said. "I know exactly where you're coming from."

"All right, fine. I won't waste your time."

"No," she said, opening the door wider and stepping to one side. "It's okay. I've got nothing else to do."

HE FOLLOWED her into the kitchen, steeling himself to receive his second scolding of the still-young day. At least this time he knew what was coming. The first one had been a sneak attack, sprung on him when he dropped Abby off at her mother's.

"Morning," Mitchell had said, greeting them in Allison's place at the front door. He tousled Abby's hair. "Welcome home, sport."

She kissed his cheek and slipped into the house, which seemed quieter than usual.

"Your wife around?" Tim inquired.

Mitchell winced, as if this were a sore subject.

"She took Logan to the playground. It's such a nice morning."

"Oh." Tim wasn't quite sure what to make of this departure from protocol. Ever since Abby had started doing overnight visits, Allison had been present for the Sunday-morning handoff. "Think she'll be back soon?"

"Why don't we go downstairs," Mitchell said. "We need to talk."

"Why? Something wrong?"

"Come on, Tim. This is serious. You got yourself way out on a limb here."

Tim had never been down to the basement before, and it was predictably impressive, a vast subterranean kingdom containing a cavernous laundry room, a carpeted play space/entertainment center for the kids with a wall-mounted wide-screen TV, and a gym equipped with a StairMaster, treadmill, stationary bike, weight bench, and sauna.

"This is something," said Tim. "You work out down here?"

"I try," Mitchell replied. "Allison uses it a lot more than me."

Mitchell's home office was smaller and funkier than Tim would have expected, with an old, clunky-looking PC hulking on a beige metal desk suitable for crawling under during a nuclear war. He was surprised to see an electric guitar propped on a stand near the three-drawer file cabinet, then taken aback to discover, upon closer inspection, that it was a vintage Telecaster.

"Jeez," he said, squatting to examine the headstock. "This isn't a reissue."

"No way." Mitchell looked pleased. "It's the real thing—1952, mint condition, all original hardware. I got it on eBay."

"I didn't even know you played."

"Just a few chords. Allison got me some lessons for my birthday, but I haven't been able to take 'em. Work's been pretty hectic lately, not that I'm complaining."

"Maybe when you retire."

"That's what I'm figuring." Mitchell grinned sheepishly and strummed an air guitar. "I'll be rocking the assisted-living facility."

Tim wouldn't have minded giving the Tele a test-drive—he'd never touched a '52 before—but he could tell by the sudden improvement in Mitchell's posture that playtime was over.

"So, uh, why don't you have a seat?"

Adopting an expression of professional sternness that must have served him well in the courtroom—if he ever set foot in a courtroom—Mitchell sat down in the Aeron desk chair and waited for Tim to get himself settled on the couch, a big, low-slung piece of furniture upholstered in outrageously soft black leather, the kind of venue on which it was all too easy to imagine your ex-wife getting fucked on a sunny weekend afternoon.

"I know this is awkward," Mitchell began, "but we have a problem."

"What is it now?" Tim smiled wearily, as if he and Mitchell had been down this road numerous times, though in actual fact, nothing like this had ever happened before.

Mitchell's face remained serious, even a bit pained. "One of the soccer parents called last night and said there's been some religious stuff going on at the games."

Tim smiled wanly, trying not to betray any surprise or concern. He'd expected complaints, but hadn't figured they'd make their way so quickly to Allison, who never came to games, and wasn't on the team e-mail or phone list.

"Just a little prayer," he said. "Totally nondenominational."

Mitchell nodded slowly, absorbing this information with an air of judicial impartiality.

"And you think that's a good idea?"

"People have been praying since the beginning of time," Tim pointed out. "If it was a bad idea, we probably would've stopped a long time ago."

"Thanks for the anthropology lesson," Mitchell told him. "But I wasn't asking what the human race as a whole thinks about prayer. I was asking about you as an individual."

Tim felt himself getting irritated. It wasn't the interrogation itself, which was gentle enough, and even mildly diverting; it was the whole situation—just being *here,* in Mitchell's palatial house, sitting on his wonderful sofa, not far from his amazing guitar, and having to account for himself and his child-rearing decisions to a man who was neither friend nor family, and who, on top of everything else, was wearing a T-shirt with Billy Joel's face on the front. It didn't help that his own gaze kept straying to a framed photograph on the wall behind the desk, an enlarged candid shot of Allison wearing a garland of flowers over a sundress, sipping a drink out of a coconut shell, and looking mighty pleased with the way things had turned out.

"It's not about what I think," he said. "It's about what God thinks."

"Come on, Tim. Don't make this difficult. Allison's pretty upset."

"I figured. Why else would she sic her lawyer on me?"

Mitchell looked hurt. "That's a cheap shot."

"Sorry, but that's what it feels like."

"I'm not your enemy," Mitchell informed him. "It may be tempting for you to think so, but if that's the case you're misreading the situation. I like you. I think you're a good father to Abby."

"Thanks," Tim muttered, pleased in spite of himself. "I appreciate it."

"But you know what the custody agreement says, and you know how Allison feels about that church of yours."

On some level, Tim understood that this would be a good moment to say something conciliatory, but his self-respect wouldn't allow it.

"If Allison's got something to say to me about our kid, tell her to at least have the courtesy to say it to my face."

"Believe me," Mitchell said, "you don't want to go there. If it was up to her, this would already be a legal matter."

"With all due respect," Tim told him, "this is none of your business."

Mitchell squeezed his eyes shut and massaged his forehead.

"Don't let this end up in court," he said. "You don't want to do that to Abby."

TIM COULD'VE used a cup of coffee, but Ruth hadn't offered, and he didn't feel comfortable asking. It didn't seem like that kind of visit, judging by the way she was staring at him from across the table.

"So." She smiled frostily, interlacing her hands in the manner of an attentive schoolgirl. "You wanted to say something?"

"Where are the girls?" he asked, trying to buy himself a little time. "Still with Frank?"

"They went to church with a nice Korean family. Something called the Living Waters Fellowship?"

"It's in Gifford," he told her. "Supposed to be pretty loose and touchy-feely."

"All I know is they serve donuts."

"We do that, too. Gives people one less excuse to stay home."

"It's funny," Ruth said, not sounding the least bit amused. "My older daughter had been planning to go all week, and then, out of the blue, Maggie decided to join her at the last minute. Apparently, she had some kind of religious experience at the game yesterday."

"Listen, Ruth, I know you're not gonna—" Tim was about to say *believe me,* but he stopped himself when he realized what she'd just said. "What do you mean?"

"She says she wants to know Jesus."

"Really?"

"You think I'd make that up?"

A strange sound came out of Tim's mouth, a kind of puzzled grunt. "That is funny," he said.

"Hilarious," Ruth replied grimly. "So I guess you should give yourself a big pat on the back. You sure made a fool of me."

Tim didn't know what to say. Some part of him was pleased to think of Maggie in church, reaching out for something that would make her stronger than she already was. And Jesus Himself had said that He'd come to turn a man against his father, and a daughter against her mother. But this wasn't what Tim would've chosen to happen—not to Ruth, and not on his account.

"If it makes you feel any better," he said, "I tried to stop her."

HE TOLD her how it unfolded, how he'd followed John Roper onto the field in that blinding rainstorm and stood by silently as the assistant coach sunk to his knees in the gigantic mud puddle in which the players of both teams were joyously splashing around, and called for the Stars to make a circle. A number of the Gifford girls retreated in confusion as John announced his intention of praising the Lord, but a handful remained behind, intrigued by the call to prayer. John had told them they were more than welcome to stay.

"Did you intervene?" Ruth said.

"No," Tim admitted. "I didn't think I had the right."

It took a while for the prayer to begin, mainly because some of the Stars refused to kneel. They were just standing there, hovering at the edge of the circle, trying to figure out what to do. Tim could see the pain and uncertainty in their eyes, the desire to merge with the group colliding with an equally powerful urge to turn their backs on something from which they felt excluded.

"There were five holdouts," he said. "Louisa, Hannah, Nadima, your daughter, and my daughter."

"Your daughter?" Ruth said. "She wouldn't pray?"

"Abby's being raised by her mother and stepfather. They're not interested in God."

The girls on the ground linked hands, smiling shyly at one another, all of them soaking wet and splattered with mud. John was staring up at Tim, not with anger, but with kindness and understanding.

*Coach,* he said. *We need you down here.*

Tim couldn't say he didn't feel a tug. John was his friend, a man he'd brought to Jesus. And the girls who were kneeling so patiently in the mud and rain—they were *his* girls, even the ones he didn't know. He took his own daughter gently by the wrist.

*Come on,* he told her. *It's okay.*

*Mom won't like it,* Abby told him. *She'll be really mad.*

*You're not a child,* he reminded her. *You can make your own decisions.*

Abby yanked her arm from her father's grasp.

*Leave me alone!* she said. *This is stupid!*

*It's not stupid,* Tim insisted.

By this point, John had already begun praying, talking about how beautiful it was to have players from both teams kneeling on the field, giving thanks and praise to the Almighty, because Jesus doesn't divide the world into teams or nations or anything else that separates one person from another.

*We're all one,* John declared. *And He loves us all.*

While he was pleading with Abby, Tim noticed Maggie drifting hesitantly forward, kneeling down between Candace and a girl from Gifford.

"I tapped her on the shoulder," Tim told Ruth. "I said, *Maggie, you shouldn't be doing this. Your mother doesn't allow it.*"

*My mother's not here,* Maggie replied.

*This really isn't a good idea,* he said.

*It's fine,* she insisted, clasping hands with the other girls, closing the circle she had opened. *I want to do this.*

Not knowing what else he could do, Tim turned back to Abby, but she was already walking away with Hannah, Nadima, and Louisa, the four of them trudging off the field with their heads down, as if they'd just suffered a heartbreaking loss.

"I was alone out there," Tim said. "I was the only one standing."

"So what did you do?"

"I got down on my knees," he told her.

RUTH WASN'T as impressed by this story as Tim had hoped.

"That's it? You tapped her on the shoulder and said I didn't approve? That's your big heroic act?"

"What'd you want me to do? Put her in a headlock? I mean, there I am, begging my own daughter to join the prayer, and in the next breath I'm telling yours she shouldn't. I felt like a total hypocrite."

"Maybe we should switch kids," Ruth suggested. "Make things a lot simpler for both of us."

Tim tried to smile, but it didn't feel too convincing. Ruth could joke about giving up her daughter, but he knew what that felt like for real. And he could already feel Abby slipping away from him again, regardless of whether Allison tried to limit his visitation rights. Even if everything stayed the same, it was all too easy to imagine a future where she barely acknowledged him and didn't need him for anything important.

"I'm just curious," he said. "What are you so afraid of? It's just a prayer. It's not gonna kill her."

"I'm not afraid. I just don't want strangers filling my kid's head with all this religious crap."

"I'm not a stranger, Ruth."

"You were. Back when this started, I didn't know you from Adam."

"Maggie's one of my favorite kids," he told her. "I wouldn't do anything to hurt her."

"I appreciate that," she said, sounding a bit calmer. "And I know she likes you, too. But that just makes it worse."

"How?"

"She trusts you, and you took advantage of that. You used your position to proselytize my kid against my wishes."

"I didn't proselytize," he said. "It's possible that John crossed the line yesterday, but you can't blame me for that."

"Don't hide behind John. You were the one who started it. And believe me, you were very effective. What'd it take to convert her? Not even two weeks. That's pretty fast work."

"I understand you're upset, but maybe this is what Maggie needs right now."

"Don't tell me what my daughter needs," Ruth snapped. "I'm not giving you any parenting advice."

"I wish you would," he told her. "I'm not doing so great on my own."

"I don't believe that," she said, her expression softening a little. "You seem like a good father."

"I try," he said. "It's just really hard. I only see Abby one night a week. Half the time I can barely get a word out of her."

"It's just the age. You shouldn't take it personally."

"It's hard not to, when she stares at me like I'm the stupidest guy on the planet."

"It can't be easy for her," she reminded him. "All that back and forth. I mean, Frank and I had a rotten marriage, but sometimes I wonder if we should've just stuck it out for the girls."

"It's not just Abby's fault," Tim conceded. "Part of it's my wife. The whole stepmother thing's kinda tense for everybody."

"Are you and your wife planning on having kids of your own?" she asked, after a brief hesitation.

Tim grimaced. "That's kind of a touchy subject."

"Sorry. I didn't mean to pry."

"It's okay. We're just having some problems lately."

"Getting pregnant?"

"No." Tim chuckled grimly. "Being married."

Ruth averted her eyes, as though she were embarrassed on his behalf. He was a little surprised to notice that she was wearing lipstick so early on Sunday morning. She didn't really seem the type.

"We got off track," she said. "I think you were telling me why church is a good thing for Maggie."

"I really can't speak for anyone else," he said, not quite sure if she was teasing him or taking pity on him. "But I know I could've used some guidance when I was her age. Say what you want about the Bible, at least it takes a clear position on right and wrong."

"See," Ruth told him. "This is what bugs me. The way you people talk, it's like you're the only ones who know how to distinguish right from wrong. Just because my moral system's different from yours, that doesn't mean I don't have one. And by the way, just because something's written down in a book that's a couple of thousand years old, that doesn't necessarily mean it's right."

"It does if it's the Word of God."

"The last I heard, the Bible wasn't written by God. It was written by human beings. And you gotta admit, some of it's a little nutty."

Tim felt a familiar sensation of uneasiness, the guilty discomfort that often afflicted him when the Bible came up in conversation. As a Christian, he felt an obligation to defend the Scripture, but he was painfully aware of how ill prepared he was to do so, given how much of it he'd managed not to read (he was conscientious enough to believe that skimming didn't count). He'd done okay with the Gospels and Psalms, but a lot of the rest of it just didn't seem as fascinating or illuminating as he might have expected, given its divine origin. Maybe that was the Lord's way of saying that nothing good was easy, but it didn't make Tim feel like any less of a fraud.

"I'm no scholar," he admitted. "I just feel like, you know, with all the moral relativism in the world, it's good to have some absolute standards."

"Like what?" she asked. "Like Thou Shalt Not Kill, except by lethal injection?"

"The Old Testament says an eye for an eye."

"And Jesus says turn the other cheek."

Tim shrugged. "Look, Ruth, I'm not gonna pretend I don't struggle with this stuff. But that doesn't mean it's all B.S."

"I'll tell you what cracks me up." She looked like she was enjoying herself. "All this heaven and hell nonsense. I mean, do you really believe that when we die we're going to sit on a cloud with the people we love while angels play harps and Jesus drops by for coffee?"

"Come on, Ruth. That's not what it says."

"I mean, how's that different from seventy virgins for every suicide bomber? It's just Santa Claus for adults."

"The Bible doesn't say anything about sitting in a cloud. Heaven's supposed to be a place where only the saved are welcome. And there's no death or pain."

"Okay, fine. But what do you do there for all of eternity?"

"I don't know," he said. "You probably don't *do* anything. You're one with God."

"Maybe it's just me, but that sounds kinda dull."

"Beats burning in hell."

"I'll let you know when I get there. We can compare notes."

"You don't have to go there," he said. "Not if you accept Jesus as your Savior."

"That's all I have to do?"

"That's what it says."

"And if I don't do that, I'll burn in hell?" Ruth shook her head in bewilderment. "Talk about the punishment not fitting the crime. I mean, I don't see why it matters so much to Jesus that I believe in Him that He'd torture me for not doing it. I mean, He's God, right? What's He so insecure about?"

"Insecure?" Tim said. "Now you're just being silly."

"*I'm* being silly? You're the one trying to sell me a theological system that puts Hitler and Gandhi on the same level."

"It does not."

"According to what you told me, they're both burning in hell for not being Christians."

"I'm sure God's capable of making a distinction between Hitler and Gandhi."

"I hope so. But somebody apparently forgot to mention that in the Bible."

"Whatever." Tim didn't even know why he was bothering to argue with her. Nothing he could say about Jesus was going to reach her ears until her heart was ready to hear. "It's easy to mock and poke holes. But it doesn't get you anywhere."

"I'm just curious," she said, her smile fading a bit. "Do you really think I deserve to go to hell?"

"It's not my call," he told her. "I mean, for what it's worth, I think you're a nice person."

"Gee, thanks."

"Look, Ruth. You can trap me in a hundred contradictions that smarter people would be able to explain away. But that's not what this is about for me."

"Well, what is it about?"

"You really want to know?"

"Sure."

He studied her for a moment, trying to detect a trace of mockery in her expression. But all he saw was curiosity, or maybe just politeness.

"You have to understand the kind of person I was. If you asked my ex-wife, she'd just tell you I was a selfish drug addict, and I'm not saying I wasn't. But it never felt like I had any kind of a choice. There was just this big dark hole in me, and all I could do was fill it with drugs and alcohol to keep it from hurting all the time. And then, after I'd pretty much fucked up everything that mattered, Jesus came into my life, and He took a lot of that pain away. It was just like He was there, holding me up, watching my back. It was a feeling, not an idea or a belief. Just this kind of physical sense that He was there and He loved me. And it changed everything."

"Okay," Ruth said, nodding the way people do when they don't really believe you, but aren't going to say so. "I can respect that."

"I can't tell you what a relief it was," he continued. "To be able to turn to Him, and say, *Here, Lord, this is my life, I've made a complete mess of it, and now I'm giving it to you.* And to just feel like a completely new person. I mean, if it wasn't for that, I'd be dead now, or at least in jail. I sure as hell wouldn't be sitting here talking to you."

Ruth didn't challenge this account, nor did she ask him to elaborate. She just let a decent interval of silence go by, then asked if he wanted some coffee.

Tim glanced at the clock above the sink.

"Yikes," he said, startled to see that it was already ten fifteen. "I'm gonna be late for church."

"It won't take long," she said. "I cleaned the coffeemaker, like you said. It's working a lot better."

"Cool." Tim grinned, oddly gratified that his diagnosis had panned out. "But I really should go."

"Come on," she said, her voice suddenly flirtatious. "Just one cup. I got this really nice French Roast."

He closed his eyes, and a vision came to him. The Praise Team was up on stage, the worshippers in their seats. Everything was all set to go, except the bass player was missing, his microphone unattended, his instrument resting on its stand. It all seemed so far away, like it had nothing to do with him.

"Ruth," he said, rising abruptly from his chair, sounding more serious than he'd meant to. "Please don't tempt me like this."

* * *

SHE SPENT the remainder of the morning back on the couch, half-heartedly trying to talk herself into going for a run, or to the super-market, or maybe just out to the backyard to rake some leaves. Even cleaning the bathroom would have been a step up from just lying there, fantasizing about making love to a man who wouldn't rule out the possibility that she was going to hell.

It was worse than embarrassing. She had every right to be furious with Tim, every right to call him to account for what he'd done. To be wasting her time thinking instead about that little cleft in his chin, or the way his eyes seemed to smile before his mouth did, or how good it would feel to have those big musician's hands on her body wasn't just foolish; it was an act of self-betrayal.

She'd felt it the moment he sat down, that strange secret thrill of being alone for the first time with someone you're physically attracted to, of realizing that the only thing separating you is a little bit of air and your own uncertainty. All she had to do was reach out and put her hand on top of his, and everything would have changed. She kept visualizing the act as they spoke to each other, clenching and un-clenching her fist, thinking about how little it would take to lift her hand off her lap and slide it across the table. But she couldn't do it, and now he was gone.

It was all for the best, of course. He was a married man, a born-again Christian, a recovering substance abuser, and a guy who clearly had is-sues with keeping his word. All they could do together was make a mess. Let him go to church with his wife, and pray to his heart's content with the people he's supposed to pray with.

If the phone hadn't rung, who knows how long she might have re-mained on her back, pondering the mystery of how she'd become so pathetic. As it was, she stood up a little too quickly and found herself wobbling on rubber legs in the middle of the living room, certain that she was about to topple over. But the head rush passed as suddenly as it came, and she was able to reach the phone before the machine picked up. The caller ID said it was Randall.

"Hi, sweetie," she said. "I was wondering when I'd hear from you."

Silence.

"Randall? Are you there?" She waited a few more seconds. "I think we have a bad connection. . . . Randall?"

She was about to hang up when he finally spoke in a soft, trembling voice.

"It's over with me and Greg."

"Oh, honey. Are you sure?"

"I threw him out," he declared, sounding proud and heartbroken at the same time. "I couldn't take it anymore."

"Maybe you just need a little time apart."

"I can't believe it. Twelve years gone to shit."

"You guys are such a good couple. I'm sure you'll work it out."

"What am I gonna do?" Randall whimpered. "I'm not good at being alone."

Ruth understood that it was her job to supply some sort of encouraging cliché, but her mind couldn't locate one. She picked up a damp yellow sponge from her countertop.

"I'm a wreck," he said.

She threw the sponge across the room as hard as she could. It barely made a sound when it struck the wall, then bounced harmlessly onto the table.

"Ruth?" he said. "Are you there?"

PART FOUR

*Presentation of Fears*

# Go Home to Your Wife

GEORGE DYKSTRA HELD HIS POKER GAMES IN THE KITCHEN OF ONE of his Fox Hollow model homes, a four-thousand-square-foot, four-bedroom unit known as The Parkhurst. He'd invited the boys there as a last resort a couple of months ago—their longtime host, a divorced guy who sold and installed high-end home-theater systems, had found himself a live-in girlfriend and abruptly quit the game—and it turned out to be a stroke of genius. A huge step up from the divorced guy's crappy condo, The Parkhurst was a luxury clubhouse where grown men could kick back in style. With Fox Hollow ("an exclusive residential enclave for the discriminating homebuyer") still under construction, there were no kids to wake with their loud voices, no wives to offend with their coarse language, no neighbors who might object to a little vomit on their front lawns, not that that happened very often. The only downsides were the no-smoking rule George had instituted after the first game—several prospective buyers had complained that the model kitchen reeked of cigar fumes—and the fact that you had to go outside to take a piss, though that wasn't such a big deal on a crisp autumn night like this.

"All right, you shitheads," said Mickey Dunleavy, a Realtor whose genial, prosperous face was plastered on FOR SALE signs all over town. "Follow the Queen, fifty-cent ante, going to Chicago, hi-lo declare."

Tim nodded along with the rest of the players, though he had only the vaguest idea what any of this meant, beyond the fifty-cent ante. He'd played a little poker when he worked at Lucky Rent-A-Car, but to the best of his recollection—he'd been high a lot in those days, so his memory wasn't always that reliable—it was just the basic stuff, five-card draw, seven-card stud, acey-deucey. So far tonight, four hands had been dealt, and they'd all had unfamiliar names like Anaconda, Razz, and Lowball. Even after the rules had been spelled out, Tim still found himself lagging behind the action, making bone-headed decisions, falling for transparent bluffs. Not even a half hour in, his twenty bucks of chips had dwindled to less than five.

Dunleavy dealt a pair of hole cards—Tim got a deuce and a king—then began flipping them faceup, as though it were an ordinary hand of stud. After everyone had received their fourth card, the dealer nodded to Tim.

"Bet's to the new guy."

"It is?"

"Pair of eights showing."

Tim looked at his up cards, an eight and a three.

"Threes are wild," George informed him. "It's Follow the Queen, remember? The first card that follows a face-up queen turns wild."

"Oh yeah, right."

"Jesus H. Christ," muttered George's cousin, Billy, the genius with the Hummer dealership. "I thought you said he was a cardplayer."

"How about you shut your mouth?" George asked him.

Billy shrugged. He was a scrawny, jittery guy in a dark suit, with such pronounced jaw muscles it looked like he was chewing gum even when he wasn't.

"Guy's a greenhorn."

"Fifty cents." Tim glared at Billy as he tossed two red chips into the pot.

"Big spender," Billy said, flashing him an unfriendly smile.

Tim wasn't sure why, but Billy seemed to have taken an instantaneous dislike to him. First he'd made a disparaging comment about Tim's Saturn—"Hey, who called Domino's?"—in the dirt parking circle outside The Parkhurst, before they'd even been introduced. Then he'd mocked Tim for bringing a six-pack of Diet Coke to a poker game.

"Careful, pardner," he'd drawled, doing a bad John Wayne. "Better go easy on that stuff."

If Billy had made these remarks in the right spirit, Tim would have been the first to laugh. It *was* sad to be drinking lukewarm diet soda when everyone else was guzzling ice-cold Heinekens—he'd caught himself more than once gazing tenderly at those sweaty green bottles—and his old car did look pretty lame out there, sandwiched between someone's BMW and a brand-new Hummer H2 with dealer plates. But underneath Billy's just-kidding smirk, Tim sensed some real hostility, and wondered what he'd done to provoke it. Pastor Dennis would have said that Billy was in deep spiritual pain and ripe for the picking, but Tim just thought the guy was an asshole.

On the next go-round, Dunleavy flipped Tim another face-up three.

"Ooh, baby," he said. "Three of a kind for the new guy."

His luck was short-lived, however.

"Looky here," Dunleavy said, dealing a queen to George, followed by a nine to Phil Kersiotis, a well-regarded contractor whose trucks Tim saw a lot around Greenwillow Estates and some of the other upscale neighborhoods in the area. "The plot thickens."

"What happens now?" Tim asked.

"Nines are wild now," George explained. "Nines and queens."

"What about threes?" Tim asked, trying to sound as though he were merely trying to nail down the rules.

"Threes are just threes," George told him. "They're not wild anymore."

"What the hell is this?" Billy said. *"Sesame Street?"*

After another round of betting—Tim stayed in just in case there was another change in wild cards—Phil dealt the final hole card. Tim drew the seven of hearts, a meaningless addition to his hand. He figured he would fold when the bet came to him, but George spoke up before he had the chance.

"Remember, you have to declare hi-lo before you place your final wager."

"Why?"

"It's Chicago," Dunleavy explained. "Low spade in the hole splits the pot. But you have to declare if you're going for the high hand or the low one."

Tim didn't have to check to know that his face-down two was a spade.

"Oh, jeez." He pretended to think over this complicated question of strategy before tossing his last four chips into the pot. "I dunno. Low, I guess. I just wish those threes were still wild."

The only other player to declare low was Billy, who had the four of spades in the hole. He wasn't too happy when Tim revealed the deuce.

"Goddammit!" he barked at George. "You were coaching him!"

"I was not," George shot back. "I was just telling him the rules."

Billy took a long pull on his beer, swishing it around like mouthwash. "He shouldn't play if he doesn't know the rules."

"He knows 'em now," Dunleavy pointed out. "Guy's a quick learner."

"Here." Kersiotis grinned at Tim as he slid two leaning towers of chips across the table. "This is your share. Not bad for a split pot."

ONCE HE got a couple of winning hands under his belt, Tim started to relax. He'd been nervous about coming here, worried that he was putting his career above his principles, willingly placing himself in one of those dicey situations Pastor Dennis had warned about—his life was suddenly full of them—in which sin seemed not only possible, but completely natural and unavoidable. Now that he'd taken the plunge, though, it didn't seem so bad.

At least part of this feeling had a theological basis. He'd done a little web surfing at the office, and had been pleasantly surprised to discover there wasn't a whole lot of biblical support for the idea that gambling was a sin. It certainly wasn't one of those open-and-shut cases like killing or adultery—there was no Commandment that read, "Thou Shalt Not Participate in a Friendly Game of Chance"—nor was it covered by one of those broad, somewhat murky prohibitions like the one in Ephesians against "obscenity, foolish talk, and coarse joking," or even one of those archaic, widely ignored taboos, like the Old Testament ban on eating pork. The authorities who believed gambling was a no-no for Christians had to go pretty far afield to justify their position, claiming it was a form of stealing, for instance, or citing a passage like, "the love of money is the root of all evil," or even suggesting that gambling was a violation of the Golden Rule, since the gambler who took an opponent's money was doing to the opponent what the gambler wouldn't wish the opponent to do to him.

But none of this struck Tim as very convincing: if everyone agreed to the rules, it was impossible to say that anyone was stealing money from anyone else, and, in any case, such small amounts were at stake that it made no sense to claim greed as a motivating force for the players. As for the Golden Rule, if you forbade poker on those grounds, you'd have to forbid soccer as well, and baseball and football and golf, and any sort of competition in business or in love—anything with a winner and a loser—and Tim couldn't see how anyone could function in a world like that, not even Pastor Dennis. You'd have to be like those saints in India who spent their whole lives trying not to swat mosquitoes or inadvertently swallow a gnat.

"Hey, George," Kersiotis said, during a lull between hands. "Ask Tim about driving."

"Oh, yeah." George grinned. "I forgot about that."

"We're taking an informal survey," Dunleavy explained.

"It's kind of a personal question," George added. "You don't have to answer if you don't want to."

Billy looked up from his shuffling.

"Don't be a pussy. Just ask the goddam question."

"I'll do it." Dunleavy wagged a finger at Tim. "Be honest now. Have you ever jerked off while driving?"

"Driving my car?"

"Yeah, you know. One hand on the wheel, the other on your johnson."

"Sounds kinda dangerous."

"You gotta pick your spot," George explained. "A nice straight country road is your best bet."

Kersiotis nodded. "Busy highways are a bad idea. That's strictly for emergencies. You know, when you got no choice."

"Can't you just pull over?"

"No way," said George's brother-in-law, Al, a big red-haired guy who'd barely said a word all night. "You'd look like a total creep, jerking off on the side of the road."

"Good way to get yourself arrested," Billy muttered.

"And forget about the rest areas," said George. "That's the one place you want to avoid at all costs. That's how you get yourself in the paper."

"Wait a second," said Tim. "Is this like a regular thing for you guys?"

"Not so much these days," Kersiotis replied. He was a good-looking guy with the self-confidence of an ex-athlete. "I mean, I got three kids, lotta responsibility. But when I was younger, hell yeah. I mean, your mind starts wandering in a certain direction, what are you gonna do?"

George gave Tim a searching look. It almost seemed like he was disappointed.

"Are you telling us you never did it? Not even once?"

"You'd be the only one," Dunleavy informed him. "Everybody else fessed up."

"Really?" Tim looked around the table at the faces of his respectable, middle-aged companions. "All of you?"

"So what about you?" Kersiotis said. "You a member of the club?"

"I'd say so if I was," Tim told them. "But it never even occurred to me." Feeling pressure to confide something, he added, "I got a handjob in a traffic jam once, a long time ago, but we weren't moving. We were just kinda stuck there, waiting for them to clear an accident."

"Handjobs don't count," Billy said disdainfully. "Everybody's done that."

"It's true," Dunleavy said. "Billy's given a lot of handjobs. That's why guys are always asking to go on test-drives with him."

"Fuck you," Billy told him.

"I had a girlfriend once who went down on me on I-95," Al reported. He glanced at George. "Don't worry, I'm not talking about your sister."

George shrugged, as if to say it didn't matter to him one way or the other if his sister performed oral sex in fast-moving cars.

"Anyway," Al continued, "it was going great, but then I had to stop short, and let me tell you, neither one of us was very happy about it. We decided we better wait till later."

"Twenty years later," Dunleavy chuckled, "and Big Al's still waiting."

"That's nothing," Billy said. "One time in high school I fucked this girl *while* I was driving her home."

"You are so full of shit." George looked at Tim. "Don't believe a word this clown says."

"I'm serious," Billy insisted. "Tina-Marie Johansen. You know, with the walleye? Her parents were really strict and she had to be home by eleven. We were running late, and the only way I could fuck her was if I drove her home at the same time."

"Come on," said Kersiotis. "The only thing you fucked in high school was your pet hamster."

"This is the God's honest truth." Billy held up his right hand like he was testifying in court. "She was wearing a skirt, so she just slid over and climbed aboard. I mean, nobody wore seat belts in those days. I just had to lean a little to the right so I could see where I was going. The only problem was the stick shift kept banging into her ass when I put it into second."

"Can you believe this?" Dunleavy said. "Now he's working the stick shift and screwing a cross-eyed girl at the same time."

"Not cross-eyed," Billy said. "Walleyed. There's a difference."

"I'm surprised you weren't juggling some bowling pins, too," Kersiotis said.

"While giving yourself a haircut," added George.

"You guys are just jealous," Billy said. He slammed the deck on the table so Al could cut the cards. "Let's play a hand of 727."

WHAT SURPRISED Tim as the night wore on wasn't the excessive drinking, or the compulsive sexual boasting, or the casual vulgarity of the conversation—he'd spent a lot of time around guys like this in his previous life, and this bunch was by no means the worst he'd encountered—what surprised him was how comfortable and unthreatened he felt in the midst of it. He'd come to Fox Hollow thinking of himself as a spy straying into enemy territory, but by the time they started the ten-dollar round of Texas Hold 'Em that was one of the evening's main events, he'd begun to feel more like a wanderer who'd accidentally found his way home.

"I'm trying to get my wife to shave her pubes," Dunleavy said, passing out white plastic markers that identified the Big Blind and the Little Blind. "But she won't do it."

"Trust me," Kersiotis told him. "You're better off. Shelley's been going Brazilian for the past couple of years, and I gotta tell you, I'm not crazy about the stubble."

"I'll tell you what I don't like," George said. "That little strip of hair some of 'em keep down there. It's like a Hitler mustache."

Big Al raised his hand in a Nazi salute. He'd loosened up quite a bit after polishing off his fourth beer.

*"Ja, mein Führer!"* he bellowed, cracking himself up.

"We're on totally different wavelengths," Dunleavy explained. "She's accusing me of wanting her to look like a little girl, like I'm some kind of pedophile or something. But that's not it. I just want her to look like a porn star, except I can't say that, 'cause she somehow got the impression that I don't look at porn."

"What?" said Billy. "She actually thinks you use that laptop for work?"

"If she does," George quipped, "then she must think you're a workaholic."

Tim was well aware of exactly how upset and disappointed Pastor Dennis would be if he could see him right then, laughing along with everyone else at the idea of a man enslaved by lust, but for some reason he couldn't manage to get himself all worked up about it. For one thing, he didn't actually believe Mickey Dunleavy was addicted to porn—if he were, they wouldn't be joking about it—and even if he did have some kind of problem, Tim was pretty sure it wasn't any of his business. All he really knew was that he was having a good time.

It was just nice to get a night off for once, a little breather from the relentless pressure he'd been living with for as long as he could remember. Sometimes it seemed like all he ever did was worry. About Abby, about Carrie, about Allison, about the soccer team, the Tabernacle, the housing market, and now about Ruth. And lately, whichever way he turned, someone else was breathing down his neck, telling him he'd screwed up, and no matter how hard he tried to fix things, he only managed to screw them up worse and make people more pissed off at him than they already were. He understood on some level that he was at fault—he wasn't going to deny it—but he couldn't always figure out what he'd done wrong, or how to go about making things better. It was just the same old story, the same old Tim: good intentions, bad results. The only real question he had about his life was just how much worse it was going to get in the next few days.

"All right," Kersiotis said. "Everybody ready?"

"Wait." George rose from his chair and opened the cooler on the counter. "Anybody want a beer?"

"I'll take one," said Big Al.

"Me too," said Dunleavy.

"What the heck," Tim said, amazed not only by what he was saying, but also by how calm he managed to sound. "One beer's not gonna kill me."

TIM AND George were the first two players to be eliminated from the Hold 'Em tournament—George because he'd gone all in on the very first hand, staking everything on the perfectly reasonable assumption that he could win with a full house of jacks over sevens (unfortunately for him, Big Al made the same guess about kings over fives), and Tim because he was so distracted by the taste of his first beer in three years that he stayed in way too long with weak cards two hands in a row and ended up bankrupt.

"The hell with these assholes," George told him. "Let's go get some air."

Tim dropped his empty in the trash bag and grabbed another Heineken from the cooler on the way out. He knew it was a bad idea, but there wasn't much sense in stopping after one. If you were going to fall off the wagon, you might as well at least get a buzz out of it.

*Here I am,* he thought. *Right back where I started.*

He thought of Pastor Dennis and felt a dull pang of regret. The guy had invested so much time and energy in saving Tim's ass, and this was what it had come to. It was the Pastor's job, of course, but even so, Tim knew he'd take it hard when he found out.

*I tried,* he thought. *I never tried so hard in my life.*

He stepped onto the back deck and sat down next to George at the top of the steps, which led down to a dirt lot that would someday be someone's backyard. Maybe there'd be a pool, Tim thought, or at least a picnic table and a gas grill, a fence and some ornamental shrubbery.

"I like it like this," George said. "Be kinda sad when the people move in."

"You'll just have to build another one somewhere else."

Tim set his beer bottle on the deck and leaned back, tilting his face to the sky. It was a stunningly clear night, the darkness speckled with stars and the blinking lights of airplanes. The planes seemed to be moving so slowly when you watched them from down here, like they had nowhere special to go.

"I'm glad you could make it," George said. "I think the guys really like you."

Tim shook his head. "I'm not much of a cardplayer."

"You're holding your own."

"Tell that to your cousin."

"Ah, don't worry about Billy. He was just born that way. Nothing anyone can do about it."

Reaching into his back pocket, George pulled out what appeared to be a cigarette case, a slender silver box that gave off a pearly sheen in the moonlight.

"You know who you should talk to?" he said, flipping open the case to reveal a single skinny joint. "Mickey Dunleavy. That guy's got the touch. He's the only real-estate agent around who's still selling houses."

"Definitely. I'd love to sit down and talk business with him."

George pinched the joint between his fingertips and withdrew it from the case, which snapped shut with a surprisingly loud report.

"I put in a good word for you," he said, sticking the joint between his lips and fishing a lighter from his hip pocket. "I think you guys might be able to get something going."

"Thanks," Tim said, riveted by the path of the flame as it moved toward the puckered tip of the joint. The paper crackled as it caught fire. "I really appreciate it."

George tucked his chin to his collarbone and sucked in the first hit with a furtive, slightly anxious expression.

"No problem," he said, in a small, strangled voice. "What goes around comes around."

After several seconds, George closed his eyes and released a shocking amount of smoke from his lungs.

"Wow," said Tim. "That smells good."

George chuckled knowingly as he passed the joint.

"Thought you might like it."

Tim got a little overeager on his first toke and ended up coughing it all out, much to George's amusement.

"Sorry," he choked, thumping his chest and wiping tears from his eyes. "I'm out of practice."

"I hear you." George inhaled another monster hit. "I've been cutting down myself. Doctor told me to watch my weight, but all bets are off when the munchies hit. Especially now that there's a Taco Bell down the road that stays open till midnight."

"I was always a White Castle man myself."

"Plus, my wife doesn't like having weed around the house. She thinks it sets a bad example for the kids. So now I gotta sneak around and hide it from her."

"Just like the good old days," Tim said, puffing more cautiously this time around. "When I was in high school, I hid my stash in a flashlight, in the compartment where the batteries were supposed to go. Kept it right on my dresser."

"That's not a bad idea."

"Yeah, except I got busted during a power failure."

George flicked his lighter on and off a few times, as if he were just getting the hang of it.

"I can always spot a fellow pothead. I bet you were into Pink Floyd, right?"

"Actually, I was more of a Deadhead."

"Oh." George couldn't quite hide his disappointment. "I was a Floyd guy."

"*Dark Side of the Moon*'s a cool album."

"No, *The Wall*," George told him. "That's a fucking masterpiece. I had this girlfriend in high school, and we used to get stoned and put on *The Wall* and dry hump until I thought my dick would melt."

"Ouch," said Tim.

"No, it was all right," George insisted. "Dry humping's got a bad rap."

"Safe sex."

"Angie Pirro," he said. "I never actually fucked her."

Tim couldn't tell if he was complaining or just stating a fact, so he let this pass without comment. They traded the joint back and forth in silence until the roach was too small to bother with, and George flicked it into the yard.

"Damn," he said, shaking his head in admiration. "That's some fucking good weed."

Tim opened his mouth to agree, but he was distracted by a powerful rush, a warm tingly surge of well-being that seemed to radiate up from the deck and into his blood. For one breathtaking moment he was weightless, untroubled by gravity. He heard himself giggle.

"So how's the soccer going?" George asked.

"Okay," Tim said, sinking back down. "We're playing for the championship on Saturday."

"Damn." George placed his hand on the back of Tim's neck and gave a friendly squeeze. "I envy you. We're lucky if we end up in fifth place."

"This was a great season," Tim said, polishing off the dregs of his beer. "I'm not gonna know what to do with myself when it's over."

"You can always sleep late on Saturday morning. Maybe even get it on with your wife."

Tim shook his head.

"I just really love this team."

George pondered this for a moment.

"Let's go back inside," he said. "See what's happening with the game."

"You go ahead," Tim told him. "I gotta make a pit stop."

AFTER GEORGE went in, Tim took a walk around Fox Hollow, ostensibly looking for a secluded place to relieve himself. He understood that this was an unnecessary precaution—aside from the poker players, there wasn't a soul around—but he kept going anyway, wandering down the hard-packed road past empty houses in varying stages of incompletion, big dumb boxes rising like monuments out of the desolate terrain, not a tree or car in sight, his head muddled, his heart beating a little too fast.

*I am so fucking stoned,* he thought.

It was almost creepy how it had happened, so smoothly and slyly, the way George had summoned him outside and offered the joint without asking, not even giving him a chance to refuse, as if he'd known all along that this was the real reason why Tim had come. Of course, Tim had already begun drinking by that point, so it was hard to blame George, or pretend he hadn't made his own decision. But for some reason, it didn't feel like that. Being stoned just felt like something that had *happened* to him, a matter of circumstance rather than will.

He just wished George hadn't mentioned soccer, because that had spoiled what had been shaping up as a pretty nice buzz. It was a nightmare—all he'd done was say a simple prayer of thanks, and now his team was in shambles. Several angry parents, including his own ex-wife, were threatening not to let their daughters play in the championship game; meanwhile, Pastor Dennis had devoted his entire Sunday sermon to what he called Tim and John's "youth sports ministry." And now it looked like the shit had really hit the fan, because he'd come home that evening to find a stern message from Bill Derzarian on his answering machine, insisting that he call back ASAP, as well as one from a friendly reporter from the *Bulletin-Chronicle,* eager to get "your side of the story."

*I'm wasted,* he thought. *That's my side of the story.*

About halfway around the main loop, he spotted a Port-A-Potty that appeared to be a pretty popular destination, judging from the foul cloud that surrounded it. He briefly considered ducking inside, but settled for standing in its shadow, peeing on it rather than in it, enjoying the sound his urine made splashing against the plastic wall of the outhouse.

He zipped up and continued around the bend, back toward The Parkhurst. The model home was all lit up, a bright island in the middle of all that darkness, but Tim felt a chill come over him as he approached the edge of what would eventually be the front lawn.

*This is a mistake,* he thought, listening to the loud voices and lewd laughter seeping through the windows. *I don't belong here.*

He turned before he could talk himself out of it and veered across the road to the parking area. He hated leaving like this, without saying good-bye or connecting with Mickey Dunleavy or offering a word of explanation for his peculiar conduct, but he didn't think there was any other way to do it. George would worry, he understood that, and the other guys would call him a flake, so he took a moment to scratch the word "JESUS" into the passenger door of Billy's Hummer with the sharp end of a key, so they'd at least have some kind of vague idea about where he was coming from.

IT WAS a school night, but Randall didn't seem to want to go home. Ruth had dropped as many hints as she could think of, clearing away the coffee cups, yawning without covering her mouth, and talking about how early she and the girls had to get up in the morning, but none of it made an impression. Randall just sat there, with that same dazed expression he'd had all evening, chewing over his long list of grievances.

"I did everything for him. The shopping, the cooking, the cleaning, all that fifties housewife crap. If he lost a button, who do you think sewed it back on?"

"You didn't have to," Ruth reminded him. "You did it because you wanted to."

"I did it because I love him," Randall admitted. "But do you think he ever thanked me?"

"I'm sure he was grateful."

"He just thought it was his due. It was his mother's fault, you know. She treated him like a little prince."

"A lot of men are like that," Ruth pointed out. "Frank sure was. If he had a cold or a tummy ache, the whole world came crashing to a halt. But if I was in bed with the flu, he'd come up and ask what I was cooking for dinner."

"It was worse because Greg's an *artiste*," Randall said, pronouncing the word with bottomless disdain. "He truly believes he has more important things to do than buy groceries or clean the toilet. That sort of thing is for lesser mortals like me. Sometimes I just wanted to grab him and say, *Hello? You're not Pablo Fucking Picasso. You're just a real-estate agent who plays with dolls!*"

"That's not fair," Ruth said in a gentle voice. "You always loved his work. And he couldn't have done it without you."

"That's not what he thinks."

"I'm sure he knows. And if he doesn't, he's going to find out the hard way."

"Oh, don't worry about him. He'll find someone else to take care of him. He just bats those big blue eyes, and the boys come running."

"Maybe they used to," Ruth said. "But he's not a kid anymore. It's not so easy to find someone new when you get to be our age."

"Good. Let him find out what it feels like to be rejected for once."

"He didn't really reject you. You kicked *him* out."

"Because he wouldn't commit."

"You've been living together for ten years. You co-own a house. How much more of a commitment could you ask for?"

"I want to get married. That's something that matters to me, okay? It didn't used to, but it does now."

"It's kind of a moot point, isn't it?"

Randall shrugged. "I just want him to propose. I want him to ask me to marry him if and when it becomes legal. He knows that, and he refuses to do it."

"It seems kind of crazy, breaking up a good relationship over a completely symbolic proposal."

"It's not symbolic," Randall insisted. "I'm talking about a real proposal. Actual words coming out of an actual person's mouth."

"I don't get it," Ruth said. "Why don't you just propose to him?"

Releasing a soft groan of frustration, Randall leaned forward, letting his forehead drop heavily into the palm of his hand.

"Have you heard a word I've said?"

There was an edge in his voice Ruth didn't appreciate. All she'd done all night was listen. She'd tried three different times to bring him up to date on Maggie and Eliza's sudden interest in Christianity, and her own uncertainty about how to deal with it—the girls had come home from church on Sunday bubbling over with excitement about the fact that Esther Park had gotten the entire Living Waters Fellowship to say a prayer for Ruth's soul—but he just kept changing the subject back to his own broken heart.

"You're tired," she told him. "You should go home and get some rest."

Randall looked up, his eyes puffy and frightened behind his smudged lenses.

"I can't go home."

"Why not?"

"If I have to spend another night alone in that bedroom, I'm gonna kill myself."

"Don't even joke about that."

Randall shook his head, as if to say he wasn't joking.

"We're gonna have to sell the house. We can't get married, but we can sure as hell get . . . *divorced.*"

For some reason, this was the word that set him off. His face tightened into a childlike mask of grief, and he burst into tears.

"Oh, honey," Ruth said, rising from her chair.

The phone rang before she could make it to the other side of the table, sounding way louder than usual. Ruth froze in her tracks, torn between her desire to comfort her friend and the natural urge to find out who could be calling at such a ridiculous hour.

"Oh, God," Randall said, in a pathetically hopeful voice. "Maybe it's him."

Ruth snatched the phone off the cradle, hoping to silence it before the third ring. The caller ID showed an unfamiliar number.

"Hello?"

There was a long silence on the other end. She repeated the greeting.

"Hey," said the staticky voice on the other end. "I didn't wake you, did I?"

"Gregory?" she said.

"No, Tim."

"Tim?"

"The soccer coach."

"I know who you are," she told him. "I just don't know why you're calling."

"Who's Gregory?"

"None of your business."

"Oh." He sounded a bit put out.

Randall mouthed the words, *Who is it?* Ruth shot him an apologetic look and wandered down the hall, out of earshot.

"Why are you calling so late?" she whispered into the phone.

"Excuse me?"

She repeated the question at a higher volume. Tim chuckled strangely.

"I was, uh, wondering if maybe I could come over."

"Now?"

"Is that all right?"

"No, it's not all right. It's eleven o'clock on Tuesday night. My kids are asleep."

"I just want to talk to you."

"We're talking now," she pointed out. "What do you want to tell me?"

He hesitated. "I don't know."

"You don't know?"

"I don't mean talk to you about anything special. I just mean talk to you talk to you. You know, like we've been doing."

Ruth's bewilderment had worn off enough for her to realize that Tim didn't quite sound like himself. There was a peculiar lilt in his voice she'd never heard before.

"Are you okay?" she asked.

"Depends how you look at it. I'm a little messed up, if that's what you mean."

"Drunk?"

"Stoned, too. A nice all-around buzz."

"I thought you didn't do that anymore."

"Me, too. Guess I was wrong."

"Is that what this is about?" she said. "You got high and decided you might like to see me?"

"Now you're catching on."

"And what? I'm supposed to be flattered?"

"I didn't really think it through that far. I was just hoping you'd be awake."

"You're not driving, are you?"

"No, actually I'm parked."

"Good."

"Right in front of your house," he added, with another cryptic chuckle.

"I hope you're kidding."

"I can honk the horn if you want."

Ruth walked to the end of the hall, pulled aside the curtain, and peered through the window of her front door. He was right where he said he was, a shadowy figure in the driver's seat.

"This isn't funny," she told him.

"No," he said. "At least we're in agreement on that."

Ruth let go of the curtain and turned around, startled by the raggedy sound of her own breathing. Randall was standing at the other end of the hall, watching her with a quizzical expression while he dabbed at his eyes with a Kleenex.

"Tim," she said. "I'm going to hang up now."

"So can I come in?"

"No," she said. "You can't."

"But I need to talk to you."

"Come back when you're sober. Right now you need to go home to your wife."

TIM DIDN'T get home until after midnight. He'd thought about heading to a bar after Ruth sent him packing, but his conscience—or maybe just some instinct of self-preservation—had kicked in, and he drove to the Tabernacle instead. The building was locked, of course, so he knelt down by the door and prayed for strength and guidance un-

til a cop pulled up in a cruiser and told him he needed to take it somewhere else.

"I hate to bother you," he said, "but no one's allowed on the prem-
ises after eleven."

"This is my church," Tim told him.

"I understand." The cop was an older guy with a mustache and a
melancholy expression. "I don't make the rules."

Tim couldn't help himself. "That's what Pontius Pilate said."

"Yeah." The cop mustered a wan smile. "Right before he busted Jesus for loitering."

Heaving an ostentatious sigh, Tim rose to his feet. His knees were
stiff, but his head was a lot clearer than when he'd started.

"I guess I can finish up at home."

"I appreciate it," the cop told him. "Have a nice night."

"You, too," Tim replied.

He'd warned Carrie that he might be late and told her not to wait
up—not wanting to mention the poker game, he'd told her he had an
"important meeting" with a big developer—so he assumed, when he
saw the light on in their bedroom, that she'd fallen asleep while reading. But she was awake and waiting for him, sitting up in bed in a
flowered bra-and-panty set he'd never seen before.

"Whoa," he said, raising both hands as if she'd pulled a gun on
him.

"You're lucky," she told him. "Five more minutes, and I would've
conked out."

She looked good, he thought, giving her a furtive once-over. The
new lingerie was sexy but reassuringly wholesome—a lot of the stuff
he'd gotten her was too slutty for her to wear with any conviction—
and there was a shy, eager smile on her face. Any man in his right
mind should've been thrilled, but Tim felt unaccountably irritated, as
if she'd spoiled his plan for a good night's sleep.

"We don't have to do anything if you're tired," he said. "I'm pretty bushed myself."

Her smile didn't go away, but he could see that her confidence was shaken. She glanced down at her lap, running a tentative hand over her belly.

"What's the matter? You don't like what I'm wearing?"

"No, it's fine. Very nice."

"You mean it?"

"I do," he said, with a little more sincerity. "You look pretty."

"Good." She patted his side of the mattress. "Then why don't you come over here and kiss me?"

Tim considered her request. It would've been so easy to lie down beside her and give her what she wanted, so pleasant and painless. But that was the problem. He'd been taking the easy way out for too long—this was one of the things he'd just been praying over—and he'd come to realize that it wasn't fair to either of them.

"Carrie," he said. "There's something I've been meaning to tell you for a while now. Something important."

"What? Is something wrong?"

He heard the fear in her voice and knew that he should sit down beside her and take her hand. But all he could think about just then was the beer on his breath and how alarmed she'd be if she smelled it.

"I had a long talk with Pastor Dennis a couple of weeks ago, and, uh, and we came to the decision that I—well, that you and I need to take a break for a while. Sexually, I mean."

"I don't understand," she said. "What does that mean, *take a break*?"

"You know, take a break. Not have sex for a while."

"But we just did. The other night."

"That was my fault," Tim explained. "I've been weak. I should've told you a long time ago."

Her voice turned wary. "Is this some kind of punishment? Did I do something wrong?"

"This is my problem," he assured her. "It has nothing to do with you. I was talking to the Pastor about my . . . spiritual condition, and he said that he didn't think I should be physically intimate with you until I took care of some issues."

She nodded, but her face expressed nothing but bewilderment.

"What issues?"

Tim found himself staring intently at the hot pink bottle of Sizzlin' Strawberry lube on the nightstand. They'd ordered it a few months ago, tried it once without much success, and then promptly forgot about it. He wondered what had possessed her to rescue it from the drawer.

"About Allison," he said. "I still have a lot of lustful feelings for her, and they're interfering with my ability to be a good husband."

Even as he said this, it occurred to him that he hadn't been thinking about Allison anywhere near as much as he used to; in any case, she certainly wasn't the worst demon he was grappling with at the moment. But the confession was out, and he couldn't just take it back.

"You think I don't know that?" Carrie asked. "You think I don't see how depressed you get every time you go over there?"

"I'm sorry. I don't think I ever really stopped loving her."

Carrie pondered this for a moment, then shrugged.

"Fine," she said. "Whatever. I don't care."

A small laugh escaped from Tim's mouth.

"Right."

"I'm serious," she insisted. "You love your ex-wife, and we're just gonna have to live with that. I mean, that's what we've been doing, right?"

"It's not that simple."

"It's not really that complicated," she replied. "It would be a problem if she still loved you, but she doesn't. She married someone else and had a kid, and you said yourself that she seems pretty happy. So it doesn't really matter, does it?"

What she said made a certain amount of sense, but Tim found himself reluctant to admit it.

"This thing we agreed to is totally biblical. A husband shouldn't have sex with his wife if his heart isn't pure. It's in Corinthians. Ask Pastor Dennis if you don't believe me."

"I'm not married to Pastor Dennis," she said.

"I didn't say you were."

"So who's he to say what goes on in our bed?"

"It's not just him, honey. It's in the Scriptures."

"Jerk!"

She snatched the lube off the table and threw it at him, harder than he expected. He barely managed to get his hand up in time to deflect it.

"Hey," he said. "Take it easy."

"Go to hell, Tim."

"I really don't see why you're so upset."

She glared at him, her eyes full of pain.

"I can't believe you're such a baby. You think I don't fantasize about other men?"

"You do?"

"Yeah. Sometimes. But I don't go crying to Pastor Dennis about it. You know why?"

Tim shook his head.

"Because I love my husband," she told him. "And all I ever wanted was for him to love me back. But he couldn't do it."

Tim didn't dispute this.

"You never did, did you?" For some mysterious reason, she was smiling, as if this knowledge brought her some kind of sad pleasure. "You never loved me one bit."

"I—" Tim began, but he faltered. "I'm trying, Carrie. I'm trying to be a good husband."

"Trying to do your Christian duty?" she taunted.

"That's not fair," he told her. "I'm really working at this."

She shook her head, slowly and for a long time. Tim felt as though some terrible judgment were being passed, and understood that there probably wouldn't be an appeal.

"If you loved me," she said, "it wouldn't seem like such a chore."

# Faith Keepers

ARRIVING AT SCHOOL ON FRIDAY MORNING, RUTH FOUND AN OFFICIAL-looking envelope tucked into her mail slot, buried beneath the usual blizzard of memos and announcements. The message it contained—a couple of lines scrawled on a piece of stationery "From the Desk of Principal Venuti"—was ominously terse.

*Ruth,* it said. *Please report to my office at the beginning of first period—J.V.*

She showed the note to Randall when she brought him his latte. He made a sympathetic noise as he mulled it over, then lapsed into a childish singsong.

"Someone's in trouble, someone's in trouble."

"Thanks for the support."

"Sorry. Just trying to inject a little levity into the proceedings."

She looked at him a little more closely. His mood seemed to have improved considerably since the previous evening, when he'd accused her of being a bad friend. Randall had cried himself to sleep on her couch for two nights in a row at that point, and hadn't taken it well when she informed him that a third night was out of the question. She hated taking a hard line when he was in such a fragile emotional state, but she felt like she needed some time alone with Maggie and Eliza, a chance for the three of them to be a family without a weepy guest underfoot. Watching the girls head off to church on Sunday with the Parks had been a wake-up call, a reminder of how easy it was for the people you love to slip away from you. It had happened with her sister, and with Frank, and with more friends than she cared to remember. She wasn't going to let it happen with her daughters, not if she could help it.

"You seem awfully cheerful this morning," she observed. "Did you get a good night's rest?"

"I wouldn't say that. Actually I was up pretty late. Greg and I had a long talk."

"And?"

Randall smiled coyly. "Are you free for dinner tonight?"

"Why?"

"There's something we want to tell you."

"*We?* Does that mean what I think it means?"

"You'll find out soon enough."

"Come on," she coaxed. "Are you back together?"

Randall's expression grew stern.

"I'm not at liberty to discuss this right now. Greg made me promise we'd break the news together."

"The suspense is killing me."

"Seven o'clock at the Indian place," he told her, handing back the summons. "Don't be late."

THIS TIME around Ruth wasn't surprised to find the Superintendent and JoAnn Marlow waiting for her in the Principal's office—they were sitting on either side of the big desk, looking professionally somber—along with sour-faced Joe Venuti, who was anxiously caressing his abdomen, as if he'd already begun to regret his breakfast.

"Hey," she said, "it's the old gang!"

Only the Superintendent felt the need to respond. He rose and offered his hand.

"Good to see you, Ruth." He jerked her arm up and down, as if congratulating her on a job well-done. "Thanks for stopping by."

JoAnn and the Principal remained seated, watching coolly as she made her way to the bronze folding chair that had been placed in front of the desk. It had the words BAND ROOM stenciled on the backrest in faded black letters.

"What's up?" Ruth asked. "Did I get Teacher of the Year?"

"Very funny," muttered Venuti.

"Now, now," cautioned Dr. Farmer, somewhat ambiguously. "No need for that."

The conversation stalled for a moment. JoAnn looked expectantly at the Principal, who did the same to the Superintendent, who pretended to be engrossed in a thorough examination of a completely ordinary ballpoint pen he'd removed from a mug on Venuti's desk.

"They want to tell you something," JoAnn explained.

Venuti nodded in confirmation. He cleared his throat and drummed a few nervous beats on the edge of his desk.

"After some, ah, administrative soul-searching, we've, ahhh, come to a decision. Dr. Farmer, would you like to have the honors?"

The Superintendent didn't look too happy to find the ball in his court.

"Right," he said, smiling sadly at Ruth. "You know we hate to do this sort of thing, but we couldn't see any alternative."

"We've received numerous complaints," Venuti added. "I can show you the file if you want."

Dr. Farmer nodded. "It seems fair to say that you're not really in synch with the new curriculum. I don't think anyone would disagree with that."

"We need team players," JoAnn chimed in. "Otherwise, we're at cross-purposes. And this pilot program is just too important for me to allow that to happen."

"I'm sorry," Ruth said. "I'm not really sure what you guys are talking about."

"You're being reassigned," Dr. Farmer informed her. "You can finish up this semester, but starting in January you're not going to be teaching Health anymore."

"We were hoping that refresher course might straighten things out," Venuti went on, "but according to the report we received, it seems like you were uncooperative at best and possibly even a bit disruptive."

"We thought about sending you to a two-week training program in Philadelphia over the summer," Dr. Farmer said, "but JoAnn sincerely feels like that would be a waste of everyone's time and the school district's resources. And in this era of across-the-board belt-tightening . . . well, I'm sure you understand."

"You can't teach something if you don't believe in it," JoAnn declared. "And clearly, you don't believe in the mission you've been entrusted with."

Ruth was stunned. She'd come here expecting a scolding, but not a three-way ambush.

"I'm being fired?" she asked meekly.

JoAnn nodded, but the Principal and Superintendent immediately took issue with this formulation.

"That's ridiculous," said Venuti. "No one's talking about firing anyone."

"You have tenure," Dr. Farmer pointed out. "We couldn't fire you if we wanted to."

"Not unless you killed someone," Venuti said, glaring at Ruth as if he wasn't ruling out this possibility.

"Even then it's dicey." Dr. Farmer allowed himself a soft bureaucratic chuckle. "You're just being reassigned, Ruth. It's nothing personal."

The fog in Ruth's head began to dissipate.

"This is outrageous," she said. "I'm going to the union."

"That's your right," Dr. Farmer assured her. "But our lawyer tells us we're on solid ground here. You're not being disciplined. You're just being redeployed in accordance with our staffing needs. We have wide latitude over that sort of thing."

"Okay," Ruth said. "Maybe you do. But who's gonna teach my classes?"

"The school board meeting's next Tuesday," Venuti said. "They're going to vote on a waiver that would allow a qualified expert to teach within her subject area without going through the onerous process of state certification."

"A qualified expert?" Ruth repeated, turning to JoAnn.

The Virginity Consultant smiled sweetly, and gave a little shrug, as if to say, *You win some, you lose some.*

"JoAnn's ABD in Public Health," Venuti pointed out. "You just have a Master's in Education."

"They've never approved one of those waivers before," Ruth said. "Didn't they turn down that retired newspaper editor who wanted to teach journalism?"

"That was four years ago," Venuti reminded her. "The board's changed a lot in the meantime. I seriously doubt that JoAnn's going to run into any problems."

"I'm sure she won't," Ruth agreed.

"Thank you for being such a good sport," Dr. Farmer said with obvious relief. "Do you have any questions about all this?"

Ruth shook her head and stood up, eager to get the hell out of there. She was almost through the door when she realized she'd forgotten something.

"Oh, wait," she said. "You didn't tell me about my reassignment."

"We're not a hundred percent sure right now," Venuti replied. "But it's starting to look like we might have an opening in the Math Department."

"Math?" She couldn't help laughing. "I don't know anything about math."

"This is remedial," Dr. Farmer assured her. "We're just talking about the basics here."

"Believe me," Venuti said. "These kids aren't rocket scientists. If you know how to put two and two together, you'll be way ahead of the curve."

THE FAITH Keepers' contingent from the Tabernacle was nine guys in all, too many to fit in John Roper's van. Tim had volunteered as the second driver and had been assigned Marty Materia and Jonathan Kim as passengers. The new guy, Jay, was originally supposed to make it four, but Pastor Dennis decided at the last minute that Jay should join him in the van.

True to form—he was an electrician who worked crazy hours to support his wife and five kids, and was renowned for his ability to nap whenever and wherever an opportunity presented itself, including at Sunday meeting—Marty started snoring in the backseat the moment Tim pulled onto the highway. Jonathan rode shotgun, staring dead ahead and plucking nervously at the sharp creases on his khakis. For the first half hour of the trip, he made the occasional random stab at conversation, asking Tim how many siblings he had and whether he intended to buy a wide-screen TV in the near future, but then he gave up, falling into a meditative silence punctuated every couple of minutes by a soft grunt of approval, as if he were agreeing with his own thoughts.

From a purely social standpoint, there was no denying that John's Odyssey was the more desirable vehicle. Trailing it from a respectful distance, Tim could see the silhouettes of the men inside; there seemed to be a lot of activity in there—heads turning, snacks getting passed around, even the odd high five. There must have been praise music on the sound system—Pastor Dennis would have insisted—and a fair amount of laughter as well, given that Steve Zelchuk appeared to be holding forth from the back row. A gifted mimic with a huge repertoire of reasonably amusing, non-dirty jokes, Steve was widely considered to be the funniest guy at the Tabernacle, not that there was a whole lot of competition for the title.

Normally, Tim would have been disappointed to find himself relegated to the dull car, but tonight he didn't mind. It was a relief to get a little time to himself, a chance to listen to his new Mavis Staples CD and let his mind wander. Things would have been a lot more problematic if he'd been stuck inside the van with Pastor Dennis and John Roper, neither of whom could contain his excitement about tomorrow's soccer game.

From what Tim could figure, the whole thing was shaping up to be a circus. The Pastor had devoted a fair amount of time over the past few days to alerting the media—not just the local and regional papers, but TV and radio stations as well—to what he said was going to be "a historic battle in the ongoing war for the hearts and minds of our children." He'd also enlisted a dozen or so volunteers from the Tabernacle to stand on the sidelines holding signs with Bible verses printed on them, which he figured would be a terrific visual if any TV reporters really did show up. These volunteers could also join the prayer circle at the end of the game, which sounded like an awesome idea to John.

It didn't sound quite so awesome to Tim, but his attempt to explain his reservations at the end of Wednesday Night Bible Study hadn't gone over too well. Pastor Dennis couldn't have cared less that Bill Derzarian and the Soccer Association would be pissed off, or that a lot of girls and their parents would be made uncomfortable, or that Tim and John would probably never be allowed to coach again.

"If it upsets people to hear the truth," he said, "so be it. Jesus told us to go into the world and preach the good news to all creation, not just the people who feel comfortable about it."

To their credit, both men were more sympathetic to Tim's fears that, by participating in another postgame prayer, he'd be violating his custody agreement and jeopardizing his relationship with his daughter.

"This is for real," he told them. "I've been put on notice."

"That's tough," John agreed. "I really don't know what I'd do in your shoes."

Pastor Dennis placed his hands on Tim's shoulders and stared directly into his eyes for several seconds, as if he were trying to give him a transfusion of courage.

"Be strong," he said. "Blessed is the man who trusts in the Lord."

John nodded in solemn agreement.

"You started this," he reminded Tim. "Let's finish it together."

THEY PARKED in a ten-dollar lot several blocks from the Civic Center and joined the parade of Christian men heading toward the arena. This was Tim's second Faith Keepers' conference, so he wasn't caught off guard the way he'd been last year, but he was still deeply impressed by the spectacle. It was disorienting, but also strangely moving, to find yourself in a demographic fun house, to look around and see nothing but kindred spirits converging from all directions, streaming out of tour buses and school buses and church vans and taxicabs, shaking hands and hugging and calling out to one another in happy voices.

Most of the Faith Keepers were white and most were on the youngish side of middle age, but there were lots of exceptions—clean-cut Asian guys, hip college dudes with soul patches and long sideburns, imposing black men with shaved heads, father-and-son duos, packs of bikers, and even a few old codgers getting around with canes and walkers. You couldn't assemble a crowd this size without attracting a handful of out-and-out weirdos—Tim saw a dreadlocked hippie in a floor-length dashiki, and a burly guy in a flannel shirt who stood by the main entrance, blowing repeatedly into a ram's horn; he was also accosted by a hollow-eyed street preacher who pressed a vile, badly photocopied pamphlet into his hand, the cover of which read, *Ten Reasons Why God Hates Fags (And We Should Too)*—but what struck him was just how few of them there were. The overwhelming majority of the conference goers were just regular guys in khakis or jeans, sweaters or leather jackets, white sneakers or brown loafers, solid citizens with steady jobs and wedding rings and maybe a little less hair and a little more belly than they'd started out with, guys who looked like they'd fit right in at the Tabernacle with Marty and Jonathan and Eddie and Jay and John and Tim and Bill and Steve and Dennis.

They picked up their official bracelets at the registration table— purple Livestrong-style rubber loops with the conference motto (UN-DAUNTED) stamped onto the side—then browsed the merchandise displays, wandering past trade-show booths selling CDs, books, T-shirts (JESUS IS AWESOME), and souvenir mugs ("got God?"), and then checking out the folding tables stacked with promotional litera-ture for Christian colleges, charities, political causes, and businesses. Examining a brochure for a company called Calvary Homebuilders, Tim winced at the memory of the bridges he'd burned at the poker game the other night, and wondered if it would be possible to set things right with George Dykstra. On the bright side, no one seemed to have connected him with the vandalism to Billy's Hummer; in any case, no one had accused him of anything. He understood all too clearly that a better man would have picked up the phone and owned up to the stupid thing he'd done, but Tim had enough problems on his plate and no stomach for kowtowing to a jerk like Billy.

The concession stands were open in the main corridor, and Tim got in line along with several other members of the Tabernacle group who hadn't had time to eat dinner. The new guy, Jay, turned to him while they waited.

"You ever been to one of these?"

"Last year," Tim told him. "I enjoyed it."

Jay looked skeptical.

"Too many guys," he said. "Feels like a gay bar."

Tim laughed in spite of himself. He'd never spoken to Jay one-on-one before, but he'd been curious about him since the day he appeared at Sunday meeting after punching Pastor Dennis in the face. He'd heard through the grapevine that the Pastor was beginning to question the strength of Jay's commitment to the Lord and expending a lot of energy trying to keep him in the fold.

"It's a little weird at first," Tim agreed. "But you'll get used to it."

As they approached the counter, Jay cast an irritated glance at the cardboard sign taped to the wall above the beer taps: NO ALCOHOL SALES AT THIS EVENT.

"That sucks," he said. "I could really use a cold one."

RUTH DID her best to put on a cheerful face as she entered Bombay Palace. She hadn't told Randall—or anyone else, for that matter— what had happened that morning in the Principal's office, and she figured the news would keep for a few more days. Right now, she just wanted to have a pleasant dinner with her friends and a drink or three to help them celebrate whatever good news it was they wanted to share with her.

Besides, now that the shock had worn off, she wasn't quite as upset about getting the axe as she'd expected to be. As angry as she was about the shabby way she'd been treated, she was also deeply relieved not to be the abstinence teacher anymore, not to have to function as the mouthpiece for an agenda that, as JoAnn rightly pointed out, she had never believed in. Remedial math would be a drag, she wasn't kidding herself about that, but at least it wouldn't make her feel unclean, like she was depriving her students of information that might help them lead happier, healthier lives. And who knew? Maybe the Wise Choices program would flop, and in another year or two, Ruth would return, vindicated, to once again preach the honest truth about human sexuality to the benighted students of Stonewood Heights. In her mind it played like a Hollywood movie, Michelle Pfeiffer standing before an audience of earnest, good-looking teenagers, rolling a condom onto a cucumber as triumphant music swelled in the background.

She headed across the dining room to join Randall and Gregory, who were sitting side by side in a booth along the back wall, holding hands—something she'd never seen them do in public—and whispering to each other with the kind of rapturous expressions you only saw on the faces of new lovers, or old couples who'd just made up after a near-death experience. As soon as she sat down, Randall poured her a glass of beer and proposed a toast.

"To our good friend, Ruth, who saved our relationship."

"Hear, hear," said Gregory.

"Me?" Ruth laughed. "What'd I do?"

"You remember when we were talking the other night?" Randall asked. "I was complaining that Greg wouldn't propose to me, and you asked why I didn't just propose to him?"

"You told me it was a stupid idea."

"He reconsidered," Gregory informed her.

Ruth turned to Randall, a smile spreading across her face. "You didn't."

Randall blushed. "I had a lot of time to think things over."

"So how'd it happen? Did you get down on your knees and all that?"

"I did it over the phone," Randall admitted. "It wasn't very romantic."

"That's not true," Gregory said. "It was *very* romantic. I could hear how hard it was for him to pop the question, how much courage it took. But it was the perfect solution. We'd fought so much about me not proposing to him that it had gotten to the point where I couldn't do it if I wanted to. Partly out of pride, I guess, but also because it would just seem like I was doing it because he wanted me to and not because I wanted to myself. You know what I'm saying?"

"Kind of," Ruth said. "I'm just really thrilled for both of you. Congratulations."

They touched glasses again. The happy couple exchanged another glance.

"But that's not why we asked you here," Randall said.

"Yeah, right."

"We're serious," Gregory insisted. "We asked you here tonight to see if you're free on August nineteenth."

"I guess." Ruth shrugged. "Probably."

"You better be," Randall told her. "Because we want you to be Best Woman at our wedding."

"Your wedding? You mean like a commitment ceremony?"

"No," Gregory said. "Our wedding. We've booked this cute little inn in the Berkshires. It'll be a legal ceremony, endorsed by the Commonwealth of Massachusetts."

"But you're not citizens. And they don't let—"

"We won't be out-of-state," Randall informed her. "We're moving to Cambridge. Or somewhere around there. Dan and Jerry said they'll help us find a nice place to live."

"You're serious?"

Her friends nodded.

"When's this gonna happen?"

"As soon as possible," Gregory said. "There's really no point in waiting."

"I-I don't understand." Ruth was still smiling, but her voice didn't match her face. "This is so . . . sudden. I didn't even know you were thinking about moving."

"It's sudden for us, too," Randall agreed. "But we know it's the right thing."

"Once we got engaged," Gregory explained, "it just seemed so obvious. You get engaged so you can get married. And right now, there's only one place where we can do that."

"And besides," Randall added. "We're getting a little tired of Stonewood Heights. We need more excitement in our lives."

Ruth wrapped her fingers around her beer glass, but couldn't seem to lift it up.

"What about me?" she asked in a soft, wounded voice. "What am I supposed to do?"

It wasn't like she expected them to say, *Come on along, come live with us in Cambridge,* but she would have appreciated something more than the blank, puzzled looks they were directing at her. They were her best friends; they should have understood how she felt. But the truth was, even Ruth didn't understand how she felt until she buried her face in her hands and heard herself sobbing like a lost child.

TIM HAD never seen the Grateful Dead perform at the Civic Center Auditorium—they tended to prefer the larger outdoor venues in the area—but he had seen a number of concerts here in his younger days, including shows by .38 Special, The English Beat, and a couple of different incarnations of the Allman Brothers. In some ways—at least if you factored out the thick cloud of pot smoke that used to hover over the festivities—it felt utterly familiar to be sitting up here in the cheap seats with his buddies, looking down on the tiny musicians rocking out on stage, completely continuous with the rest of his life. He wondered how many other Faith Keepers could say the same thing, how many of them had batted beach balls into the air while waiting for Supertramp to take the stage, or passed drunk girls overhead while Little Feat played a third encore.

After four songs, the Faith Keepers band yielded the stage to the emcee, Brother Biggs—Tim remembered him from last year—a rotund, light-skinned black man with impish charm and a booming voice. He got the crowd going with some stadium-style call-and-response, pitting the floor against the mezzanine, the left side of the arena against the right.

"Who loves Jesus?"

"WE DO!"

"Who hates sin?"

"WE DO!"

"Who do we love?"

"JESUS!"

"What do we hate?"

"SIN!"

"All right." Brother Biggs grinned, his face enormous on the jumbo screens mounted on either side of the stage. "Now I know y'all got a bracelet when you came in tonight, am I right? That's a pretty good deal, don't you think? Don't ever say we're not taking care of you. I'm not sure if you noticed, but there's a word printed on that bracelet, and it's our motto for tonight. Why don't you tell me what it is?"

"Undaunted," the crowd replied, but the response seemed hesitant and disorganized, even though the word was flashing on the big screens.

"Oh, my goodness," said Brother Biggs with a sad chuckle. "I don't want to insult nobody, but that was kind of sissy-sounding. I thought y'all were a bunch of red-blooded Christian men, but you sounded more like a Brownie troop or something. So let me ask you again. What's our motto for tonight?"

"UNDAUNTED!"

Brother Biggs mopped his forehead with a handkerchief and released a big sigh of relief.

"That's much better. Y'all had me worried there for a minute. Thought I'd wandered into the wrong event. Not that I got anything against Brownies, but you guys just not cute enough to wear those sweet little dresses."

Brother Biggs wandered up to the edge of the stage. On the screens, his face grew serious.

"Now I know y'all came here for a good time tonight, a celebration of our shared love for Jesus Christ. Get you some of that good, old-fashioned praise and fellowship with a couple thousand like-minded Christian guys. Trust me, fellas, we gonna give you that experience. But first we got a little work to do on confronting our fears. Oh, I know, that doesn't sound like much fun, but it makes sense when you think about it. Because you can't feel true joy when you're afraid, can you? You gotta conquer your fear. And that's what *undaunted* means. It means you may be scared, but you don't run. You stand tall and keep walking, right straight into that fear. Because the Lord's right there, He's walking with you. Say Amen."

The crowd said it.

"So like I told you, we got a great event planned for you. But before we get to that, I want to give you your mission for the night. Three simple tasks. Not two, not four. Three. I put 'em in a little rhyme so they're easy to remember. The first thing we gonna do, we gonna *face* our fear. Then—and this is the hard part—we gonna *embrace* our fear. And after that, with the help of Jesus, we gonna *erase* our fear. You got that? *Face, Embrace, Erase.* Why don't you say it with me? What are we gonna do first?"

"FACE!"

"That's right! What comes next?"

"EMBRACE!"

"And then?"

"ERASE!"

"Excellent," said Brother Biggs. "You guys are starting to get the hang of this. Sounds like we got a bunch of strong, undaunted Christian men in the house! Now let's get this party staaaarteeeed!"

MIDWAY THROUGH the keynote address—"Optimizing Jesus: Seven Ways to Put Your Faith to Work in the Workplace"—Tim got up to use the restroom. It wasn't an emergency, but a half hour into the lecture, "former corporate CEO and sought-after Christian motivational speaker, Bob Mallott" had only made it through three of the seven ways, and Tim was starting to get a little restless.

He killed a few minutes in the bathroom, splashing cold water on his face and chafing his hands together beneath the automatic dryer long after there was any need for it. When he finally emerged, he wasn't completely startled to find Jay waiting for him in the hallway, a cardboard boat of nachos in his hand. All evening long, Tim had felt the new guy sneaking glances at him, making faces and generally trying to get his attention, despite the fact that Pastor Dennis and Youth Pastor Eddie were sitting between them.

"There you are," Jay said, in a weirdly accusing tone. "I thought maybe you ditched me."

Tim was puzzled by his word choice. How could you ditch someone who had no claim on you whatsoever?

"I was just using the men's room," he said.

Jay nodded, but he didn't seem fully convinced. He leaned in close to Tim, keeping his voice soft.

"You enjoying this?"

"It's okay. I mean, it's not the most exciting night I've ever had."

Jay made a soft, incredulous noise.

"I'd rather drive a spike into my head than listen to this shit."

"It was better last year," Tim assured him. "They had a comedian."

Jay held out his nachos. Tim waved him off.

"Come on, don't be shy. Take a cheesy one."

"All right. Thanks."

Tim selected a particularly goopy chip with a jalapeño slice on it. Jay watched him chew with an interest that verged on rudeness.

"What?" Tim said.

"Nothing." Jay gave a cryptic shrug. He had a plump babyish face, but there was a shrewdness in his eyes Tim hadn't noticed before. "I'm just glad we're finally getting a chance to talk."

"Me, too," Tim said, though he was beginning to feel a bit uncomfortable.

Jay glanced left and right. There were a fair number of guys wandering around the corridor, but none of them were from the Tabernacle.

"From what I hear," he said, "we've got some things in common. You know, issues in our past. Struggles and whatnot."

"That's possible," Tim allowed. "I've had my share of issues."

Jay hung his head.

"It's not easy," he said.

"Tell me about it."

"I wanna be good, don't get me wrong." Jay looked up. "But it's so fucking boring."

"That can be a problem," Tim agreed.

Jay rubbed his chin with the tip of his thumb. "All I know is it's a good thing I'm not driving tonight. 'Cause there's a pretty great strip club a couple miles from here, and if I had a car—"

Jay caught Tim's warning glance and clammed up. John Roper had just emerged from the exit ramp and was heading straight for them.

"Hey, guys," he said, in a voice full of false cheer. "Whassup?"

Tim pursed his lips. Jay muttered something indecipherable.

"You were gone for a long time," John told them. "The Pastor was getting worried."

"We're fine," Tim assured him.

"Just having a little chat," Jay added. "Getting to know each other a bit."

"That's cool," John replied. "I didn't mean to intrude."

"No problem," Tim said. "We were just about to head back in anyway."

RUTH DIDN'T cry for long, but the guys still felt terrible.

"I'm really sorry," Gregory said. "We should've been more considerate."

Randall agreed. "We were so caught up in our good news that we didn't stop and think about how it might affect you."

"It's not your fault," Ruth told them. "I really don't know why it upset me so much. I guess you just caught me off guard or something."

Randall reached across the table and patted her hand.

"I know it's been a tough year. Things are bound to get better."

"I don't see how," she said. "My job sucks, my kids are ashamed of me, I'm not in a relationship, and my best friends are leaving town."

"You can visit us whenever you want," Gregory told her. "It's not that far."

"Thanks." Ruth forced a smile. "I'm really happy for you. I know you'll have a beautiful wedding, and I'm honored to be included."

The guys assured her they wouldn't have it any other way. Ruth blew her nose in a cloth napkin.

"Hey, wait a minute," said Gregory. "What happened on your big date the other night? Nobody told me."

Ruth shook her head. "It was a bust. Paul's a nice guy, but we don't have anything in common."

"Too bad," said Gregory. "He sounded promising."

"You'll meet someone," Randall said. "It's time to get cracking on those internet dating services."

"I've done that," Ruth reminded him. "It's a wasteland. There were seventy-year-old men who wouldn't date a woman over forty."

"This time we'll do it right," Gregory said. "We're gonna get you all dressed up and take some sexy pictures. You know, good lighting, flattering angles. Then we're gonna put our heads together and write you a new profile. And you know what? If you want to say you're thirty-four, I won't tell on you."

Ruth tried to smile, but it just made her tired.

"Whatever," she said. "I don't even care anymore."

"Can't hurt to try," Randall reminded her.

"What's the point? There just aren't a lot of decent guys out there."

Gregory brushed his fingers across Randall's cheek and looked at Ruth.

"Honey," he said. "All it takes is one."

"Besides, it's not like your phone's not ringing." Randall turned to Gregory. "Some married guy drunk-dialed her at eleven o'clock the other night. He wanted to stop by for a little chat."

"My daughter's soccer coach."

"The Christian guy?" Gregory said. "The one who makes the girls pray?"

"Yup, that one."

Gregory's eyes widened with interest.

"Is he cute?"

"What difference does it make?" Ruth asked. "He's a drunk married Christian."

Randall pondered this for a moment.

"Nobody's perfect," he told her.

AFTER THE lecture, there was a brief, enigmatic theater piece about two troubled superheroes dressed in full leotard-and-cape regalia who meet in a psychiatrist's waiting room. Jetman used to be able to fly, but has recently been plagued by a crippling fear of heights ("I looked down one day and it just didn't seem safe, way up there in the sky like that."); Mr. Asbestos, famous for his ability to walk through flames, has developed a sudden aversion to fire ("That stuff is hot!" he tells Jetman, flapping his wrist at the memory). After sharing their sad stories, they flip through magazines and glance impatiently at their watches.

"What time do you have?" Jetman asks.

"One thirty," says Mr. Asbestos.

"It's strange," Jetman replies. "My appointment was for one o'clock."

"Couldn't be," says Mr. Asbestos. "*My* appointment was for one o'clock."

Puzzled by this coincidence, they search for the receptionist but can't find one. Finally, they decide to take drastic action, and pound on the psychiatrist's door, which has a huge DO NOT DISTURB sign hanging on it. When they get no reply, they crash through the door and into the office, only to emerge seconds later, more puzzled than before.

"The room's completely empty," Mr. Asbestos says, scratching his head.

"You know what that means?" Jetman says in an ominous voice.

"I do," says a frightened Mr. Asbestos. "It means we're on our own."

The spotlight lingered for a moment on the forlorn superheroes, then went dark. Moments later, the stage lights came on to reveal that the band had returned. They were playing a simple chord progression, their heads tilted heavenward, the music soft and comforting. Just when Tim expected the singer to burst into song, Brother Biggs walked onto the stage. His swagger was gone; he seemed uncharacteristically solemn.

"I gotta tell you guys. Jetman and Mr. Asbestos might be alone with their fears, but we're not. We got someone watching our backs way more powerful than any superhero. And that's why every single one of us can walk through the valley of the shadow of death, and we will fear no evil. Because He's with us! I can feel Him here tonight!

"A little while ago, I told you about our mission. Before we can truly be undaunted men of God, we got to deal with our fears. And that's what we gonna do now. If you'll open your program to page eight, you'll see a white card. I want you to rip it out at the perforation."

Tim detached his card. It was blank, except for a single phrase printed across the top—MY GREATEST FEAR IS:

"Now guys," Brother Biggs continued, "what I need is for you to be completely honest. Don't be writing down stupid stuff like, *I'm afraid the world will run out of ice cream.* We really need you to look into your hearts and face your fears. Some of you got work problems, and some of you got problems with your wives, or maybe your kids. And a lot of you—oh, I know it, because I know you guys, you're my brothers— some of you got appetites and addictions that are keeping you from being the kind of man God wants you to be. And by the way, don't be telling me you can't fill out the card because you didn't bring anything to write with. We got volunteers spread throughout the auditorium even as I speak, and they got a pencil for anyone who needs one."

It was true. Guys in neon green traffic safety vests were moving up and down the stairways, handing out fistfuls of stubby, eraserless pencils from plastic buckets. Bill Spooner took a bunch and passed them down the aisle.

AFTER THE Faith Keepers had filled out their cards, Brother Biggs invited them to come down to the area in front of the stage for what he called the Presentation of Fears.

"Come on now, let's do this together. You done the facing and the embracing just by looking into yourself and writing down what you saw there. Now we gotta take this one last step. We got to erase these fears by giving them to God."

The procession started slowly, individual guys rising from their seats and moving toward the stage.

"Okay," said Brother Biggs. "That's a start. I know it's not easy to be a pioneer. But we're with Jesus. Ain't nothing can scare us."

There was a big open pit in front of the stage. Once the first group of volunteers made it that far, they raised their hands, waving their cards overhead as they approached a row of plastic trash cans with the words FEAR RECEPTACLE painted on them.

"Go ahead, guys. Put those cards in the barrels. Give those fears to God! He can handle anything you got!"

The band had been repeating the same dreamy chords for several minutes, but the music suddenly grew louder. The singer launched into an eighties-style power ballad, with a quiet verse that swelled to a stirring chorus:

> *Fear not!*
> *The day is breaking*
> *Fear not!*

*Stop your shaking*
*Fear not!*
*The Lord is with us, and we've got nothing to fear*

"Come join us!" Brother Biggs called out during an instrumental break. "Let's show the world what it means to be undaunted!"

Pastor Dennis stood first, and the rest of the Tabernacle guys followed, filing down the aisle and into the stairway, which was starting to get pretty congested.

"Take courage," Brother Biggs told them. "Remember what Jesus said. 'Be not afraid, for I am with you!'"

All over the auditorium more men were leaving their seats and joining the procession. Tim was caught at a bottleneck near the entrance to the floor when a torrent of confetti suddenly dropped from the ceiling over the pit.

"Do you know what that is?" Brother Biggs said. "Those are the cards we collected last week in Baltimore! We took those fears and turned them into something joyful! And next week your cards will rain down on the good men of Albany!"

By the time he reached the edge of the pit, Tim had his hands up; he was waving his card and singing along with the band.

"Fear not! Day is breaking. . . ."

He hung back for a moment, letting his comrades go ahead of him. It was chaos down there, confetti and swirling lights, a surging mass of bodies coming and going, packed as tight as a rush hour subway car. All around him, guys were weeping and falling to their knees. Tim watched Bill Spooner and Steve Zelchuk let go of their fears—Bill wiped a tear away afterward, and Steve pumped his fist into the air—before stepping up to a barrel himself.

"You know what?" Brother Biggs shouted. "I want you to turn to the man next to you and say, *I'm not afraid anymore!*"

Tim hadn't found it easy to put a name to his fear, partly because he had so many of them. He thought about Abby first, and how he might never get to know her the way he wanted to, and then of Carrie, because he knew how much he'd hurt her. He thought about tomorrow's soccer game, and how badly he wanted a drink. But when he actually put his pencil to the paper, it was Pastor Dennis he was thinking about, and John Roper, and all the guys he'd come here with tonight, guys he'd worshipped and prayed with these past three years. The guys who'd accepted him despite all his flaws and helped him back on his feet. They were gathered behind him now in a confetti blizzard, hugging one another and saying they weren't afraid anymore. And Tim was standing in a daze by the trash can, a white card trembling in his hand.

"MY GREATEST FEAR IS:," it said, "that I'm not part of this anymore."

BRUSHING BITS of paper off his shoulders, Tim stepped through the exit door and into the fresh night air. As far as he could tell, no one seemed to be following him. He'd sensed Pastor Dennis's eyes on him as he lingered by the barrel, unable to let go of his card, but he'd taken advantage of the whiteout caused by a fresh confetti drop to slip out of the pit and make his getaway.

He wasn't alone out there. There must have been a dozen Faith Keepers loitering around the cement plaza outside the Civic Center. A couple were smokers who'd stepped outside for a cigarette break, but most of the others appeared to be in some sort of spiritual turmoil, muttering to themselves or staring uncertainly at their cell phones, doing their best to avoid eye contact with anyone else.

Keeping his head down, Tim veered across the plaza, stopping by the taxi stand to strip off his purple bracelet. He cast a quick fearful glance over his shoulder—he wasn't sure why; he wasn't doing anything wrong—before dropping it into a trash can.

He crossed Fountain Boulevard and darted down a side street, power-walking as though late for an appointment. As he approached the parking lot it suddenly occurred to him how badly he was inconveniencing the guys he'd left behind. There were eight of them and John's van fit only seven, which meant that somebody was going to have to sit on somebody's lap. It would be a long, uncomfortable ride home.

For a second or two, Tim felt so bad about this that he considered turning around and going back, but he couldn't make himself do it. The Civic Center seemed impossibly far away, and his car was right around the corner. Even so, the thought of all those guys—all his *friends*—squeezed into the Odyssey, their big night ruined by Tim's selfishness, was so vivid in his mind, and so disturbing, that he actually felt relieved, upon entering the parking lot, to find Jay leaning against the trunk of his Saturn, arms crossed impatiently on his chest.

"Damn," he said. "You sure took your time."

"A LITTLE more?" Randall asked.

"Why not?" Ruth replied. "I'm not the one who has to drive home."

To make up for her less-than-festive behavior at the restaurant, Ruth had picked up a bottle of Champagne at the Liquor Mart and invited the guys back to her house for a do-over celebration. They were more than happy to accept, and even bought a second bottle, on the grounds that "you never knew when it might come in handy." It was this bottle that Randall used to refill Ruth's glass and top off Gregory's.

"Better be careful," Gregory warned his fiancé. "We're the ones who do."

"Not necessarily," Randall said, gazing at Ruth with a smile full of drunken goodwill. "I'm always happy to sleep on Ruth's couch."

"Feel free," she assured him. "You're always welcome."

"I know," he said, then turned to Gregory. "But I'd really like to sleep in my own bed tonight."

"If you want to do more than sleep," Gregory said, "we better not drink much more."

"Doesn't matter," Randall said. "Drunken sex tonight or hangover sex in the morning. It's all good."

"Oh yeah." Gregory laughed. "Nothing beats hangover sex. Except maybe flu sex. That's superhot."

"Believe it or not," Randall said, "I do tend to get horny when I'm sick."

Gregory nodded. "He had strep last year and kept begging me for a blowjob every time I took his temperature."

"See?" said Ruth. "This is why I'm gonna be lost without you guys. You think I'm gonna hear stories like this from Donna DiNardo?"

"Good old Donna," Randall said. "I'm gonna miss her."

"Oh well," Ruth said. "Once you find a new job, you'll meet a whole new cast of characters."

"Randall's not getting a new job," Gregory said. "At least not for a while."

"Really?" Ruth said.

"I'm going to start an eBay business from home," Randall told her. "It's already like a part-time job."

"Plus," Gregory pointed out, "someone's got to stay at home with the kid."

Ruth laughed, but stopped when she realized that Gregory hadn't been joking.

"Or kids," Randall added. "We think two's a nice round number."

"You serious?" she asked. In all the time she'd known the guys, they'd never expressed even the slightest inclination to raise a child.

"Kind of," Gregory said. "Right now we're just thinking out loud. But once you get married, it just kind of makes sense to have kids, don't you think?"

"It's definitely worth considering," Ruth said. "I think you two would make great parents."

They agreed that they wanted an older girl and a younger boy, not that you always got to choose. Randall liked the names Fiona and Jake, while Gregory preferred Isabelle and Liam. They were throwing around some other possibilities—Maria and Luke, Nina and Josh, Madeline and Ernesto—when the doorbell rang. They looked at one another in puzzlement.

"Expecting anyone?" Randall asked.

"No," Ruth said, rising hesitantly from her chair.

"Maybe it's the drunk dialer," Gregory suggested. "Maybe his phone broke."

"It can't be," Ruth said, inching toward the hall. "You can't just show up on somebody's doorstep at this time of night."

"Invite him in," Randall said. "We'd like to meet him."

"It's not him," Ruth insisted.

But it was. She knew it before she put her hand on the knob, before she opened the door and saw him standing right in front of her, his big hands jammed into the pockets of his jean jacket and a pleading look in his eyes. The only things she couldn't have predicted were the confetti in his hair and her own inability to speak.

# Good Morning

RUTH USUALLY SLEPT NAKED ON FRIDAY NIGHT, BUT IT DIDN'T feel right with Tim on the downstairs couch. Her everyday sweatpants-and-extra-large-T-shirt combo seemed depressingly frumpy under the circumstances, so she dug deep in her underwear drawer and dredged up a satiny black nightie with a plunging neckline that Frank used to like. It smelled a bit musty when she slipped it on—it hadn't been in contact with fresh air for quite a while—but it was the best she could do on such short notice. At least this way she wouldn't be at too much of a disadvantage if Tim decided to knock on her bedroom door in the middle of the night, not that there seemed to be much danger of that.

She still hadn't fully recovered from the shock of seeing him on the porch, the sudden force and clarity of her own feelings. It felt like she'd stared at him for a full minute before recovering the power of speech.

"What are you doing here?"

His eyes drifted, as if drawn by a magnetic force, to the Champagne glass in her hand.

"You told me to come back when I was sober."

"It's late," she said. "I have some friends over."

He shut his eyes, as if he needed a moment to absorb this.

"So you want me to go?"

Ruth pretended to think this over, but she already knew the answer. She'd spent the last three days regretting her decision not to invite him in on Tuesday night—it just wasn't possible, not with the girls upstairs and Randall crying in the kitchen—and she wasn't about to repeat the mistake.

"Come join us," she said.

To her surprise, Tim got along pretty well with Randall and Gregory. He congratulated them on their engagement, and didn't say or do anything to suggest that he disapproved of their relationship or felt any squeamishness in their company. The only awkward moment came when she had to intervene to prevent Randall from pouring Tim a glass of champagne.

"No," she said, a bit more sharply than she meant to. "Don't do that."

"But we're celebrating," Randall protested.

"He shouldn't drink."

Tim didn't look too happy about this, but he didn't contradict her.

"Sometimes I forget," he told Randall.

"You know what?" Gregory rose from his seat, shooting a meaningful glance at his partner. "I think it's time for us to go."

"No, no," Tim told him. "Don't leave on my account."

"Not at all," Gregory assured him. "It's past our bedtime."

Ruth was pretty sure he'd make a move on her once they were alone—she was wholeheartedly in favor of the idea—but all he did was ask if he could spend the night on her couch.

"I hate to bother you," he said. "But I have nowhere else to go."

"What about your wife?"

He shook his head, as if this were no longer an option.

"Did you guys have a fight?"

His cell phone started buzzing before he could answer. He pulled it out of his pocket and winced at what he saw on the display.

"Come on," he muttered. "Just leave me alone."

"Is something wrong?"

He shoved the phone back into his pocket and tried to smile.

"My life's a mess."

She wanted to ask him how he'd gotten all that confetti in his hair, but he didn't seem to be in the mood for conversation.

"I'll get your sheets," she said. "There's an extra toothbrush in the medicine cabinet."

RUTH TRIED to read in bed, but it was hopeless. She was too busy listening through the not-quite-closed door, trying to figure out what Tim was up to in the living room, wondering if he'd gotten undressed, if he was thinking the same thoughts about her that she was thinking about him. She put down the book, turned off the lamp, and slid her hand between her legs, but her heart wasn't in it.

*Help me,* she thought. *I'm right upstairs.*

She wasn't quite sure why she didn't just go downstairs and kiss him. After all, wasn't that the advice she'd given Randall, to stop waiting around and take matters into your own hands? And besides, Tim had done most of the work simply by showing up. Maybe now it was her turn.

But she couldn't do it. Not only because he was still married—even if the marriage was hanging by a thread—or because he seemed to be going through some sort of larger crisis that involved a relapse with alcohol and drugs. And not even because she was still pissed at him about the trouble he'd caused with his prayers at the soccer games. It was mainly just that she was scared—scared he'd say no, and scared of how she'd feel if he did.

After tossing and turning for what felt like hours, she finally must have dozed off. She only realized this was the case because she was conscious, sometime later, of being startled awake by a creaking door.

"Ruth?" he whispered. "Are you asleep?"

"No," she said. "Not anymore."

Tim was standing on the threshold, illuminated from behind by the hall light, his silhouette compact, oddly familiar, deeply thrilling.

"I hate to do this," he said, "but can I use your computer?"

HE FELT a little weird, scrolling through Ruth's inbox at two in the morning, but he didn't really have a choice. In any case, it didn't take too long to find what he was looking for, a reminder he'd sent to the team on Tuesday morning—"Re: This Week's Practice Re-Scheduled." He hit Reply All, erased the old subject line, and typed in a new one: "IMPORTANT MESSAGE FROM COACH TIM."

*Dear Stars,* he wrote, *I regret to inform you that due to an unavoidable personal situation, I won't be with you at tomorrow's game against Green Valley. Assistant Coach John Roper will lead the charge in my absence.*

He had prayed long and hard before making this decision, which ran counter to his deepest principles and desires. But a sense of calm certainty came over him as he reread his words on the screen, a spiritual clarity he hadn't experienced in a long time, as if Jesus were looking over his shoulder, nodding in approval.

The irony of the situation wasn't lost on him. Just a few hours earlier, in the parking lot of a "gentleman's club" called Eyeballs, Tim had found himself tongue-tied, struggling to respond to Jay's claim that Pastor Dennis had tricked him.

"I mean, don't get me wrong," he said. "I felt something that first night, when the Pastor prayed with me in the parking lot. I'm not denying that I was shit-faced at the time, but I swear to you—and I've thought a lot about this—I felt like I was enveloped in this beautiful cloud of love and, you know, forgiveness. And the Pastor told me that feeling was Jesus.

"And I believed him," Jay continued in a bitter tone. "I accepted Christ and told everybody I knew that I was a different person. I gave away my porn, dumped out my liquor, and tried to stop saying *fuck* all the time.

"But guess what? That feeling never came back. Not once. I didn't feel it in church, or at Bible Study, and I definitely didn't feel it tonight at that fucking *event*, whatever they call it. I was just sitting there, looking around, and it hit me: that feeling wasn't Jesus, it was just *me*, hoping for something better."

"There's nothing wrong with that," Tim told him.

"Maybe not," Jay conceded. "But it's not gonna save anyone."

"It's only been a couple of weeks. You need to have a little more patience."

Jay turned to Tim with an expression that seemed scared and defiant at the same time. They were idling in the fire lane, a short distance away from the entrance of the club.

"You think I'm making a mistake?"

"I . . . I really don't know," Tim told him. "I'm a little mixed up myself."

Jay opened the passenger door but didn't get out.

"You sure you don't wanna come in? They got this Brazilian girl, I swear—"

"I don't think so."

Reluctantly, Jay got out of the car. Instead of heading for the club, though, he just stood there, staring at Tim, pleading almost, as if he wanted to be talked out of what he was about to do. But it was his choice, and Tim couldn't make it for him.

"See you around," he said.

Tim got on the highway and drove straight home, steeling himself for what he knew was going to be another painful conversation with Carrie. He got as far as the parking lot of their condo complex before losing his nerve and winding up here at Ruth's.

*Girls, you know how much I love our team, and what a privilege it's been for me to be your coach this season. So I probably don't have to tell you how much it breaks my heart to have to miss the game tomorrow.*

The conversation with Jay was still echoing in his mind when he got down on his knees in Ruth's living room. He honestly didn't know if he was praying out of habit, or desperation, or because he actually expected to communicate with God. It didn't help that he had no idea what he was praying *for*. His troubles were all just gathered up into one big convoluted knot, and he couldn't even figure out which end to pull on first. On top of that he was distracted by his cell phone—Pastor Dennis and John Roper kept calling every few minutes, trying to track him down—and by the knowledge that Ruth was right upstairs in her bedroom, not to mention the recurring thought that there was probably some liquor in the house and he wouldn't have to look too hard to find it.

He was close to throwing in the towel and trying to get some sleep—he'd been feeling that way pretty much since he started praying—when a voice sounded in his head, way louder and clearer than the confused muttering of his own thoughts.

"DON'T GO," it said.

He understood the meaning of this, and he didn't like it. He couldn't miss the game. It wouldn't be fair to the girls.

"IT'S THE ONLY WAY."

And it was. He'd known it for a long time, but hadn't been able to admit it to himself.

*I'm truly sorry if I've done anything to cause divisions among you. We're a team. We need to stick together tomorrow. Whatever happens, just know that I'll be there in spirit, and I'll be proud of you whether we win or lose.*

It was such a relief just to make a decision, to get one problem out of the way so he could begin to tackle the others. The important thing, he realized, was not to get overwhelmed, to take things one at a time. After this he would write an e-mail to Pastor Dennis, thanking him for all his help, the heroic efforts he'd made on behalf of a lost soul, and offering his eternal gratitude. Then he'd bite the bullet and call Carrie to let her know that he wouldn't be coming home, though she'd probably figured that out for herself by now. But first, he had a little more to say to the girls.

*Green Valley is a tough opponent. We need to play our game—fast, smart, unselfish soccer.*

*Nomad—you're a wonderful ball handler, but you have a tendency to dribble into traffic. Please look for the early pass.*

*Slinky—you kick with great power. But don't clump. Move to the open space.*

*Loopy—no fear in the goal. NO FEAR.*

*Monkey—You're my warrior. We need your fire.*

*Hangman—it's okay to push up on D, but please hustle back into position if necessary.*

*Caddyshack—Don't hesitate. If you get a shot, take it. We need you to step up on offense.*

*Abba—I love you so much. Play as hard as you can, and don't lose your focus. Please call me after the game.*


AFTER A night of uneasy sleep, Ruth was awakened by the doorbell. She sat up in bed, aware of both a sense of incipient panic and the early-warning signs of a hangover. The bell sounded again, one long buzz followed by two shorter ones.

"All right," she said, throwing off the covers and standing up more quickly than was advisable. "I'm coming."

She glanced at the clock. It was 6:47 in the morning. Saturday. The girls were at Frank's. She made it to the top of the stairs before remembering she had a guest and wasn't decently dressed, her memory jogged by the sight of the guest in question coming up the stairs in boxer shorts and a T-shirt, looking at her with a worried expression. At almost the same moment their eyes met, the doorbell went crazy, buzzing repeatedly and insistently, as if it were an emergency.

"It's for me," he told her.

"Well, could you get it?"

He grimaced and shook his head.

"I really can't handle this right now."

"Is it your wife?"

As if to answer her question, the caller gave up on the bell and started pounding on the door, demanding to be let in. Ruth couldn't make out the words, but she could hear enough to know that it was a man doing the shouting.

"He's gonna wake up the whole neighborhood," she said, squeezing past Tim on her way downstairs.

She opened the door a crack, just wide enough to show her face. The man on the porch was smaller and younger-looking in person than he was in her memory. Of course, she'd only seen him a couple of times at public meetings and had never gotten this close to him.

"Can I help you?" she asked.

Pastor Dennis stared at her through his wire-rimmed glasses. His eyes looked bloodshot and haunted, like he'd been up all night.

"I need to speak to Tim."

"He doesn't want to talk to you."

"Let me in," the Pastor insisted, craning his neck to get a better view into her house. "Tim's afraid, and he needs my help."

Ruth was startled by the anguish in his voice. In public, Pastor Dennis was always so strident and angry, but he now seemed to be on the verge of tears.

"I'm sorry," she said. "You really need to go now."

The Pastor shook his head.

"I came for Tim, and I'm not leaving without him. He doesn't belong here."

"Please," Ruth said. "I'm asking you politely."

"Just bring him to the door. If he wants me to leave, let him say it to my face."

"You have to go," she told him. "*Now.* I don't want to argue about it."

The Pastor must have heard the implicit threat in her voice.

"Fine," he said. "But do me a favor. Tell him I've been praying for him all night. And I'm not going to stop until he talks to me."

Feeling an unexpected pang of guilt, Ruth shut the door, twisted the dead bolt, and headed back upstairs. Tim was crouching by her bedroom window, peering down at the front lawn.

"I told him to go away," she reported. "He wasn't too happy about it."

He stood up and looked at her, his eyes lingering on her body. She should've been embarrassed, standing there in the kind of nightgown you only wore for a lover, but the feeling didn't materialize. It helped that he was in his underwear, too, as close to naked as she was.

"Believe me," he told her. "The Pastor's not going anywhere."

"What do you mean?"

He beckoned her to the window. It was a bright morning, a beautiful day for a soccer game. A stiff breeze must have been blowing, because the air was full of red and yellow leaves, detaching themselves from trees, floating dreamily to the earth, blowing sideways across the grass. Tim's Saturn was parked right in front of Ruth's house, beneath the sugar maple, and Pastor Dennis was sitting on the hood, arms crossed on his chest, staring right back at them.

"He's a stubborn guy," Tim said. "He'll stay there all day if he has to."

"What time do you have to leave for the game?"

"I'm not going. I have to sit this one out."

"Really? But isn't this for the championship of, uh, what is it, Division B-3?"

"Yeah," he said. "I'm trying not to think about it."

"Sorry."

"That's okay. It's not your fault."

Ruth wasn't sure this was true, but she kept it to herself.

"What about you?" he said. "You going?"

"Not today. Maggie asked me to stay home. She thinks I'm a troublemaker."

Tim shook his head. "She's a good kid, Ruth."

"I know."

A few seconds went by. Tim's voice was soft, a bit fearful.

"I guess I should get going soon. I'm sure you have things to do."

They were standing side by side, not quite touching, but close enough that she could breathe in the sleepy smell of his body and feel a gentle current moving between them. They kept staring straight ahead for a long time, almost as if they were afraid of looking at each other, the silence gathering around them, thickening, until the world outside the window disappeared—the sky, the houses, the trees, the airborne leaves, even the man on the car—and they were alone.

"Stay as long as you want," she told him.